# BATMAN '66

VOL. 1

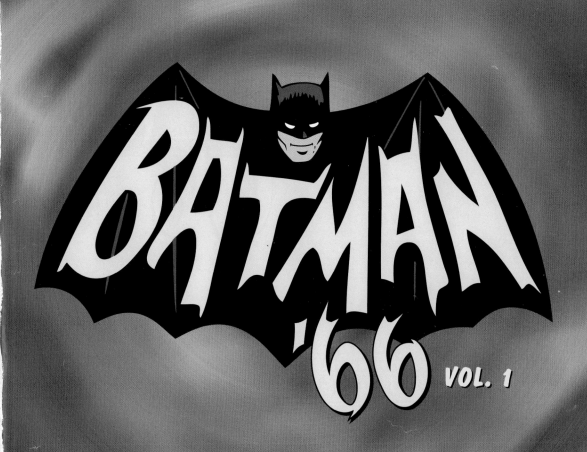

# BATMAN '66 VOL. 1

Written by
**JEFF PARKER**

Art by
**JONATHAN CASE   TY TEMPLETON
JOE QUINONES   SANDY JARRELL
RUBEN PROCOPIO   COLLEEN COOVER**

Colors by
**WES HARTMAN   JONATHAN CASE
MARIS WICKS   RICO RENZI
TONY AVIÑA   MATTHEW WILSON
COLLEEN COOVER**

Letters by
**WES ABBOTT**

Cover Art & Original Series Covers by
**MICHAEL & LAURA ALLRED**

BATMAN created by
**BOB KANE**

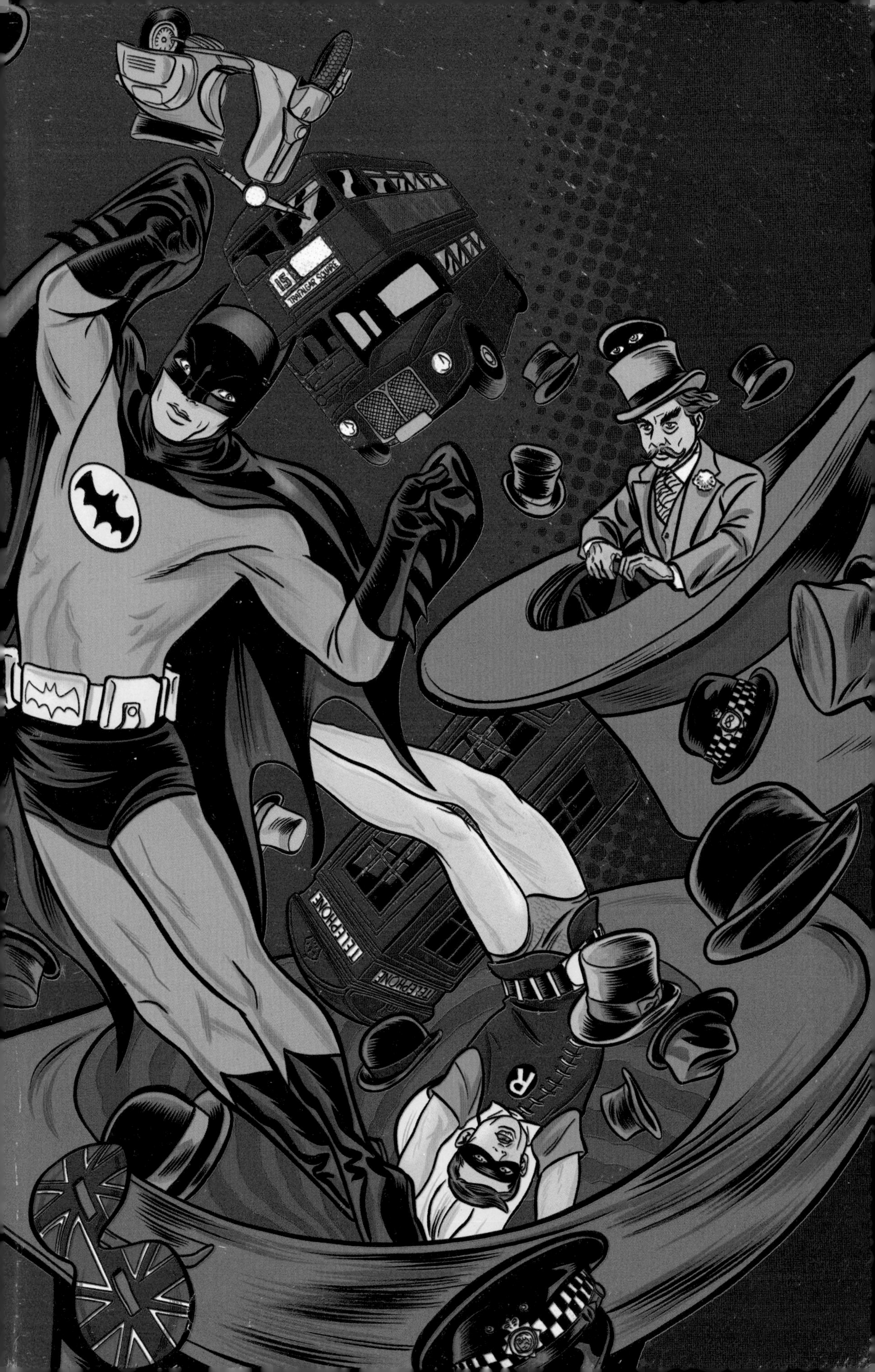
15
TRAFALGAR SQUARE
TELEPHONE
TELEPHONE

**JIM CHADWICK**
Editor — Original Series

**ANIZ ANSARI**
Assistant Editor — Original Series

**SCOTT NYBAKKEN**
Editor

**ROBBIN BROSTERMAN**
Design Director - Books

**CURTIS KING JR.**
Publication Design

**HANK KANALZ**
Senior VP — Vertigo & Integrated Publishing

**DIANE NELSON**
President

**DAN DIDIO** and **JIM LEE**
Co-Publishers

**GEOFF JOHNS**
Chief Creative Officer

**JOHN ROOD**
Executive VP — Sales, Marketing & Business Development

**AMY GENKINS**
Senior VP — Business & Legal Affairs

**NAIRI GARDINER**
Senior VP — Finance

**JEFF BOISON**
VP — Publishing Planning

**MARK CHIARELLO**
VP — Art Direction & Design

**JOHN CUNNINGHAM**
VP — Marketing

**TERRI CUNNINGHAM**
VP — Editorial Administration

**ALISON GILL**
Senior VP — Manufacturing & Operations

**BOB HARRAS**
Senior VP — Editor-in-Chief, DC Comics

**JAY KOGAN**
VP — Business & Legal Affairs, Publishing

**JACK MAHAN**
VP — Business Affairs, Talent

**NICK NAPOLITANO**
VP — Manufacturing Administration

**SUE POHJA**
VP — Book Sales

**COURTNEY SIMMONS**
Senior VP — Publicity

**BOB WAYNE**
Senior VP — Sales

**BATMAN '66 VOL. 1**
Published by DC Comics.
Copyright © 2014 DC Comics. All Rights Reserved.

Originally published in single magazine form as BATMAN '66 1-5 and online as
BATMAN '66 Chapters 1-15. Copyright © 2013, 2014 DC Comics. All Rights
Reserved. All characters, their distinctive likenesses and related elements
featured in this publication are trademarks of DC Comics. The stories, characters
and incidents featured in this publication are entirely fictional. DC Comics
does not read or accept unsolicited submissions of ideas, stories or artwork.

DC Comics, 1700 Broadway, New York, NY 10019
A Warner Bros. Entertainment Company.
Printed by RR Donnelley, Salem, VA, USA. 2/28/14. First Printing.
HC ISBN: 978-1-4012-4721-8
SC ISBN: 978-1-4012-4931-1

SUSTAINABLE
FORESTRY
INITIATIVE

Certified Chain of Custody
At Least 20% Certified Forest Content
www.sfiprogram.org
SFI-01042
APPLIES TO TEXT STOCK ONLY

Library of Congress Cataloging-in-Publication Data

Parker, Jeff, 1966- author.
  Batman '66. Volume 1 / Jeff Parker ; [illustrated by] Richard Case.
     pages cm
  ISBN 978-1-4012-4721-8 (hardback)
  1. Graphic novels. I. Case, Richard, illustrator. II. Title.
PN6728.B36P37 2014
741.5'973—dc23
                                    2013049627

# TABLE OF CONTENTS

# BATMAN '66

## VOL. 1

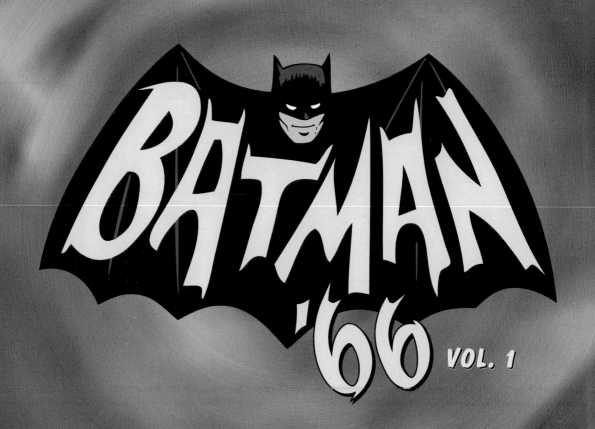

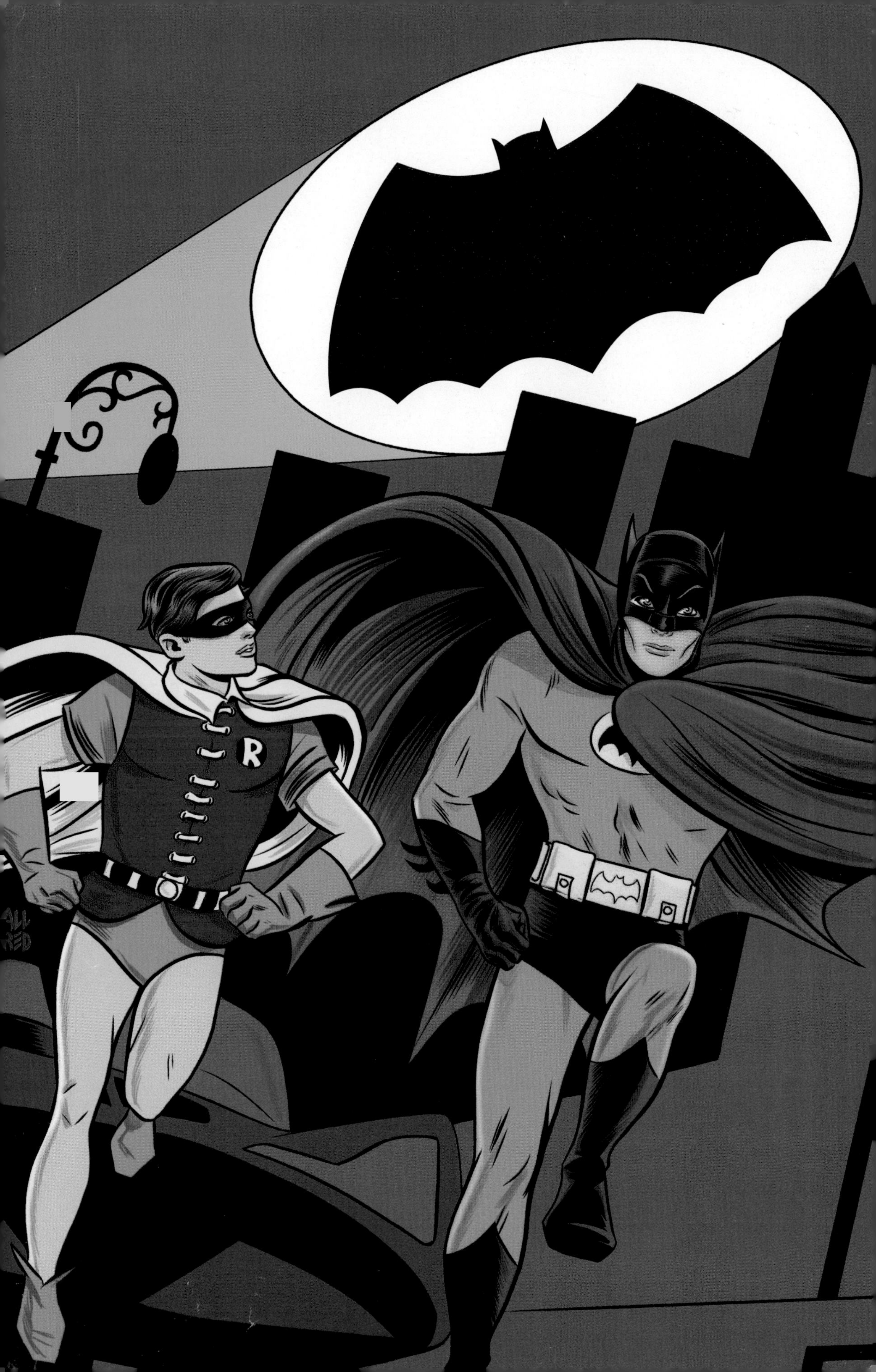

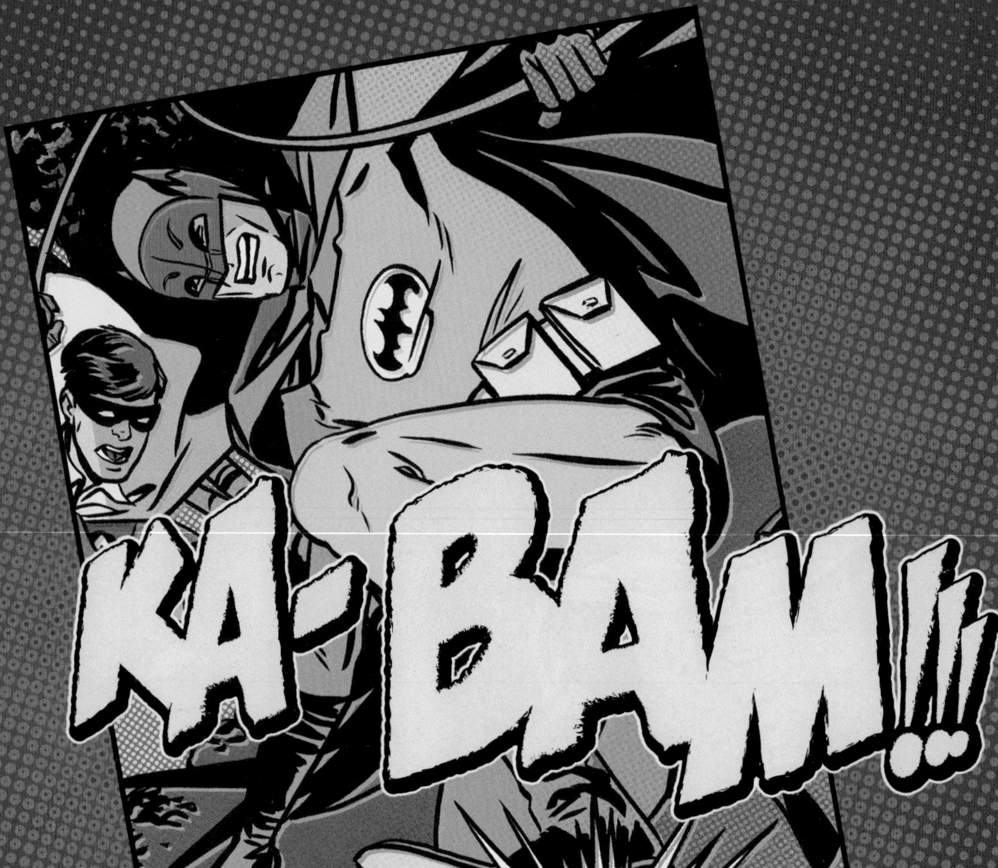
KA-BAM!!!

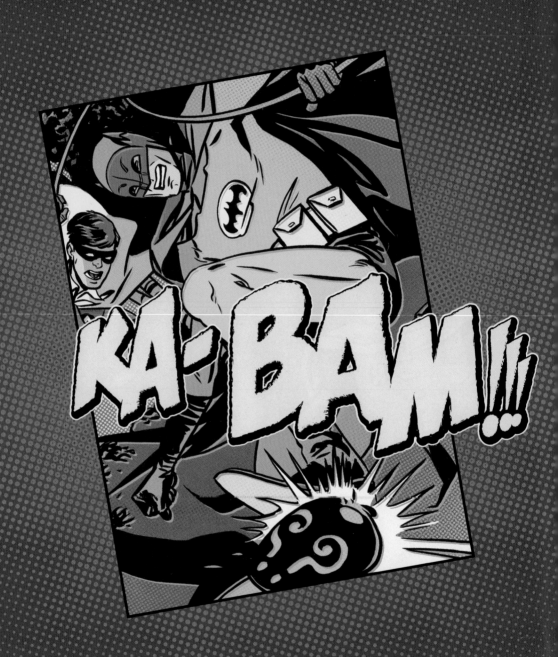

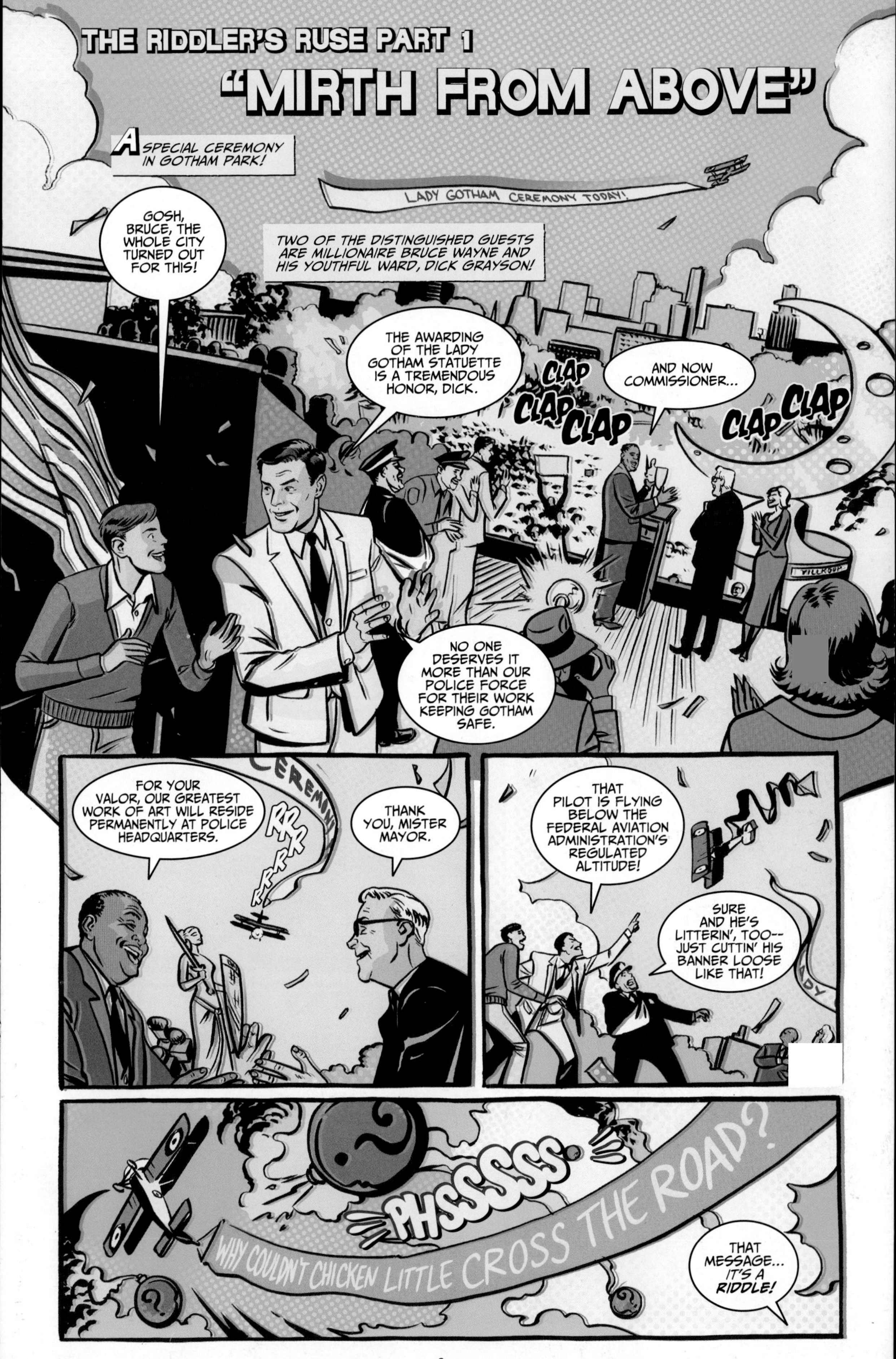
THE RIDDLER'S RUSE PART 1
"MIRTH FROM ABOVE"
A SPECIAL CEREMONY IN GOTHAM PARK!
LADY GOTHAM CEREMONY TODAY!
GOSH, BRUCE, THE WHOLE CITY TURNED OUT FOR THIS!
TWO OF THE DISTINGUISHED GUESTS ARE MILLIONAIRE BRUCE WAYNE AND HIS YOUTHFUL WARD, DICK GRAYSON!
THE AWARDING OF THE LADY GOTHAM STATUETTE IS A TREMENDOUS HONOR, DICK.
CLAP CLAP CLAP
AND NOW COMMISSIONER...
CLAP CLAP
NO ONE DESERVES IT MORE THAN OUR POLICE FORCE FOR THEIR WORK KEEPING GOTHAM SAFE.
FOR YOUR VALOR, OUR GREATEST WORK OF ART WILL RESIDE PERMANENTLY AT POLICE HEADQUARTERS.
CEREMONY
RRRRR
THANK YOU, MISTER MAYOR.
THAT PILOT IS FLYING BELOW THE FEDERAL AVIATION ADMINISTRATION'S REGULATED ALTITUDE!
SURE AND HE'S LITTERIN', TOO-- JUST CUTTIN' HIS BANNER LOOSE LIKE THAT!
PHSSSSS
WHY COULDN'T CHICKEN LITTLE CROSS THE ROAD?
THAT MESSAGE... IT'S A *RIDDLE!*

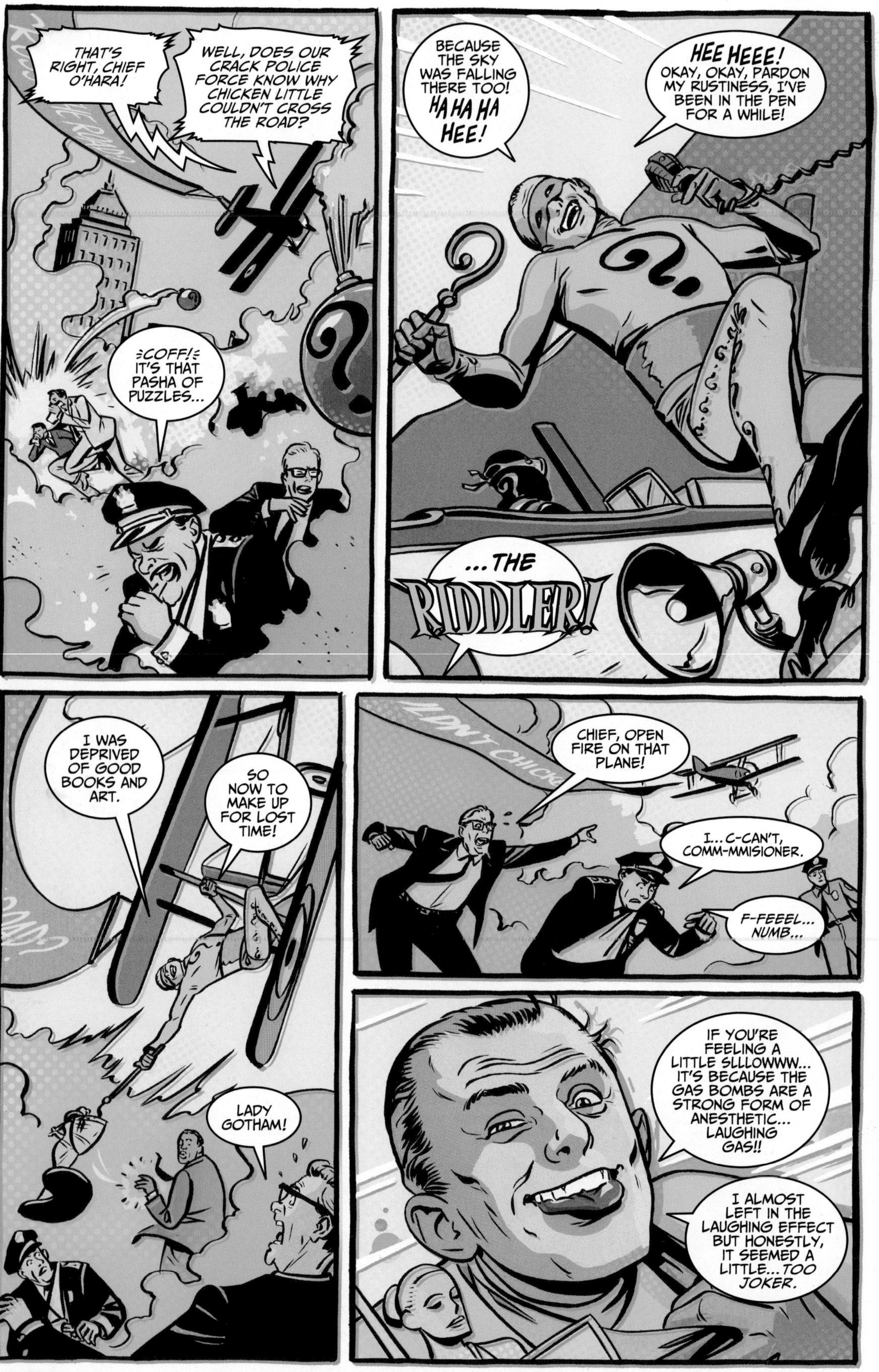
THAT'S RIGHT, CHIEF O'HARA!
WELL, DOES OUR CRACK POLICE FORCE KNOW WHY CHICKEN LITTLE COULDN'T CROSS THE ROAD?
*COFF!* IT'S THAT PASHA OF PUZZLES...
BECAUSE THE SKY WAS FALLING THERE TOO! HA HA HA HEE!
HEE HEEE! OKAY, OKAY, PARDON MY RUSTINESS, I'VE BEEN IN THE PEN FOR A WHILE!
...THE RIDDLER!
I WAS DEPRIVED OF GOOD BOOKS AND ART.
SO NOW TO MAKE UP FOR LOST TIME!
LADY GOTHAM!
CHIEF, OPEN FIRE ON THAT PLANE!
I...C-CAN'T, COMM-MMISIONER.
F-FEEEL... NUMB...
IF YOU'RE FEELING A LITTLE SLLLOWWW... IT'S BECAUSE THE GAS BOMBS ARE A STRONG FORM OF ANESTHETIC... LAUGHING GAS!!
I ALMOST LEFT IN THE LAUGHING EFFECT BUT HONESTLY, IT SEEMED A LITTLE... TOO JOKER.

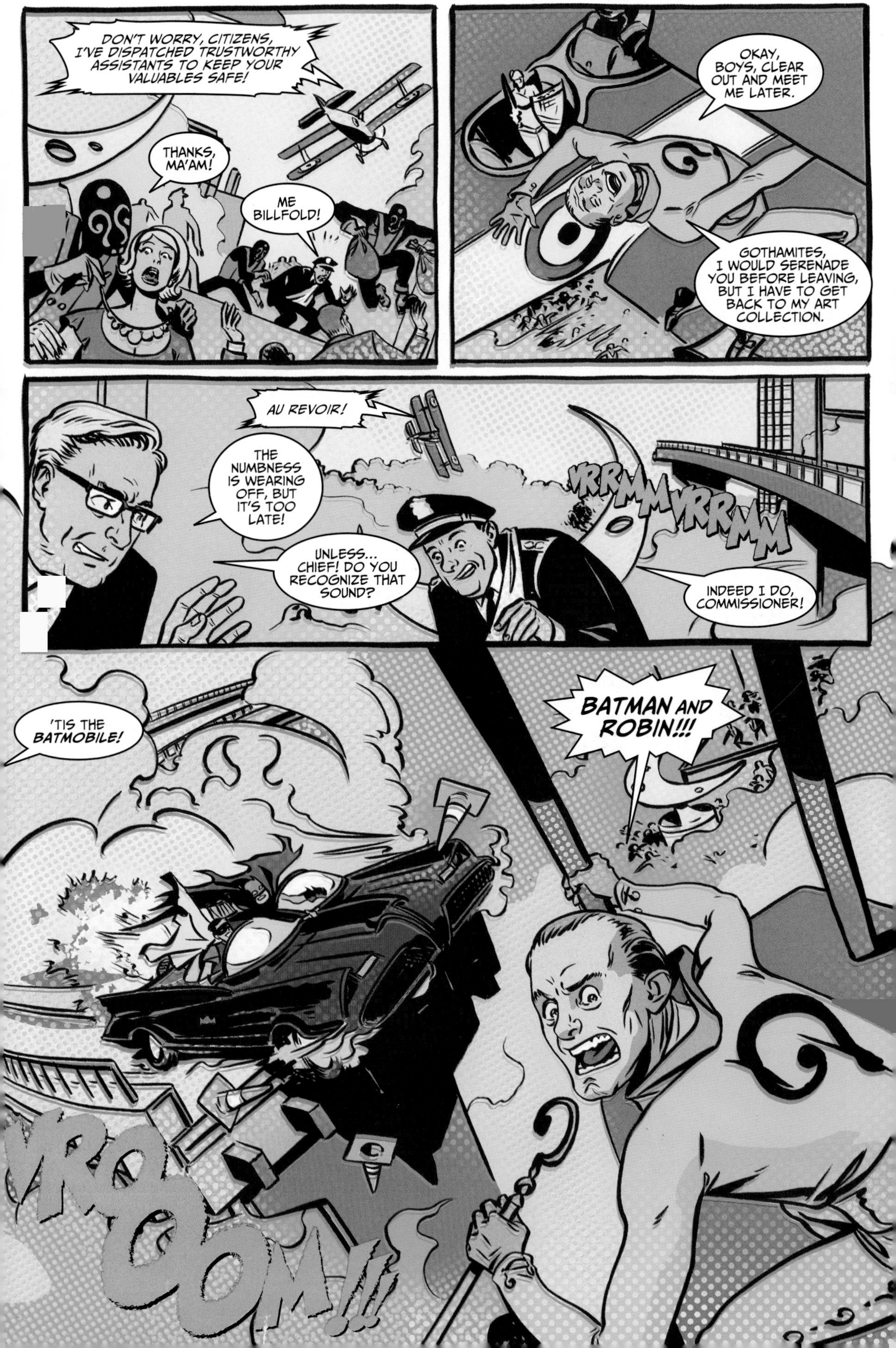
DON'T WORRY, CITIZENS, I'VE DISPATCHED TRUSTWORTHY ASSISTANTS TO KEEP YOUR VALUABLES SAFE!
THANKS, MA'AM!
ME BILLFOLD!
OKAY, BOYS, CLEAR OUT AND MEET ME LATER.
GOTHAMITES, I WOULD SERENADE YOU BEFORE LEAVING, BUT I HAVE TO GET BACK TO MY ART COLLECTION.
AU REVOIR!
THE NUMBNESS IS WEARING OFF, BUT IT'S TOO LATE!
VRRMMMVRRMM
UNLESS... CHIEF! DO YOU RECOGNIZE THAT SOUND?
INDEED I DO, COMMISSIONER!
'TIS THE BATMOBILE!
BATMAN AND ROBIN!!!
VROOOM!!!

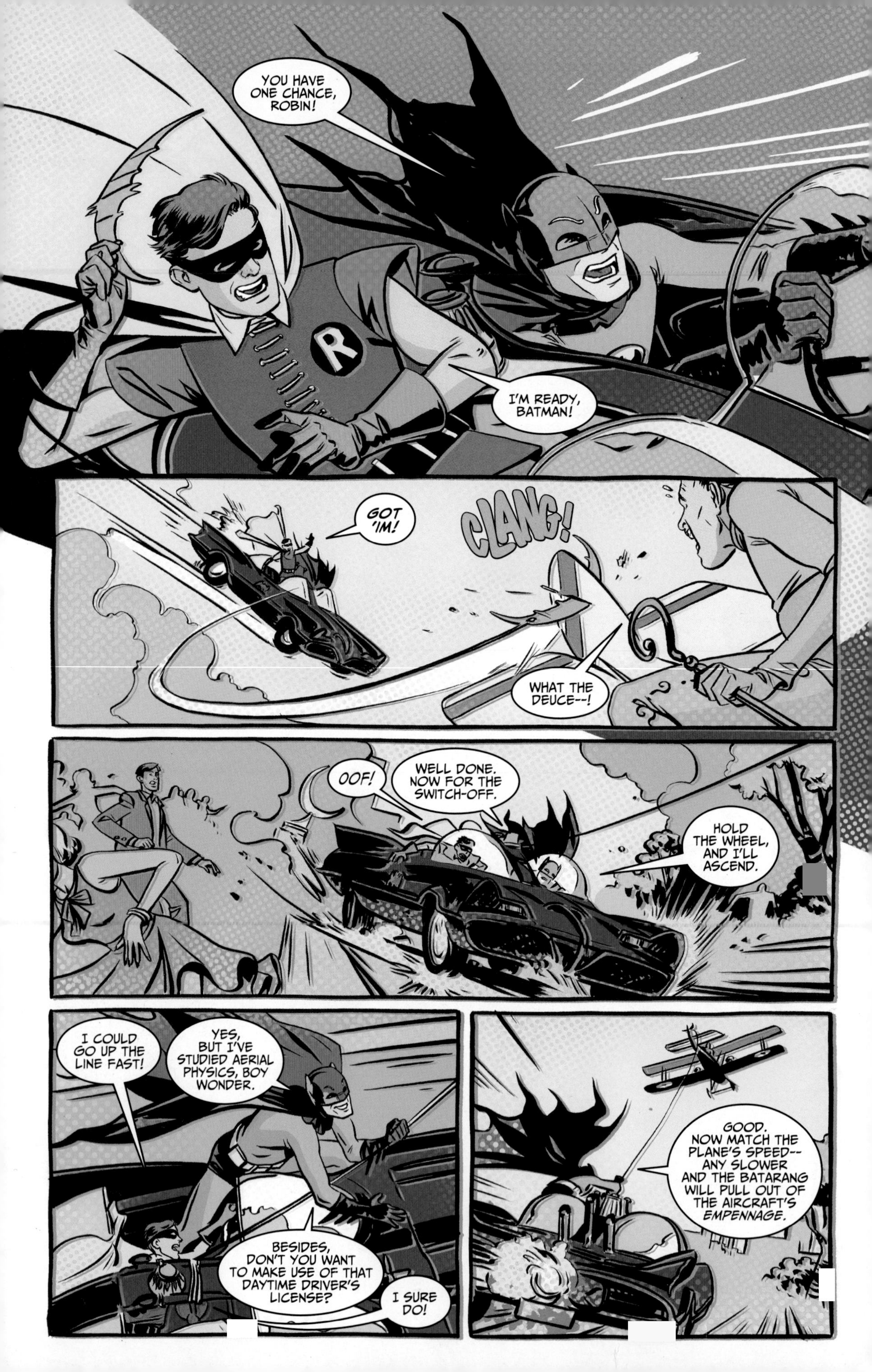
YOU HAVE ONE CHANCE, ROBIN!
I'M READY, BATMAN!
GOT 'IM!
CLANG!
WHAT THE DEUCE--!
OOF!
WELL DONE. NOW FOR THE SWITCH-OFF.
HOLD THE WHEEL, AND I'LL ASCEND.
I COULD GO UP THE LINE FAST!
YES, BUT I'VE STUDIED AERIAL PHYSICS, BOY WONDER.
BESIDES, DON'T YOU WANT TO MAKE USE OF THAT DAYTIME DRIVER'S LICENSE?
I SURE DO!
GOOD. NOW MATCH THE PLANE'S SPEED-- ANY SLOWER AND THE BATARANG WILL PULL OUT OF THE AIRCRAFT'S EMPENNAGE.

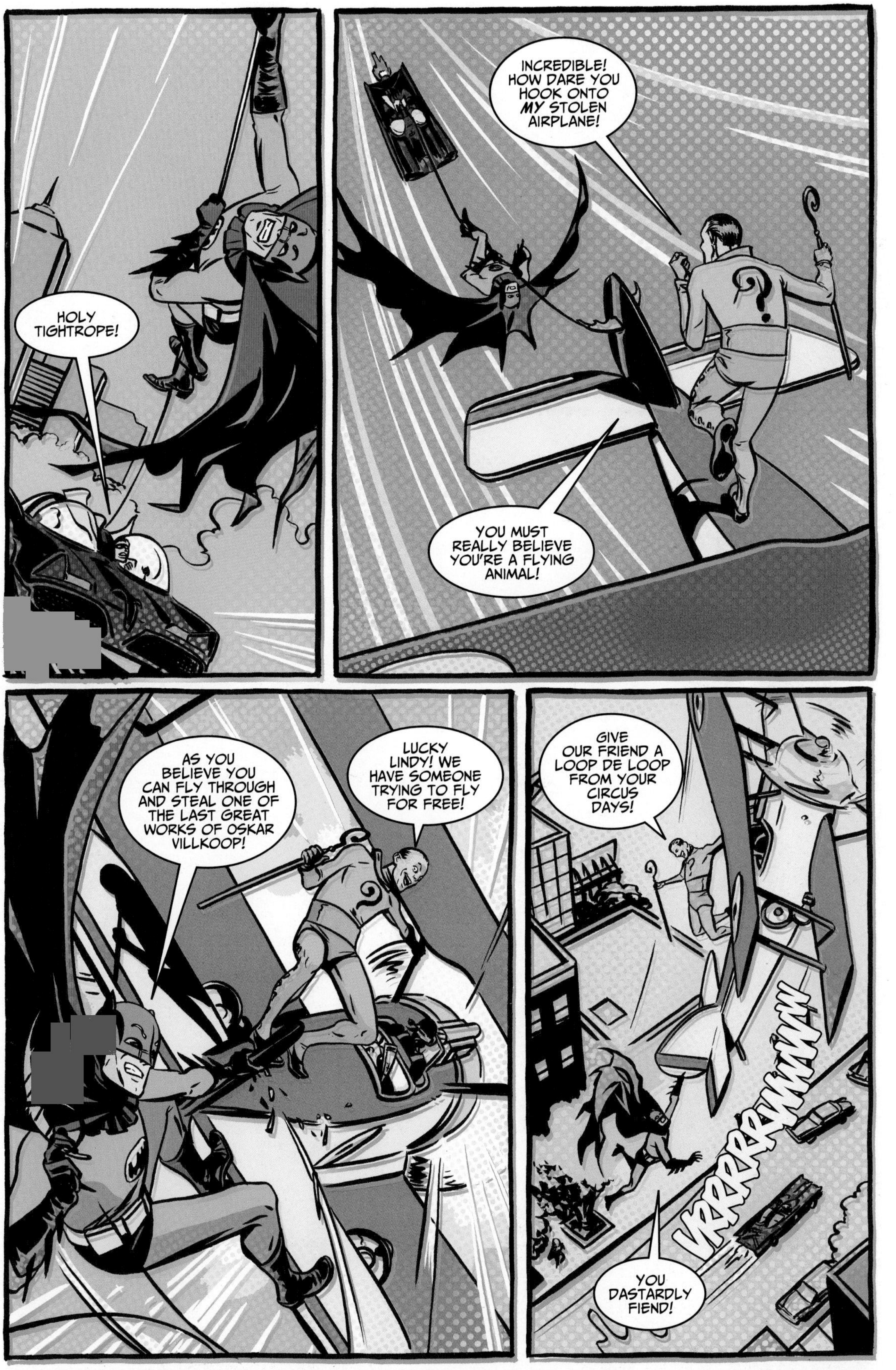
HOLY TIGHTROPE!
INCREDIBLE! HOW DARE YOU HOOK ONTO *MY* STOLEN AIRPLANE!
YOU MUST REALLY BELIEVE YOU'RE A FLYING ANIMAL!
AS YOU BELIEVE YOU CAN FLY THROUGH AND STEAL ONE OF THE LAST GREAT WORKS OF OSKAR VILLKOOP!
LUCKY LINDY! WE HAVE SOMEONE TRYING TO FLY FOR FREE!
GIVE OUR FRIEND A LOOP DE LOOP FROM YOUR CIRCUS DAYS!
VRRRRRWWWWWW
YOU DASTARDLY FIEND!

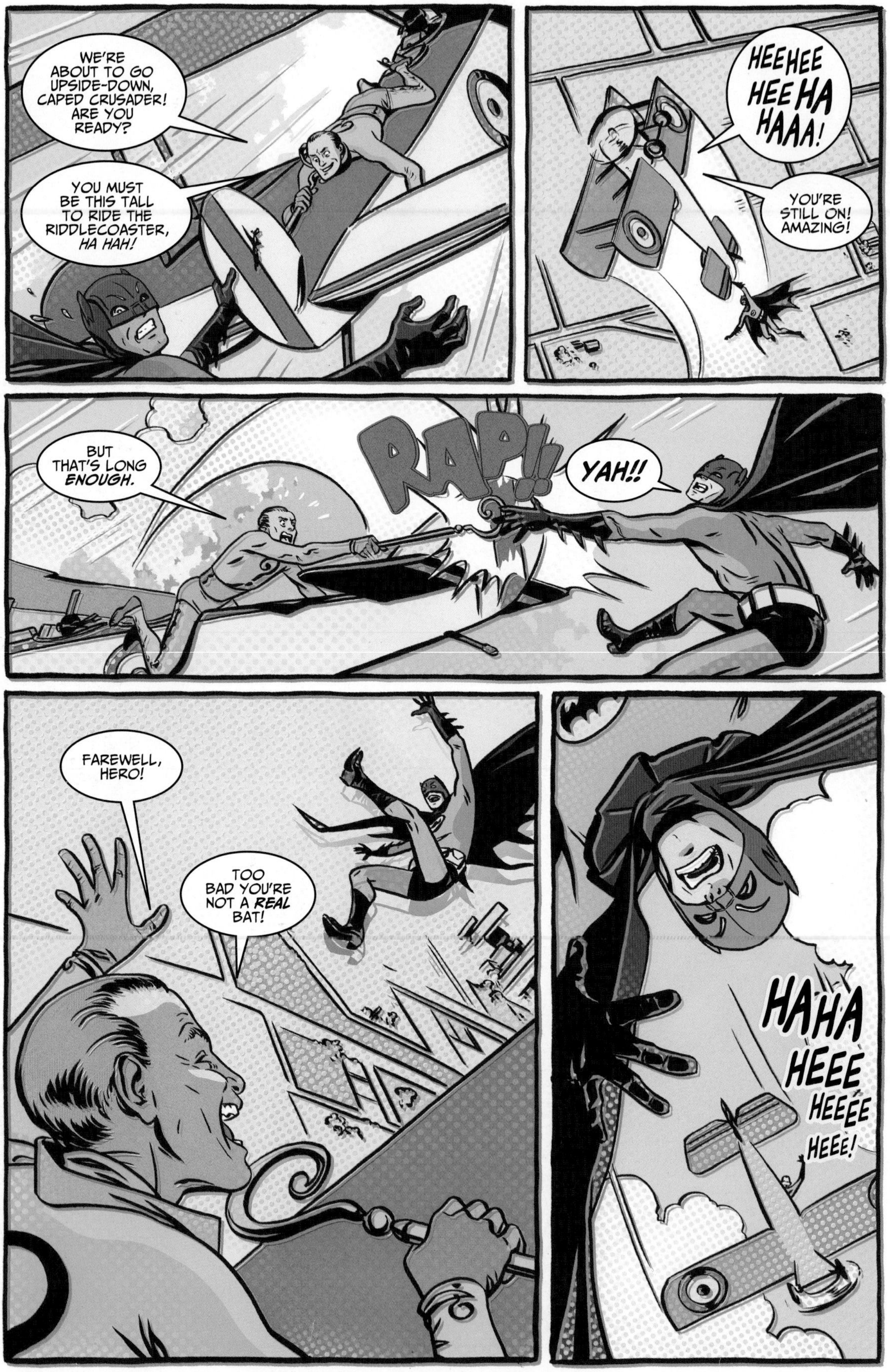
WE'RE ABOUT TO GO UPSIDE-DOWN, CAPED CRUSADER! ARE YOU READY?
YOU MUST BE THIS TALL TO RIDE THE RIDDLECOASTER, HA HAH!
HEE HEE HEE HA HAAA!
YOU'RE STILL ON! AMAZING!
BUT THAT'S LONG ENOUGH.
RAP!!
YAH!!
FAREWELL, HERO!
TOO BAD YOU'RE NOT A REAL BAT!
HAHA HEEE HEEEE HEEE!

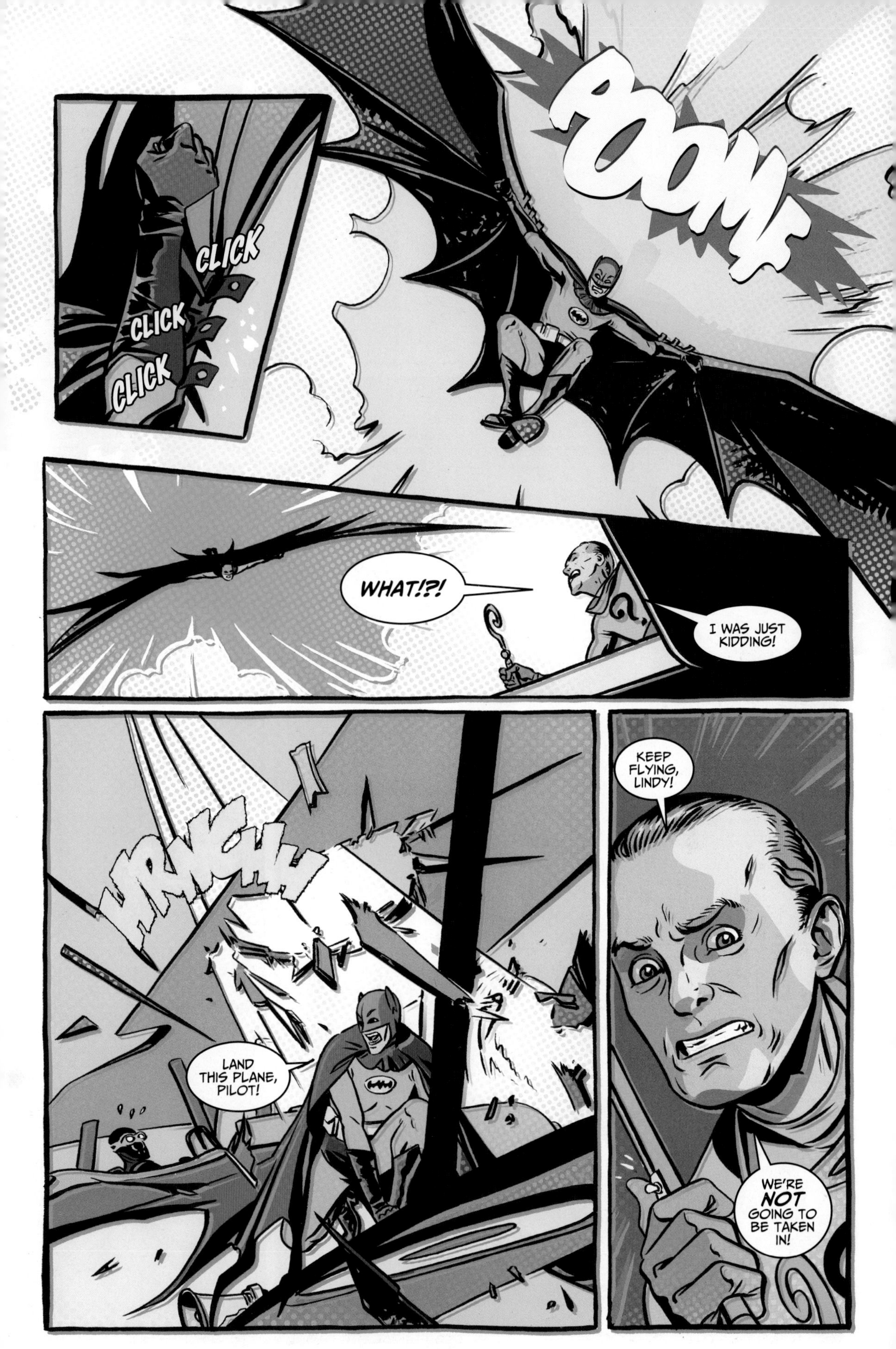
CLICK
CLICK
CLICK
BOOM!
WHAT!?!
I WAS JUST KIDDING!
LAND THIS PLANE, PILOT!
KEEP FLYING, LINDY!
WE'RE NOT GOING TO BE TAKEN IN!

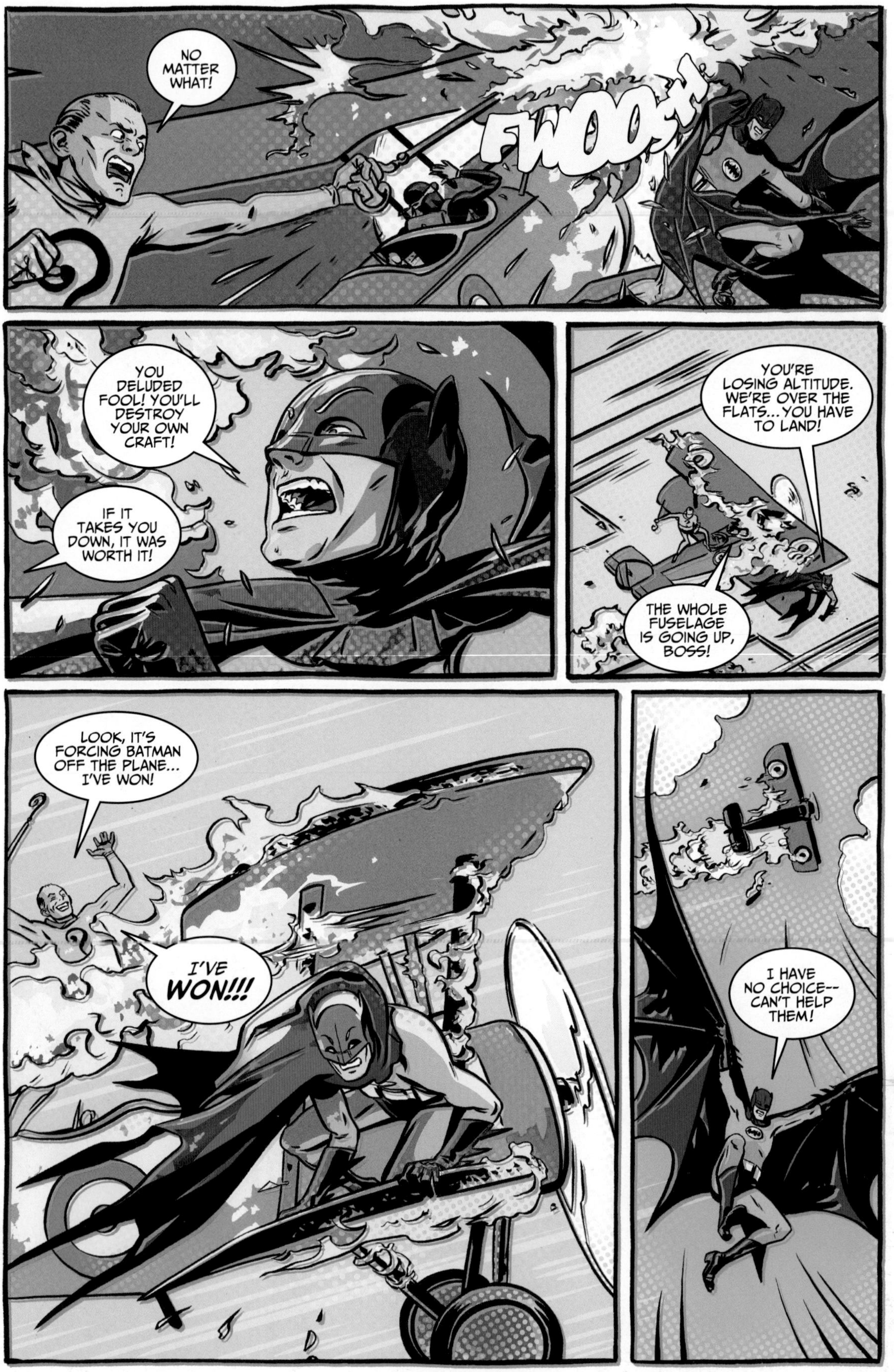
NO MATTER WHAT!
FWOOSH
YOU DELUDED FOOL! YOU'LL DESTROY YOUR OWN CRAFT!
IF IT TAKES YOU DOWN, IT WAS WORTH IT!
YOU'RE LOSING ALTITUDE. WE'RE OVER THE FLATS...YOU HAVE TO LAND!
THE WHOLE FUSELAGE IS GOING UP, BOSS!
LOOK, IT'S FORCING BATMAN OFF THE PLANE... I'VE WON!
I'VE WON!!!
I HAVE NO CHOICE-- CAN'T HELP THEM!

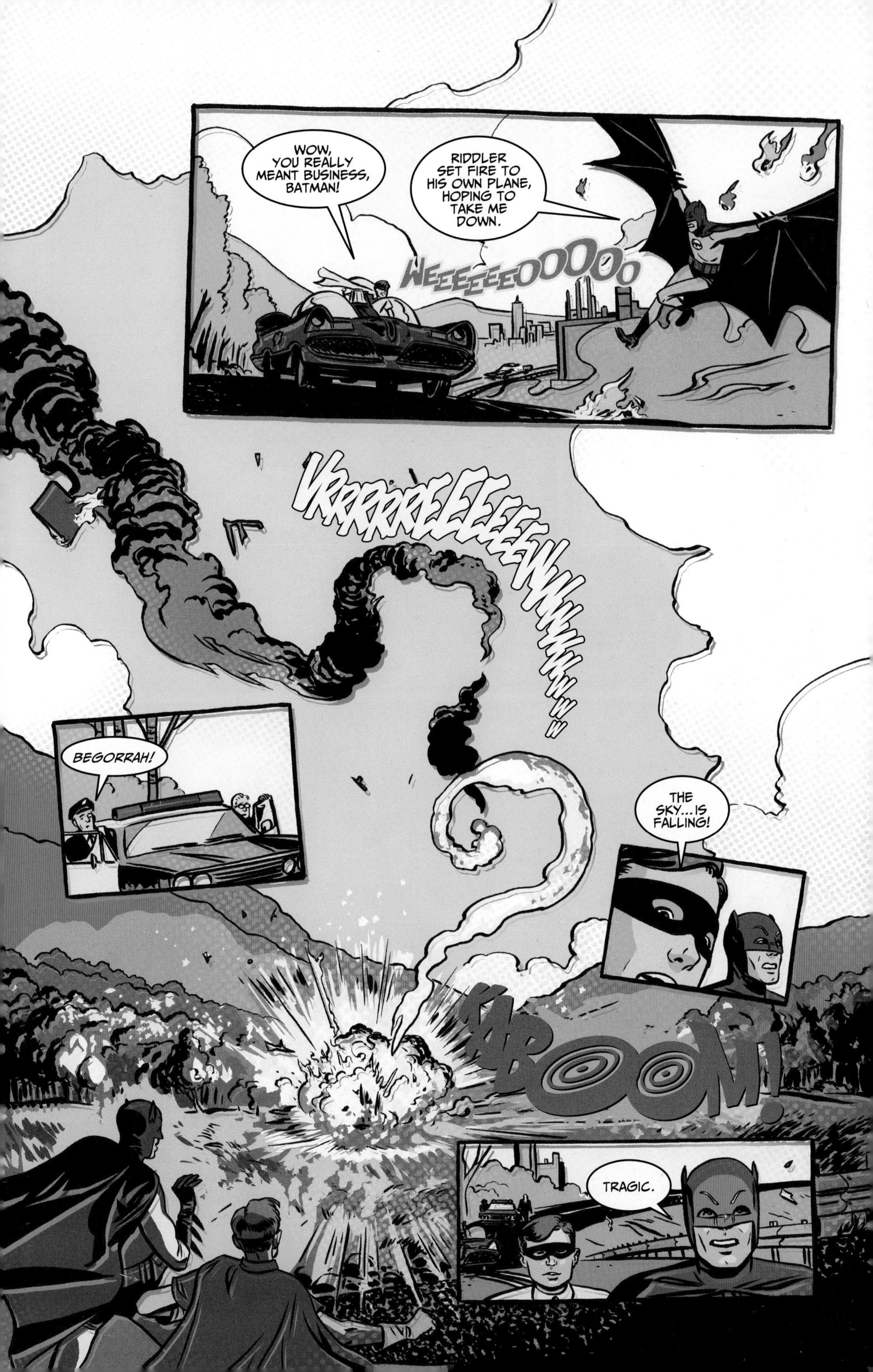
WOW, YOU REALLY MEANT BUSINESS, BATMAN!
RIDDLER SET FIRE TO HIS OWN PLANE, HOPING TO TAKE ME DOWN.
WEEEEEEOOOOo
VRRRRREEEEEEWWWWWWWW
BEGORRAH!
THE SKY...IS FALLING!
KABOOM!
TRAGIC.

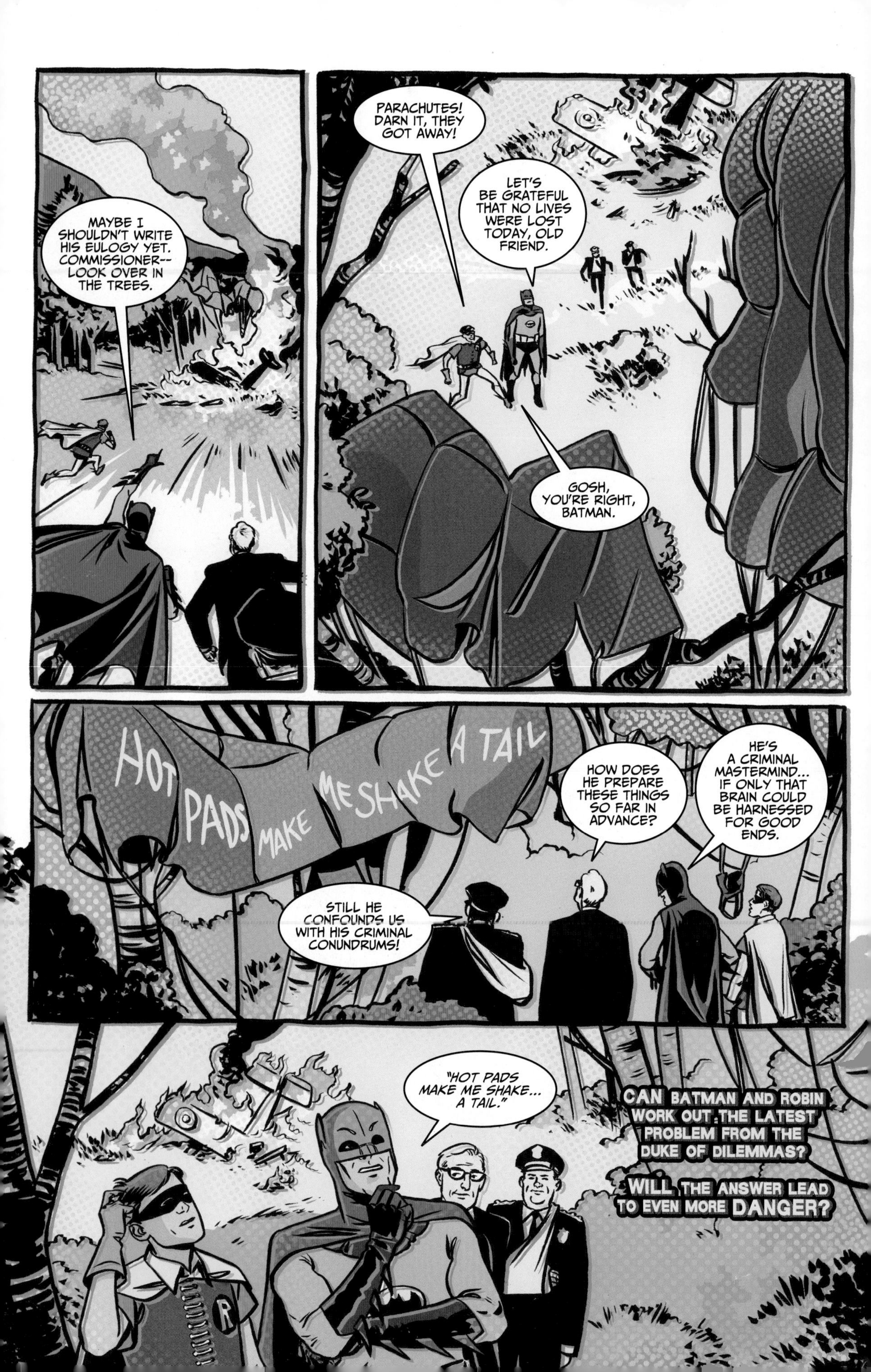
MAYBE I SHOULDN'T WRITE HIS EULOGY YET. COMMISSIONER-- LOOK OVER IN THE TREES.
PARACHUTES! DARN IT, THEY GOT AWAY!
LET'S BE GRATEFUL THAT NO LIVES WERE LOST TODAY, OLD FRIEND.
GOSH, YOU'RE RIGHT, BATMAN.
HOT PADS MAKE ME SHAKE A TAIL
STILL HE CONFOUNDS US WITH HIS CRIMINAL CONUNDRUMS!
HOW DOES HE PREPARE THESE THINGS SO FAR IN ADVANCE?
HE'S A CRIMINAL MASTERMIND... IF ONLY THAT BRAIN COULD BE HARNESSED FOR GOOD ENDS.
"HOT PADS MAKE ME SHAKE... A TAIL."
CAN BATMAN AND ROBIN WORK OUT THE LATEST PROBLEM FROM THE DUKE OF DILEMMAS?
WILL THE ANSWER LEAD TO EVEN MORE DANGER?

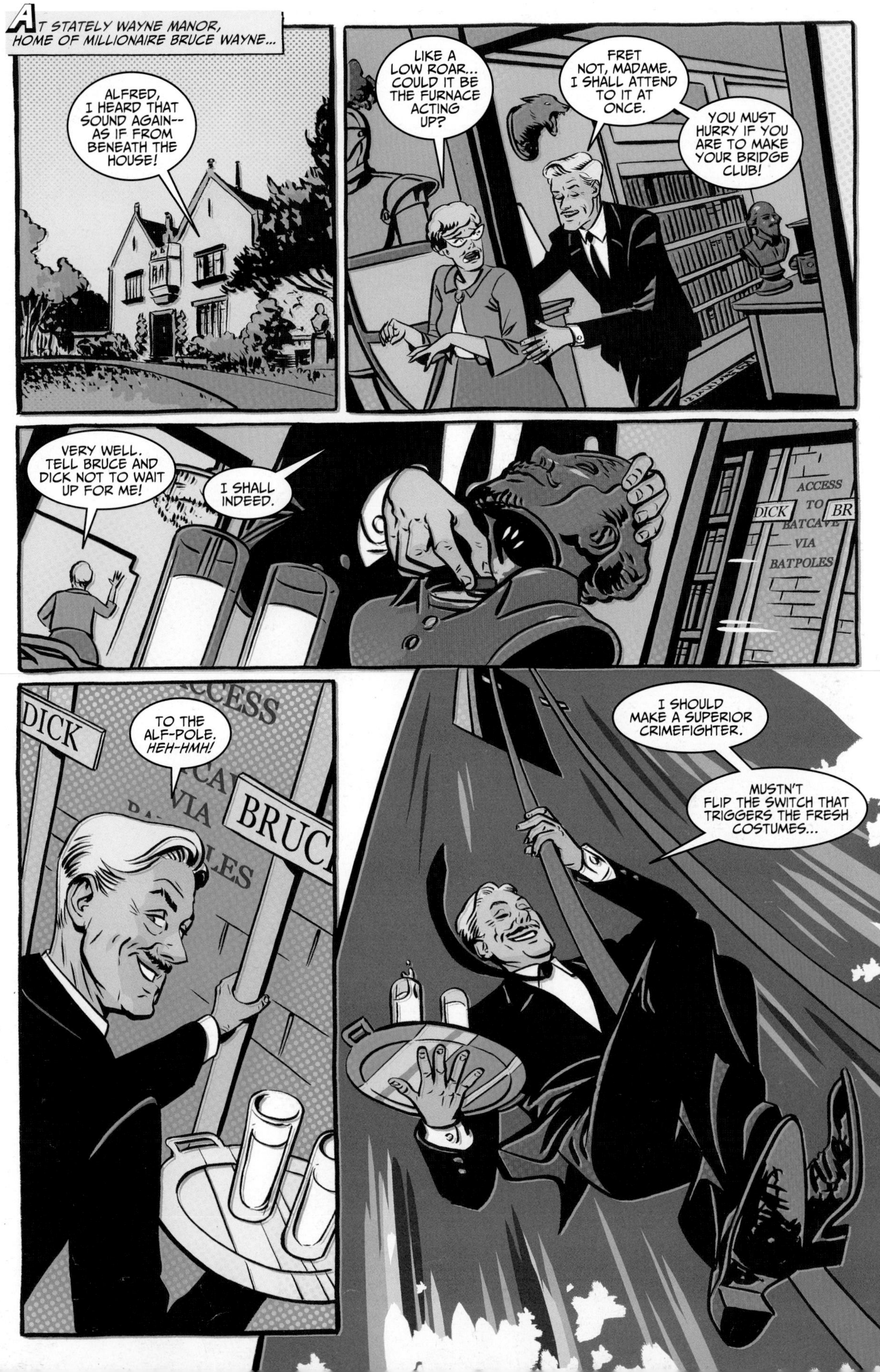
AT STATELY WAYNE MANOR, HOME OF MILLIONAIRE BRUCE WAYNE...
ALFRED, I HEARD THAT SOUND AGAIN-- AS IF FROM BENEATH THE HOUSE!
LIKE A LOW ROAR... COULD IT BE THE FURNACE ACTING UP?
FRET NOT, MADAME. I SHALL ATTEND TO IT AT ONCE.
YOU MUST HURRY IF YOU ARE TO MAKE YOUR BRIDGE CLUB!
VERY WELL. TELL BRUCE AND DICK NOT TO WAIT UP FOR ME!
I SHALL INDEED.
DICK
ACCESS TO BATCAVE VIA BATPOLES
BR
DICK
TO THE ALF-POLE. HEH-HMH!
BRUC
I SHOULD MAKE A SUPERIOR CRIMEFIGHTER.
MUSTN'T FLIP THE SWITCH THAT TRIGGERS THE FRESH COSTUMES...

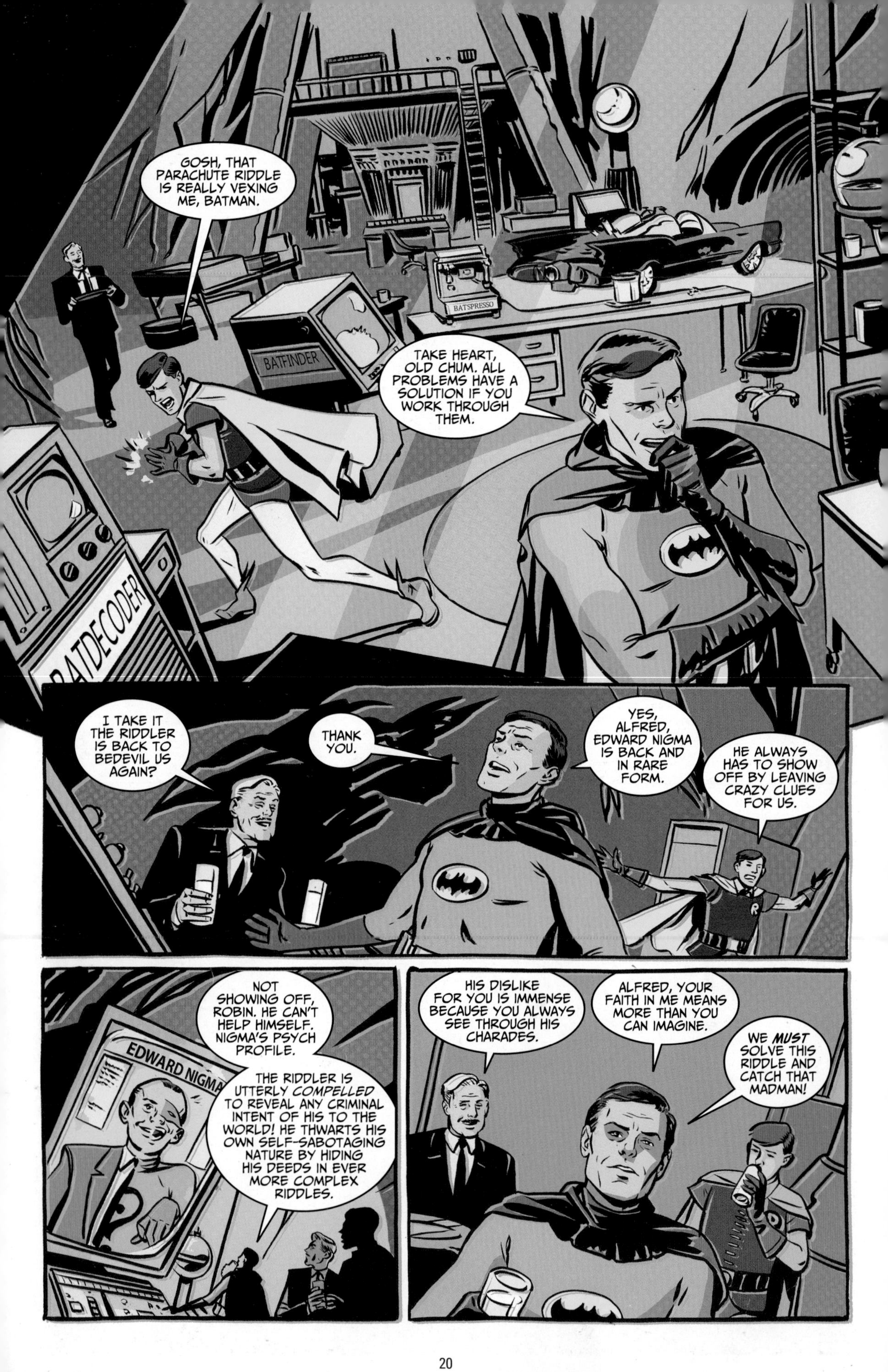
GOSH, THAT PARACHUTE RIDDLE IS REALLY VEXING ME, BATMAN.
BATFINDER
BATSPRESSO
TAKE HEART, OLD CHUM. ALL PROBLEMS HAVE A SOLUTION IF YOU WORK THROUGH THEM.
BATDECODER
I TAKE IT THE RIDDLER IS BACK TO BEDEVIL US AGAIN?
THANK YOU.
YES, ALFRED, EDWARD NIGMA IS BACK AND IN RARE FORM.
HE ALWAYS HAS TO SHOW OFF BY LEAVING CRAZY CLUES FOR US.
NOT SHOWING OFF, ROBIN. HE CAN'T HELP HIMSELF. NIGMA'S PSYCH PROFILE.
EDWARD NIGMA
THE RIDDLER IS UTTERLY *COMPELLED* TO REVEAL ANY CRIMINAL INTENT OF HIS TO THE WORLD! HE THWARTS HIS OWN SELF-SABOTAGING NATURE BY HIDING HIS DEEDS IN EVER MORE COMPLEX RIDDLES.
HIS DISLIKE FOR YOU IS IMMENSE BECAUSE YOU ALWAYS SEE THROUGH HIS CHARADES.
ALFRED, YOUR FAITH IN ME MEANS MORE THAN YOU CAN IMAGINE.
WE *MUST* SOLVE THIS RIDDLE AND CATCH THAT MADMAN!

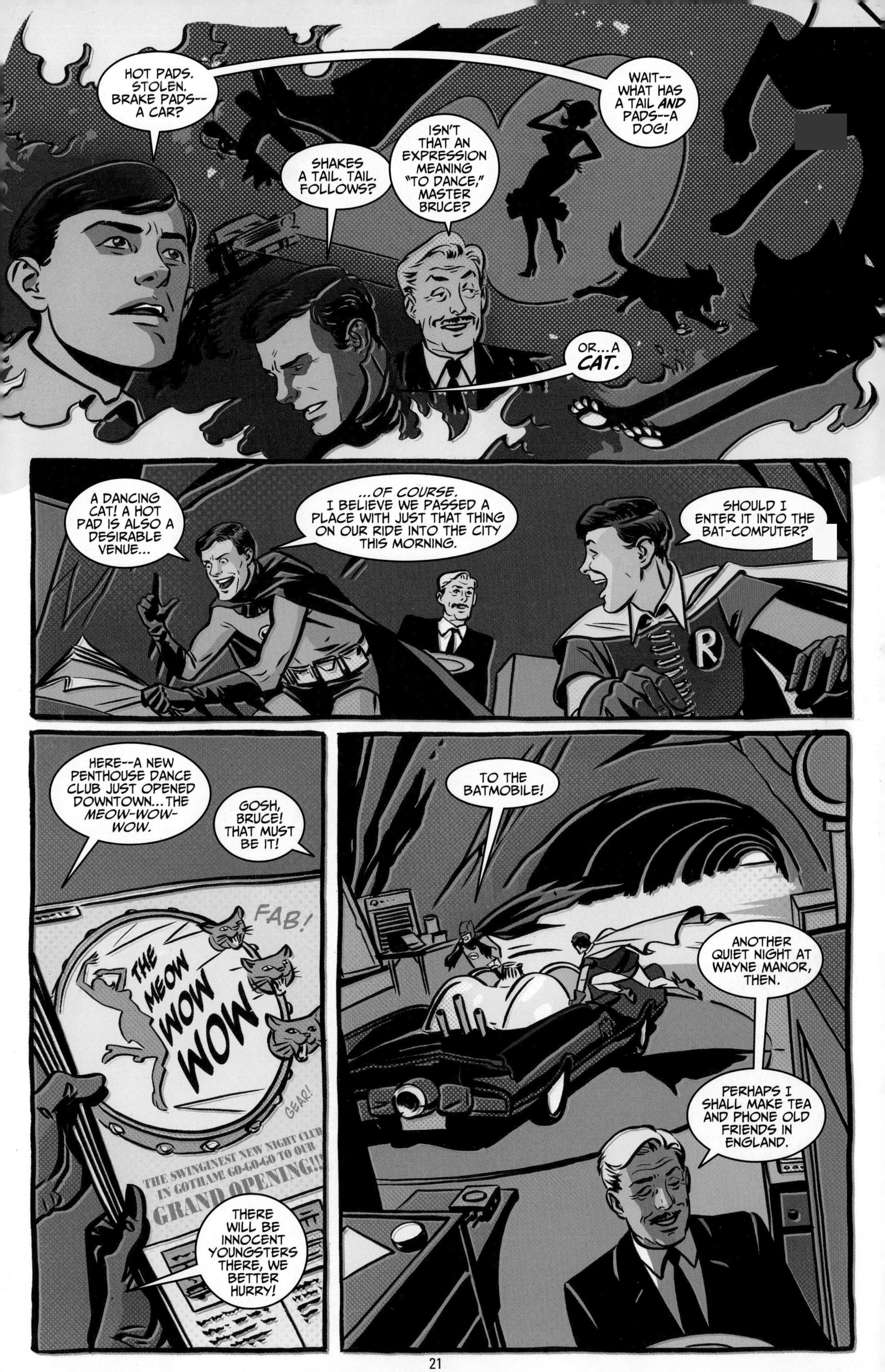
HOT PADS. STOLEN. BRAKE PADS-- A CAR?
WAIT-- WHAT HAS A TAIL AND PADS--A DOG!
SHAKES A TAIL. TAIL. FOLLOWS?
ISN'T THAT AN EXPRESSION MEANING "TO DANCE," MASTER BRUCE?
OR...A CAT.
A DANCING CAT! A HOT PAD IS ALSO A DESIRABLE VENUE...
...OF COURSE. I BELIEVE WE PASSED A PLACE WITH JUST THAT THING ON OUR RIDE INTO THE CITY THIS MORNING.
SHOULD I ENTER IT INTO THE BAT-COMPUTER?
HERE--A NEW PENTHOUSE DANCE CLUB JUST OPENED DOWNTOWN...THE MEOW-WOW-WOW.
GOSH, BRUCE! THAT MUST BE IT!
FAB!
THE MEOW WOW WOW
GEAR!
THE SWINGINEST NEW NIGHT CLUB IN GOTHAM! GO-GO-GO TO OUR GRAND OPENING!!!
THERE WILL BE INNOCENT YOUNGSTERS THERE, WE BETTER HURRY!
TO THE BATMOBILE!
ANOTHER QUIET NIGHT AT WAYNE MANOR, THEN.
PERHAPS I SHALL MAKE TEA AND PHONE OLD FRIENDS IN ENGLAND.

LATER THAT NIGHT AT THE MEOW-WOW-WOW!

CLINK

WHY DO YOU THINK RIDDLER WOULD PICK SUCH A BUSY PLACE TO STORE HIS LOOT, BATMAN?

PERHAPS HE MEANS TO KEEP THE LOOT FROM HIS OWN GANG.

HOLY DOUBLE-CROSS!

VHAT!? VHERE IS A HOLY-- AH!

SO I DID HEAR FOOTFALLS ON THE VALL.

SORRY TO DISTURB YOU, SIR.

I TAKE IT YOU ARE NEW TO AMERICA, VISITOR?

YES, I JUST ARRIVED FROM THE OLD COUNTRY... TO FIND MEN DRESSED AS BATS OUTSIDE VINDOWS.

I THOUGHT I WAS GETTING AWAY FROM... COMPETITION.

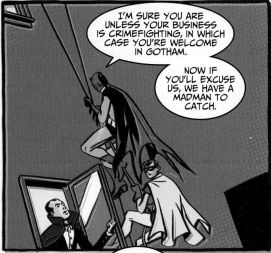

I'M SURE YOU ARE UNLESS YOUR BUSINESS IS CRIMEFIGHTING, IN WHICH CASE YOU'RE WELCOME IN GOTHAM.

NOW IF YOU'LL EXCUSE US, WE HAVE A MADMAN TO CATCH.

EXQUISITE TASTE IN CAPES.

PERHAPS VE SHALL MEET AGAIN.

22

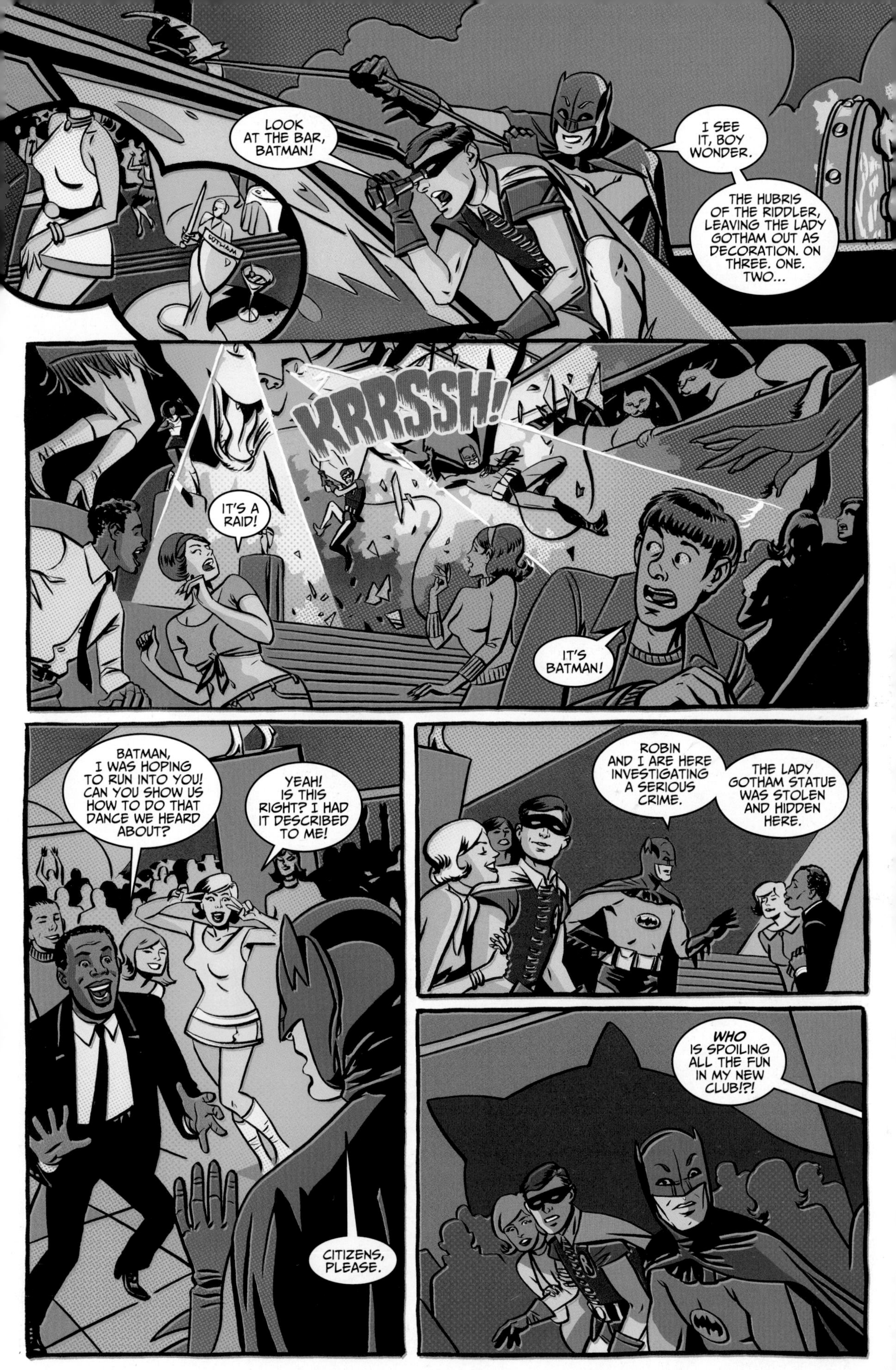
LOOK AT THE BAR, BATMAN!
I SEE IT, BOY WONDER.
THE HUBRIS OF THE RIDDLER, LEAVING THE LADY GOTHAM OUT AS DECORATION. ON THREE. ONE. TWO...
KRRSSH!
IT'S A RAID!
IT'S BATMAN!
BATMAN, I WAS HOPING TO RUN INTO YOU! CAN YOU SHOW US HOW TO DO THAT DANCE WE HEARD ABOUT?
YEAH! IS THIS RIGHT? I HAD IT DESCRIBED TO ME!
CITIZENS, PLEASE.
ROBIN AND I ARE HERE INVESTIGATING A SERIOUS CRIME.
THE LADY GOTHAM STATUE WAS STOLEN AND HIDDEN HERE.
*WHO* IS SPOILING ALL THE FUN IN MY NEW CLUB!?!

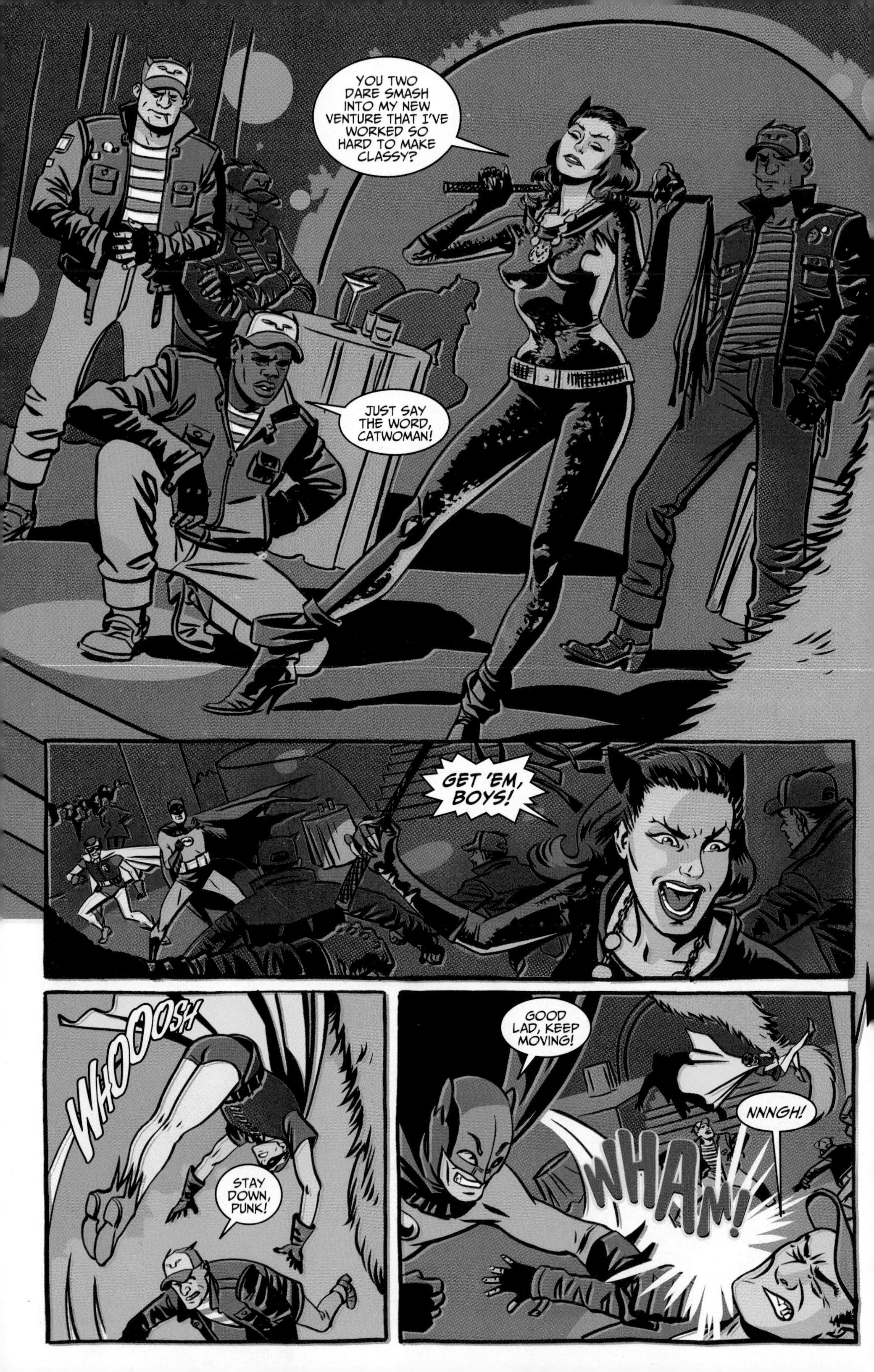
YOU TWO DARE SMASH INTO MY NEW VENTURE THAT I'VE WORKED SO HARD TO MAKE CLASSY?
JUST SAY THE WORD, CATWOMAN!
GET 'EM, BOYS!
WHOOOOSH
STAY DOWN, PUNK!
GOOD LAD, KEEP MOVING!
NNNGH!
WHAM!

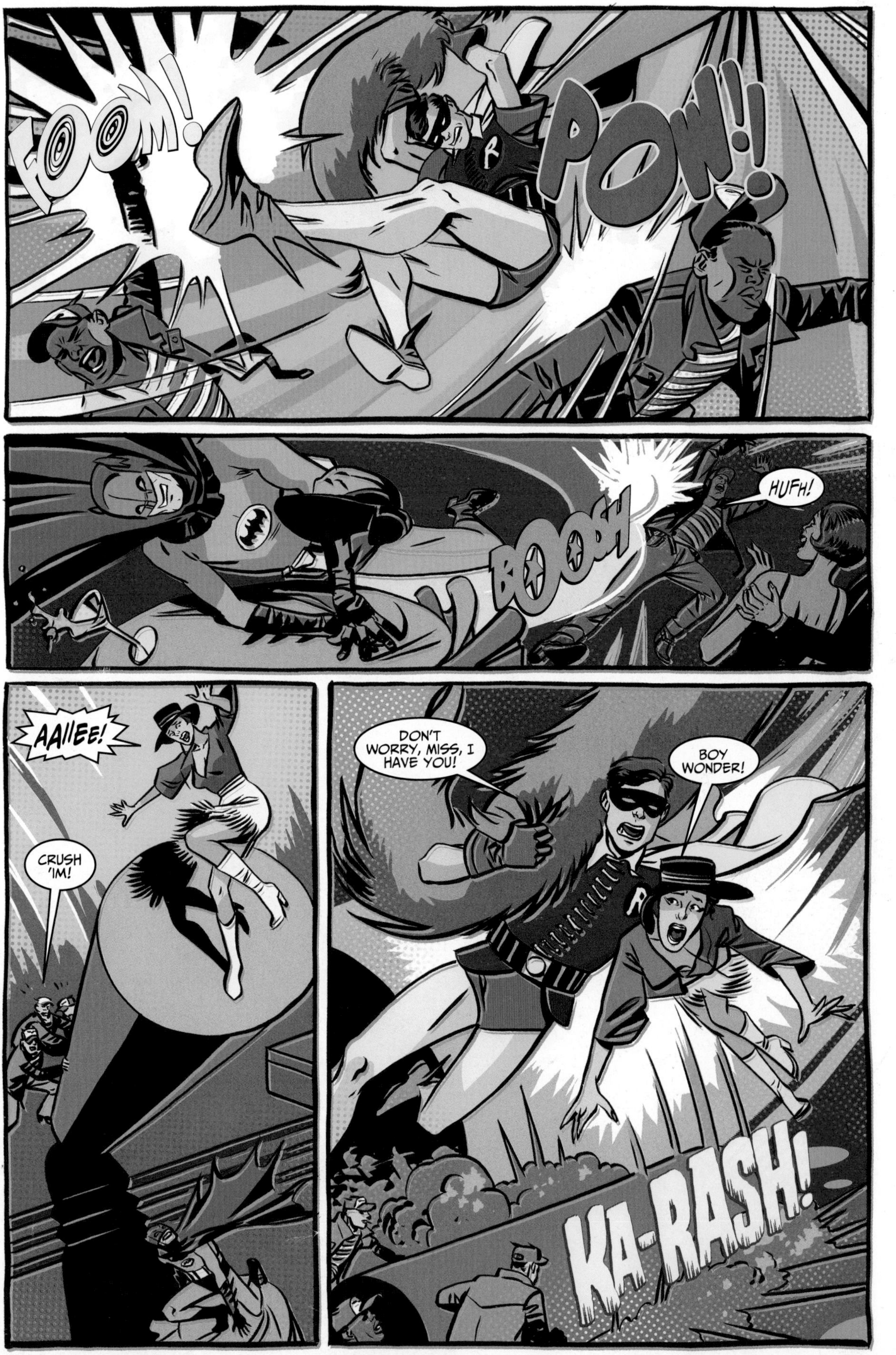
FOOM!
POW!!
BOOSH
HUFH!
AAIIEE!
CRUSH 'IM!
DON'T WORRY, MISS, I HAVE YOU!
BOY WONDER!
KA-RASH!

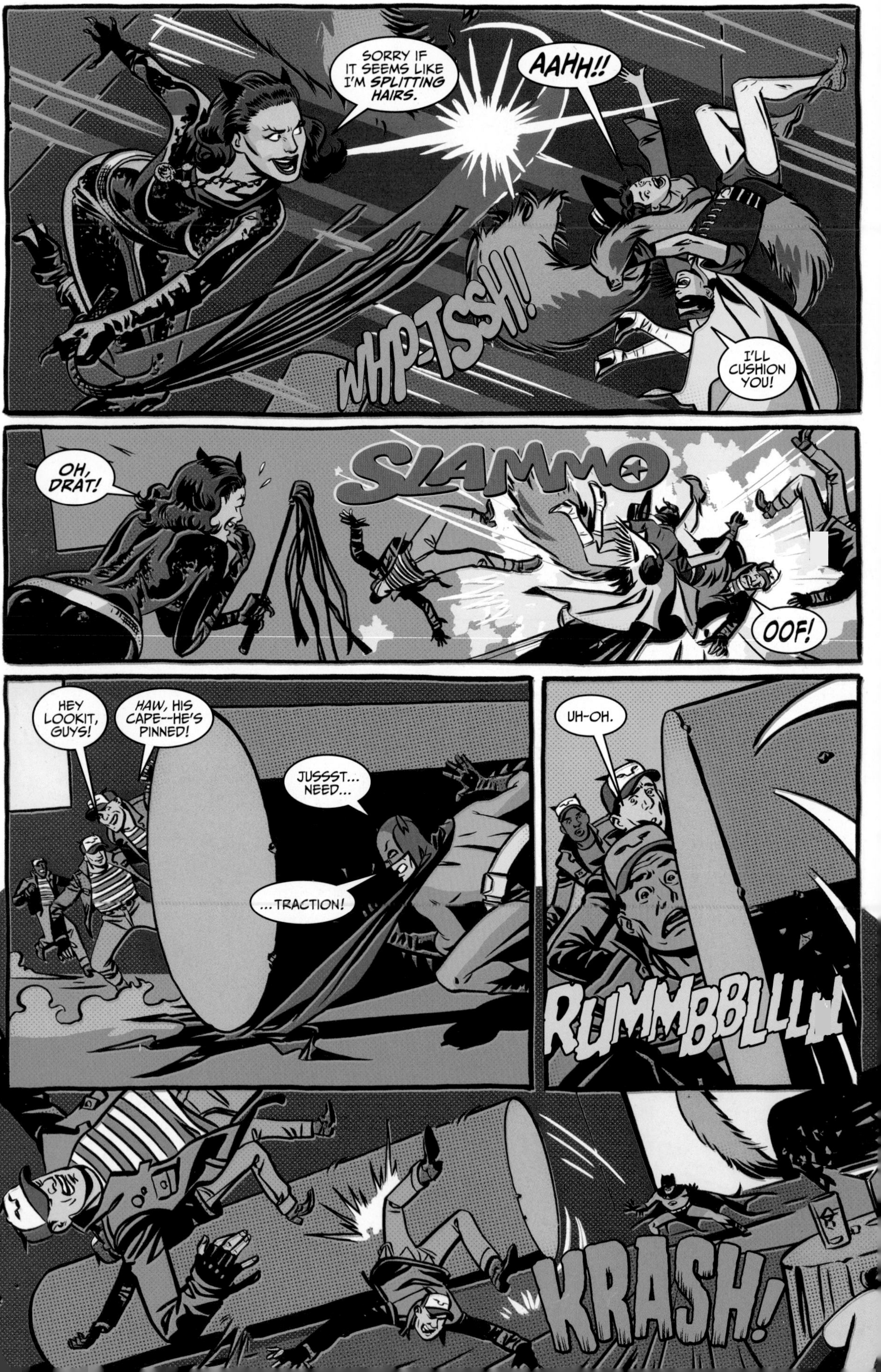
SORRY IF IT SEEMS LIKE I'M SPLITTING HAIRS.
AAHH!!
WHP-TSSH!
I'LL CUSHION YOU!
OH, DRAT!
SLAMMO
OOF!
HEY LOOKIT, GUYS!
HAW, HIS CAPE--HE'S PINNED!
JUSSST... NEED...
...TRACTION!
UH-OH.
RUMMBBLLLL
KRASH!

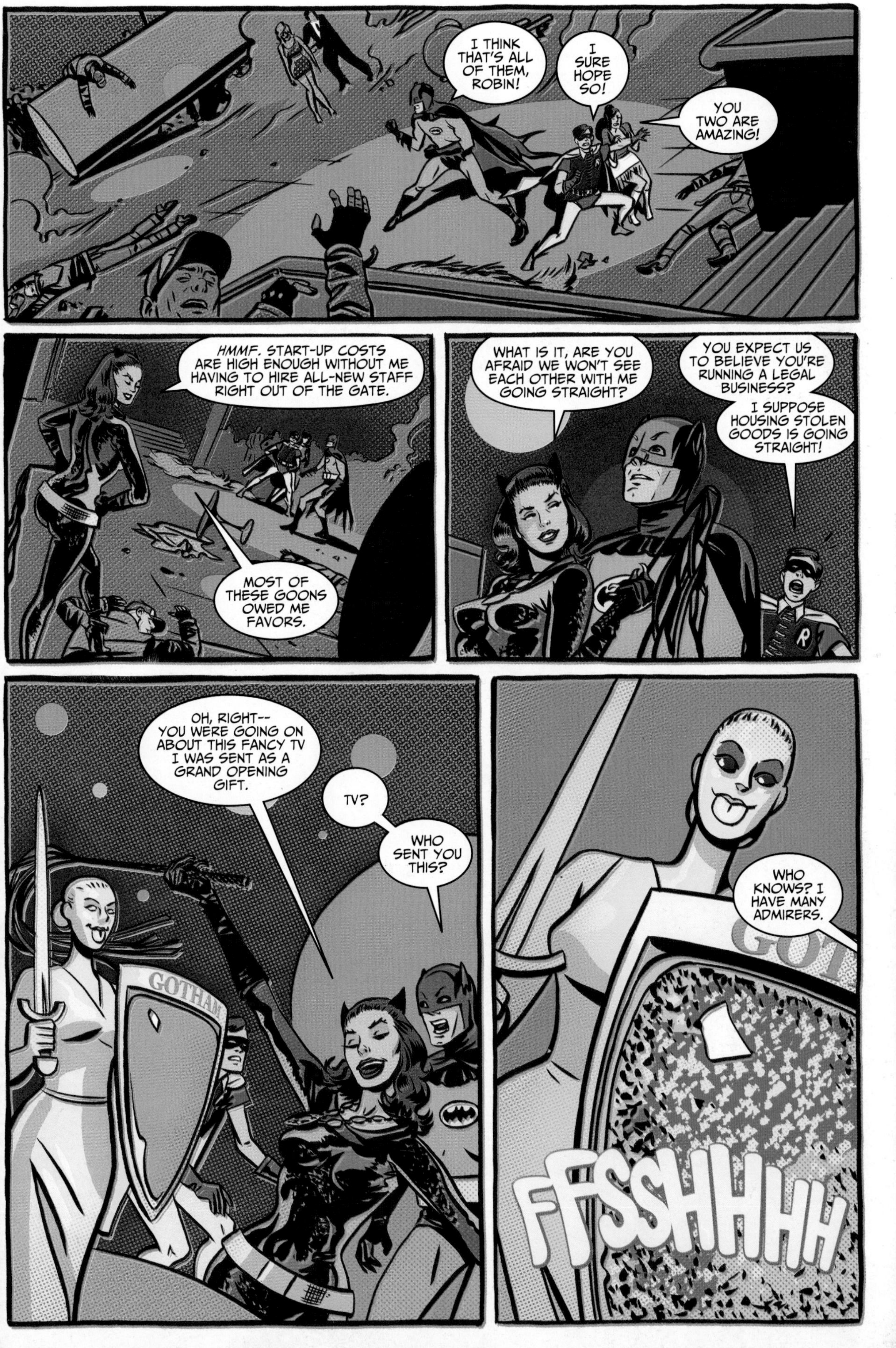
I THINK THAT'S ALL OF THEM, ROBIN!
I SURE HOPE SO!
YOU TWO ARE AMAZING!
HMMF. START-UP COSTS ARE HIGH ENOUGH WITHOUT ME HAVING TO HIRE ALL-NEW STAFF RIGHT OUT OF THE GATE.
MOST OF THESE GOONS OWED ME FAVORS.
WHAT IS IT, ARE YOU AFRAID WE WON'T SEE EACH OTHER WITH ME GOING STRAIGHT?
YOU EXPECT US TO BELIEVE YOU'RE RUNNING A LEGAL BUSINESS?
I SUPPOSE HOUSING STOLEN GOODS IS GOING STRAIGHT!
OH, RIGHT-- YOU WERE GOING ON ABOUT THIS FANCY TV I WAS SENT AS A GRAND OPENING GIFT.
TV?
WHO SENT YOU THIS?
GOTHAM
WHO KNOWS? I HAVE MANY ADMIRERS.
FFSSHHHH

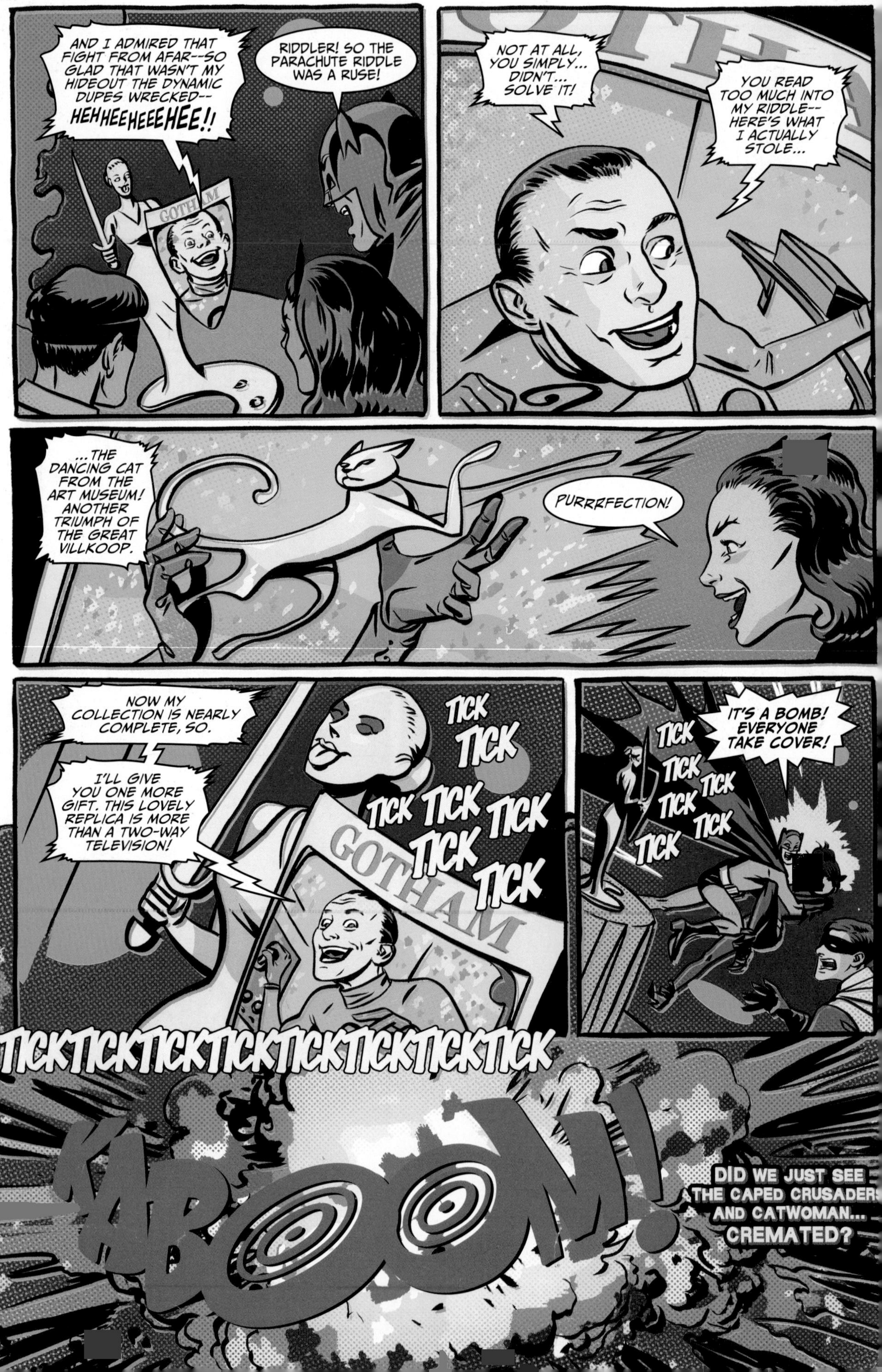
AND I ADMIRED THAT FIGHT FROM AFAR--SO GLAD THAT WASN'T MY HIDEOUT THE DYNAMIC DUPES WRECKED-- HEHHEEHEEEHEE!!
GOTHAM
RIDDLER! SO THE PARACHUTE RIDDLE WAS A RUSE!
NOT AT ALL, YOU SIMPLY... DIDN'T... SOLVE IT!
YOU READ TOO MUCH INTO MY RIDDLE-- HERE'S WHAT I ACTUALLY STOLE...
...THE DANCING CAT FROM THE ART MUSEUM! ANOTHER TRIUMPH OF THE GREAT VILLKOOP.
PURRRFECTION!
NOW MY COLLECTION IS NEARLY COMPLETE, SO.
I'LL GIVE YOU ONE MORE GIFT. THIS LOVELY REPLICA IS MORE THAN A TWO-WAY TELEVISION!
TICK TICK TICK TICK TICK TICK TICK
GOTHAM
IT'S A BOMB! EVERYONE TAKE COVER!
TICK TICK TICK TICK TICK TICK
TICKTICKTICKTICKTICKTICKTICKTICK
KABOOM!
DID WE JUST SEE THE CAPED CRUSADERS AND CATWOMAN... CREMATED?

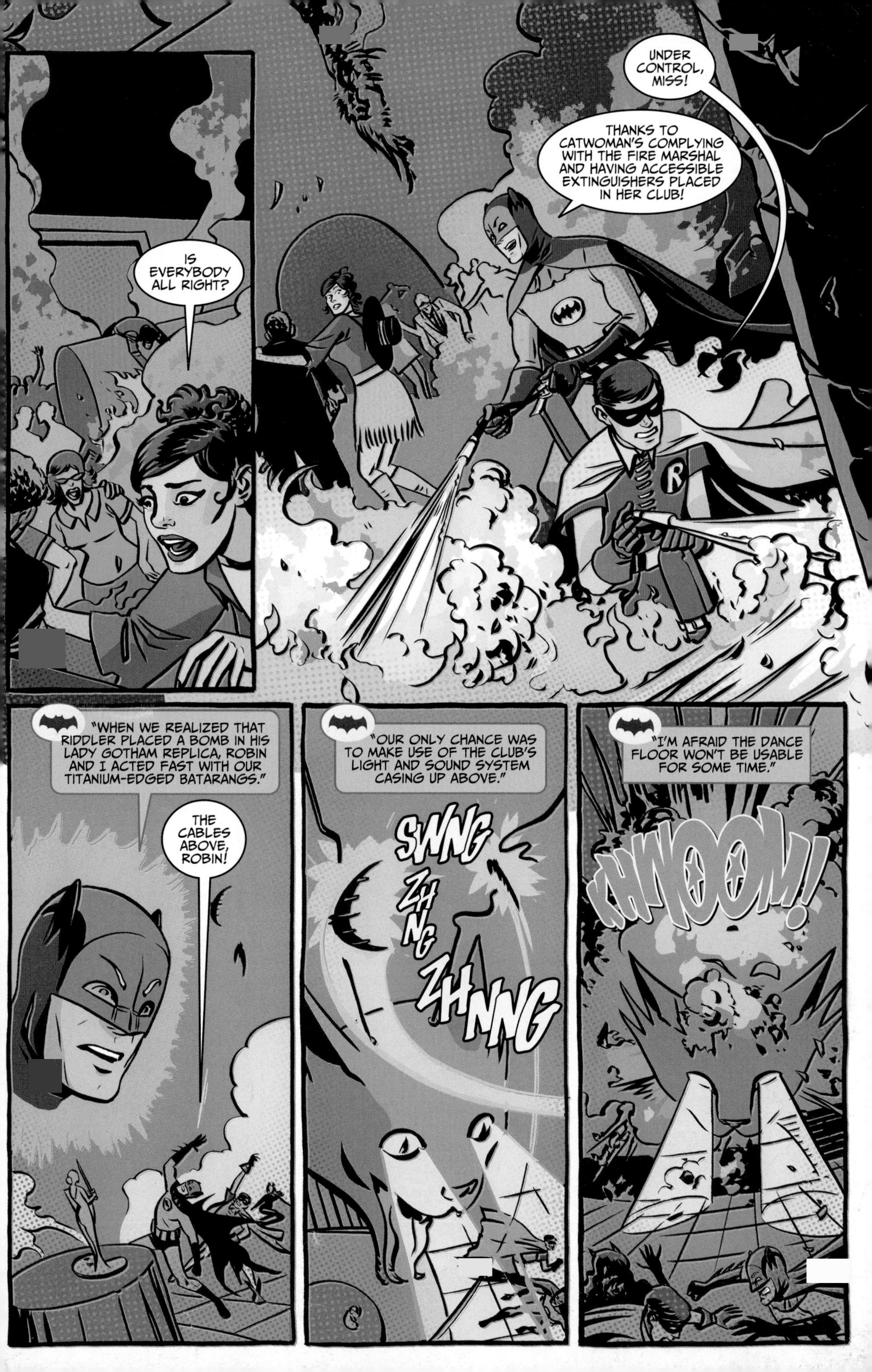
IS EVERYBODY ALL RIGHT?
UNDER CONTROL, MISS!
THANKS TO CATWOMAN'S COMPLYING WITH THE FIRE MARSHAL AND HAVING ACCESSIBLE EXTINGUISHERS PLACED IN HER CLUB!
"WHEN WE REALIZED THAT RIDDLER PLACED A BOMB IN HIS LADY GOTHAM REPLICA, ROBIN AND I ACTED FAST WITH OUR TITANIUM-EDGED BATARANGS."
THE CABLES ABOVE, ROBIN!
"OUR ONLY CHANCE WAS TO MAKE USE OF THE CLUB'S LIGHT AND SOUND SYSTEM CASING UP ABOVE."
SWNG
ZHNG
ZHNNG
"I'M AFRAID THE DANCE FLOOR WON'T BE USABLE FOR SOME TIME."
KHWOOM!

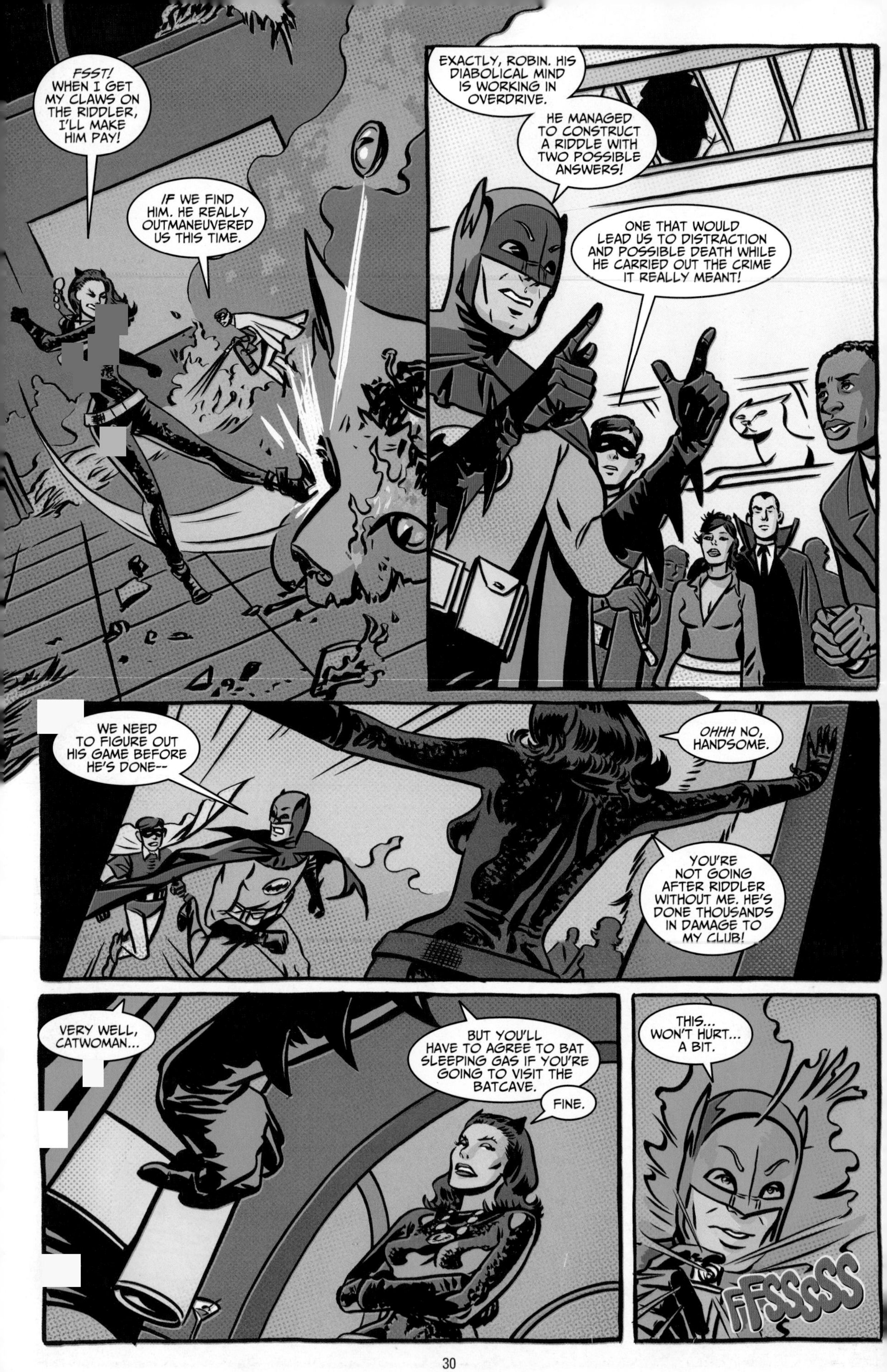
FSST! WHEN I GET MY CLAWS ON THE RIDDLER, I'LL MAKE HIM PAY!
IF WE FIND HIM. HE REALLY OUTMANEUVERED US THIS TIME.
EXACTLY, ROBIN. HIS DIABOLICAL MIND IS WORKING IN OVERDRIVE.
HE MANAGED TO CONSTRUCT A RIDDLE WITH TWO POSSIBLE ANSWERS!
ONE THAT WOULD LEAD US TO DISTRACTION AND POSSIBLE DEATH WHILE HE CARRIED OUT THE CRIME IT REALLY MEANT!
WE NEED TO FIGURE OUT HIS GAME BEFORE HE'S DONE--
OHHH NO, HANDSOME.
YOU'RE NOT GOING AFTER RIDDLER WITHOUT ME. HE'S DONE THOUSANDS IN DAMAGE TO MY CLUB!
VERY WELL, CATWOMAN...
BUT YOU'LL HAVE TO AGREE TO BAT SLEEPING GAS IF YOU'RE GOING TO VISIT THE BATCAVE.
FINE.
THIS... WON'T HURT... A BIT.
FFSSSSS

YOU CAN WAKE UP NOW.

FFSSSSS

YAAAAWWWNN... WHAT A CAT NAP--SAY!

OH, RIGHT...THE BATCAVE!

WHEN YOU'RE READY TO STAND, BATMAN WANTS US OVER BY THE BAT-COMPUTER.

WHEN IN ROME-- HEY, WHERE WERE YOU SITTING IF WE WERE ALL IN THE CAR?

HOW'S IT COMING?

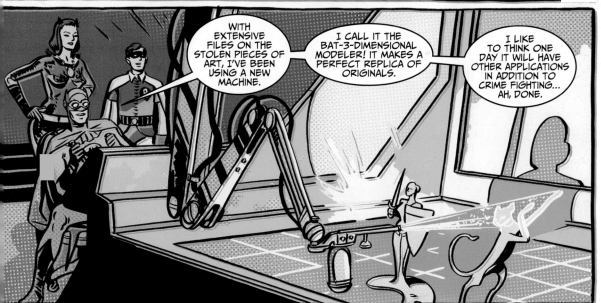

WITH EXTENSIVE FILES ON THE STOLEN PIECES OF ART, I'VE BEEN USING A NEW MACHINE.

I CALL IT THE BAT-3-DIMENSIONAL MODELER! IT MAKES A PERFECT REPLICA OF ORIGINALS.

I LIKE TO THINK ONE DAY IT WILL HAVE OTHER APPLICATIONS IN ADDITION TO CRIME FIGHTING... AH, DONE.

RIDDLER SAID HE WANTED TO COMPLETE HIS COLLECTION. I DID SOME RESEARCH--THESE WERE TO BE A SERIES OF THREE PIECES BY VILLKOOP.

YET IT WAS BELIEVED HE DIED BEFORE MAKING THE LAST ONE.

GOSH, RIDDLER MUST THINK DIFFERENT.

LADY GOTHAM #1

DANCI AT

?

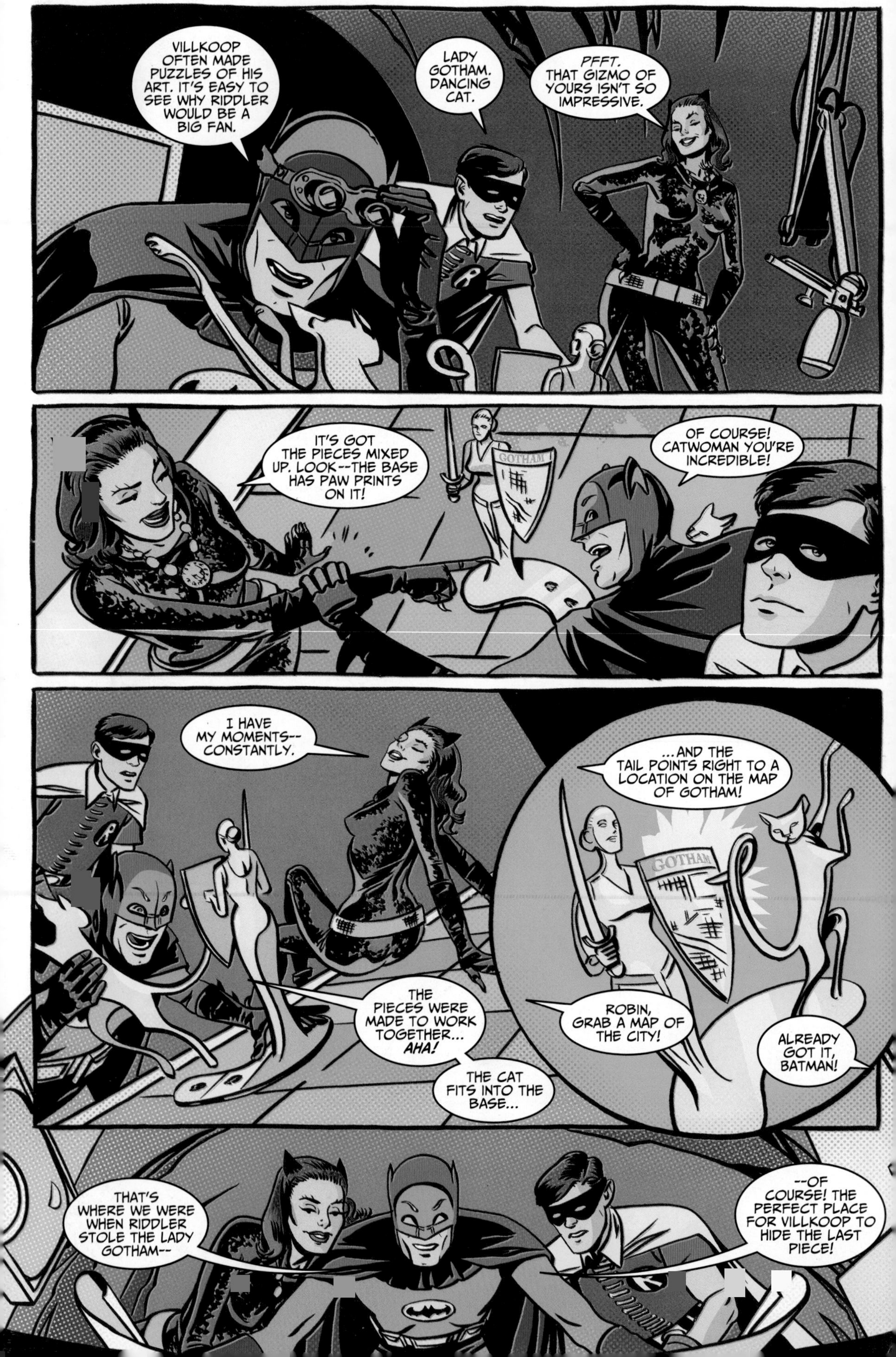
VILLKOOP OFTEN MADE PUZZLES OF HIS ART. IT'S EASY TO SEE WHY RIDDLER WOULD BE A BIG FAN.
LADY GOTHAM. DANCING CAT.
PFFT. THAT GIZMO OF YOURS ISN'T SO IMPRESSIVE.
IT'S GOT THE PIECES MIXED UP. LOOK--THE BASE HAS PAW PRINTS ON IT!
GOTHAM
OF COURSE! CATWOMAN YOU'RE INCREDIBLE!
I HAVE MY MOMENTS-- CONSTANTLY.
THE PIECES WERE MADE TO WORK TOGETHER... AHA!
THE CAT FITS INTO THE BASE...
...AND THE TAIL POINTS RIGHT TO A LOCATION ON THE MAP OF GOTHAM!
GOTHAM
ROBIN, GRAB A MAP OF THE CITY!
ALREADY GOT IT, BATMAN!
THAT'S WHERE WE WERE WHEN RIDDLER STOLE THE LADY GOTHAM--
--OF COURSE! THE PERFECT PLACE FOR VILLKOOP TO HIDE THE LAST PIECE!

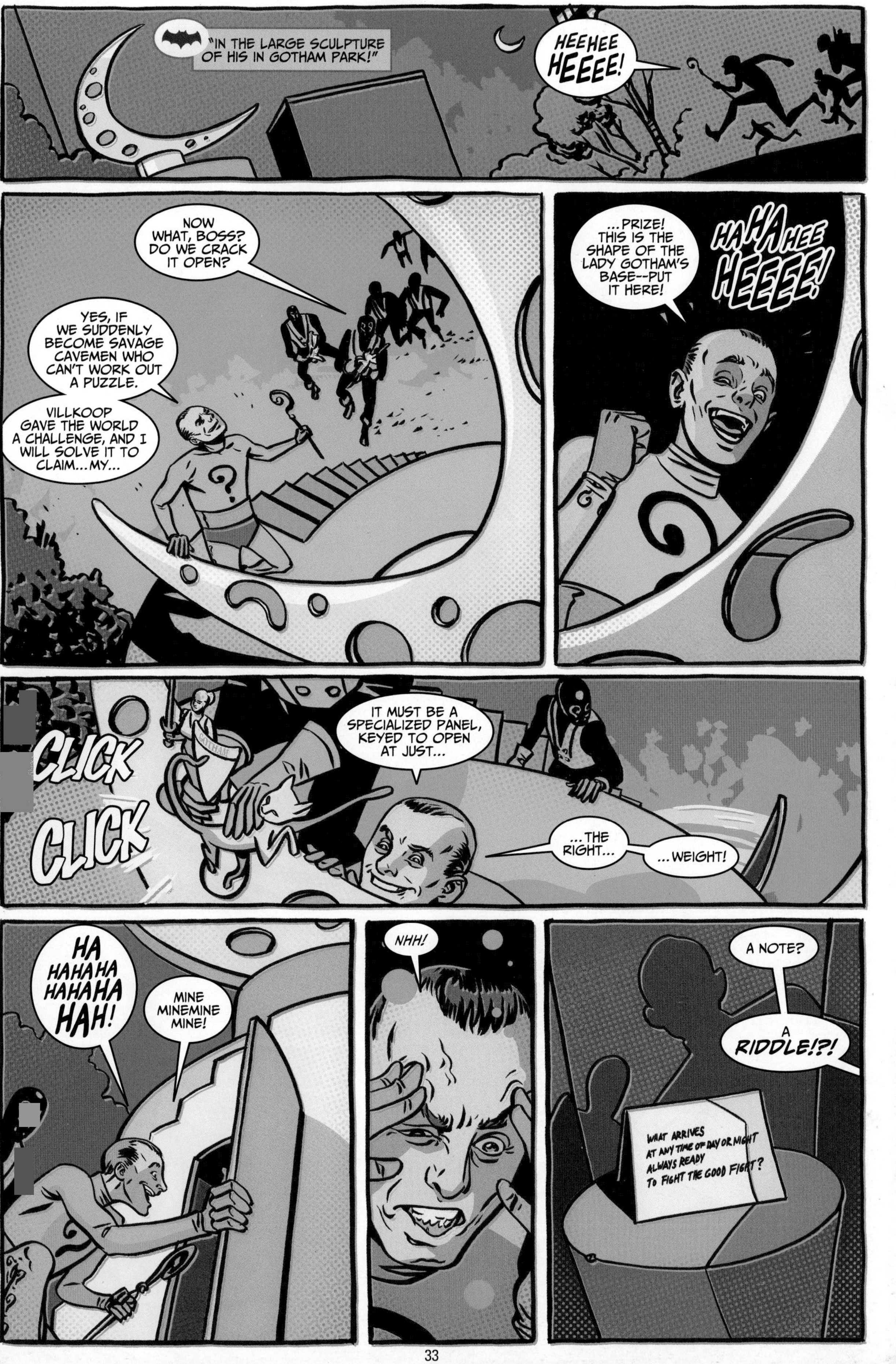
"IN THE LARGE SCULPTURE OF HIS IN GOTHAM PARK!"
HEE HEE HEEEE!
NOW WHAT, BOSS? DO WE CRACK IT OPEN?
YES, IF WE SUDDENLY BECOME SAVAGE CAVEMEN WHO CAN'T WORK OUT A PUZZLE.
VILLKOOP GAVE THE WORLD A CHALLENGE, AND I WILL SOLVE IT TO CLAIM...MY...
...PRIZE! THIS IS THE SHAPE OF THE LADY GOTHAM'S BASE--PUT IT HERE!
HA HA HEE HEEEE!
CLICK
CLICK
GOTHAM
IT MUST BE A SPECIALIZED PANEL, KEYED TO OPEN AT JUST...
...THE RIGHT...
...WEIGHT!
HA HAHAHA HAHAHA HAH!
MINE MINEMINE MINE!
NHH!
A NOTE?
A RIDDLE!?!
WHAT ARRIVES AT ANY TIME OF DAY OR NIGHT ALWAYS READY TO FIGHT THE GOOD FIGHT?

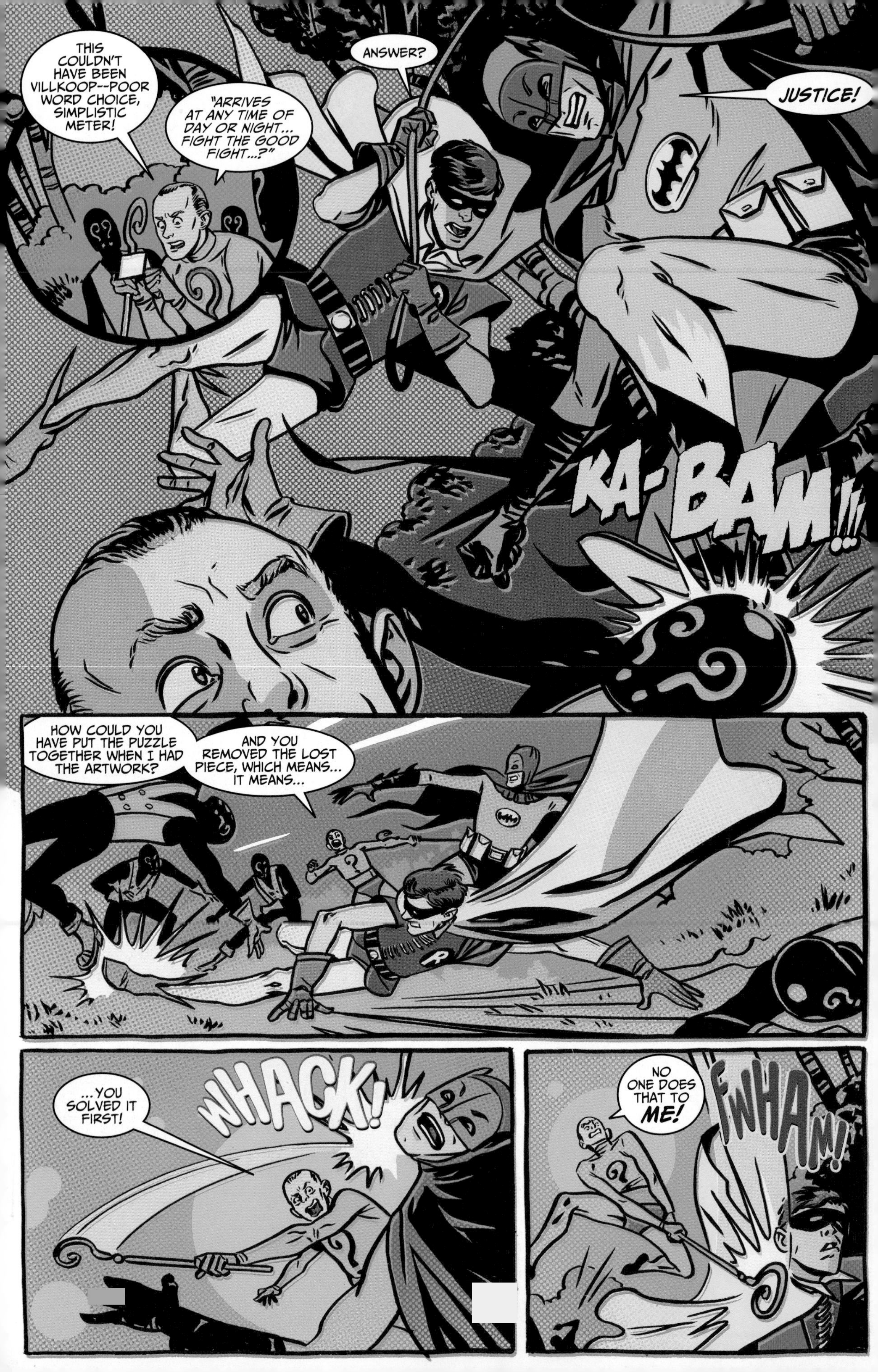
THIS COULDN'T HAVE BEEN VILLKOOP--POOR WORD CHOICE, SIMPLISTIC METER!
"ARRIVES AT ANY TIME OF DAY OR NIGHT... FIGHT THE GOOD FIGHT...?"
ANSWER?
JUSTICE!
KA-BAM!!!
HOW COULD YOU HAVE PUT THE PUZZLE TOGETHER WHEN I HAD THE ARTWORK?
AND YOU REMOVED THE LOST PIECE, WHICH MEANS... IT MEANS...
...YOU SOLVED IT FIRST!
WHACK!
NO ONE DOES THAT TO ME!
FWHAM!

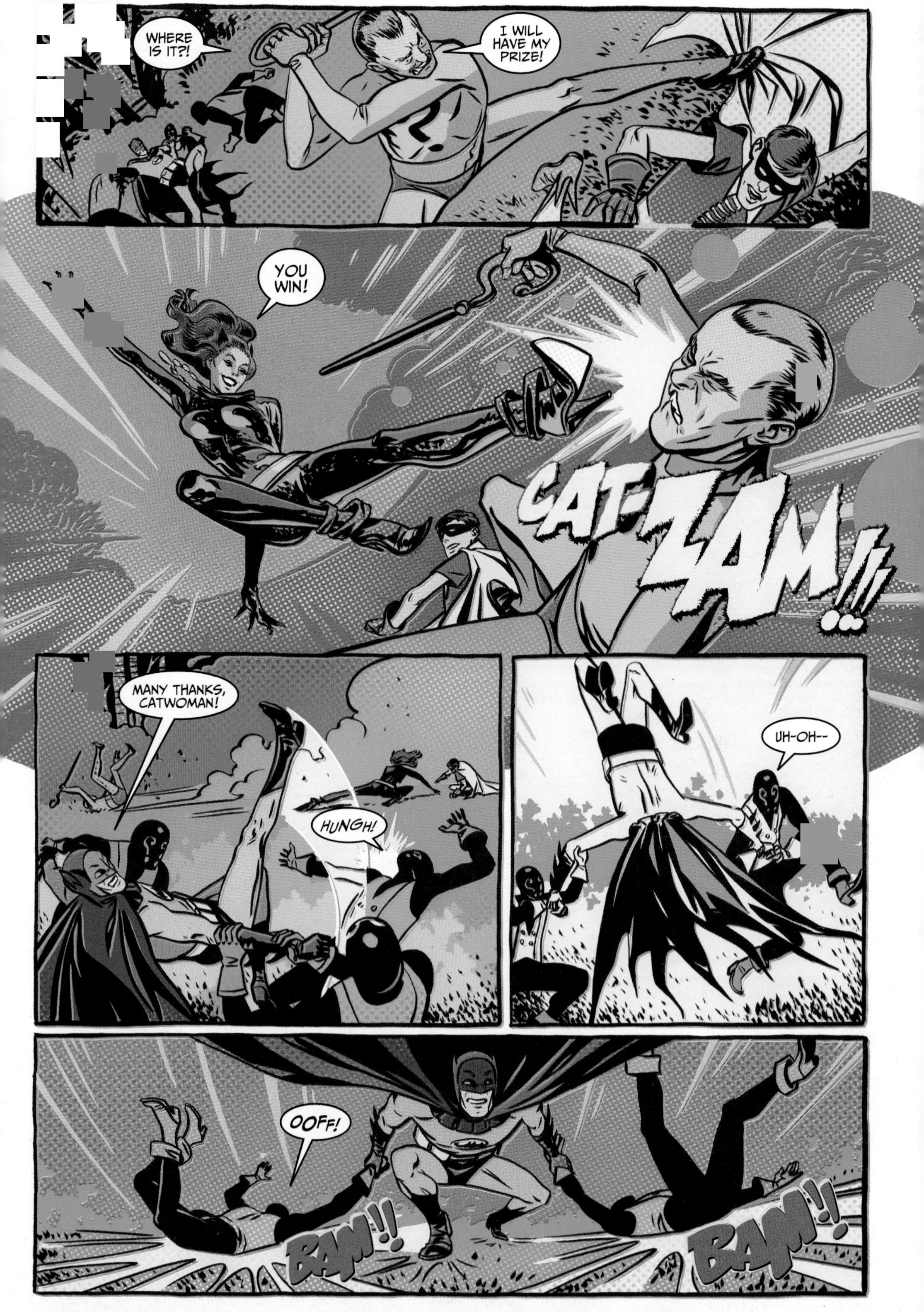
WHERE IS IT?!
I WILL HAVE MY PRIZE!
YOU WIN!
CAT-ZAM!!
MANY THANKS, CATWOMAN!
HUNGH!
UH-OH--
OOFF!
BAM!!
BAM!!

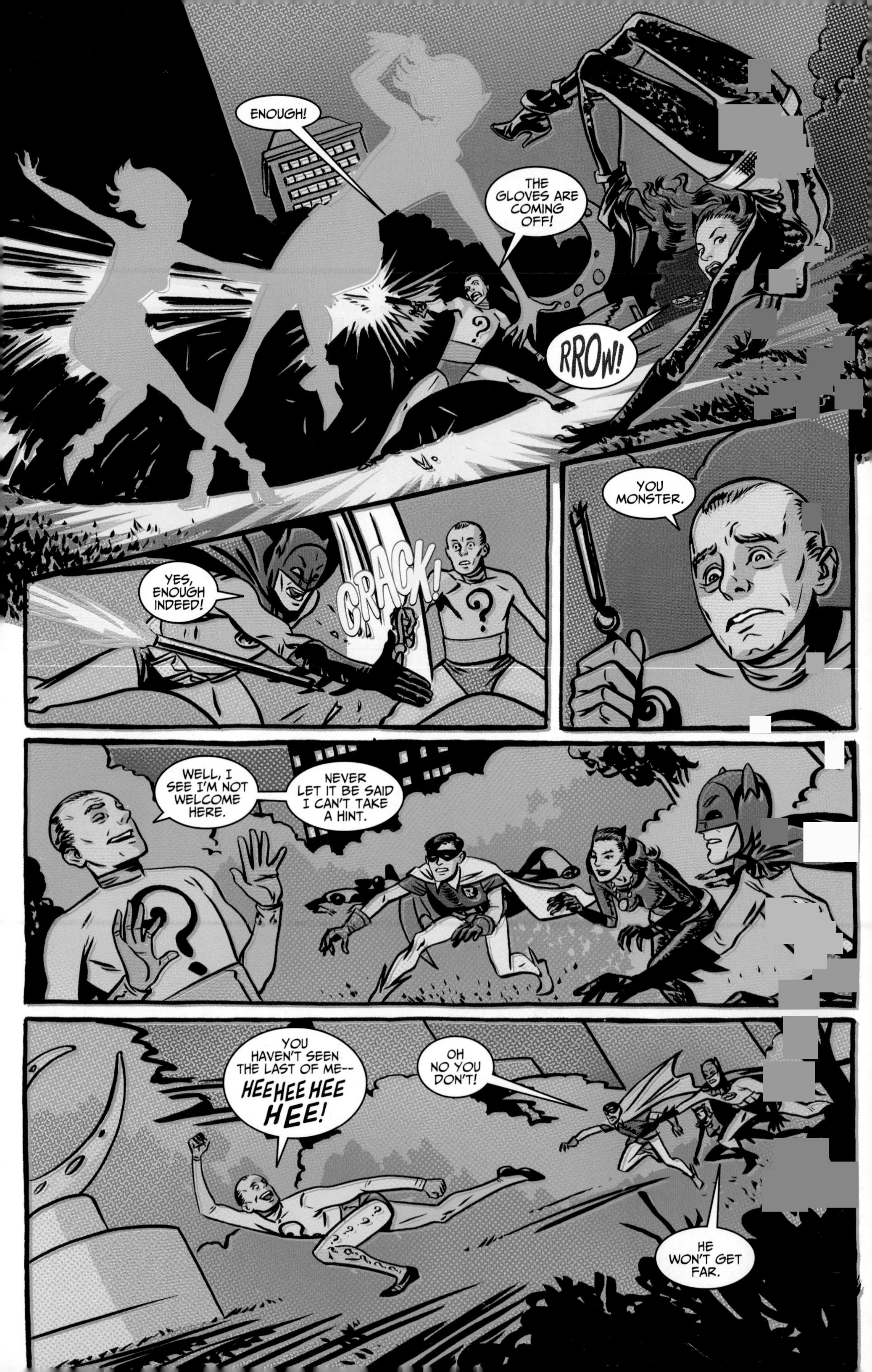
ENOUGH!
THE GLOVES ARE COMING OFF!
RROW!
YES, ENOUGH INDEED!
CRACK!
YOU MONSTER.
WELL, I SEE I'M NOT WELCOME HERE.
NEVER LET IT BE SAID I CAN'T TAKE A HINT.
YOU HAVEN'T SEEN THE LAST OF ME-- HEE HEE HEE HEE!
OH NO YOU DON'T!
HE WON'T GET FAR.

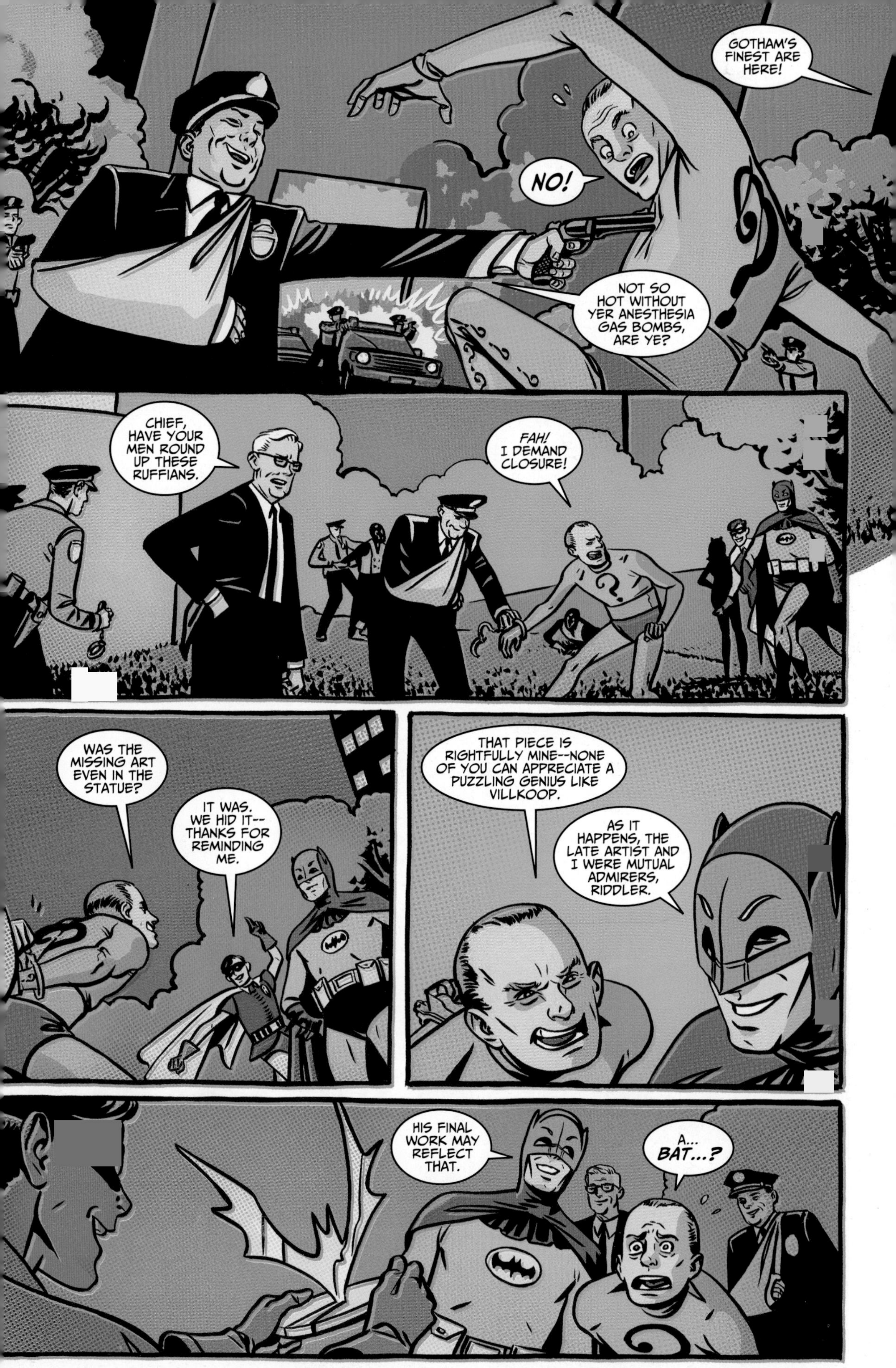
GOTHAM'S FINEST ARE HERE!
NO!
NOT SO HOT WITHOUT YER ANESTHESIA GAS BOMBS, ARE YE?
CHIEF, HAVE YOUR MEN ROUND UP THESE RUFFIANS.
FAH! I DEMAND CLOSURE!
WAS THE MISSING ART EVEN IN THE STATUE?
IT WAS. WE HID IT-- THANKS FOR REMINDING ME.
THAT PIECE IS RIGHTFULLY MINE--NONE OF YOU CAN APPRECIATE A PUZZLING GENIUS LIKE VILLKOOP.
AS IT HAPPENS, THE LATE ARTIST AND I WERE MUTUAL ADMIRERS, RIDDLER.
HIS FINAL WORK MAY REFLECT THAT.
A... BAT...?

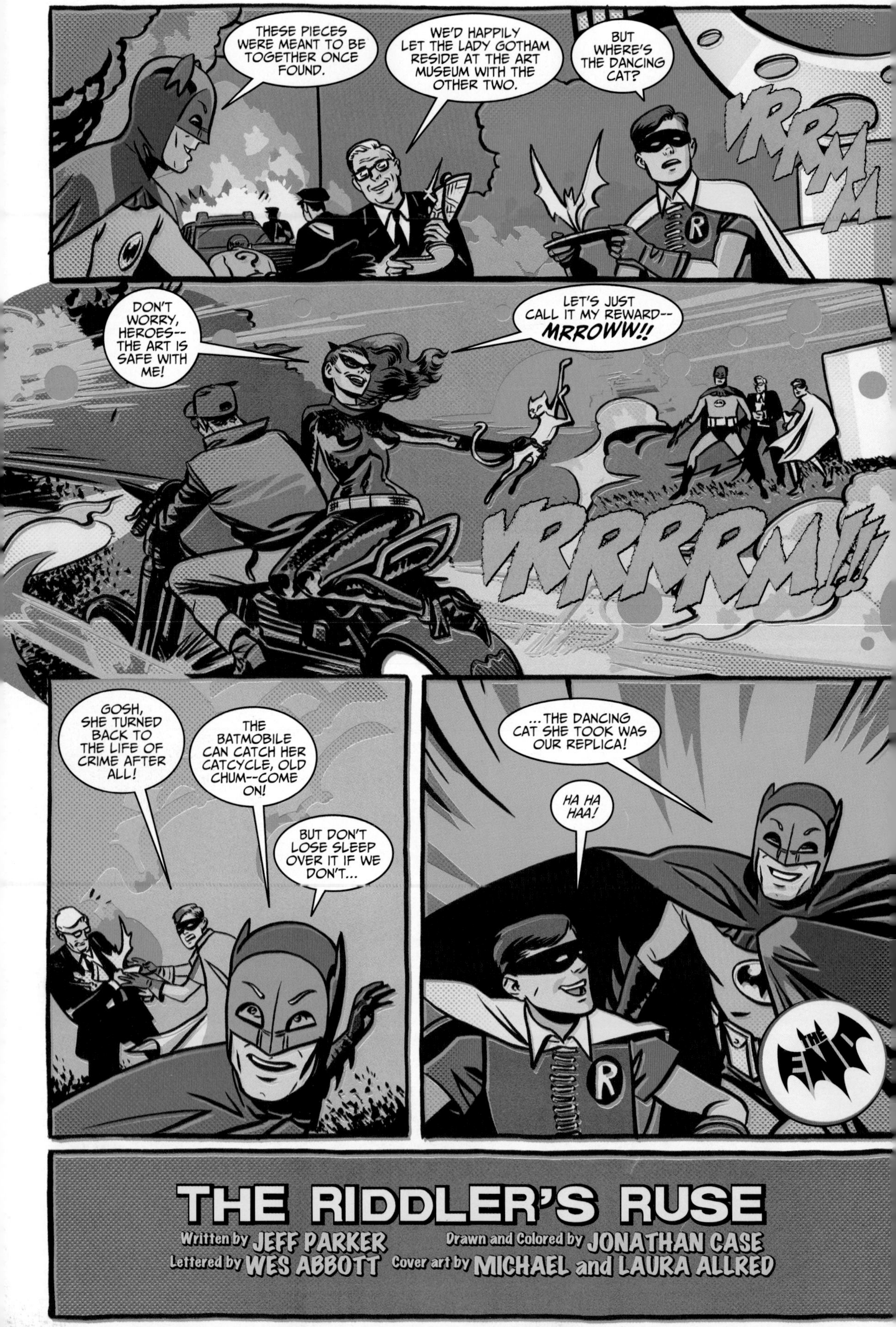
THESE PIECES WERE MEANT TO BE TOGETHER ONCE FOUND.
WE'D HAPPILY LET THE LADY GOTHAM RESIDE AT THE ART MUSEUM WITH THE OTHER TWO.
BUT WHERE'S THE DANCING CAT?
VRRMM
DON'T WORRY, HEROES-- THE ART IS SAFE WITH ME!
LET'S JUST CALL IT MY REWARD-- MRROWW!!
VRRRRM!!
GOSH, SHE TURNED BACK TO THE LIFE OF CRIME AFTER ALL!
THE BATMOBILE CAN CATCH HER CATCYCLE, OLD CHUM--COME ON!
BUT DON'T LOSE SLEEP OVER IT IF WE DON'T...
...THE DANCING CAT SHE TOOK WAS OUR REPLICA!
HA HA HAA!
THE END

# THE RIDDLER'S RUSE

Written by JEFF PARKER Drawn and Colored by JONATHAN CASE
Lettered by WES ABBOTT Cover art by MICHAEL and LAURA ALLRED

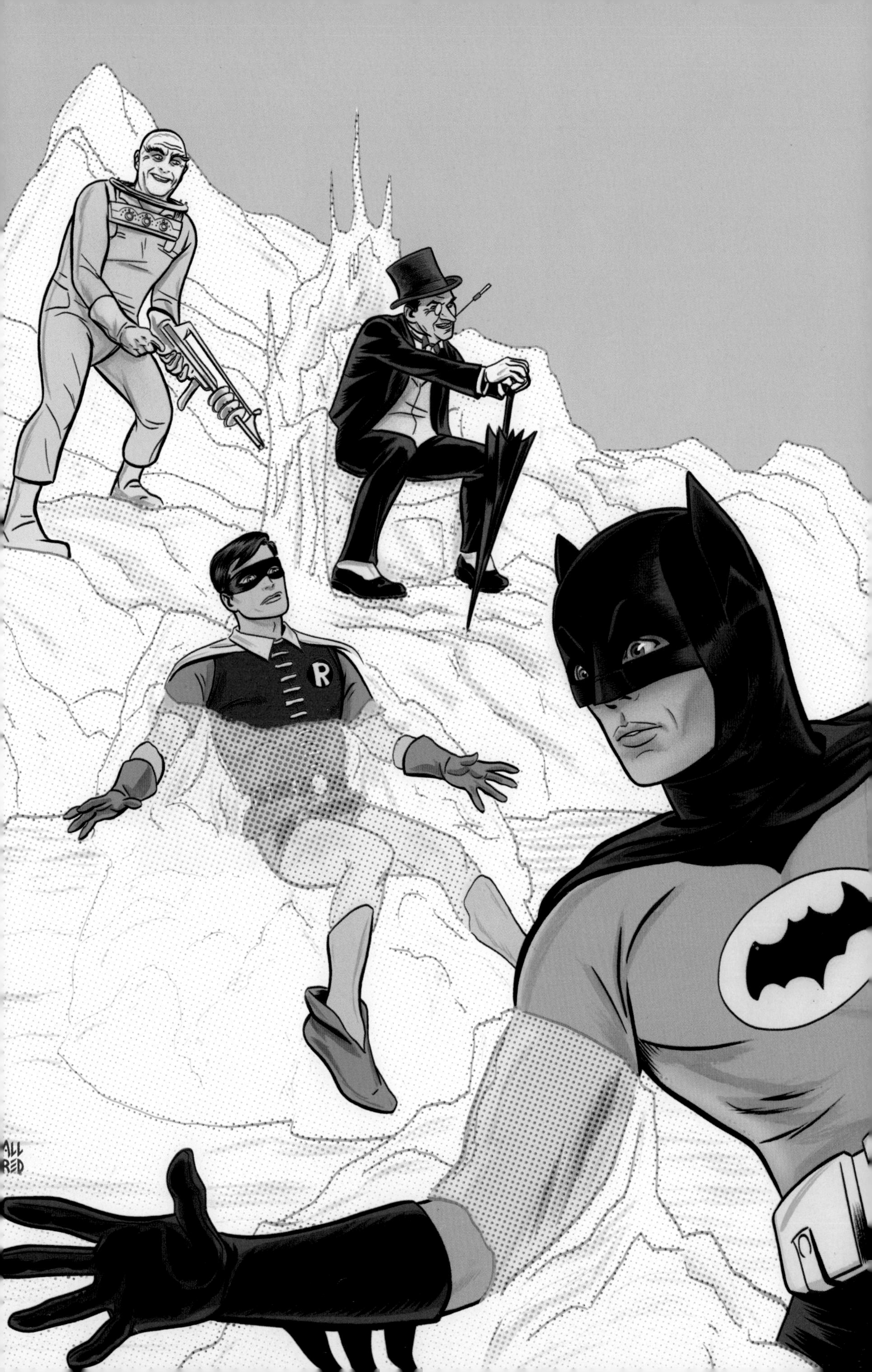

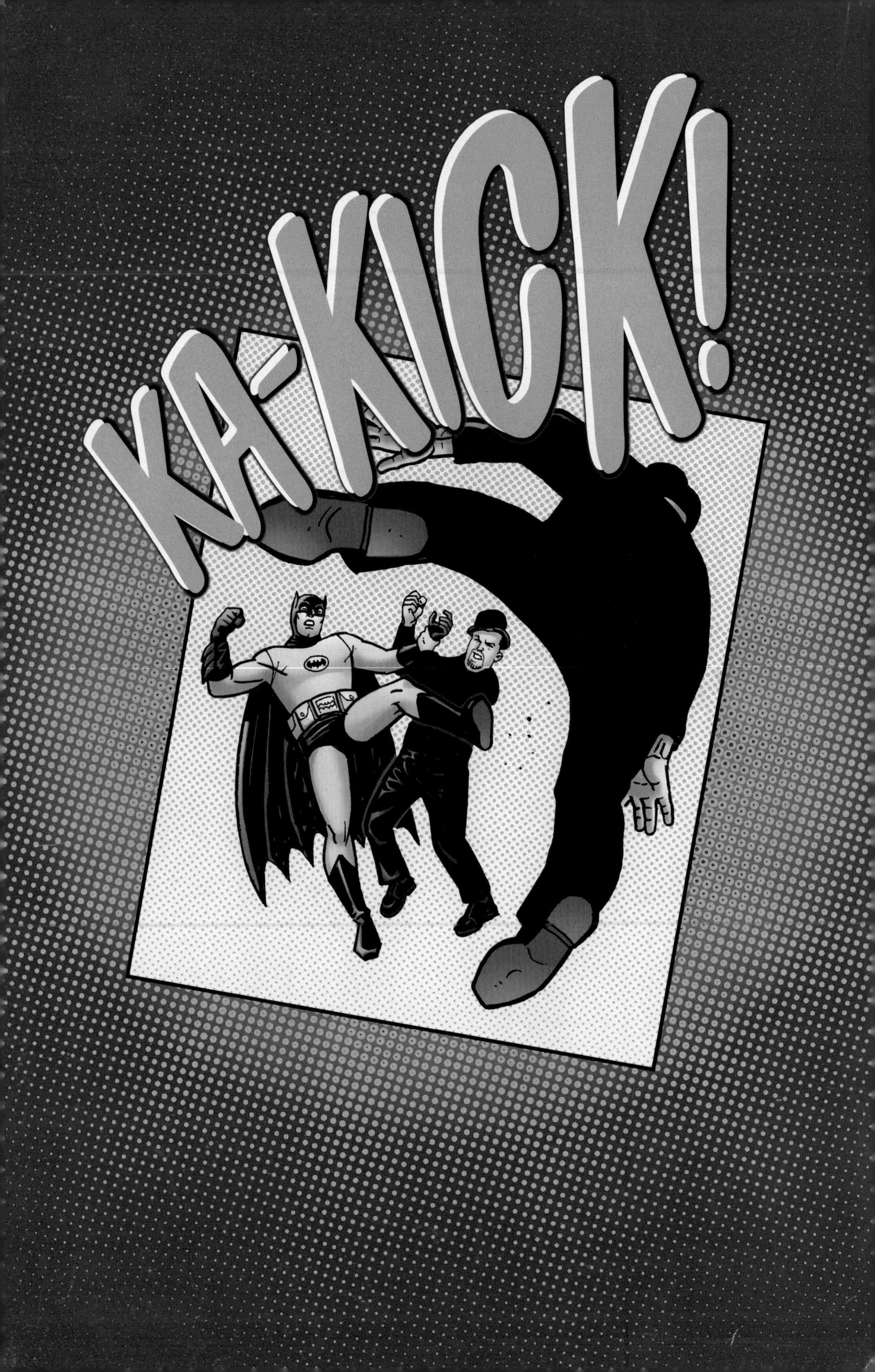
KA-KICK!

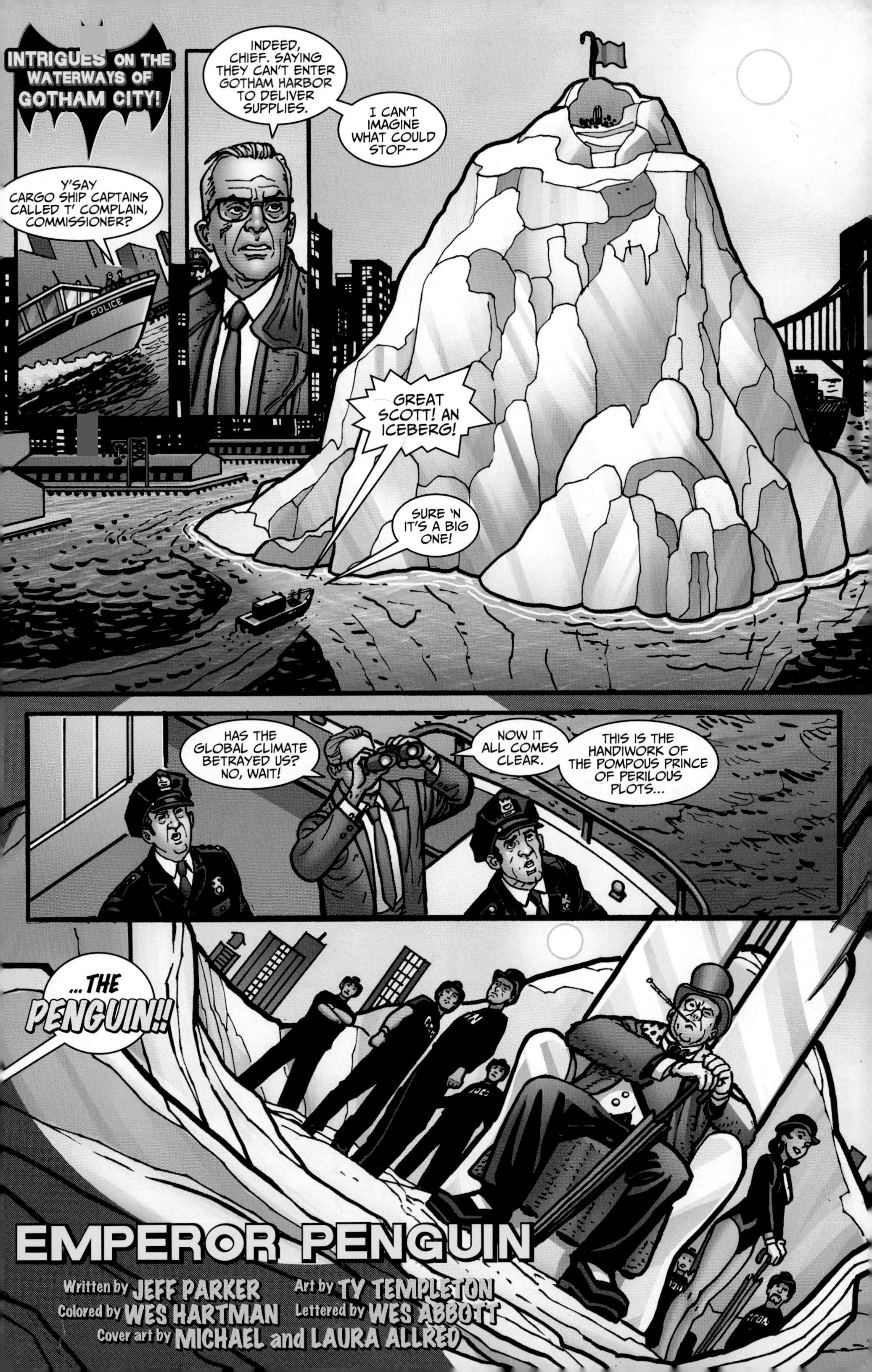
INTRIGUES ON THE WATERWAYS OF GOTHAM CITY!
Y'SAY CARGO SHIP CAPTAINS CALLED T' COMPLAIN, COMMISSIONER?
INDEED, CHIEF. SAYING THEY CAN'T ENTER GOTHAM HARBOR TO DELIVER SUPPLIES.
I CAN'T IMAGINE WHAT COULD STOP--
POLICE
GREAT SCOTT! AN ICEBERG!
SURE 'N IT'S A BIG ONE!
HAS THE GLOBAL CLIMATE BETRAYED US? NO, WAIT!
NOW IT ALL COMES CLEAR.
THIS IS THE HANDIWORK OF THE POMPOUS PRINCE OF PERILOUS PLOTS...
...THE PENGUIN!!
EMPEROR PENGUIN
Written by JEFF PARKER Art by TY TEMPLETON
Colored by WES HARTMAN Lettered by WES ABBOTT
Cover art by MICHAEL and LAURA ALLRED

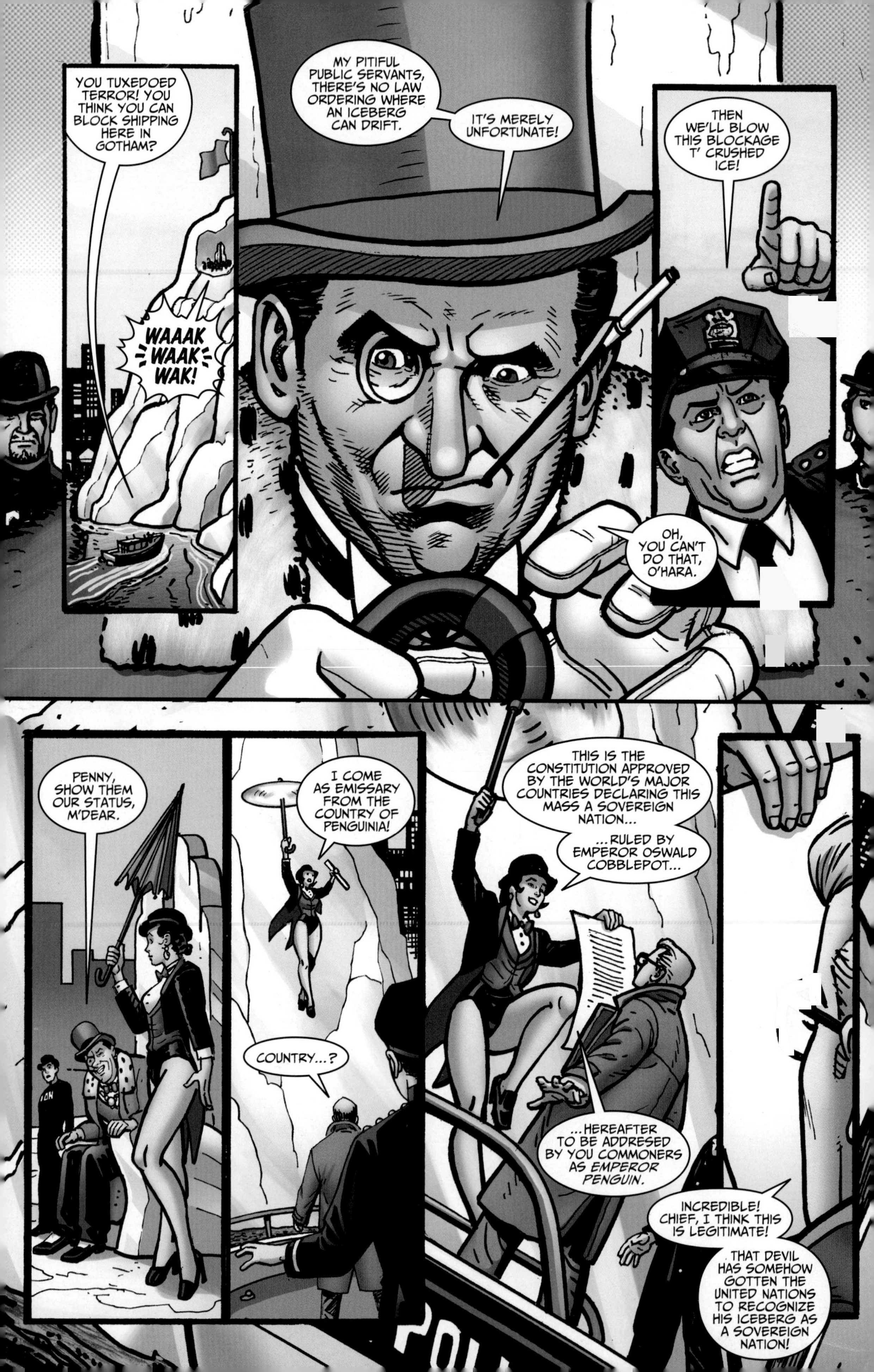

YOU TUXEDOED TERROR! YOU THINK YOU CAN BLOCK SHIPPING HERE IN GOTHAM?
WAAAK WAAK WAK!
MY PITIFUL PUBLIC SERVANTS, THERE'S NO LAW ORDERING WHERE AN ICEBERG CAN DRIFT.
IT'S MERELY UNFORTUNATE!
THEN WE'LL BLOW THIS BLOCKAGE T' CRUSHED ICE!
OH, YOU CAN'T DO THAT, O'HARA.
PENNY, SHOW THEM OUR STATUS, M'DEAR.
I COME AS EMISSARY FROM THE COUNTRY OF PENGUINIA!
COUNTRY...?
THIS IS THE CONSTITUTION APPROVED BY THE WORLD'S MAJOR COUNTRIES DECLARING THIS MASS A SOVEREIGN NATION...
...RULED BY EMPEROR OSWALD COBBLEPOT...
...HEREAFTER TO BE ADDRESED BY YOU COMMONERS AS *EMPEROR PENGUIN.*
INCREDIBLE! CHIEF, I THINK THIS IS LEGITIMATE!
THAT DEVIL HAS SOMEHOW GOTTEN THE UNITED NATIONS TO RECOGNIZE HIS ICEBERG AS A SOVEREIGN NATION!

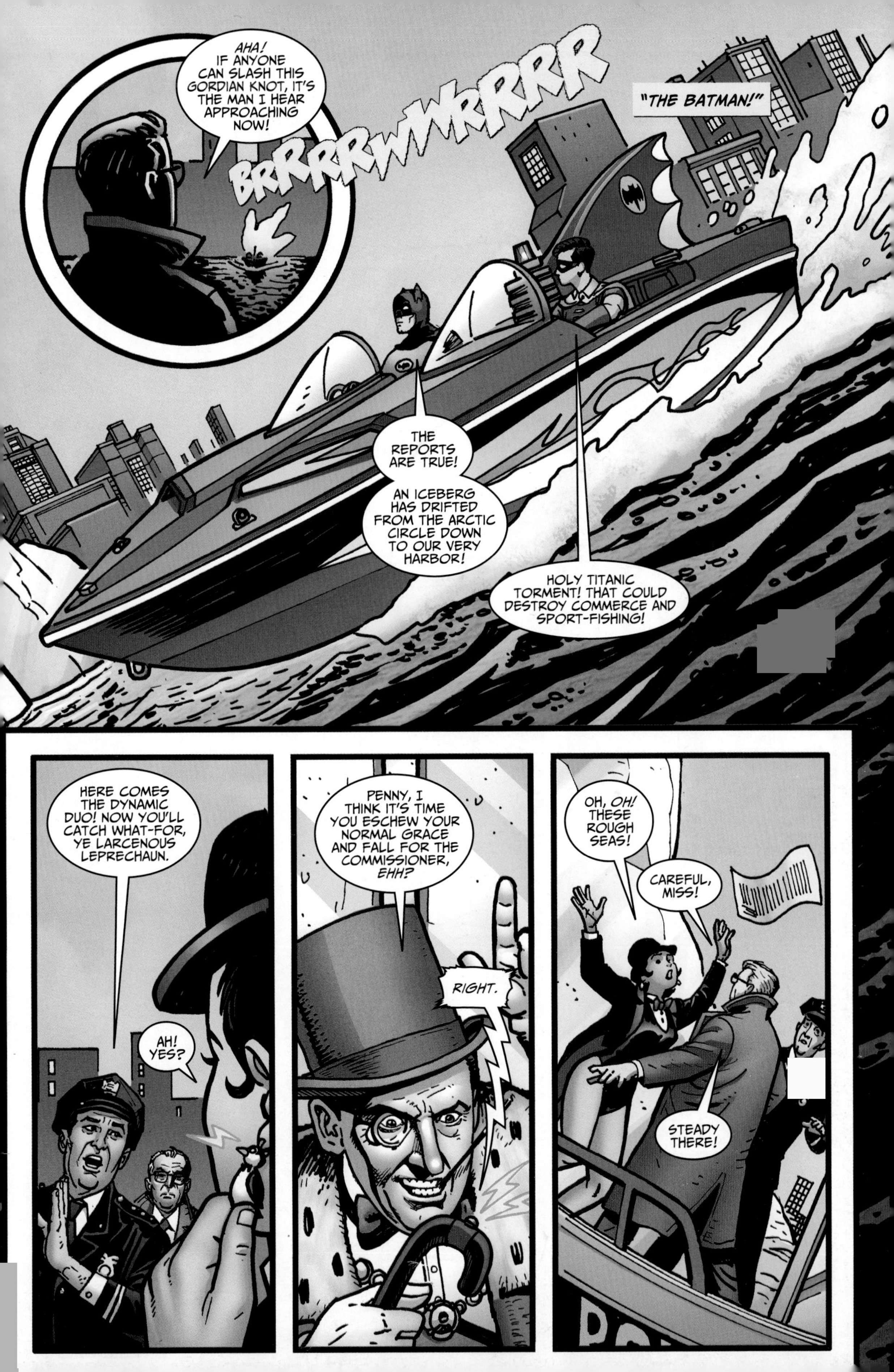
AHA! IF ANYONE CAN SLASH THIS GORDIAN KNOT, IT'S THE MAN I HEAR APPROACHING NOW!
BRRRRWWRRRR
"THE BATMAN!"
THE REPORTS ARE TRUE!
AN ICEBERG HAS DRIFTED FROM THE ARCTIC CIRCLE DOWN TO OUR VERY HARBOR!
HOLY TITANIC TORMENT! THAT COULD DESTROY COMMERCE AND SPORT-FISHING!
HERE COMES THE DYNAMIC DUO! NOW YOU'LL CATCH WHAT-FOR, YE LARCENOUS LEPRECHAUN.
AH! YES?
PENNY, I THINK IT'S TIME YOU ESCHEW YOUR NORMAL GRACE AND FALL FOR THE COMMISSIONER, EHH?
RIGHT.
OH, OH! THESE ROUGH SEAS!
CAREFUL, MISS!
STEADY THERE!

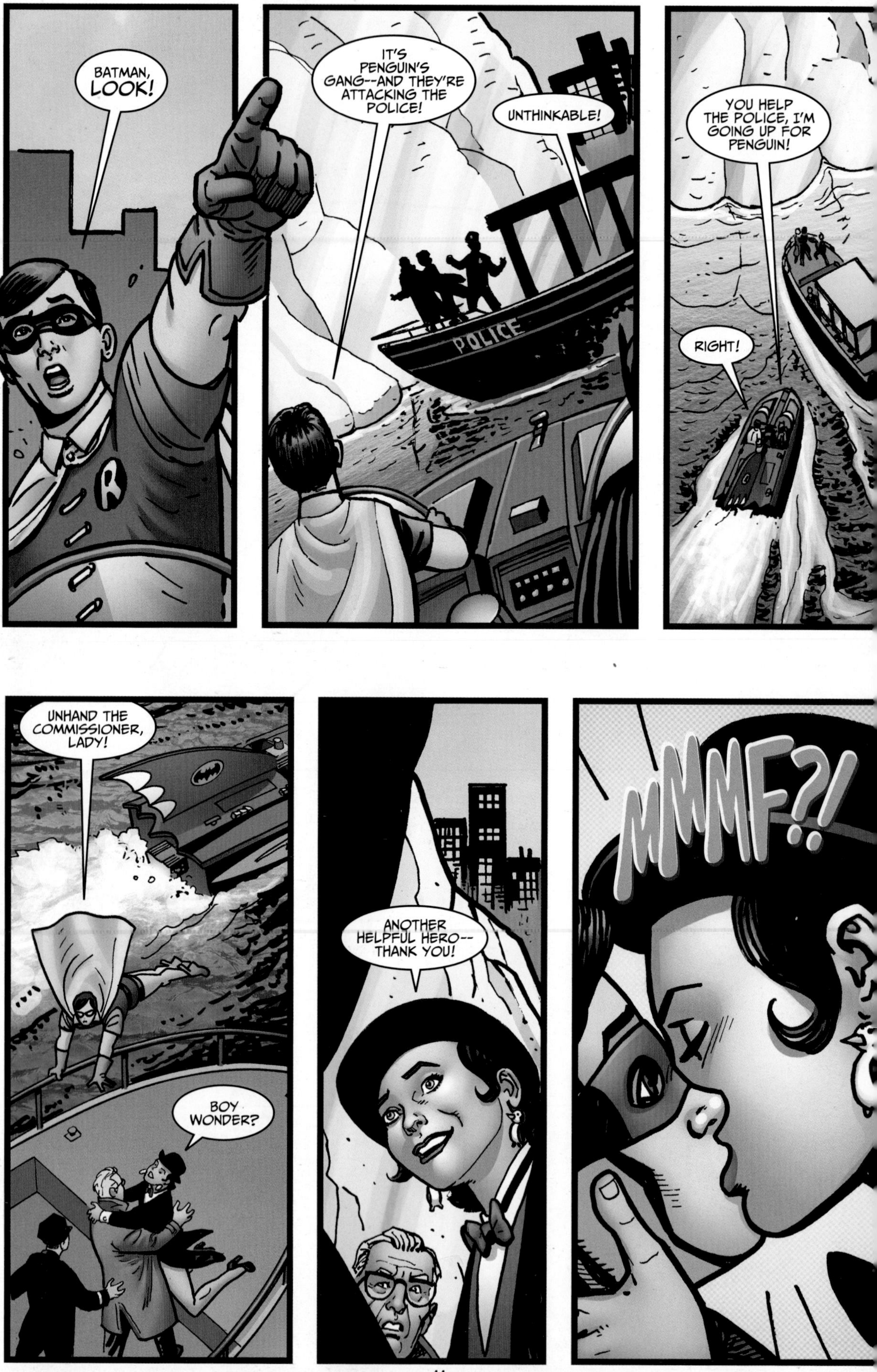
BATMAN, LOOK!
IT'S PENGUIN'S GANG--AND THEY'RE ATTACKING THE POLICE!
POLICE
UNTHINKABLE!
YOU HELP THE POLICE, I'M GOING UP FOR PENGUIN!
RIGHT!
UNHAND THE COMMISSIONER, LADY!
BOY WONDER?
ANOTHER HELPFUL HERO--THANK YOU!
MMMF?!

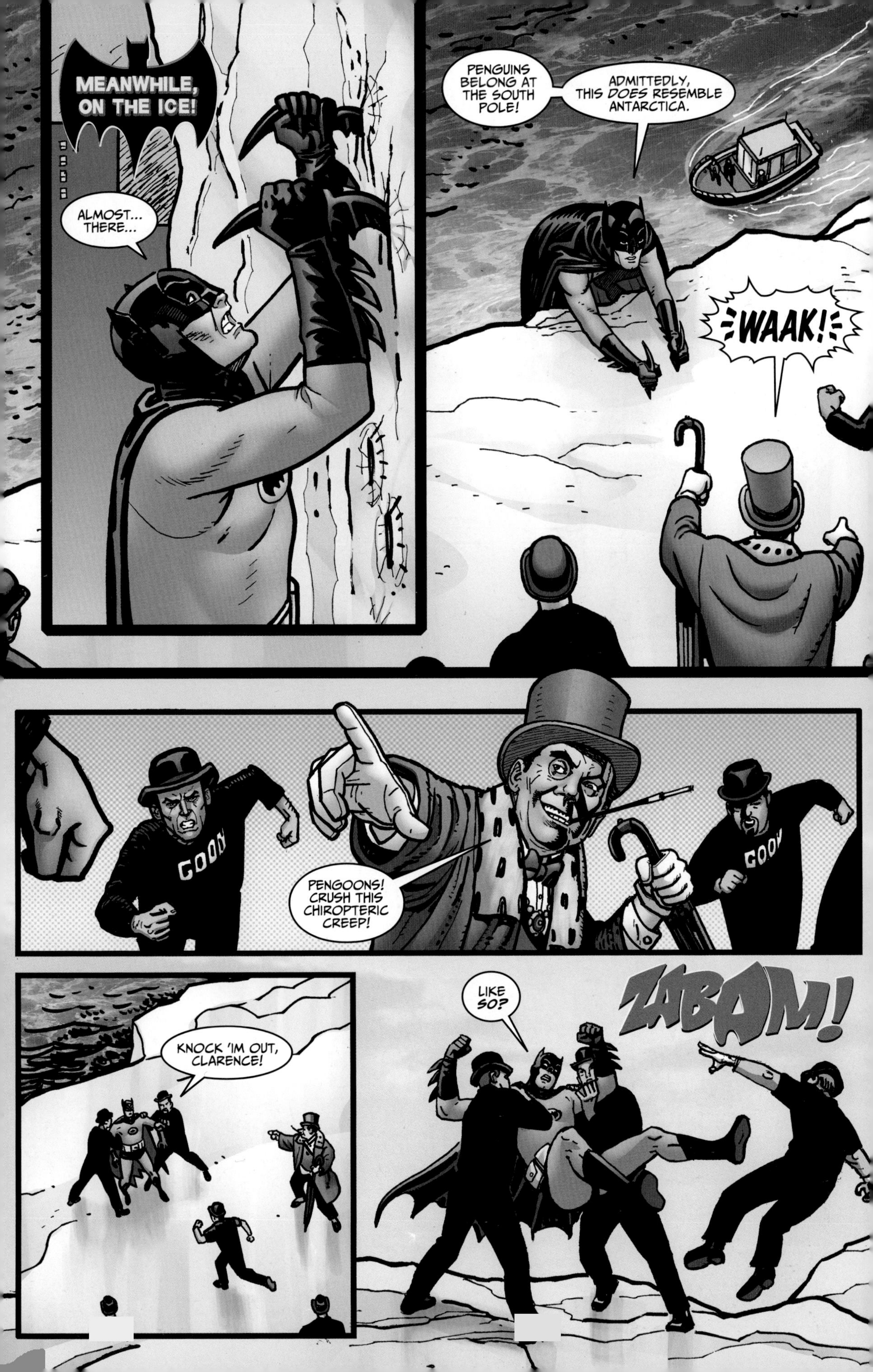
MEANWHILE, ON THE ICE!
ALMOST... THERE...
PENGUINS BELONG AT THE SOUTH POLE!
ADMITTEDLY, THIS DOES RESEMBLE ANTARCTICA.
WAAK!
GOON
GOON
PENGOONS! CRUSH THIS CHIROPTERIC CREEP!
KNOCK 'IM OUT, CLARENCE!
LIKE SO?
ZABAM!

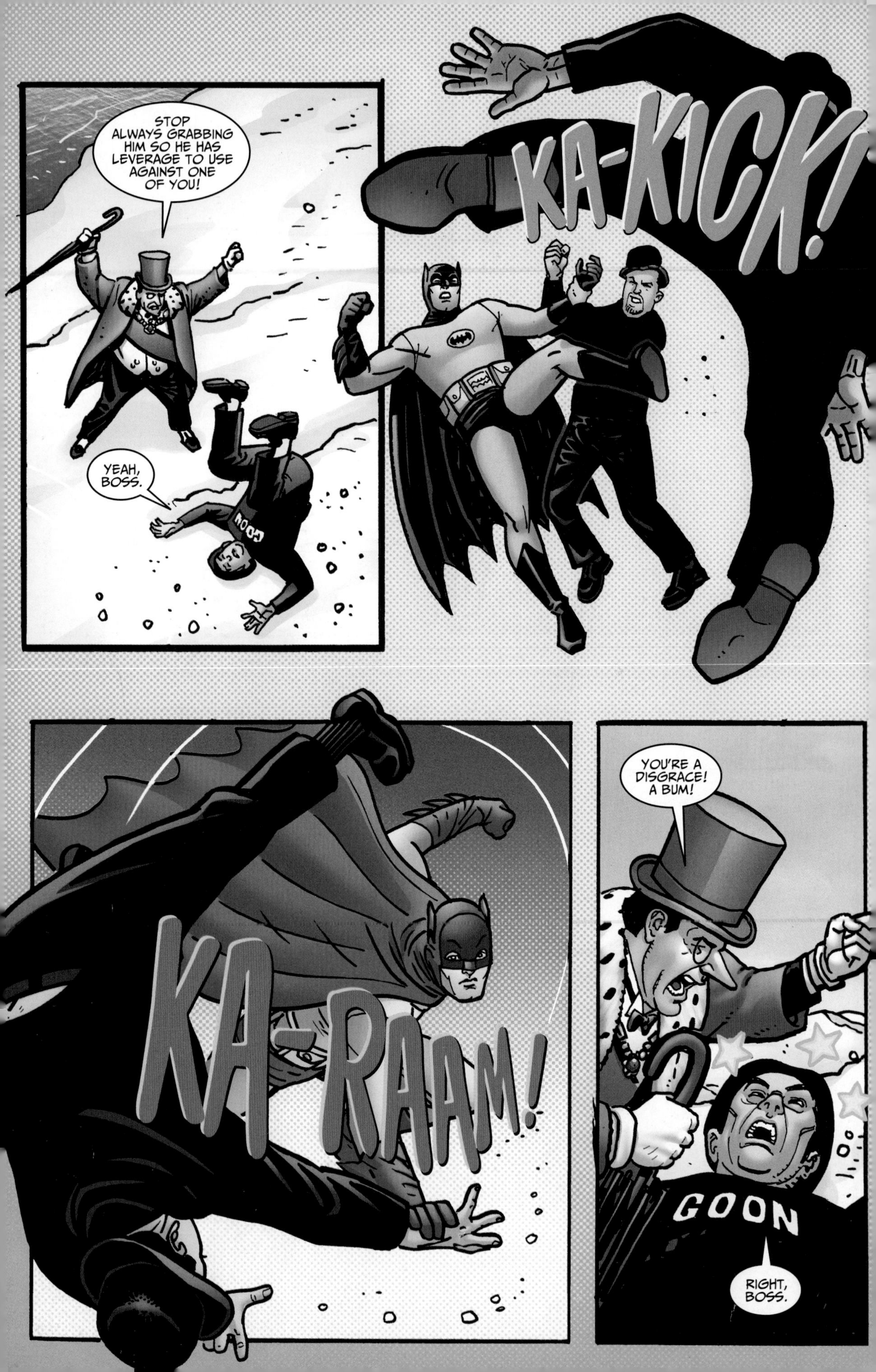
STOP ALWAYS GRABBING HIM SO HE HAS LEVERAGE TO USE AGAINST ONE OF YOU!
YEAH, BOSS.
GOON
KA-KICK!
KA-RAAM!
YOU'RE A DISGRACE! A BUM!
GOON
RIGHT, BOSS.

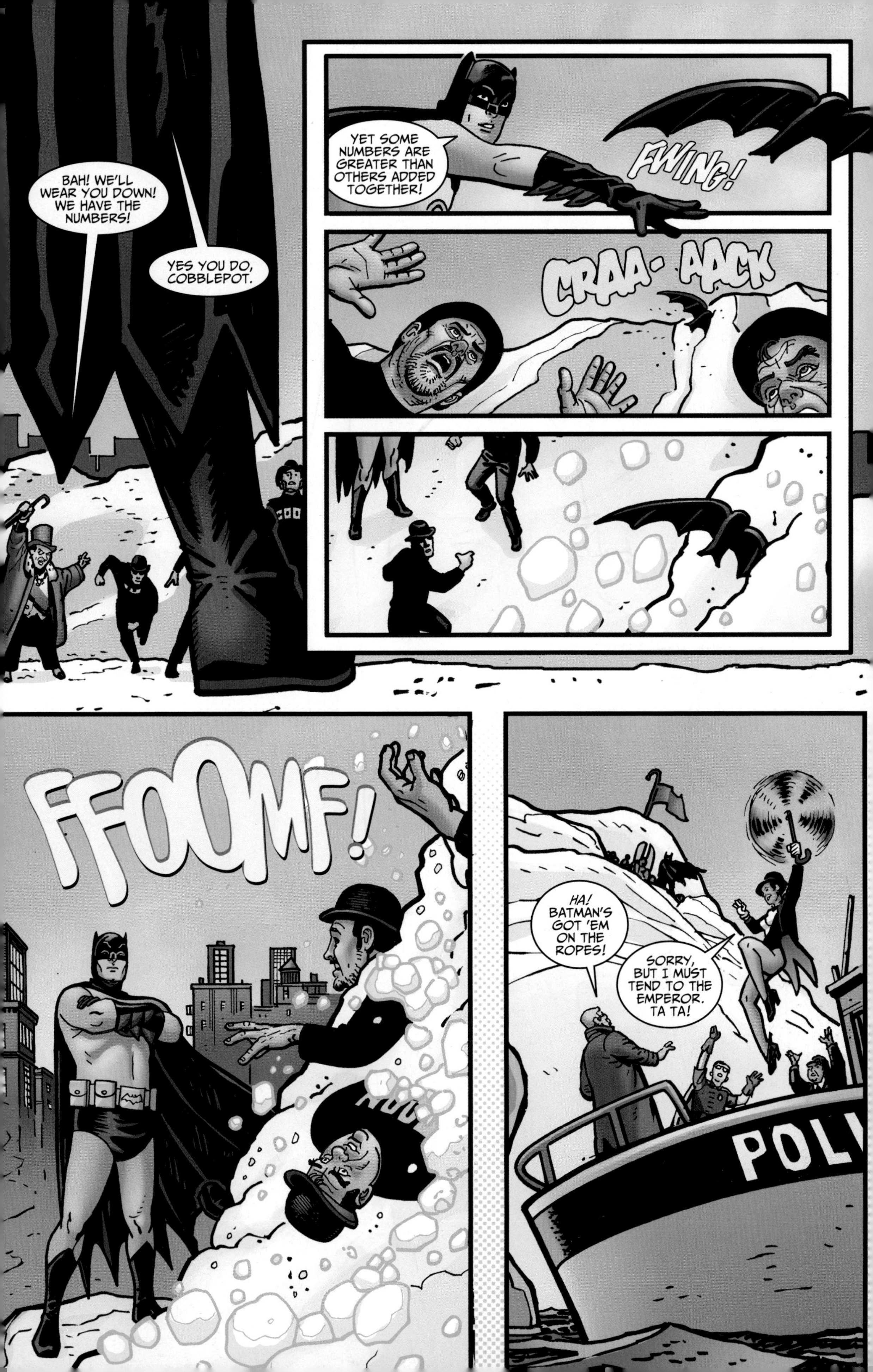
BAH! WE'LL WEAR YOU DOWN! WE HAVE THE NUMBERS!
YES YOU DO, COBBLEPOT.
YET SOME NUMBERS ARE GREATER THAN OTHERS ADDED TOGETHER!
FWING!
CRAA- AACK
FFOOMF!
HA! BATMAN'S GOT 'EM ON THE ROPES!
SORRY, BUT I MUST TEND TO THE EMPEROR. TA TA!
POLI

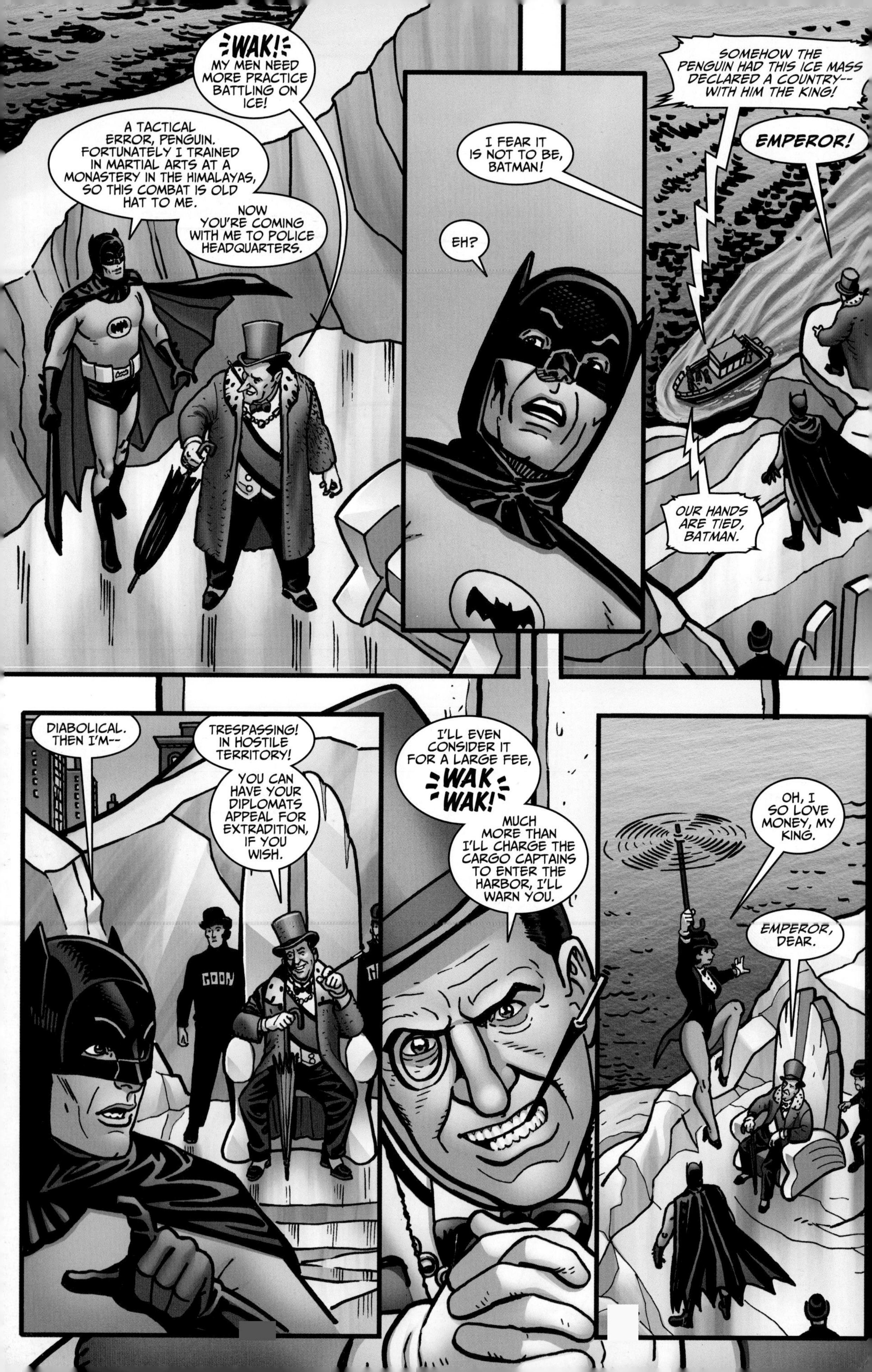
WAK! MY MEN NEED MORE PRACTICE BATTLING ON ICE!
A TACTICAL ERROR, PENGUIN. FORTUNATELY I TRAINED IN MARTIAL ARTS AT A MONASTERY IN THE HIMALAYAS, SO THIS COMBAT IS OLD HAT TO ME.
NOW YOU'RE COMING WITH ME TO POLICE HEADQUARTERS.
I FEAR IT IS NOT TO BE, BATMAN!
EH?
SOMEHOW THE PENGUIN HAD THIS ICE MASS DECLARED A COUNTRY-- WITH HIM THE KING!
EMPEROR!
OUR HANDS ARE TIED, BATMAN.
DIABOLICAL. THEN I'M--
TRESPASSING! IN HOSTILE TERRITORY!
YOU CAN HAVE YOUR DIPLOMATS APPEAL FOR EXTRADITION, IF YOU WISH.
GOON
I'LL EVEN CONSIDER IT FOR A LARGE FEE, WAK WAK!
MUCH MORE THAN I'LL CHARGE THE CARGO CAPTAINS TO ENTER THE HARBOR, I'LL WARN YOU.
OH, I SO LOVE MONEY, MY KING.
EMPEROR, DEAR.

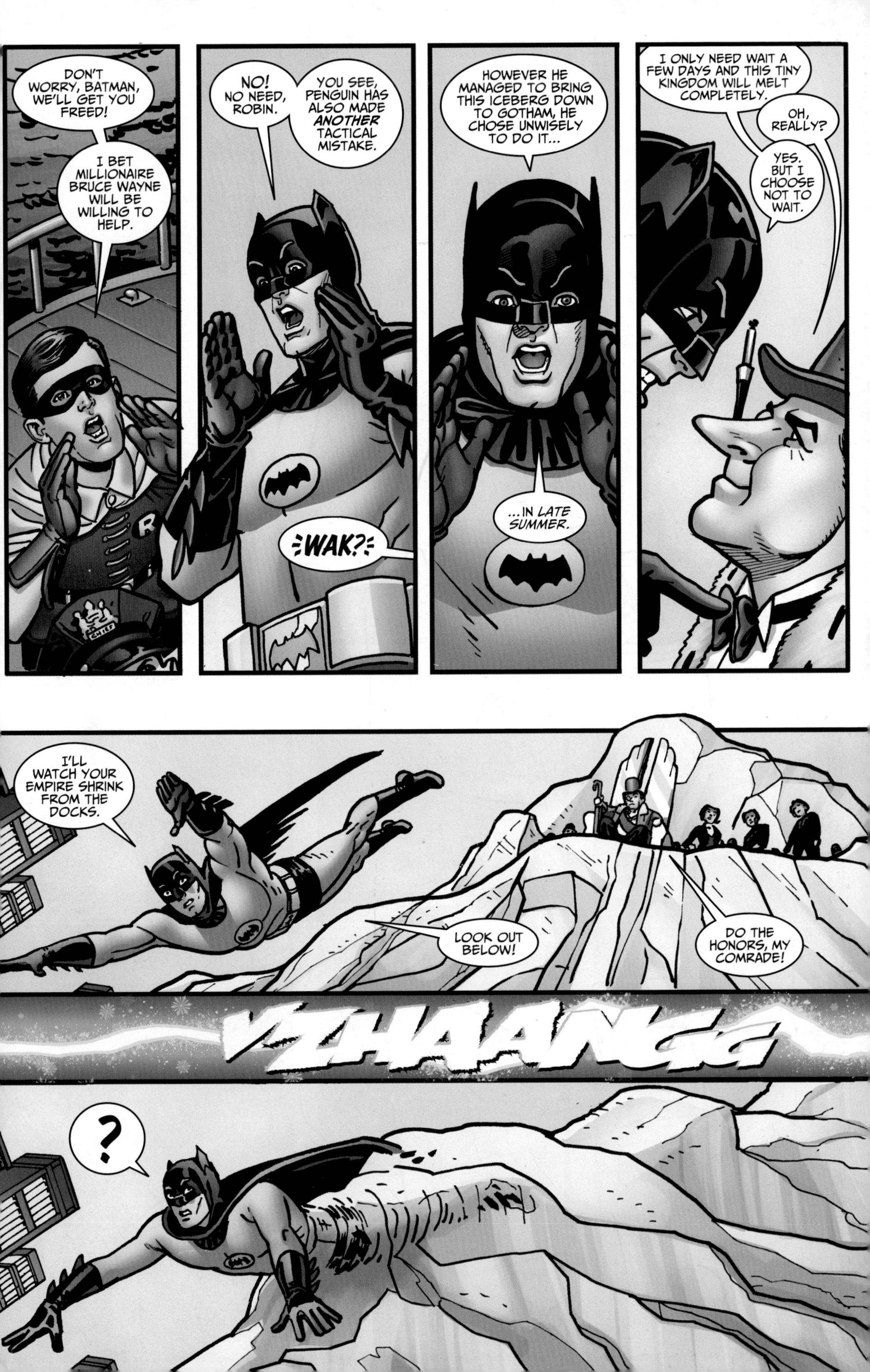
DON'T WORRY, BATMAN, WE'LL GET YOU FREED!
I BET MILLIONAIRE BRUCE WAYNE WILL BE WILLING TO HELP.
NO! NO NEED, ROBIN.
YOU SEE, PENGUIN HAS ALSO MADE ANOTHER TACTICAL MISTAKE.
WAK?
HOWEVER HE MANAGED TO BRING THIS ICEBERG DOWN TO GOTHAM, HE CHOSE UNWISELY TO DO IT...
...IN LATE SUMMER.
I ONLY NEED WAIT A FEW DAYS AND THIS TINY KINGDOM WILL MELT COMPLETELY.
OH, REALLY?
YES. BUT I CHOOSE NOT TO WAIT.
I'LL WATCH YOUR EMPIRE SHRINK FROM THE DOCKS.
LOOK OUT BELOW!
DO THE HONORS, MY COMRADE!
VZHAANGG
?

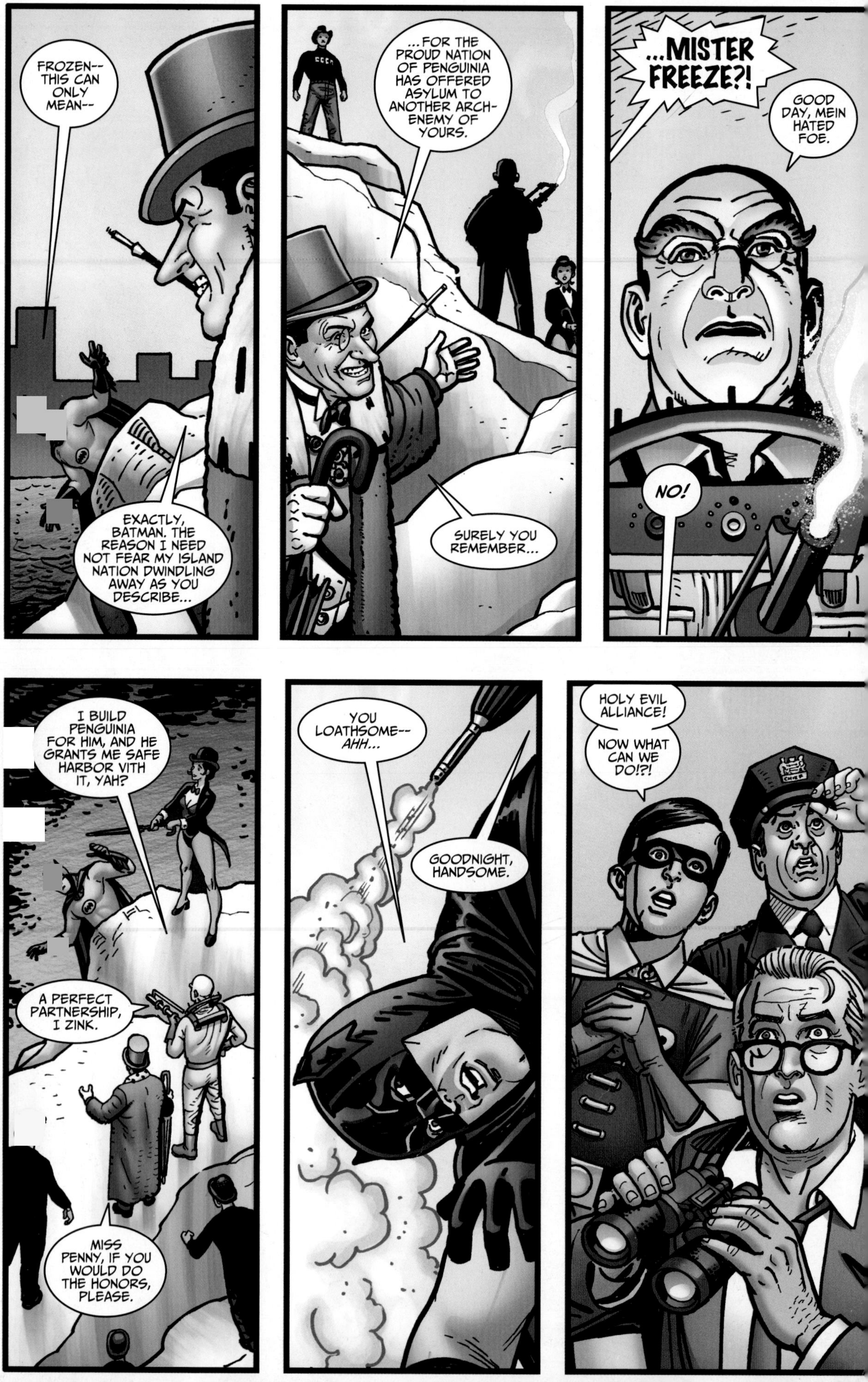
FROZEN-- THIS CAN ONLY MEAN--
EXACTLY, BATMAN. THE REASON I NEED NOT FEAR MY ISLAND NATION DWINDLING AWAY AS YOU DESCRIBE...
...FOR THE PROUD NATION OF PENGUINIA HAS OFFERED ASYLUM TO ANOTHER ARCH-ENEMY OF YOURS.
SURELY YOU REMEMBER...
...MISTER FREEZE?!
GOOD DAY, MEIN HATED FOE.
NO!
I BUILD PENGUINIA FOR HIM, AND HE GRANTS ME SAFE HARBOR VITH IT, YAH?
A PERFECT PARTNERSHIP, I ZINK.
MISS PENNY, IF YOU WOULD DO THE HONORS, PLEASE.
YOU LOATHSOME-- AHH...
GOODNIGHT, HANDSOME.
HOLY EVIL ALLIANCE!
NOW WHAT CAN WE DO!?!

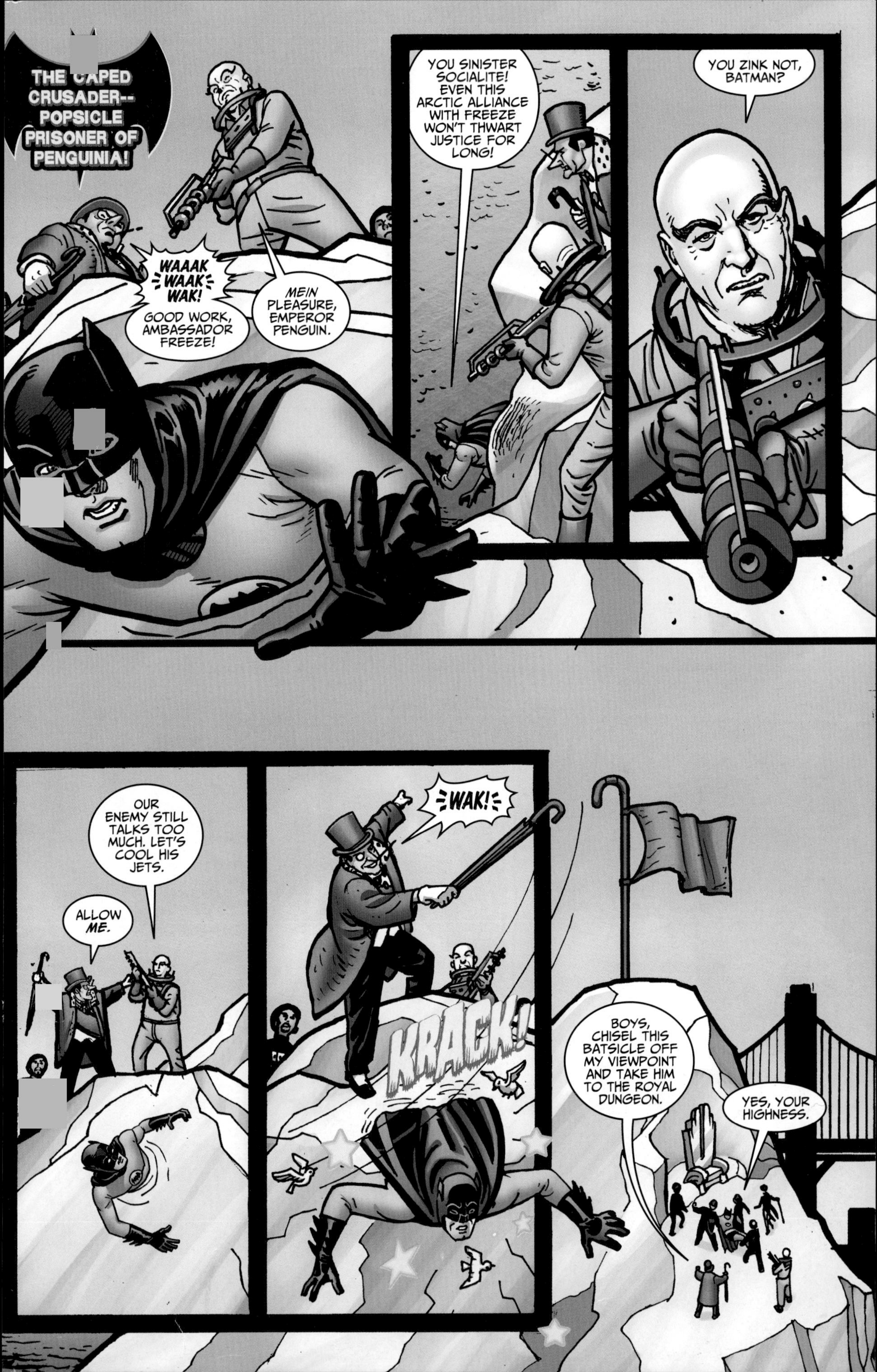

THE CAPED CRUSADER--POPSICLE PRISONER OF PENGUINIA!
WAAAK WAAK WAK!
GOOD WORK, AMBASSADOR FREEZE!
MEIN PLEASURE, EMPEROR PENGUIN.
YOU SINISTER SOCIALITE! EVEN THIS ARCTIC ALLIANCE WITH FREEZE WON'T THWART JUSTICE FOR LONG!
YOU ZINK NOT, BATMAN?
OUR ENEMY STILL TALKS TOO MUCH. LET'S COOL HIS JETS.
ALLOW ME.
WAK!
KRACK!
BOYS, CHISEL THIS BATSICLE OFF MY VIEWPOINT AND TAKE HIM TO THE ROYAL DUNGEON.
YES, YOUR HIGHNESS.

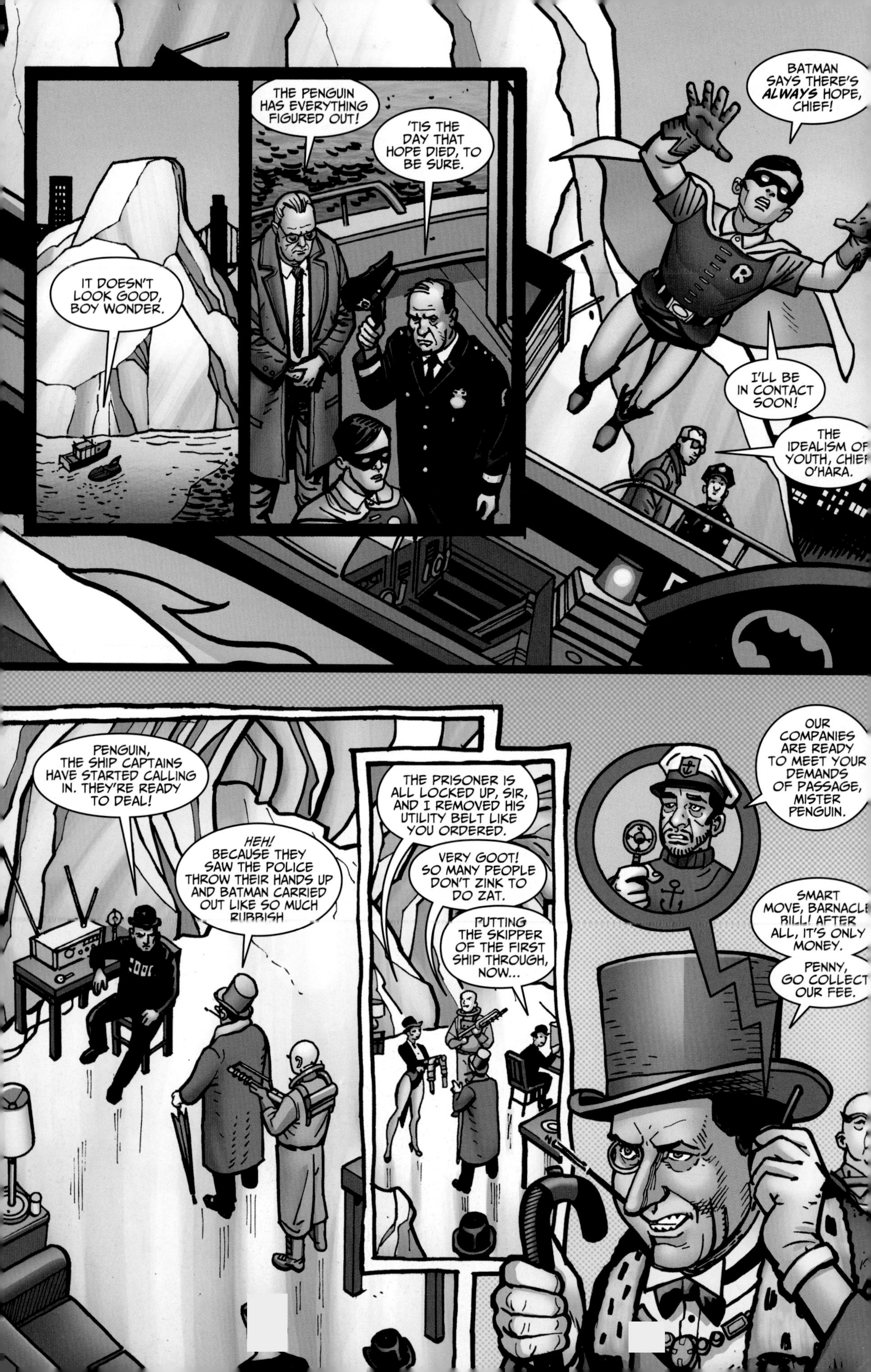

IT DOESN'T LOOK GOOD, BOY WONDER.
THE PENGUIN HAS EVERYTHING FIGURED OUT!
'TIS THE DAY THAT HOPE DIED, TO BE SURE.
BATMAN SAYS THERE'S *ALWAYS* HOPE, CHIEF!
I'LL BE IN CONTACT SOON!
THE IDEALISM OF YOUTH, CHIEF O'HARA.
PENGUIN, THE SHIP CAPTAINS HAVE STARTED CALLING IN. THEY'RE READY TO DEAL!
*HEH!* BECAUSE THEY SAW THE POLICE THROW THEIR HANDS UP AND BATMAN CARRIED OUT LIKE SO MUCH RUBBISH.
THE PRISONER IS ALL LOCKED UP, SIR, AND I REMOVED HIS UTILITY BELT LIKE YOU ORDERED.
VERY GOOT! SO MANY PEOPLE DON'T ZINK TO DO ZAT.
PUTTING THE SKIPPER OF THE FIRST SHIP THROUGH, NOW...
OUR COMPANIES ARE READY TO MEET YOUR DEMANDS OF PASSAGE, MISTER PENGUIN.
SMART MOVE, BARNACLE BILL! AFTER ALL, IT'S ONLY MONEY.
PENNY, GO COLLECT OUR FEE.

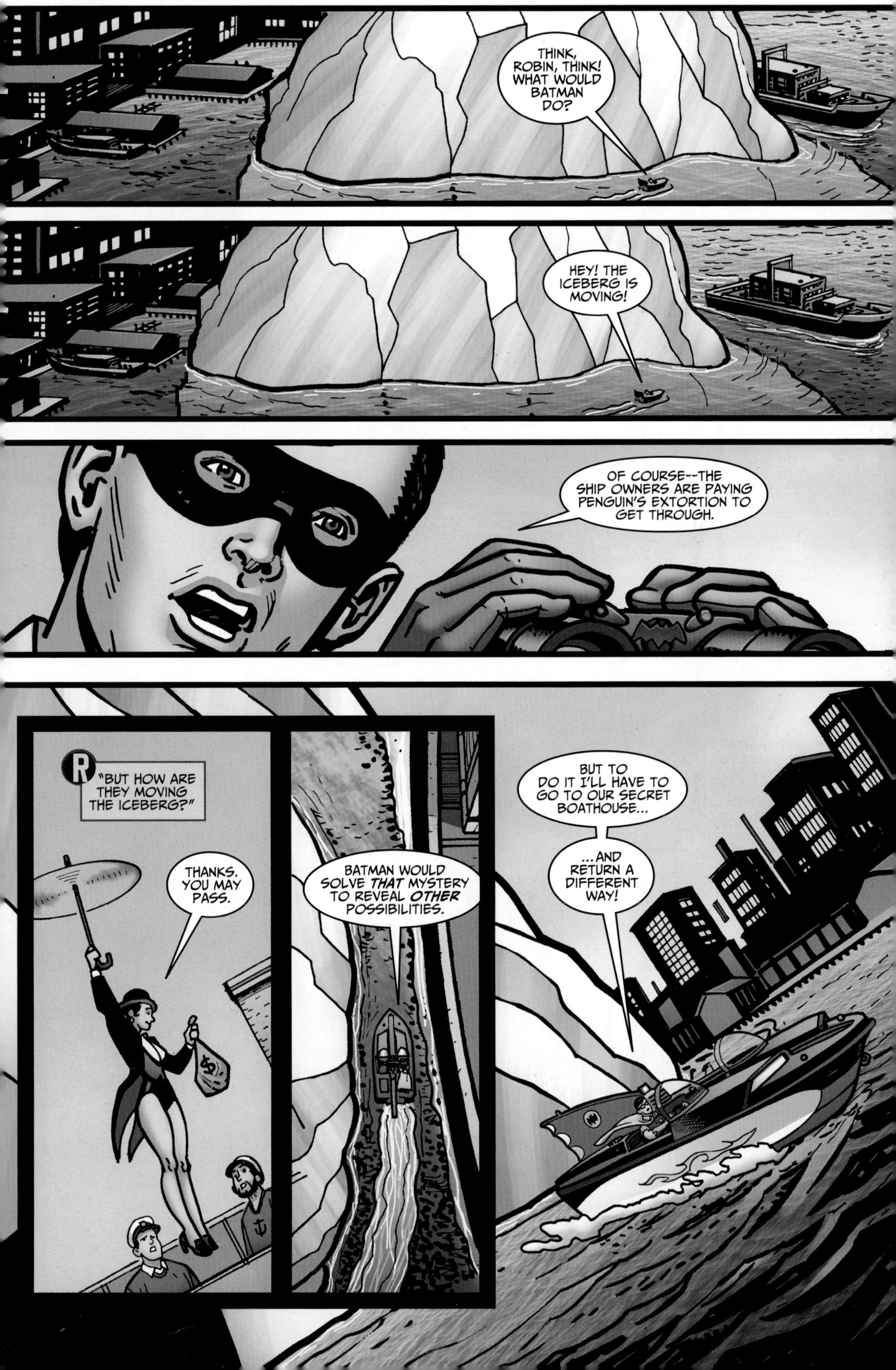
THINK, ROBIN, THINK! WHAT WOULD BATMAN DO?
HEY! THE ICEBERG IS MOVING!
OF COURSE--THE SHIP OWNERS ARE PAYING PENGUIN'S EXTORTION TO GET THROUGH.
"BUT HOW ARE THEY MOVING THE ICEBERG?"
THANKS. YOU MAY PASS.
BATMAN WOULD SOLVE THAT MYSTERY TO REVEAL OTHER POSSIBILITIES.
BUT TO DO IT I'LL HAVE TO GO TO OUR SECRET BOATHOUSE...
...AND RETURN A DIFFERENT WAY!

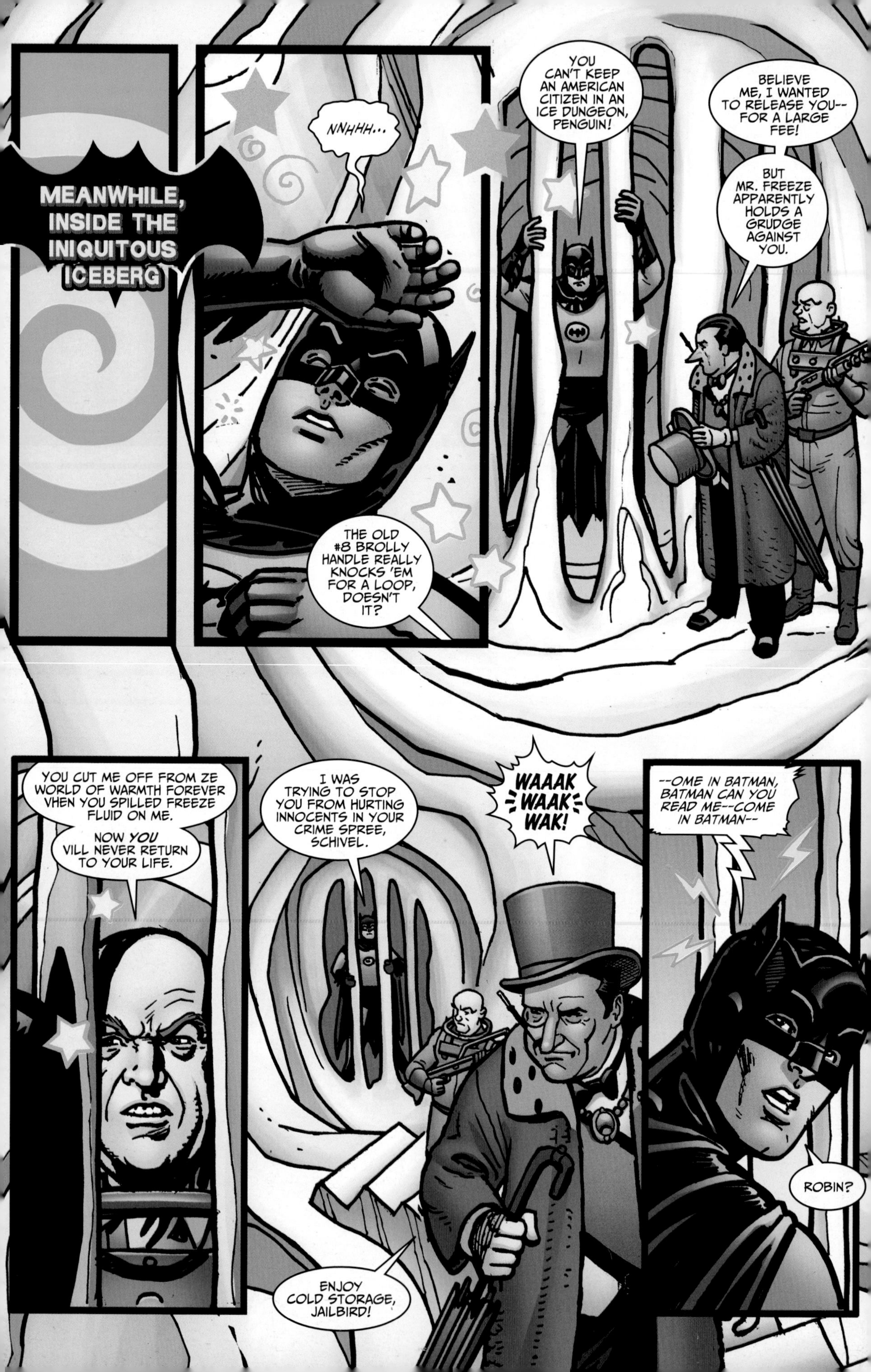
MEANWHILE, INSIDE THE INIQUITOUS ICEBERG
NNHHH...
THE OLD #8 BROLLY HANDLE REALLY KNOCKS 'EM FOR A LOOP, DOESN'T IT?
YOU CAN'T KEEP AN AMERICAN CITIZEN IN AN ICE DUNGEON, PENGUIN!
BELIEVE ME, I WANTED TO RELEASE YOU--FOR A LARGE FEE!
BUT MR. FREEZE APPARENTLY HOLDS A GRUDGE AGAINST YOU.
YOU CUT ME OFF FROM ZE WORLD OF WARMTH FOREVER VHEN YOU SPILLED FREEZE FLUID ON ME.
NOW YOU VILL NEVER RETURN TO YOUR LIFE.
I WAS TRYING TO STOP YOU FROM HURTING INNOCENTS IN YOUR CRIME SPREE, SCHIVEL.
WAAAK WAAK WAK!
ENJOY COLD STORAGE, JAILBIRD!
--COME IN BATMAN, BATMAN CAN YOU READ ME--COME IN BATMAN--
ROBIN?

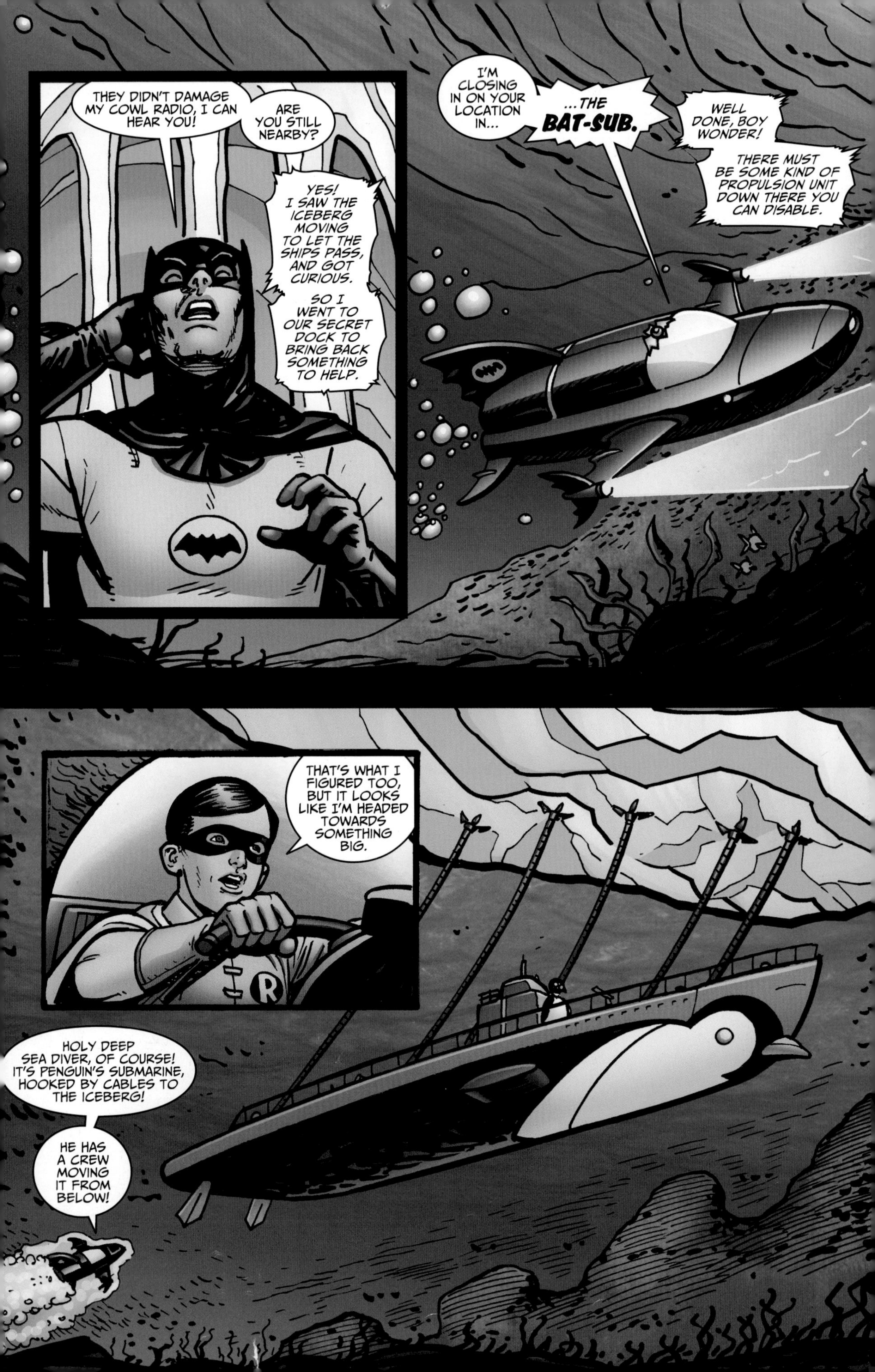
THEY DIDN'T DAMAGE MY COWL RADIO, I CAN HEAR YOU!
ARE YOU STILL NEARBY?
YES! I SAW THE ICEBERG MOVING TO LET THE SHIPS PASS, AND GOT CURIOUS.
SO I WENT TO OUR SECRET DOCK TO BRING BACK SOMETHING TO HELP.
I'M CLOSING IN ON YOUR LOCATION IN...
...THE BAT-SUB.
WELL DONE, BOY WONDER!
THERE MUST BE SOME KIND OF PROPULSION UNIT DOWN THERE YOU CAN DISABLE.
THAT'S WHAT I FIGURED TOO, BUT IT LOOKS LIKE I'M HEADED TOWARDS SOMETHING BIG.
HOLY DEEP SEA DIVER, OF COURSE! IT'S PENGUIN'S SUBMARINE, HOOKED BY CABLES TO THE ICEBERG!
HE HAS A CREW MOVING IT FROM BELOW!

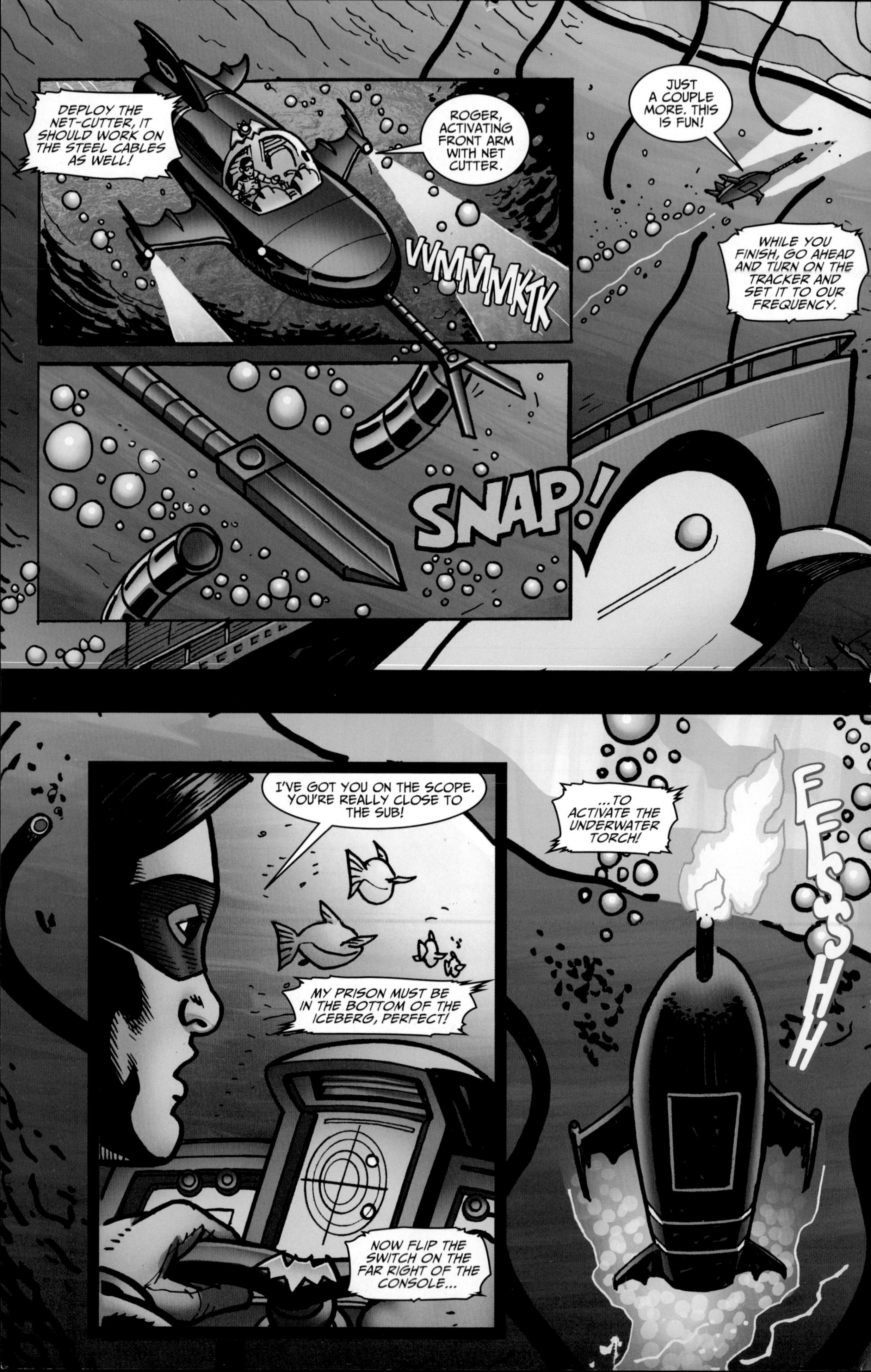

DEPLOY THE NET-CUTTER, IT SHOULD WORK ON THE STEEL CABLES AS WELL!
ROGER, ACTIVATING FRONT ARM WITH NET CUTTER.
VVMMMKTK
JUST A COUPLE MORE. THIS IS FUN!
WHILE YOU FINISH, GO AHEAD AND TURN ON THE TRACKER AND SET IT TO OUR FREQUENCY.
SNAP!
I'VE GOT YOU ON THE SCOPE. YOU'RE REALLY CLOSE TO THE SUB!
MY PRISON MUST BE IN THE BOTTOM OF THE ICEBERG, PERFECT!
NOW FLIP THE SWITCH ON THE FAR RIGHT OF THE CONSOLE...
...TO ACTIVATE THE UNDERWATER TORCH!
FFSSHHH

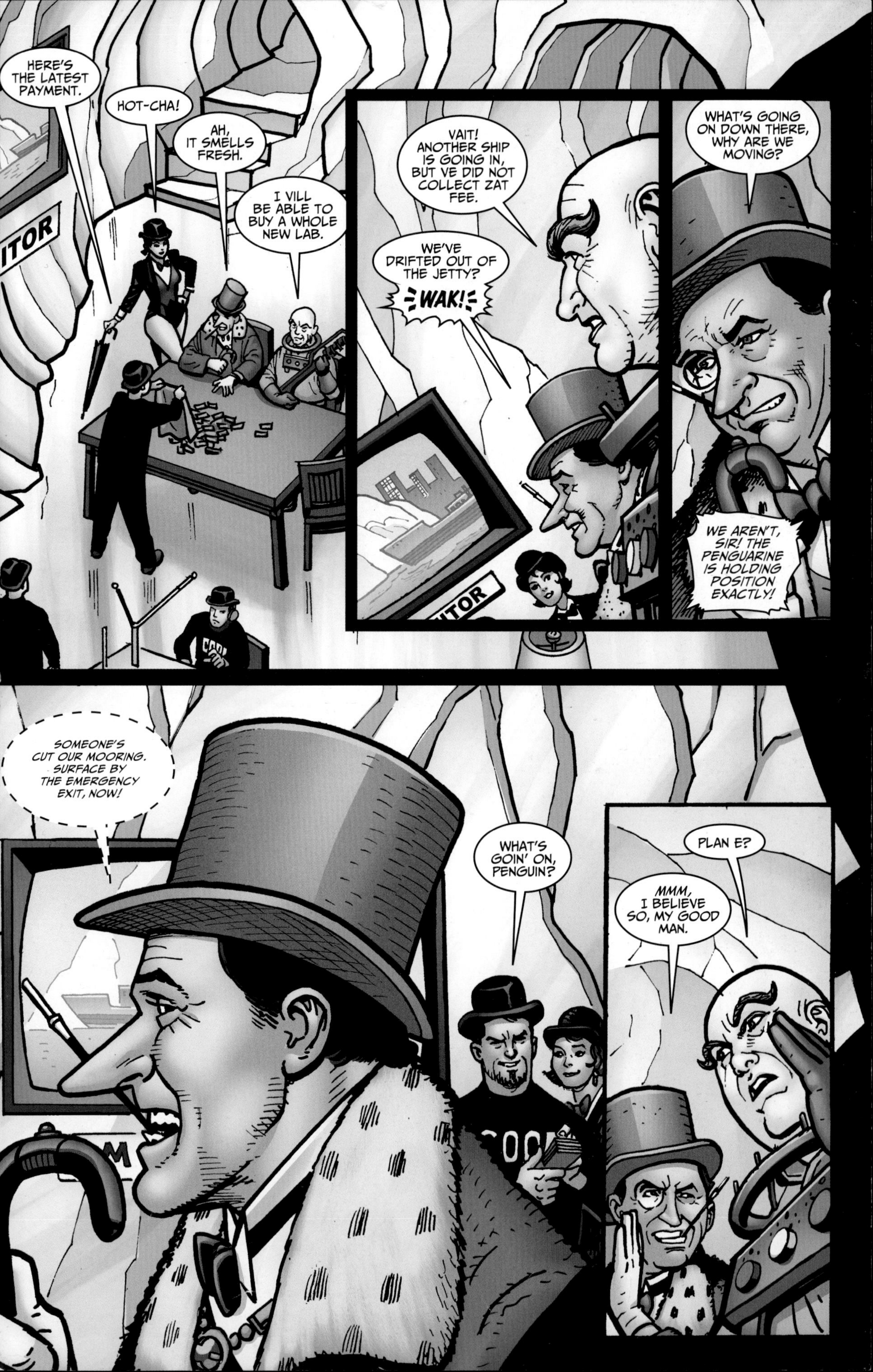
HERE'S THE LATEST PAYMENT.
HOT-CHA!
AH, IT SMELLS FRESH.
I VILL BE ABLE TO BUY A WHOLE NEW LAB.
ITOR
VAIT! ANOTHER SHIP IS GOING IN, BUT VE DID NOT COLLECT ZAT FEE.
WE'VE DRIFTED OUT OF THE JETTY?
WAK!
ITOR
WHAT'S GOING ON DOWN THERE, WHY ARE WE MOVING?
WE AREN'T, SIR! THE PENGUARINE IS HOLDING POSITION EXACTLY!
SOMEONE'S CUT OUR MOORING. SURFACE BY THE EMERGENCY EXIT, NOW!
WHAT'S GOIN' ON, PENGUIN?
PLAN E?
MMM, I BELIEVE SO, MY GOOD MAN.

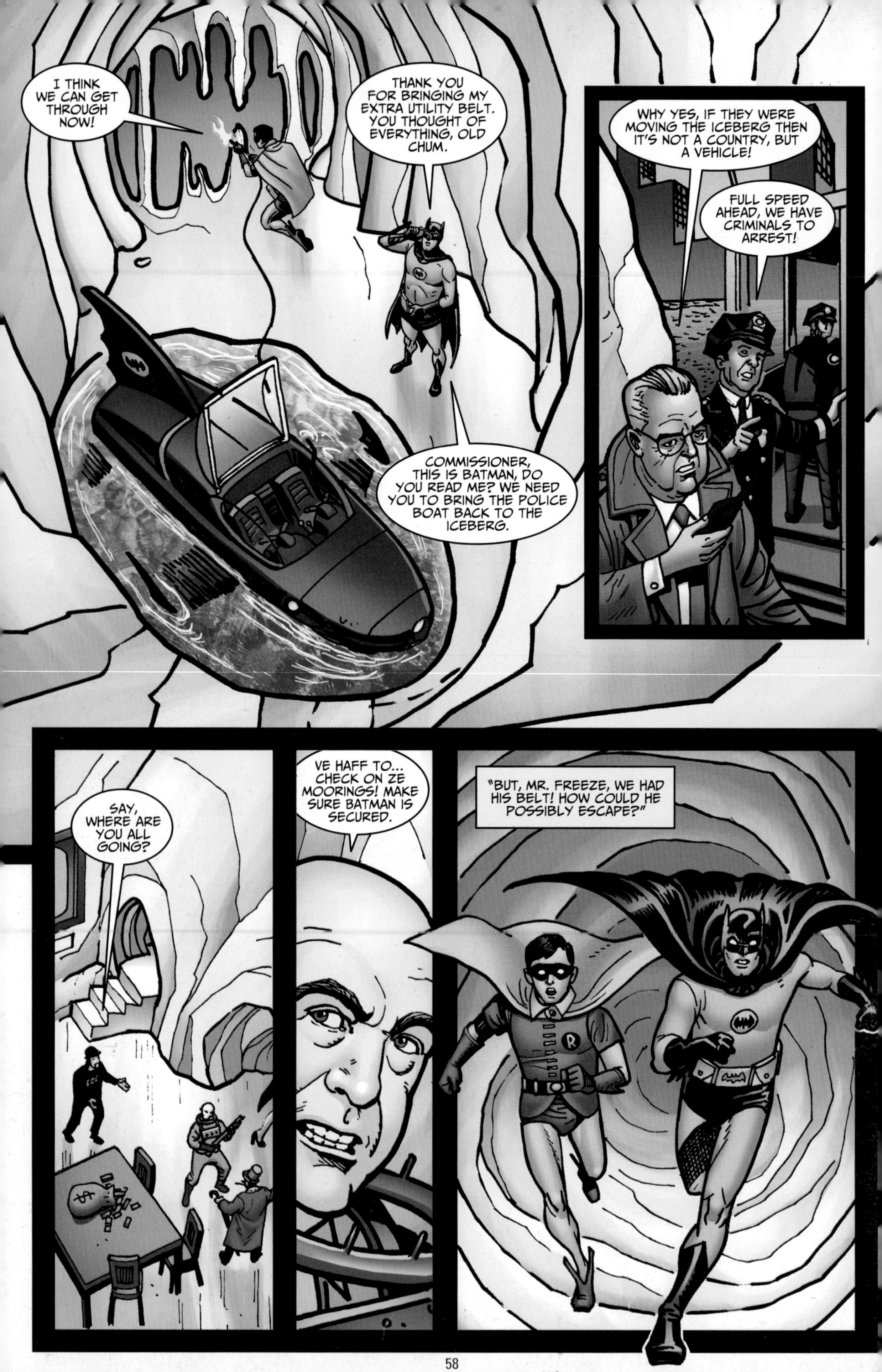
I THINK WE CAN GET THROUGH NOW!
THANK YOU FOR BRINGING MY EXTRA UTILITY BELT. YOU THOUGHT OF EVERYTHING, OLD CHUM.
COMMISSIONER, THIS IS BATMAN, DO YOU READ ME? WE NEED YOU TO BRING THE POLICE BOAT BACK TO THE ICEBERG.
WHY YES, IF THEY WERE MOVING THE ICEBERG THEN IT'S NOT A COUNTRY, BUT A VEHICLE!
FULL SPEED AHEAD, WE HAVE CRIMINALS TO ARREST!
SAY, WHERE ARE YOU ALL GOING?
VE HAFF TO... CHECK ON ZE MOORINGS! MAKE SURE BATMAN IS SECURED.
"BUT, MR. FREEZE, WE HAD HIS BELT! HOW COULD HE POSSIBLY ESCAPE?"

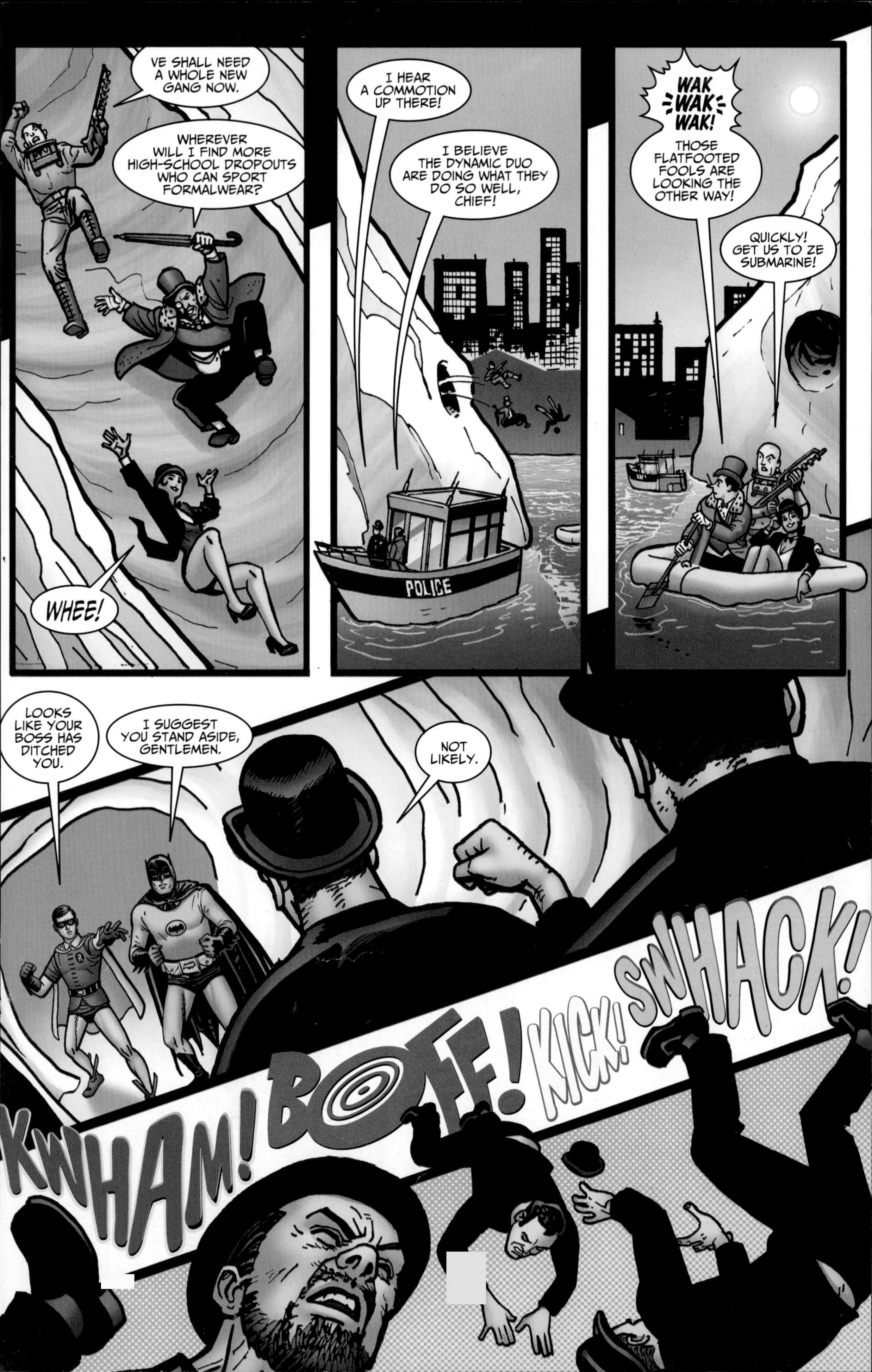
VE SHALL NEED A WHOLE NEW GANG NOW.
WHEREVER WILL I FIND MORE HIGH-SCHOOL DROPOUTS WHO CAN SPORT FORMALWEAR?
WHEE!
I HEAR A COMMOTION UP THERE!
I BELIEVE THE DYNAMIC DUO ARE DOING WHAT THEY DO SO WELL, CHIEF!
POLICE
WAK WAK WAK!
THOSE FLATFOOTED FOOLS ARE LOOKING THE OTHER WAY!
QUICKLY! GET US TO ZE SUBMARINE!
LOOKS LIKE YOUR BOSS HAS DITCHED YOU.
I SUGGEST YOU STAND ASIDE, GENTLEMEN.
NOT LIKELY.
KWHAM! BOFF! KICK! SWHACK!

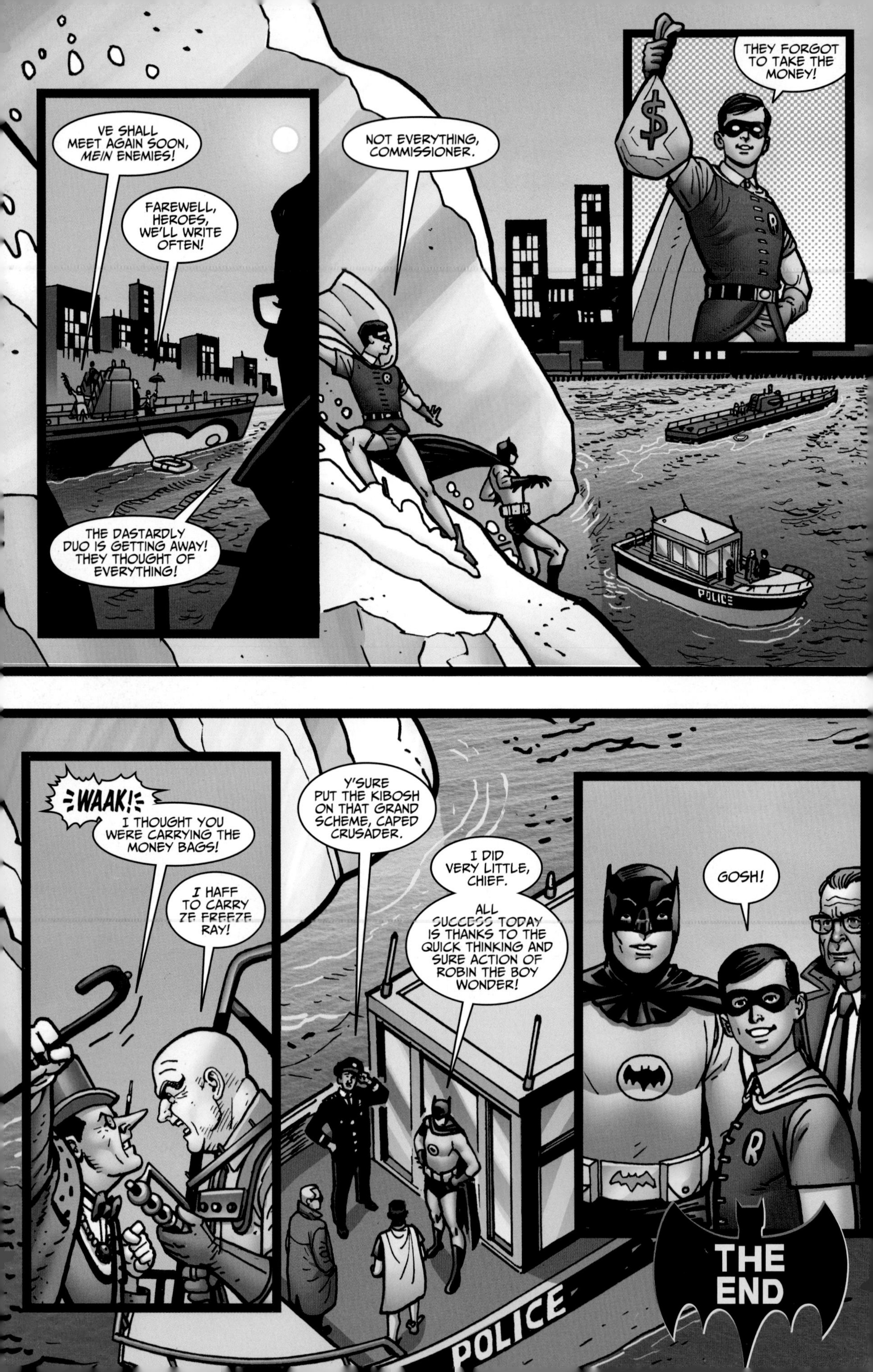

VE SHALL MEET AGAIN SOON, *MEIN* ENEMIES!
FAREWELL, HEROES, WE'LL WRITE OFTEN!
THE DASTARDLY DUO IS GETTING AWAY! THEY THOUGHT OF EVERYTHING!
NOT EVERYTHING, COMMISSIONER.
THEY FORGOT TO TAKE THE MONEY!
POLICE
WAAK!
I THOUGHT YOU WERE CARRYING THE MONEY BAGS!
*I* HAFF TO CARRY ZE FREEZE RAY!
Y'SURE PUT THE KIBOSH ON THAT GRAND SCHEME, CAPED CRUSADER.
I DID VERY LITTLE, CHIEF.
ALL SUCCESS TODAY IS THANKS TO THE QUICK THINKING AND SURE ACTION OF ROBIN THE BOY WONDER!
GOSH!
POLICE
THE END

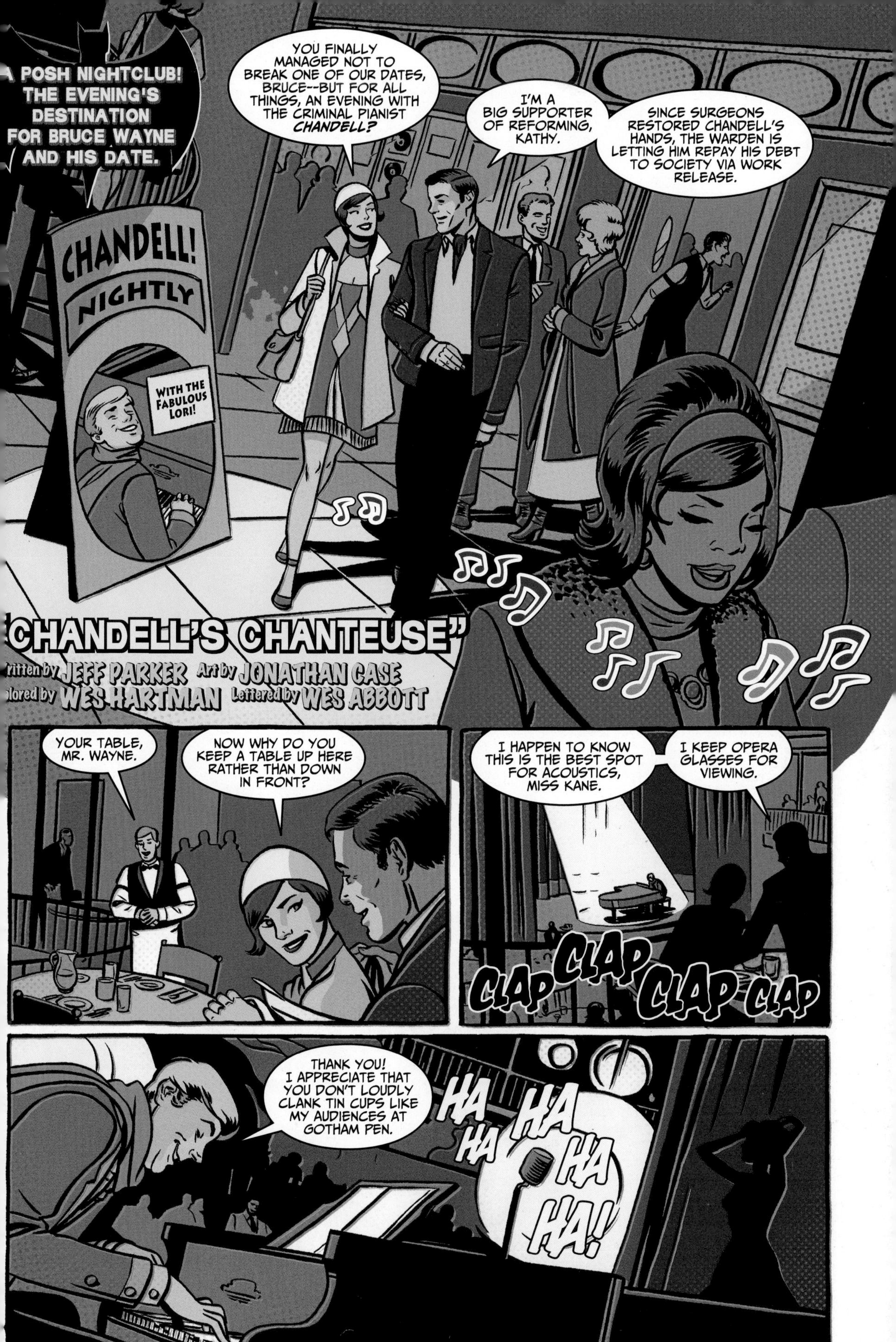
A POSH NIGHTCLUB! THE EVENING'S DESTINATION FOR BRUCE WAYNE AND HIS DATE.
YOU FINALLY MANAGED NOT TO BREAK ONE OF OUR DATES, BRUCE--BUT FOR ALL THINGS, AN EVENING WITH THE CRIMINAL PIANIST CHANDELL?
I'M A BIG SUPPORTER OF REFORMING, KATHY.
SINCE SURGEONS RESTORED CHANDELL'S HANDS, THE WARDEN IS LETTING HIM REPAY HIS DEBT TO SOCIETY VIA WORK RELEASE.
CHANDELL! NIGHTLY
WITH THE FABULOUS LORI!
"CHANDELL'S CHANTEUSE"
Written by JEFF PARKER Art by JONATHAN CASE
Colored by WES HARTMAN Lettered by WES ABBOTT
YOUR TABLE, MR. WAYNE.
NOW WHY DO YOU KEEP A TABLE UP HERE RATHER THAN DOWN IN FRONT?
I HAPPEN TO KNOW THIS IS THE BEST SPOT FOR ACOUSTICS, MISS KANE.
I KEEP OPERA GLASSES FOR VIEWING.
CLAP CLAP CLAP CLAP
THANK YOU! I APPRECIATE THAT YOU DON'T LOUDLY CLANK TIN CUPS LIKE MY AUDIENCES AT GOTHAM PEN.
HA HA HA HA HA!

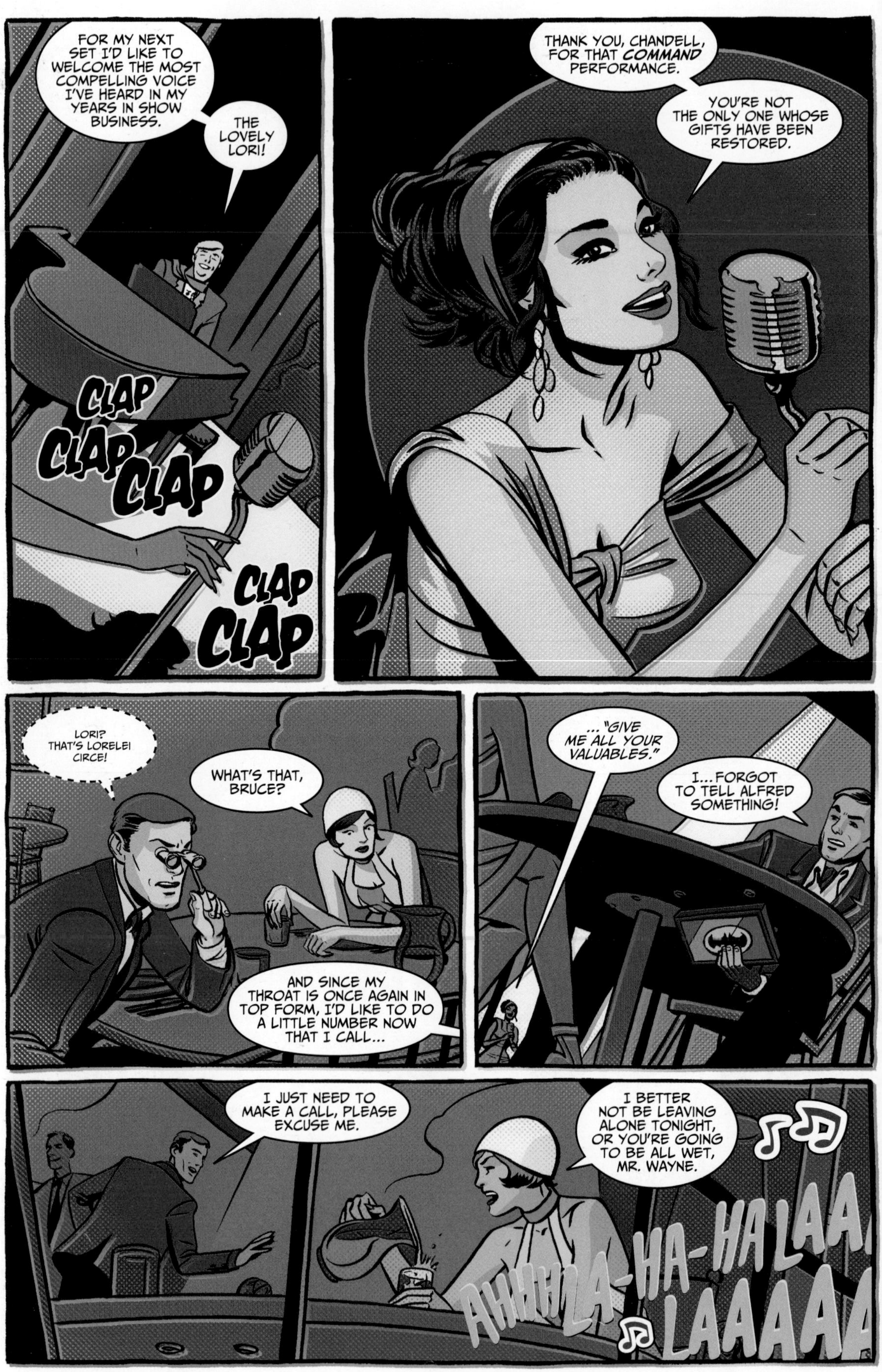
FOR MY NEXT SET I'D LIKE TO WELCOME THE MOST COMPELLING VOICE I'VE HEARD IN MY YEARS IN SHOW BUSINESS.
THE LOVELY LORI!
CLAP CLAP CLAP
CLAP CLAP
THANK YOU, CHANDELL, FOR THAT *COMMAND* PERFORMANCE.
YOU'RE NOT THE ONLY ONE WHOSE GIFTS HAVE BEEN RESTORED.
LORI? THAT'S LORELEI CIRCE!
WHAT'S THAT, BRUCE?
AND SINCE MY THROAT IS ONCE AGAIN IN TOP FORM, I'D LIKE TO DO A LITTLE NUMBER NOW THAT I CALL...
..."GIVE ME ALL YOUR VALUABLES."
I...FORGOT TO TELL ALFRED SOMETHING!
I JUST NEED TO MAKE A CALL, PLEASE EXCUSE ME.
I BETTER NOT BE LEAVING ALONE TONIGHT, OR YOU'RE GOING TO BE ALL WET, MR. WAYNE.
AHHHLA-HA-HA LAA LAAAAA

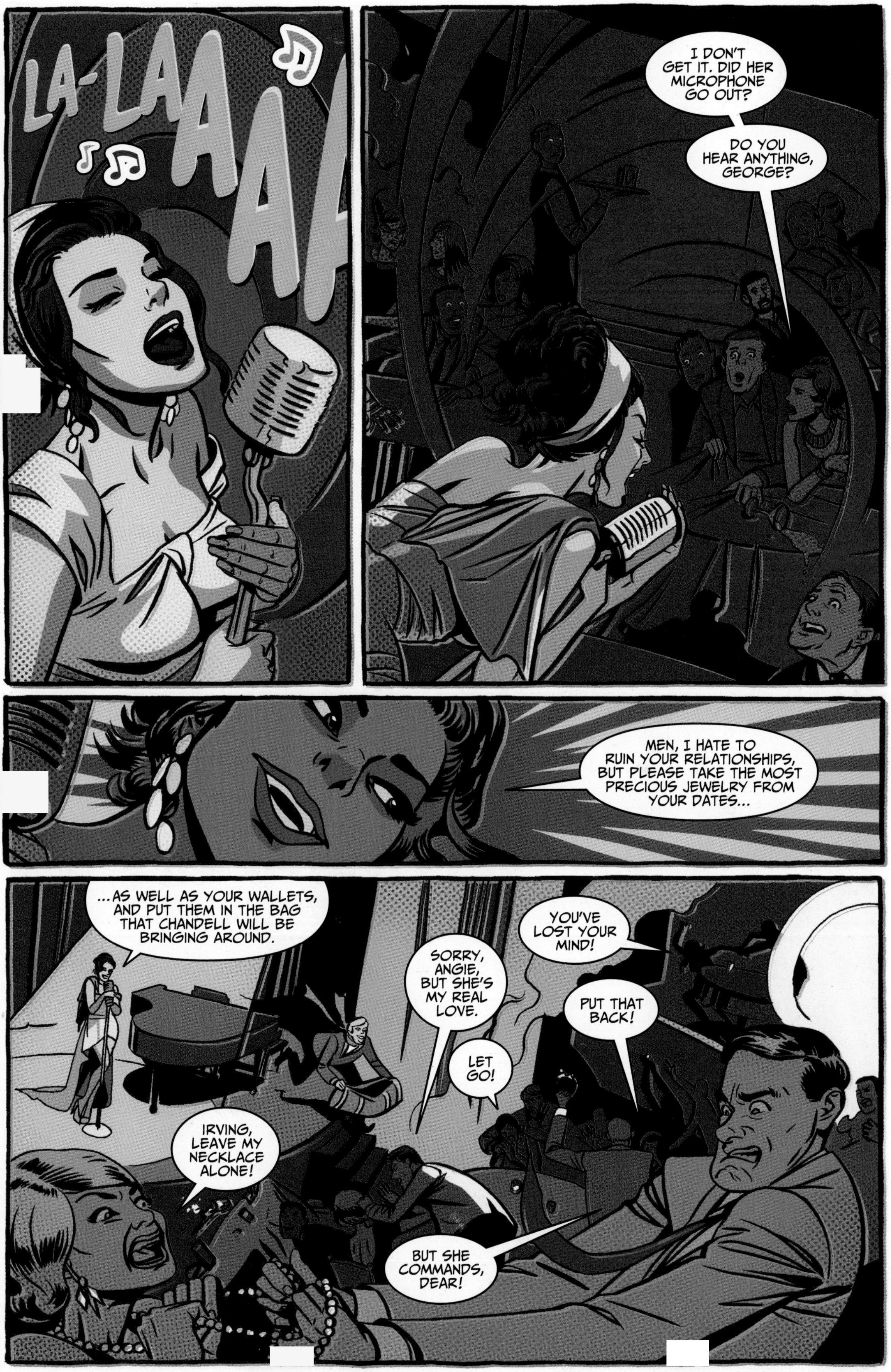
LA-LAAAA
I DON'T GET IT. DID HER MICROPHONE GO OUT?
DO YOU HEAR ANYTHING, GEORGE?
MEN, I HATE TO RUIN YOUR RELATIONSHIPS, BUT PLEASE TAKE THE MOST PRECIOUS JEWELRY FROM YOUR DATES...
...AS WELL AS YOUR WALLETS, AND PUT THEM IN THE BAG THAT CHANDELL WILL BE BRINGING AROUND.
SORRY, ANGIE, BUT SHE'S MY REAL LOVE.
YOU'VE LOST YOUR MIND!
PUT THAT BACK!
LET GO!
IRVING, LEAVE MY NECKLACE ALONE!
BUT SHE COMMANDS, DEAR!

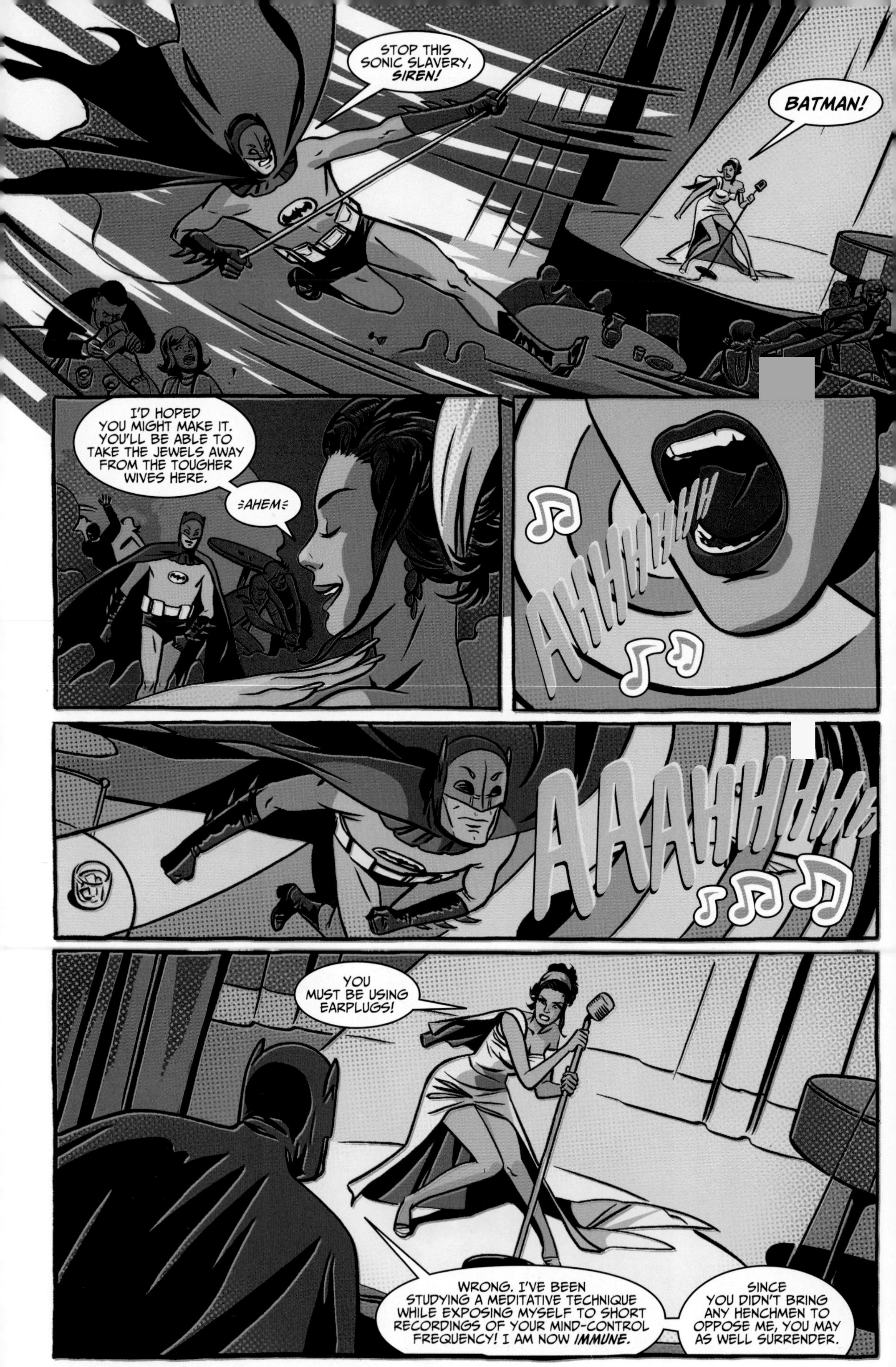
STOP THIS SONIC SLAVERY, SIREN!
BATMAN!
I'D HOPED YOU MIGHT MAKE IT. YOU'LL BE ABLE TO TAKE THE JEWELS AWAY FROM THE TOUGHER WIVES HERE.
AHEM
AHHHHHHH
AAAHHHHH
YOU MUST BE USING EARPLUGS!
WRONG. I'VE BEEN STUDYING A MEDITATIVE TECHNIQUE WHILE EXPOSING MYSELF TO SHORT RECORDINGS OF YOUR MIND-CONTROL FREQUENCY! I AM NOW IMMUNE.
SINCE YOU DIDN'T BRING ANY HENCHMEN TO OPPOSE ME, YOU MAY AS WELL SURRENDER.

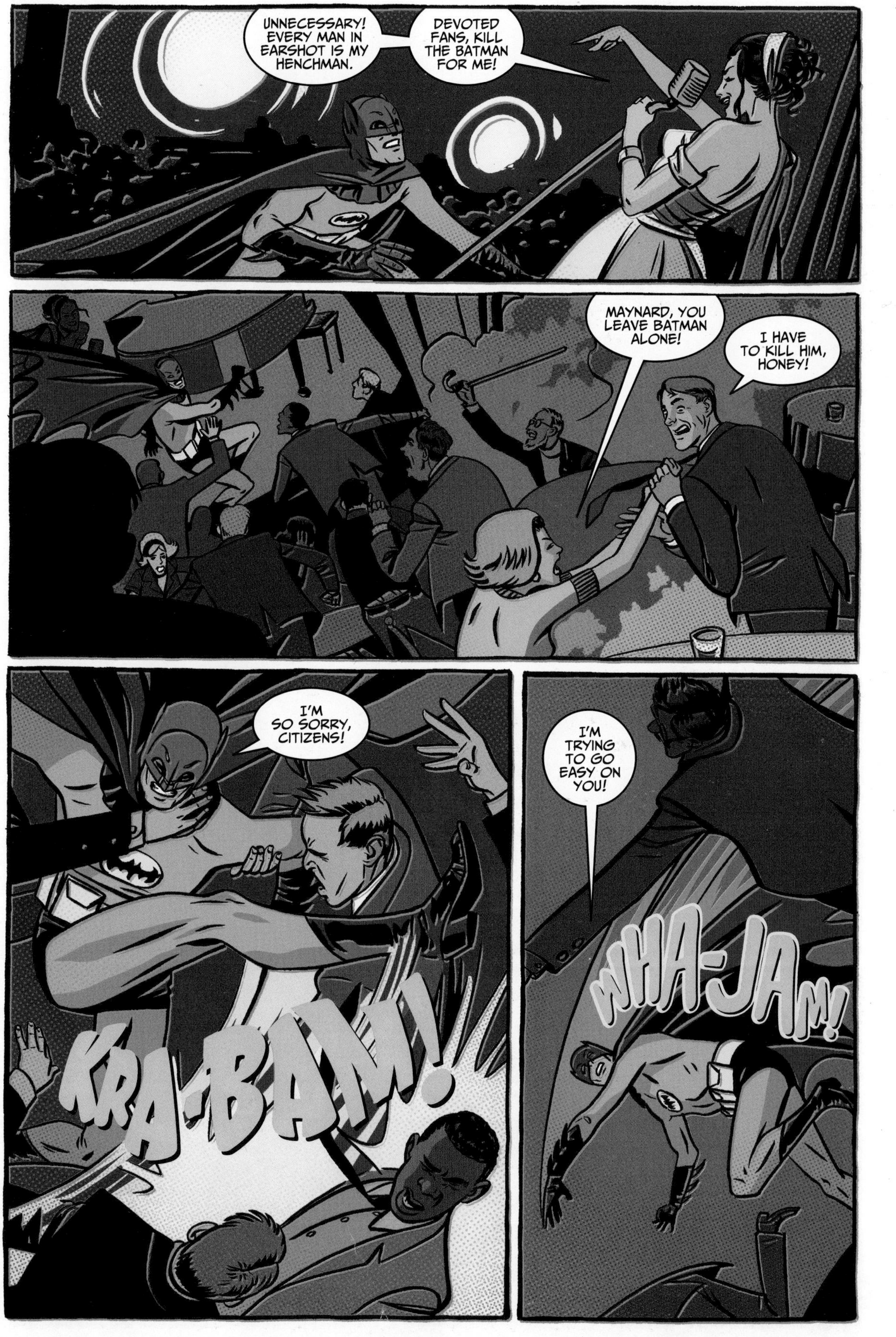
UNNECESSARY! EVERY MAN IN EARSHOT IS MY HENCHMAN.
DEVOTED FANS, KILL THE BATMAN FOR ME!
MAYNARD, YOU LEAVE BATMAN ALONE!
I HAVE TO KILL HIM, HONEY!
I'M SO SORRY, CITIZENS!
KRA-BAM!
I'M TRYING TO GO EASY ON YOU!
WHA-JAM!

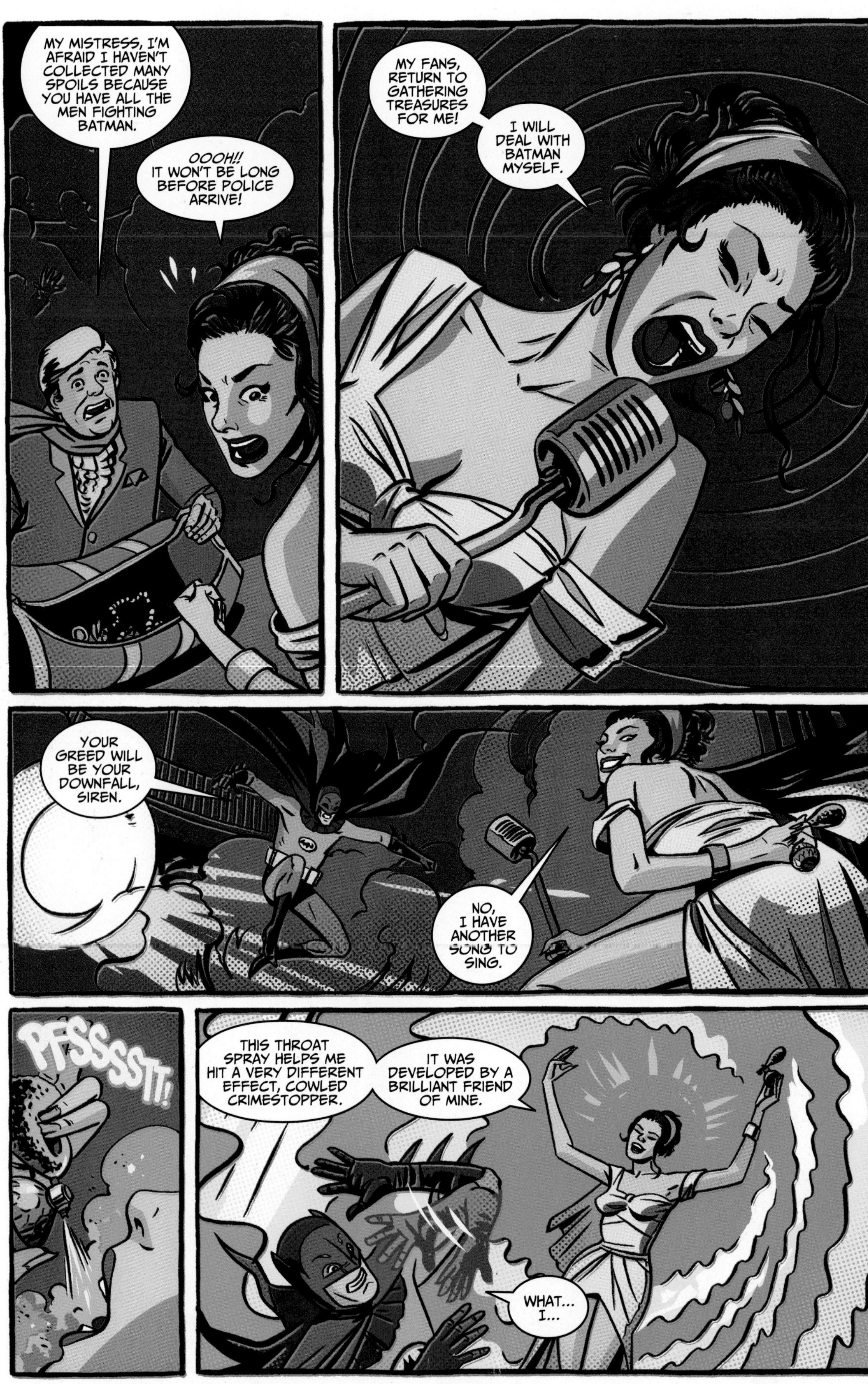
MY MISTRESS, I'M AFRAID I HAVEN'T COLLECTED MANY SPOILS BECAUSE YOU HAVE ALL THE MEN FIGHTING BATMAN.
OOOH!! IT WON'T BE LONG BEFORE POLICE ARRIVE!
MY FANS, RETURN TO GATHERING TREASURES FOR ME!
I WILL DEAL WITH BATMAN MYSELF.
YOUR GREED WILL BE YOUR DOWNFALL, SIREN.
NO, I HAVE ANOTHER SONG TO SING.
PFSSSSTT!
THIS THROAT SPRAY HELPS ME HIT A VERY DIFFERENT EFFECT, COWLED CRIMESTOPPER.
IT WAS DEVELOPED BY A BRILLIANT FRIEND OF MINE.
WHAT... I...

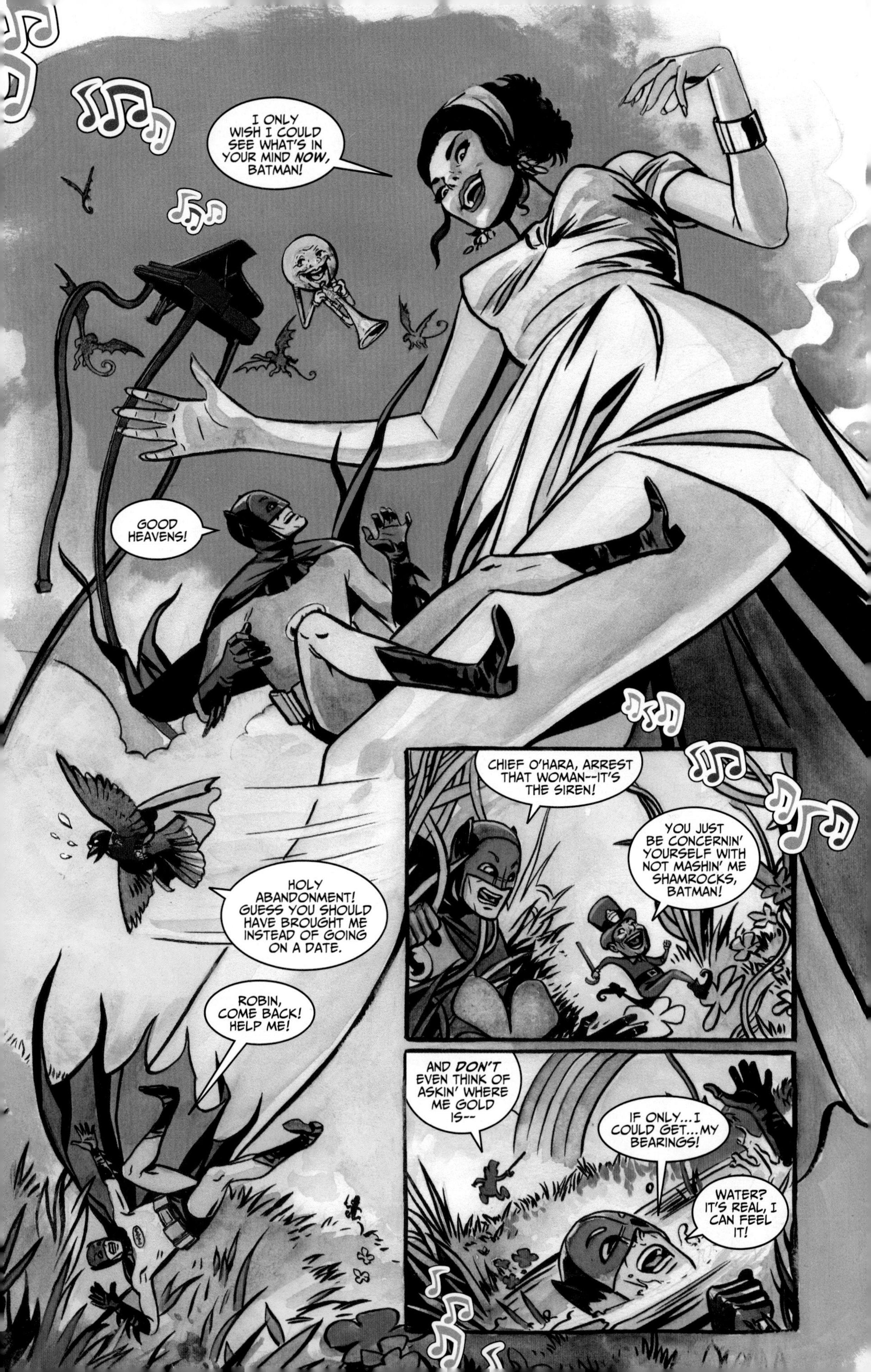
I ONLY WISH I COULD SEE WHAT'S IN YOUR MIND NOW, BATMAN!
GOOD HEAVENS!
HOLY ABANDONMENT! GUESS YOU SHOULD HAVE BROUGHT ME INSTEAD OF GOING ON A DATE.
ROBIN, COME BACK! HELP ME!
CHIEF O'HARA, ARREST THAT WOMAN--IT'S THE SIREN!
YOU JUST BE CONCERNIN' YOURSELF WITH NOT MASHIN' ME SHAMROCKS, BATMAN!
AND DON'T EVEN THINK OF ASKIN' WHERE ME GOLD IS--
IF ONLY... I COULD GET... MY BEARINGS!
WATER? IT'S REAL, I CAN FEEL IT!

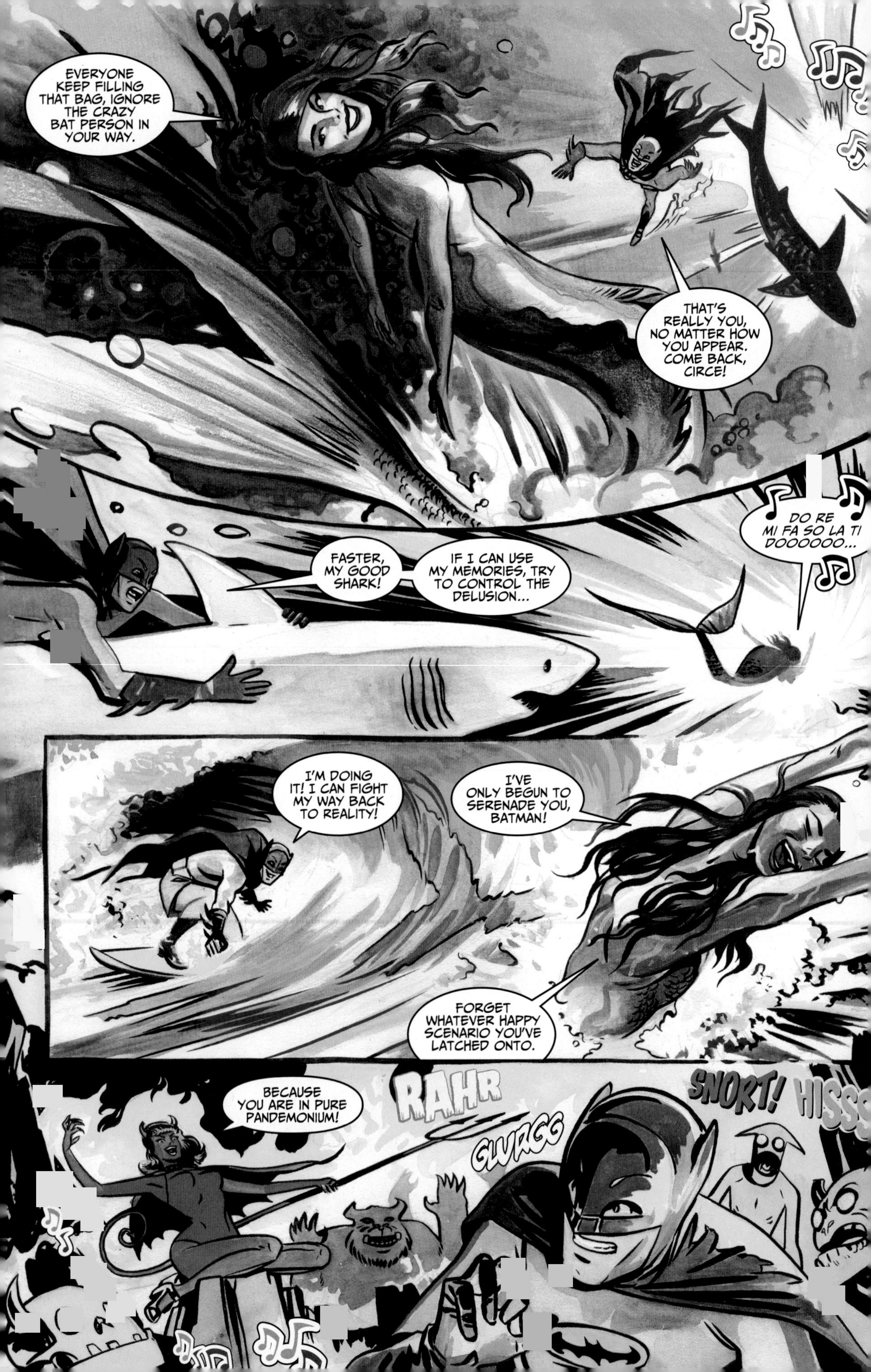
EVERYONE KEEP FILLING THAT BAG, IGNORE THE CRAZY BAT PERSON IN YOUR WAY.
THAT'S REALLY YOU, NO MATTER HOW YOU APPEAR. COME BACK, CIRCE!
FASTER, MY GOOD SHARK!
IF I CAN USE MY MEMORIES, TRY TO CONTROL THE DELUSION...
DO RE MI FA SO LA TI DOOOOOO...
I'M DOING IT! I CAN FIGHT MY WAY BACK TO REALITY!
I'VE ONLY BEGUN TO SERENADE YOU, BATMAN!
FORGET WHATEVER HAPPY SCENARIO YOU'VE LATCHED ONTO.
BECAUSE YOU ARE IN PURE PANDEMONIUM!
RAHR
SNORT!
HISSS
GLURGG

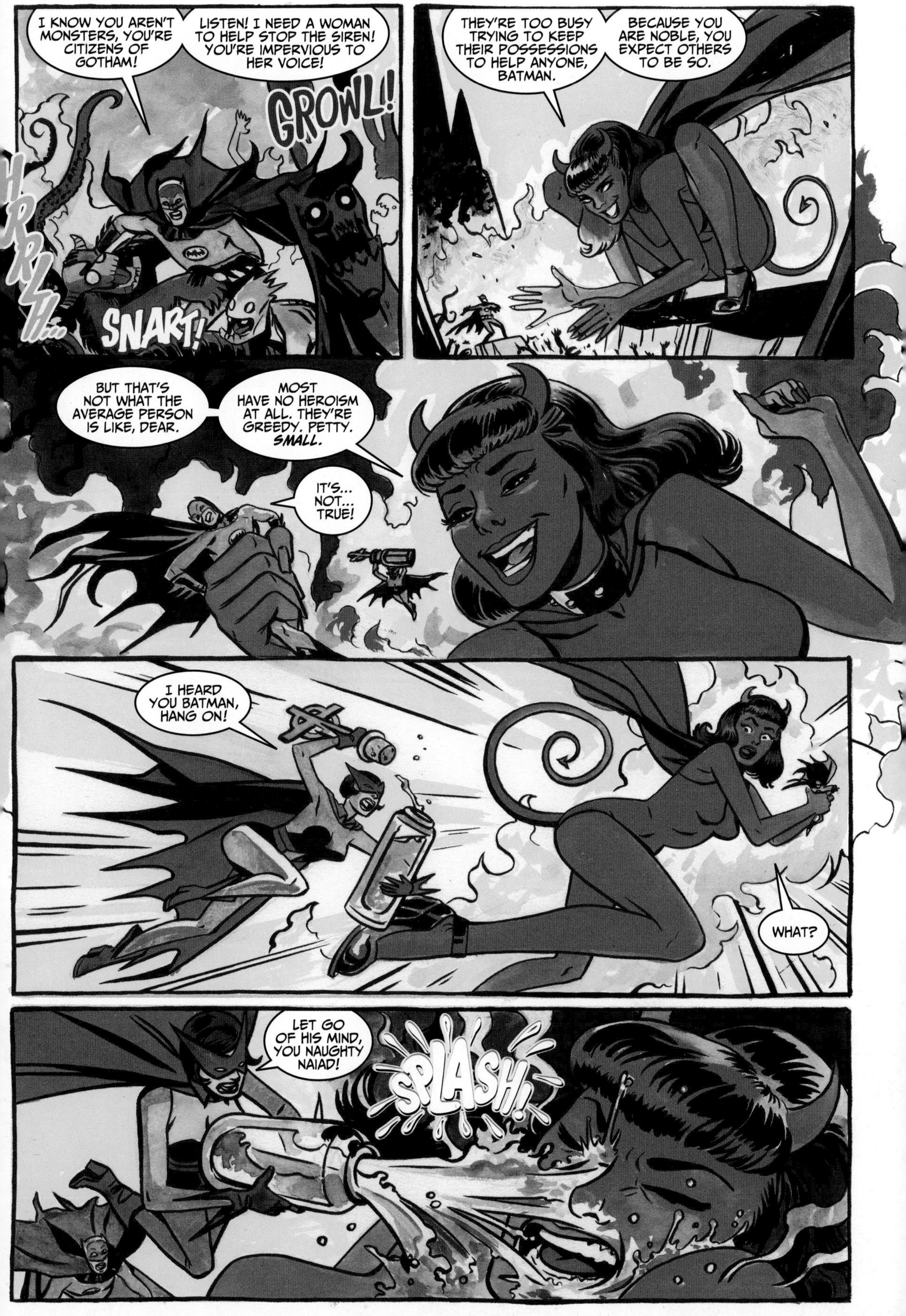
I KNOW YOU AREN'T MONSTERS, YOU'RE CITIZENS OF GOTHAM!
LISTEN! I NEED A WOMAN TO HELP STOP THE SIREN! YOU'RE IMPERVIOUS TO HER VOICE!
GROWL!
HRRLH...
SNART!
THEY'RE TOO BUSY TRYING TO KEEP THEIR POSSESSIONS TO HELP ANYONE, BATMAN.
BECAUSE YOU ARE NOBLE, YOU EXPECT OTHERS TO BE SO.
BUT THAT'S NOT WHAT THE AVERAGE PERSON IS LIKE, DEAR.
MOST HAVE NO HEROISM AT ALL. THEY'RE GREEDY. PETTY. SMALL.
IT'S... NOT... TRUE!
I HEARD YOU BATMAN, HANG ON!
WHAT?
LET GO OF HIS MIND, YOU NAUGHTY NAIAD!
SPLASH!

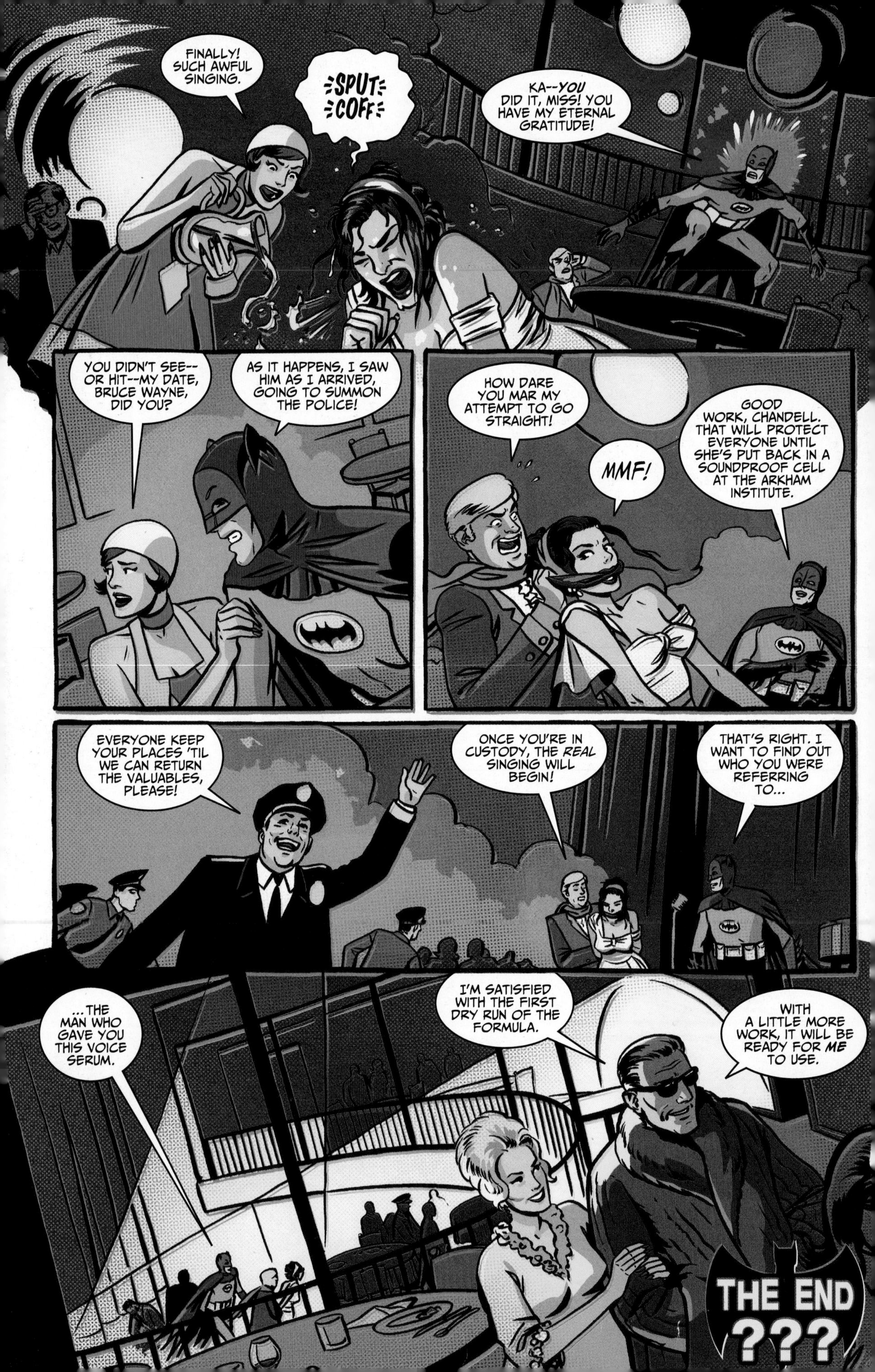
FINALLY! SUCH AWFUL SINGING.
SPUT COFF
KA--YOU DID IT, MISS! YOU HAVE MY ETERNAL GRATITUDE!
YOU DIDN'T SEE-- OR HIT--MY DATE, BRUCE WAYNE, DID YOU?
AS IT HAPPENS, I SAW HIM AS I ARRIVED, GOING TO SUMMON THE POLICE!
HOW DARE YOU MAR MY ATTEMPT TO GO STRAIGHT!
MMF!
GOOD WORK, CHANDELL. THAT WILL PROTECT EVERYONE UNTIL SHE'S PUT BACK IN A SOUNDPROOF CELL AT THE ARKHAM INSTITUTE.
EVERYONE KEEP YOUR PLACES 'TIL WE CAN RETURN THE VALUABLES, PLEASE!
ONCE YOU'RE IN CUSTODY, THE REAL SINGING WILL BEGIN!
THAT'S RIGHT. I WANT TO FIND OUT WHO YOU WERE REFERRING TO...
...THE MAN WHO GAVE YOU THIS VOICE SERUM.
I'M SATISFIED WITH THE FIRST DRY RUN OF THE FORMULA.
WITH A LITTLE MORE WORK, IT WILL BE READY FOR ME TO USE.
THE END ???

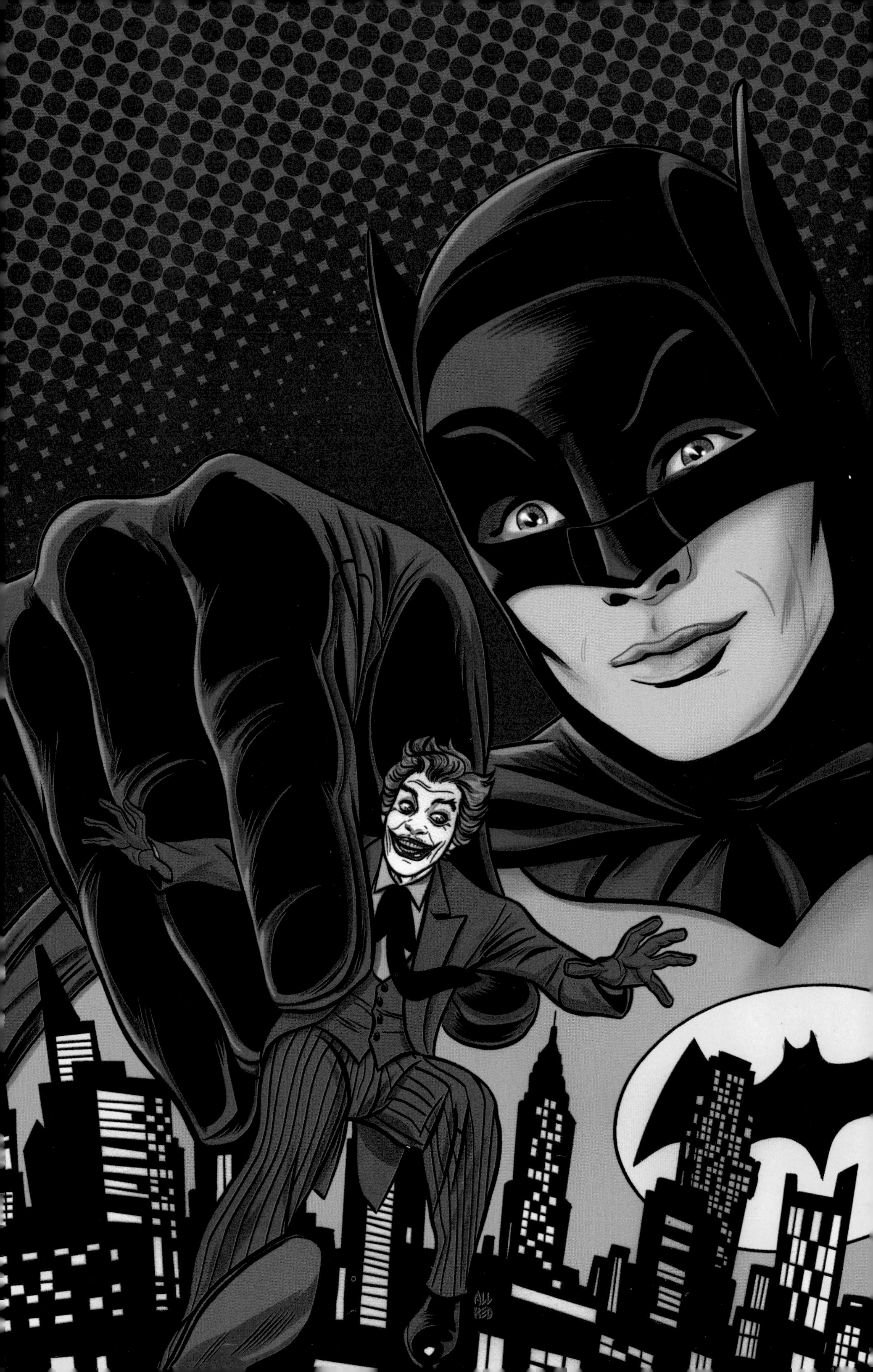
ALL
RED

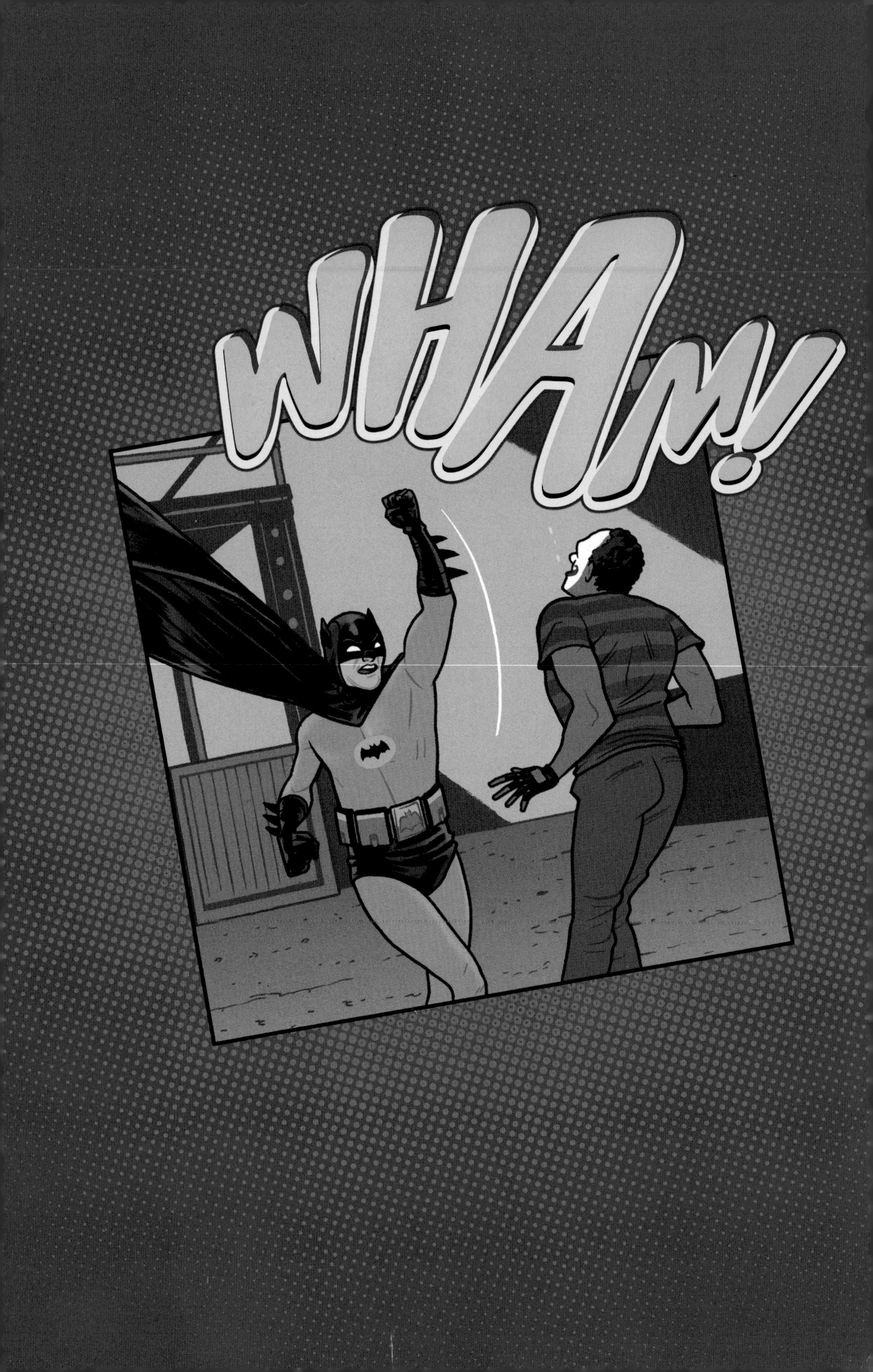
WHAM!

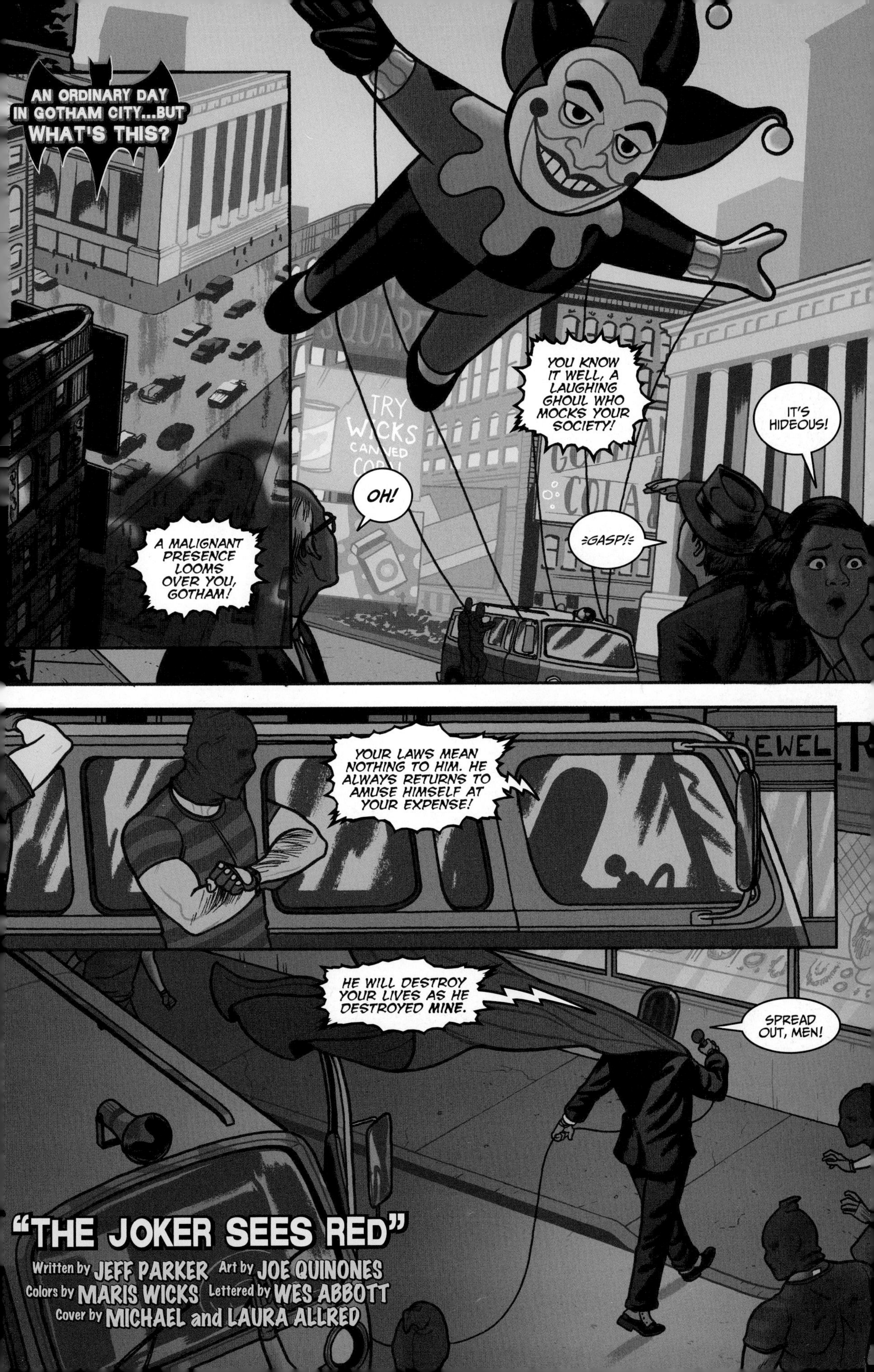
AN ORDINARY DAY IN GOTHAM CITY...BUT WHAT'S THIS?
TRY WICKS CANNED CORN
YOU KNOW IT WELL, A LAUGHING GHOUL WHO MOCKS YOUR SOCIETY!
IT'S HIDEOUS!
OH!
=GASP!=
A MALIGNANT PRESENCE LOOMS OVER YOU, GOTHAM!
YOUR LAWS MEAN NOTHING TO HIM. HE ALWAYS RETURNS TO AMUSE HIMSELF AT YOUR EXPENSE!
HE WILL DESTROY YOUR LIVES AS HE DESTROYED MINE.
SPREAD OUT, MEN!
"THE JOKER SEES RED"
Written by JEFF PARKER Art by JOE QUINONES
Colors by MARIS WICKS Lettered by WES ABBOTT
Cover by MICHAEL and LAURA ALLRED

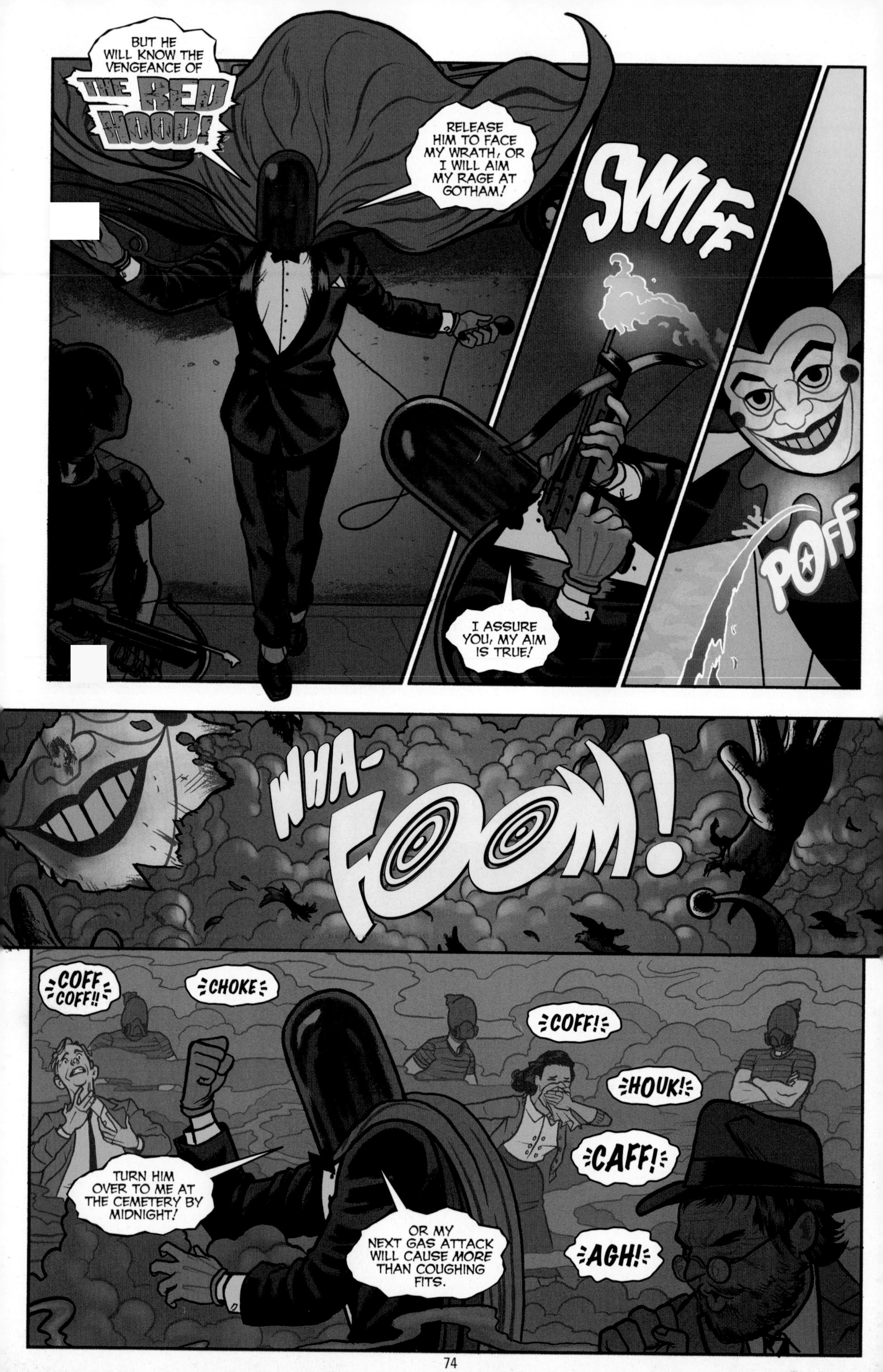

BUT HE WILL KNOW THE VENGEANCE OF THE RED HOOD!
RELEASE HIM TO FACE MY WRATH, OR I WILL AIM MY RAGE AT GOTHAM!
SWIFF
I ASSURE YOU, MY AIM IS TRUE!
POFF
WHA-FOOM!
COFF COFF!!
CHOKE
COFF!
HOUK!
CAFF!
TURN HIM OVER TO ME AT THE CEMETERY BY MIDNIGHT!
OR MY NEXT GAS ATTACK WILL CAUSE MORE THAN COUGHING FITS.
AGH!

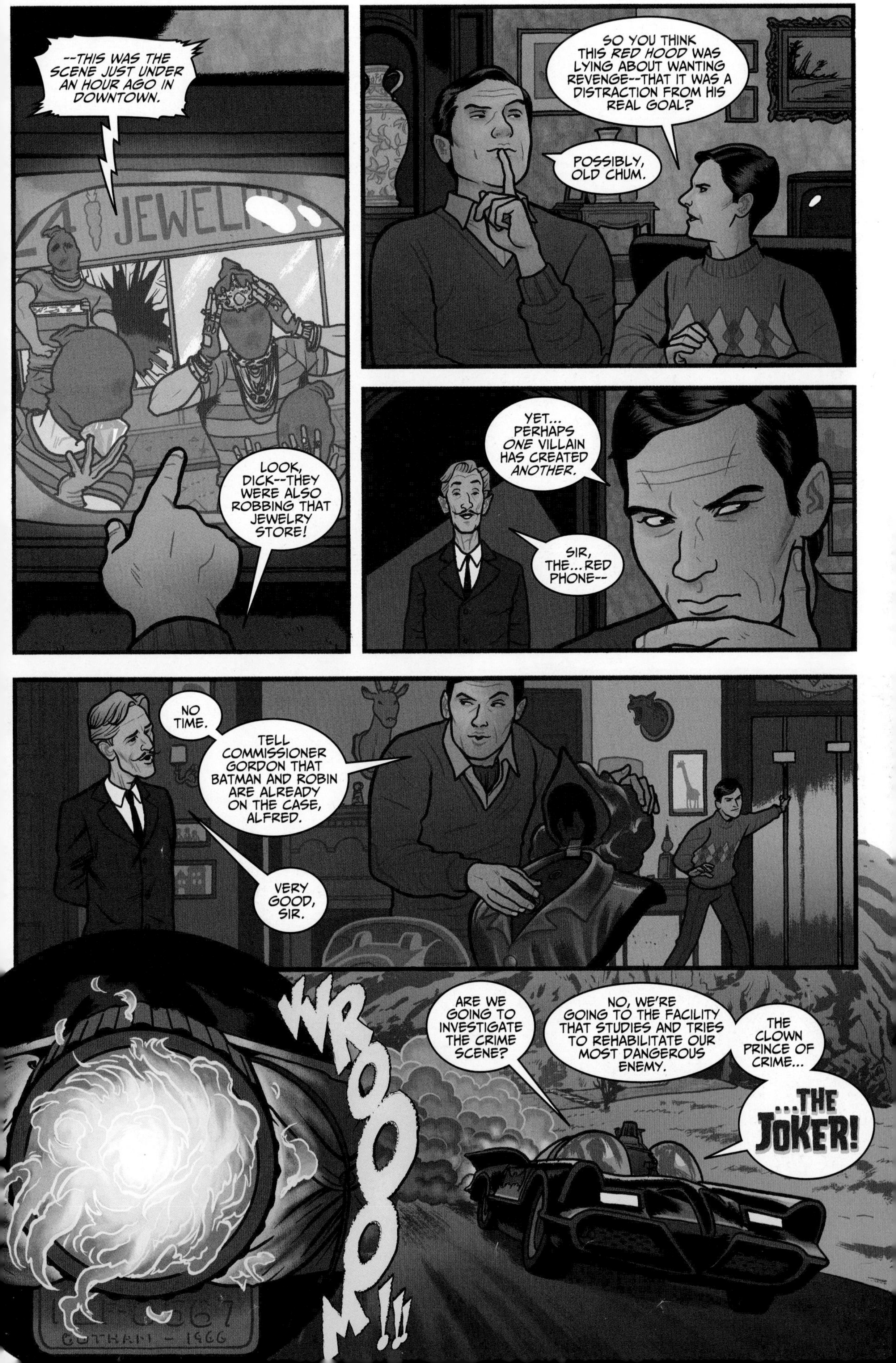
--THIS WAS THE SCENE JUST UNDER AN HOUR AGO IN DOWNTOWN.
JEWEL
LOOK, DICK--THEY WERE ALSO ROBBING THAT JEWELRY STORE!
SO YOU THINK THIS RED HOOD WAS LYING ABOUT WANTING REVENGE--THAT IT WAS A DISTRACTION FROM HIS REAL GOAL?
POSSIBLY, OLD CHUM.
YET... PERHAPS ONE VILLAIN HAS CREATED ANOTHER.
SIR, THE... RED PHONE--
NO TIME.
TELL COMMISSIONER GORDON THAT BATMAN AND ROBIN ARE ALREADY ON THE CASE, ALFRED.
VERY GOOD, SIR.
WROOOOM!!!
ARE WE GOING TO INVESTIGATE THE CRIME SCENE?
NO, WE'RE GOING TO THE FACILITY THAT STUDIES AND TRIES TO REHABILITATE OUR MOST DANGEROUS ENEMY.
THE CLOWN PRINCE OF CRIME...
...THE JOKER!

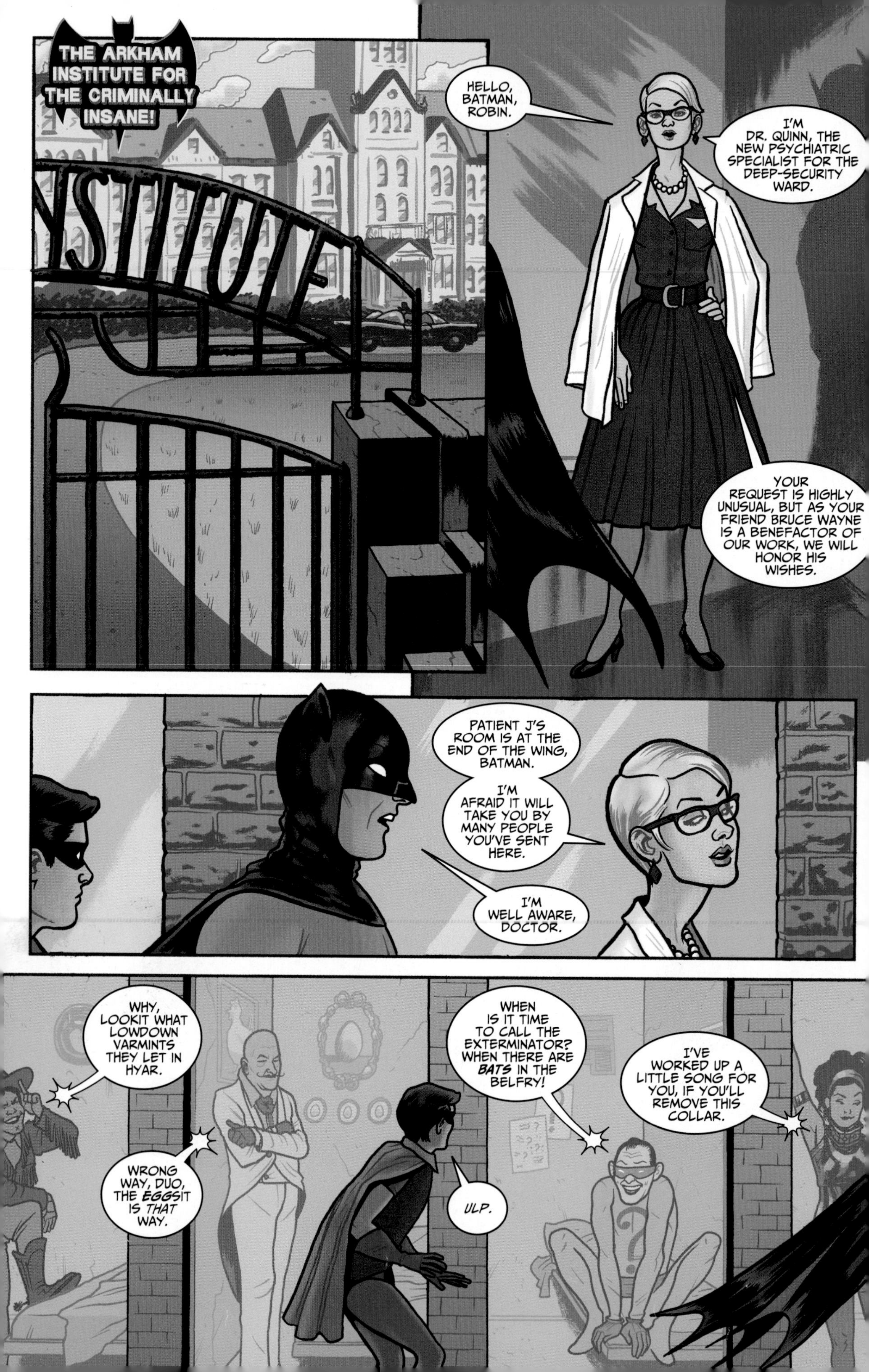
THE ARKHAM INSTITUTE FOR THE CRIMINALLY INSANE!
HELLO, BATMAN, ROBIN.
I'M DR. QUINN, THE NEW PSYCHIATRIC SPECIALIST FOR THE DEEP-SECURITY WARD.
YOUR REQUEST IS HIGHLY UNUSUAL, BUT AS YOUR FRIEND BRUCE WAYNE IS A BENEFACTOR OF OUR WORK, WE WILL HONOR HIS WISHES.
PATIENT J'S ROOM IS AT THE END OF THE WING, BATMAN.
I'M AFRAID IT WILL TAKE YOU BY MANY PEOPLE YOU'VE SENT HERE.
I'M WELL AWARE, DOCTOR.
WHY, LOOKIT WHAT LOWDOWN VARMINTS THEY LET IN HYAR.
WRONG WAY, DUO, THE *EGGS*IT IS *THAT* WAY.
ULP.
WHEN IS IT TIME TO CALL THE EXTERMINATOR? WHEN THERE ARE *BATS* IN THE BELFRY!
I'VE WORKED UP A LITTLE SONG FOR YOU, IF YOU'LL REMOVE THIS COLLAR.

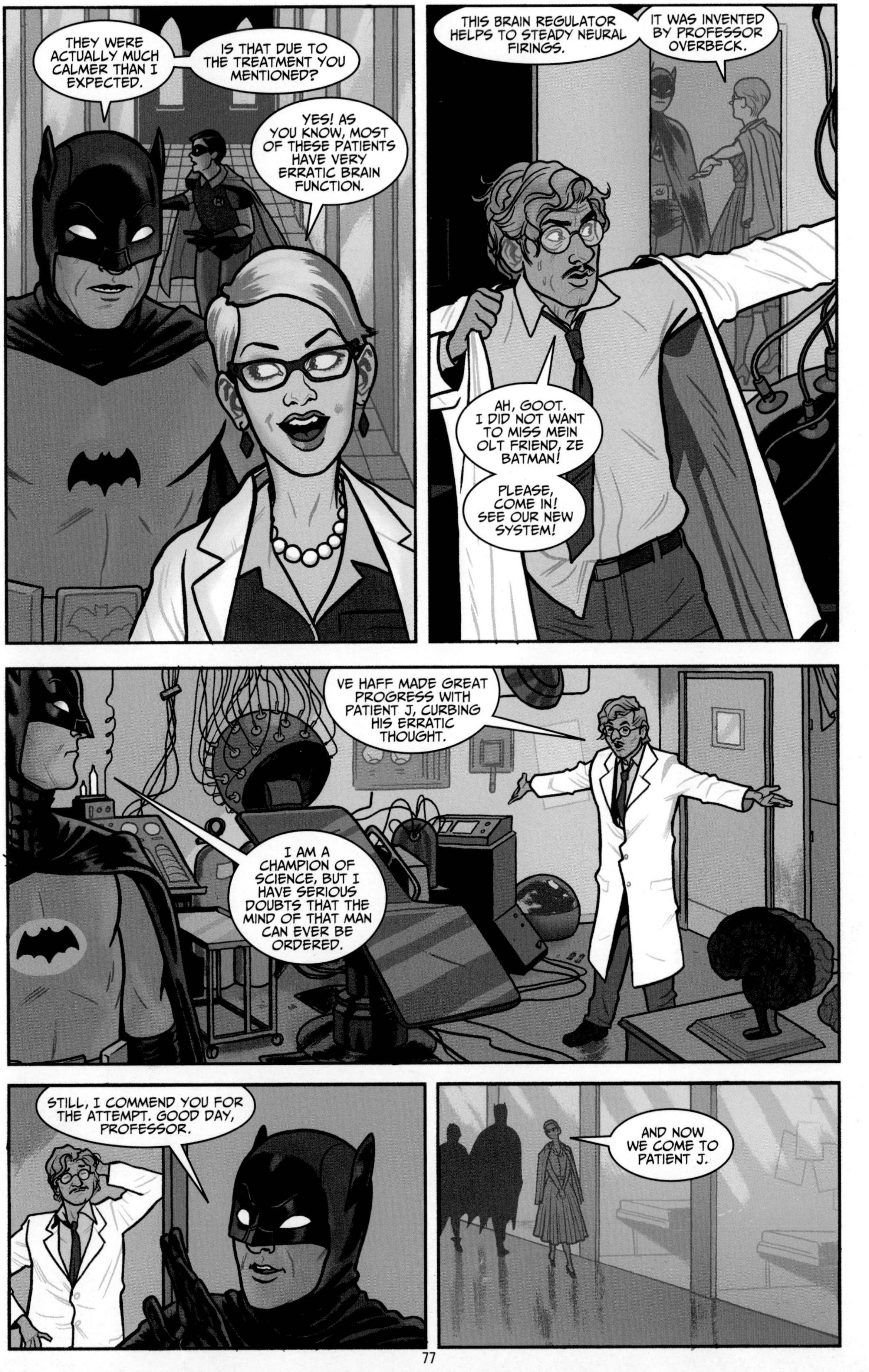
THEY WERE ACTUALLY MUCH CALMER THAN I EXPECTED.
IS THAT DUE TO THE TREATMENT YOU MENTIONED?
YES! AS YOU KNOW, MOST OF THESE PATIENTS HAVE VERY ERRATIC BRAIN FUNCTION.
THIS BRAIN REGULATOR HELPS TO STEADY NEURAL FIRINGS.
IT WAS INVENTED BY PROFESSOR OVERBECK.
AH, GOOT. I DID NOT WANT TO MISS MEIN OLT FRIEND, ZE BATMAN!
PLEASE, COME IN! SEE OUR NEW SYSTEM!
VE HAFF MADE GREAT PROGRESS WITH PATIENT J, CURBING HIS ERRATIC THOUGHT.
I AM A CHAMPION OF SCIENCE, BUT I HAVE SERIOUS DOUBTS THAT THE MIND OF THAT MAN CAN EVER BE ORDERED.
STILL, I COMMEND YOU FOR THE ATTEMPT. GOOD DAY, PROFESSOR.
AND NOW WE COME TO PATIENT J.

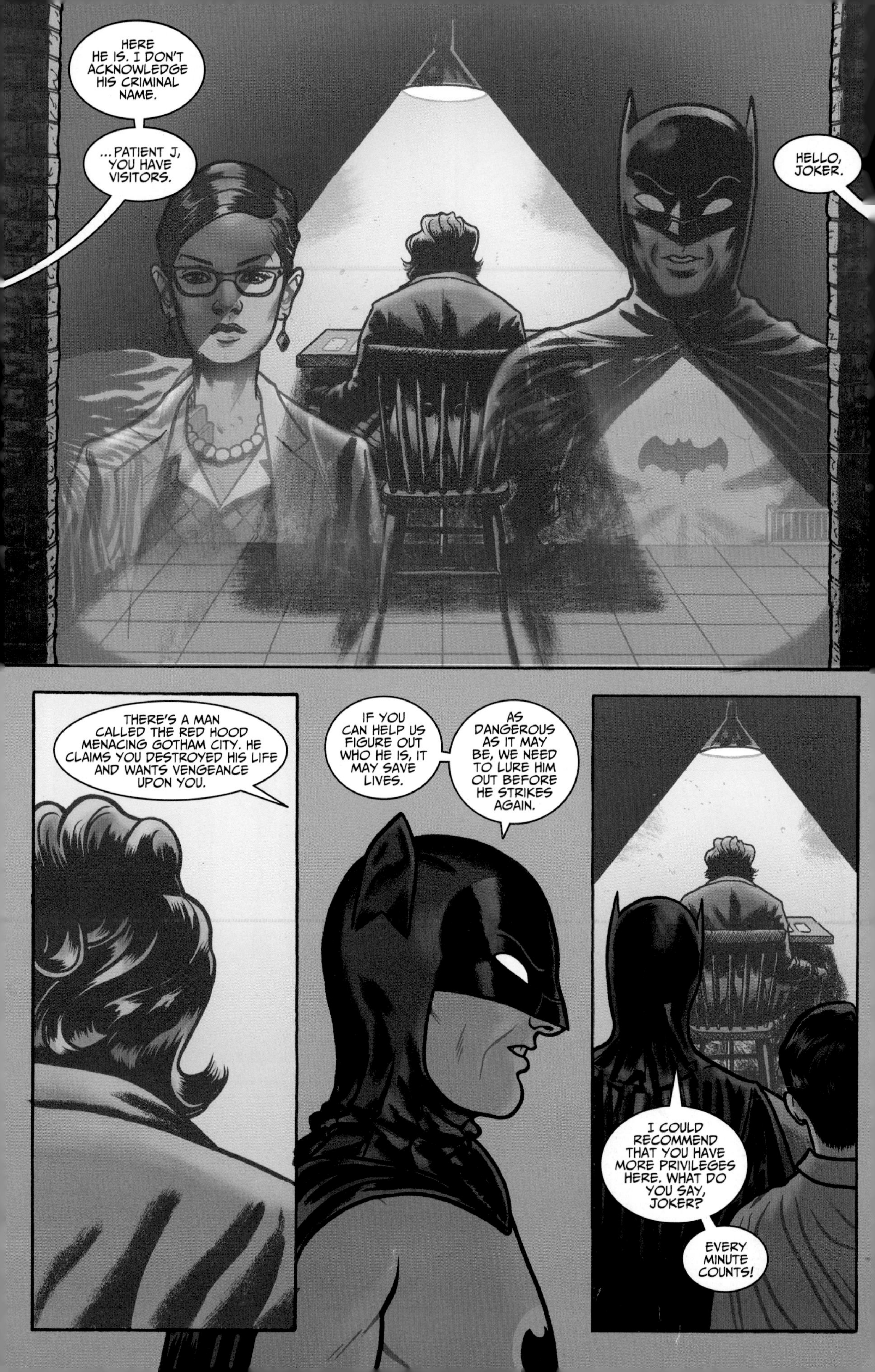
HERE HE IS. I DON'T ACKNOWLEDGE HIS CRIMINAL NAME.
...PATIENT J, YOU HAVE VISITORS.
HELLO, JOKER.
THERE'S A MAN CALLED THE RED HOOD MENACING GOTHAM CITY. HE CLAIMS YOU DESTROYED HIS LIFE AND WANTS VENGEANCE UPON YOU.
IF YOU CAN HELP US FIGURE OUT WHO HE IS, IT MAY SAVE LIVES.
AS DANGEROUS AS IT MAY BE, WE NEED TO LURE HIM OUT BEFORE HE STRIKES AGAIN.
I COULD RECOMMEND THAT YOU HAVE MORE PRIVILEGES HERE. WHAT DO YOU SAY, JOKER?
EVERY MINUTE COUNTS!

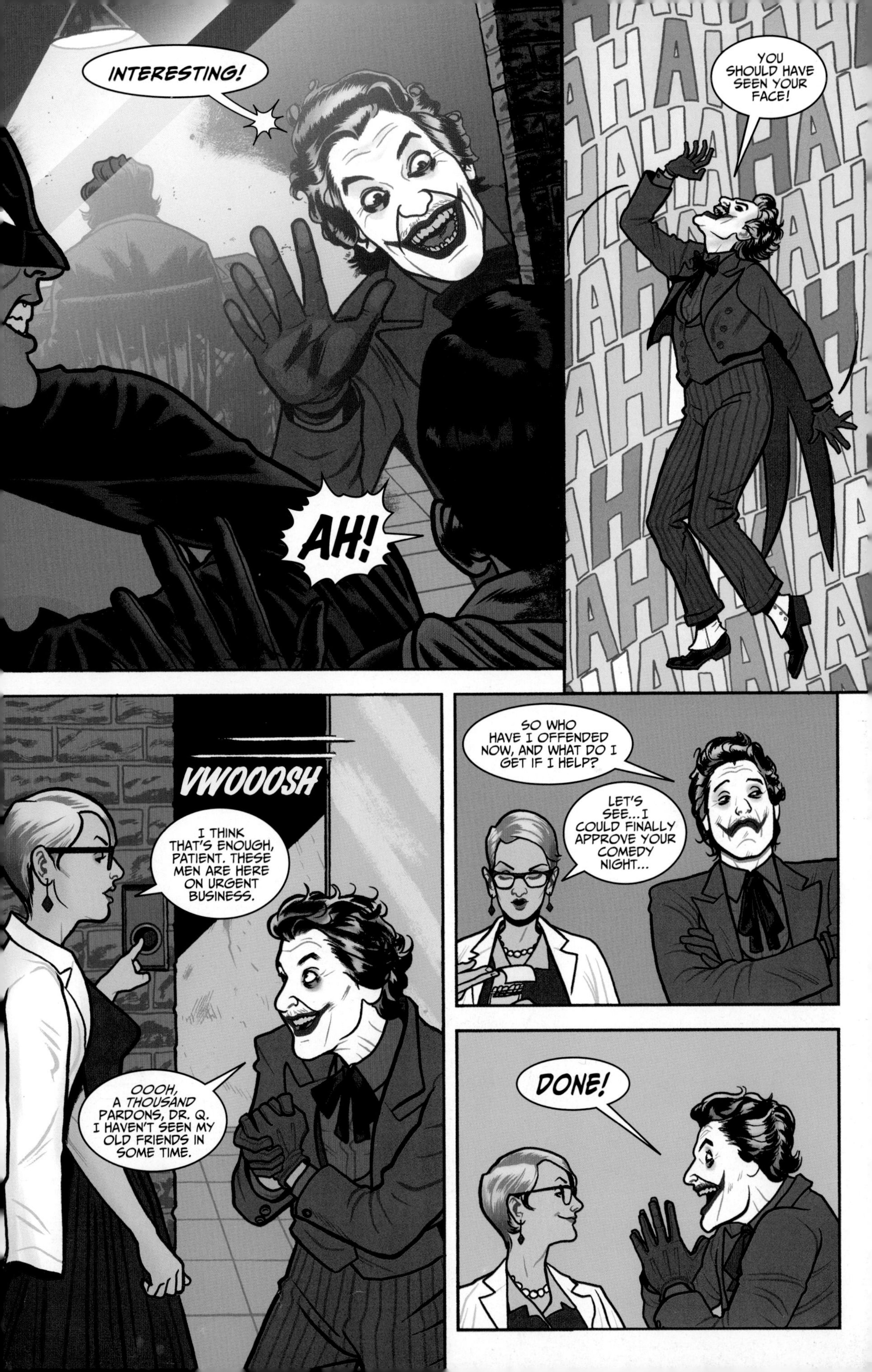

INTERESTING!
AH!
YOU SHOULD HAVE SEEN YOUR FACE!
HAHAHAHAHA
VWOOOSH
I THINK THAT'S ENOUGH, PATIENT. THESE MEN ARE HERE ON URGENT BUSINESS.
OOOH, A *THOUSAND* PARDONS, DR. Q. I HAVEN'T SEEN MY OLD FRIENDS IN SOME TIME.
SO WHO HAVE I OFFENDED NOW, AND WHAT DO I GET IF I HELP?
LET'S SEE...I COULD FINALLY APPROVE YOUR COMEDY NIGHT...
DONE!

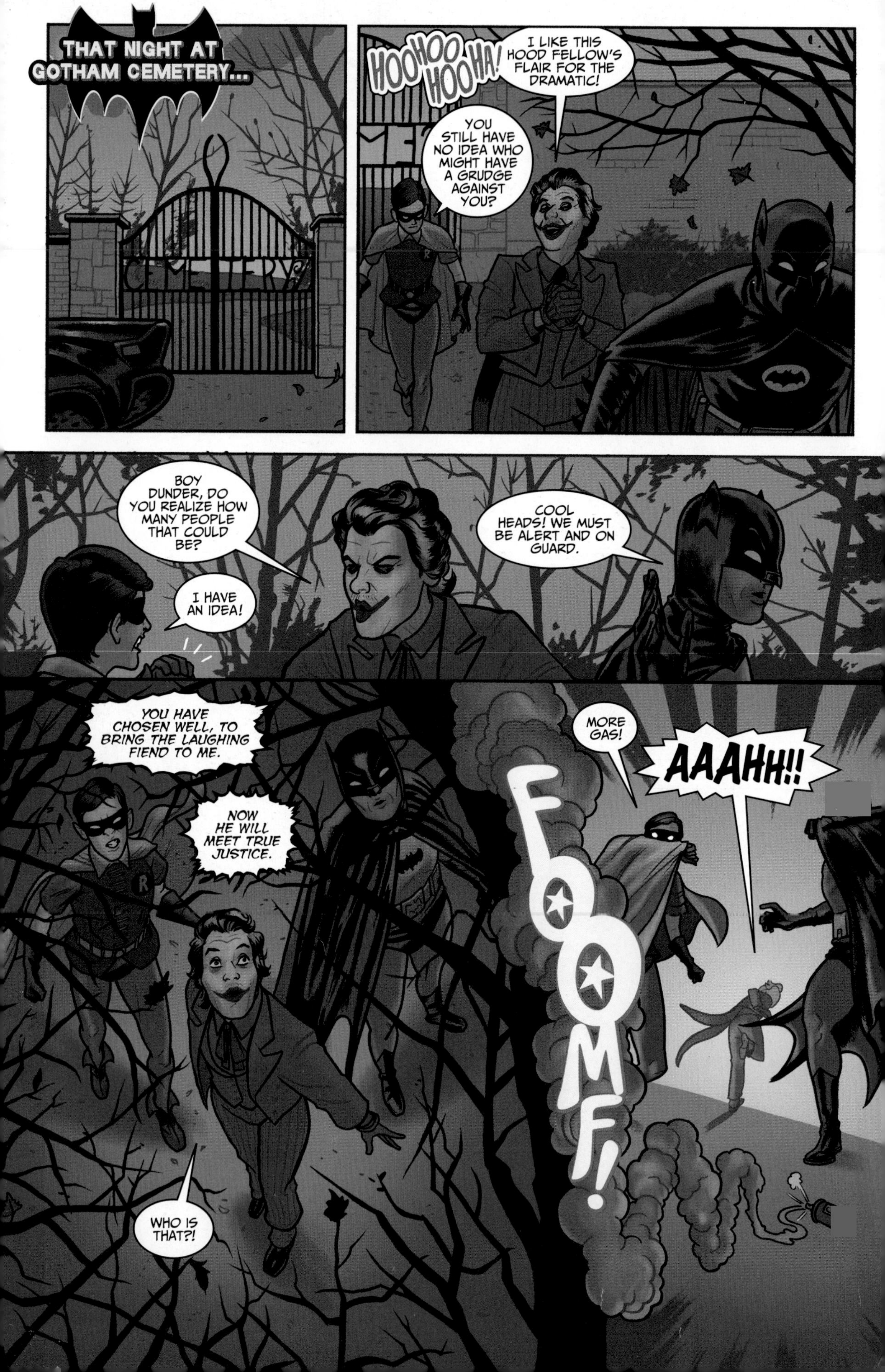
THAT NIGHT AT GOTHAM CEMETERY...
CEMETERY
HOOHOO HOOHOOHA!
I LIKE THIS HOOD FELLOW'S FLAIR FOR THE DRAMATIC!
YOU STILL HAVE NO IDEA WHO MIGHT HAVE A GRUDGE AGAINST YOU?
BOY DUNDER, DO YOU REALIZE HOW MANY PEOPLE THAT COULD BE?
I HAVE AN IDEA!
COOL HEADS! WE MUST BE ALERT AND ON GUARD.
YOU HAVE CHOSEN WELL, TO BRING THE LAUGHING FIEND TO ME.
NOW HE WILL MEET TRUE JUSTICE.
WHO IS THAT?!
FOOMF!
MORE GAS!
AAAHH!!

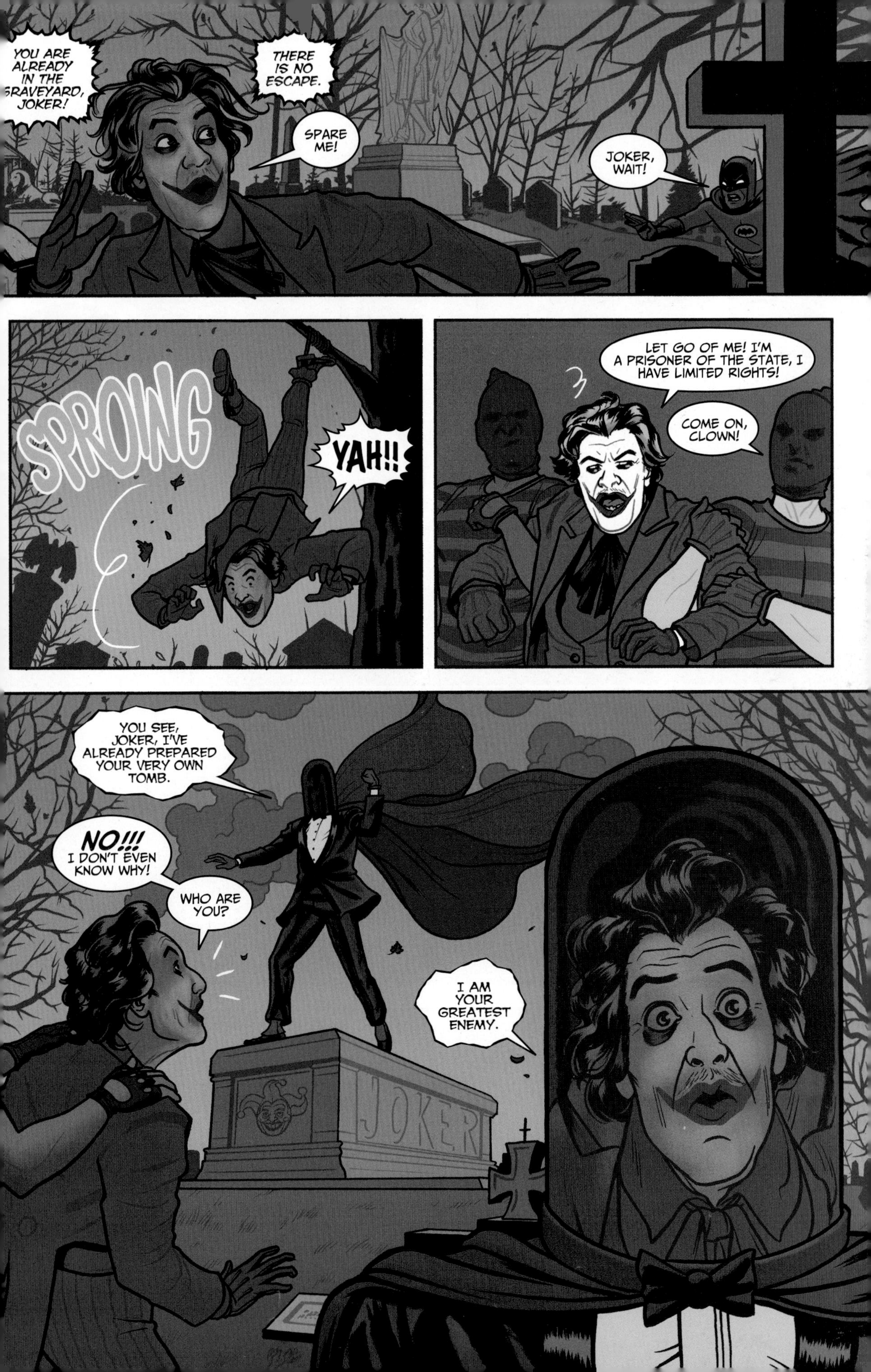

YOU ARE ALREADY IN THE GRAVEYARD, JOKER!
THERE IS NO ESCAPE.
SPARE ME!
JOKER, WAIT!
SPROING
YAH!!
LET GO OF ME! I'M A PRISONER OF THE STATE, I HAVE LIMITED RIGHTS!
COME ON, CLOWN!
YOU SEE, JOKER, I'VE ALREADY PREPARED YOUR VERY OWN TOMB.
NO!!! I DON'T EVEN KNOW WHY!
WHO ARE YOU?
I AM YOUR GREATEST ENEMY.
JOKER

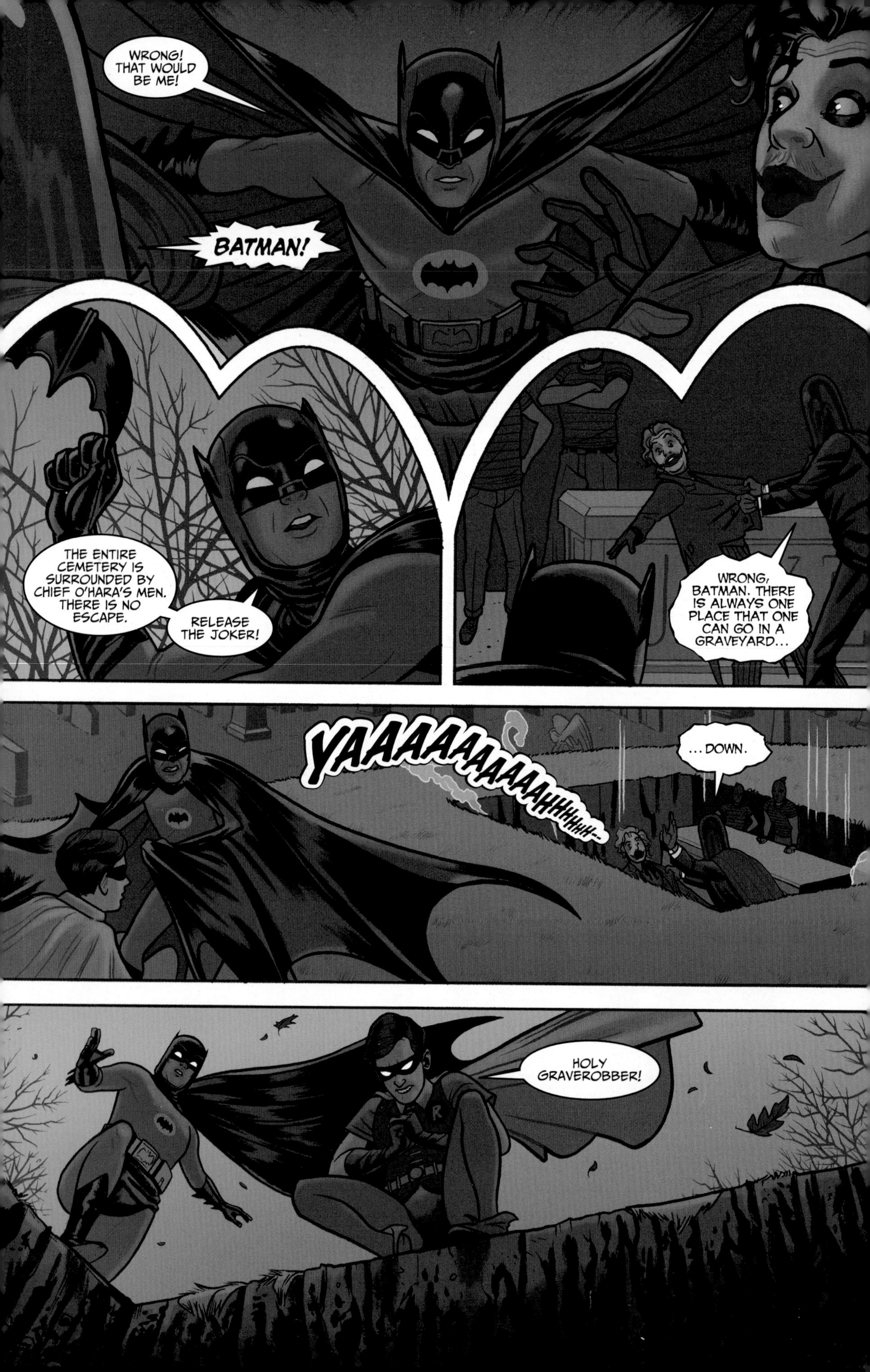
WRONG! THAT WOULD BE ME!
BATMAN!
THE ENTIRE CEMETERY IS SURROUNDED BY CHIEF O'HARA'S MEN. THERE IS NO ESCAPE.
RELEASE THE JOKER!
WRONG, BATMAN. THERE IS ALWAYS ONE PLACE THAT ONE CAN GO IN A GRAVEYARD...
YAAAAAAAAAAAHHHHHH-
...DOWN.
HOLY GRAVEROBBER!

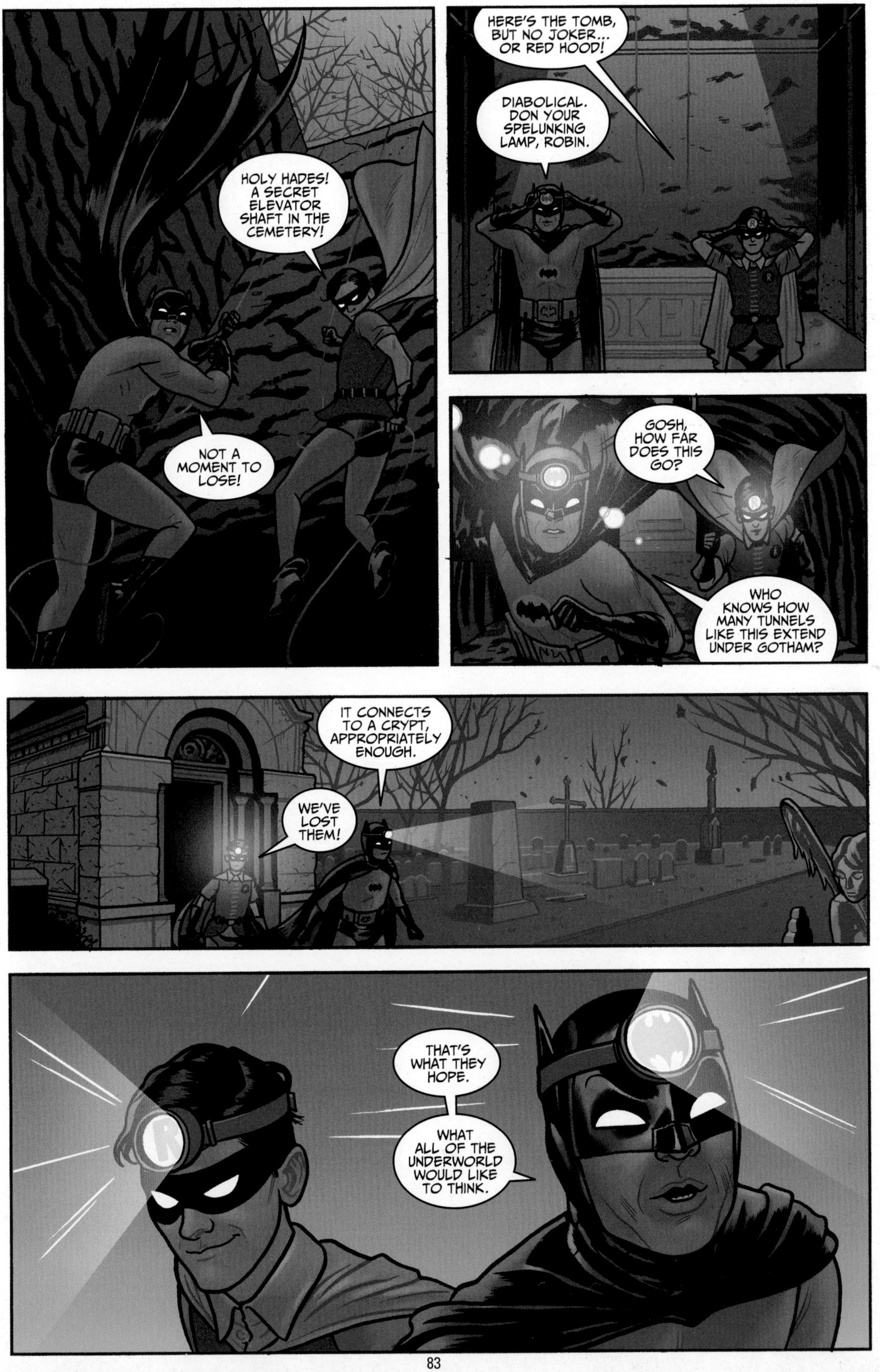
HOLY HADES! A SECRET ELEVATOR SHAFT IN THE CEMETERY!
NOT A MOMENT TO LOSE!
HERE'S THE TOMB, BUT NO JOKER... OR RED HOOD!
DIABOLICAL. DON YOUR SPELUNKING LAMP, ROBIN.
GOSH, HOW FAR DOES THIS GO?
WHO KNOWS HOW MANY TUNNELS LIKE THIS EXTEND UNDER GOTHAM?
WE'VE LOST THEM!
IT CONNECTS TO A CRYPT, APPROPRIATELY ENOUGH.
THAT'S WHAT THEY HOPE.
WHAT ALL OF THE UNDERWORLD WOULD LIKE TO THINK.

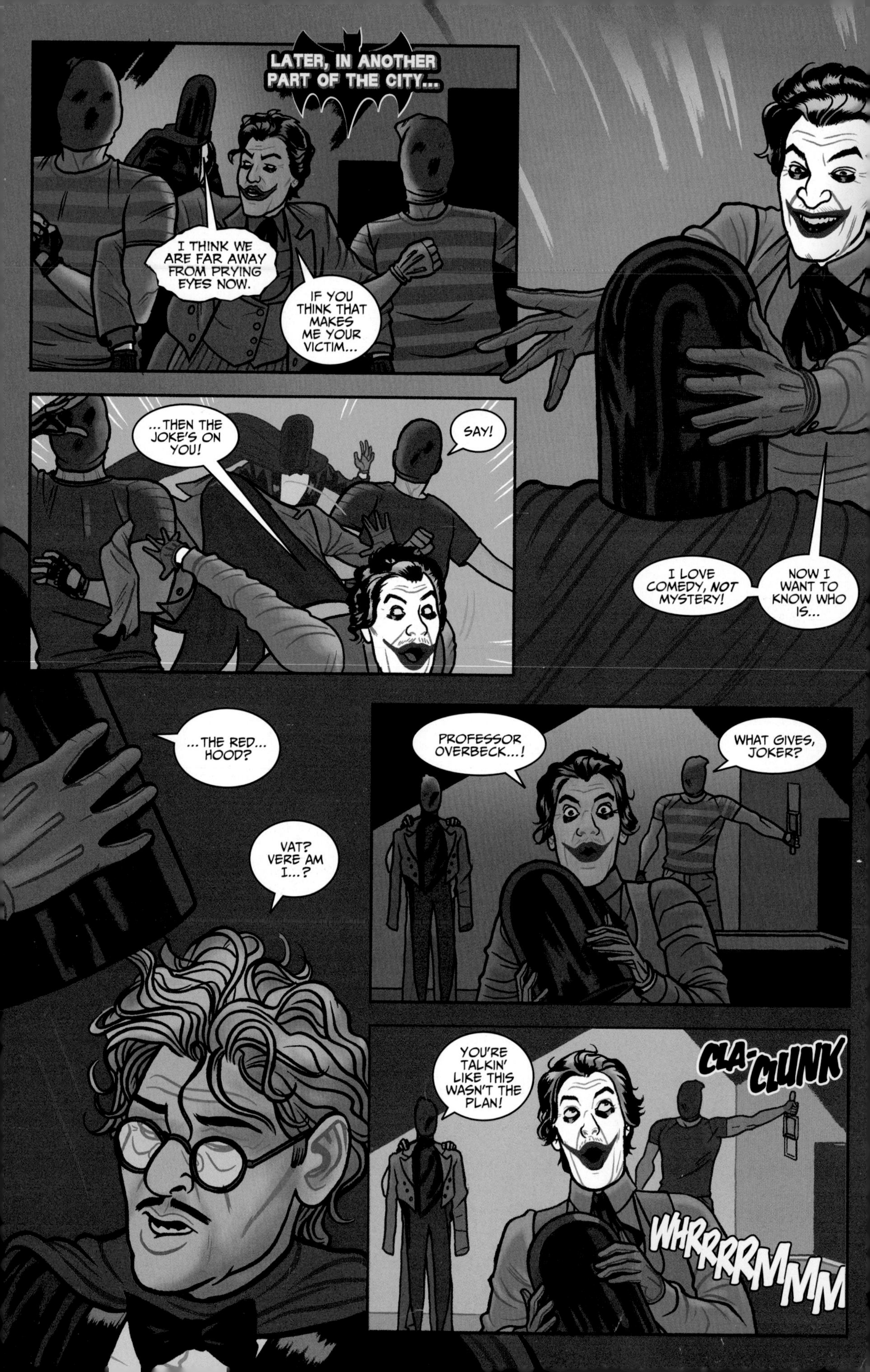

LATER, IN ANOTHER PART OF THE CITY...
I THINK WE ARE FAR AWAY FROM PRYING EYES NOW.
IF YOU THINK THAT MAKES ME YOUR VICTIM...
...THEN THE JOKE'S ON YOU!
SAY!
I LOVE COMEDY, *NOT* MYSTERY!
NOW I WANT TO KNOW WHO IS...
...THE RED... HOOD?
VAT? VERE AM I...?
PROFESSOR OVERBECK...!
WHAT GIVES, JOKER?
YOU'RE TALKIN' LIKE THIS WASN'T THE PLAN!
CLA-CLUNK
WHRRRRMMMM

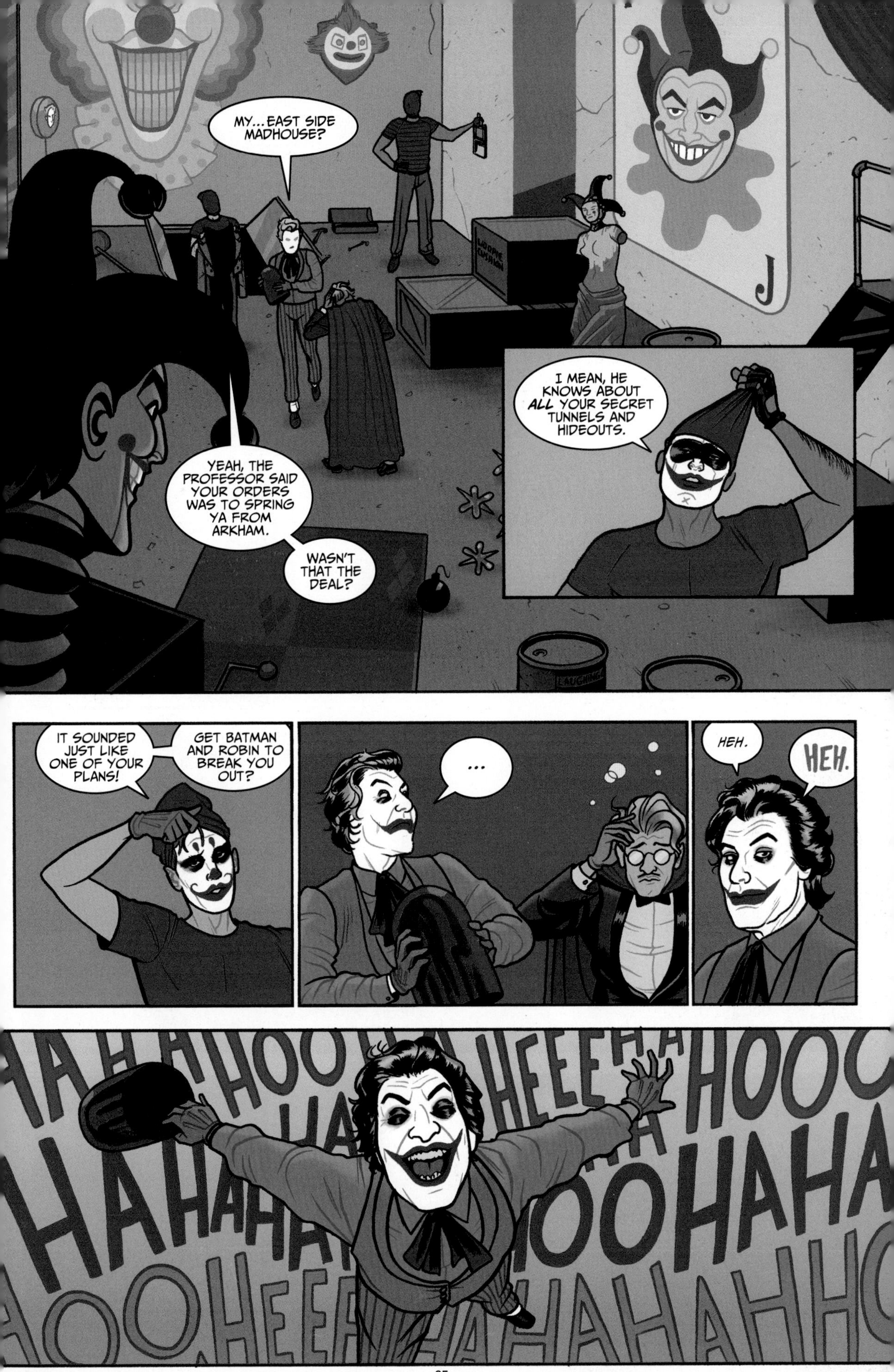

MY...EAST SIDE MADHOUSE?
YEAH, THE PROFESSOR SAID YOUR ORDERS WAS TO SPRING YA FROM ARKHAM.
WASN'T THAT THE DEAL?
I MEAN, HE KNOWS ABOUT ***ALL*** YOUR SECRET TUNNELS AND HIDEOUTS.
IT SOUNDED JUST LIKE ONE OF YOUR PLANS!
GET BATMAN AND ROBIN TO BREAK YOU OUT?
...
HEH.
HEH.

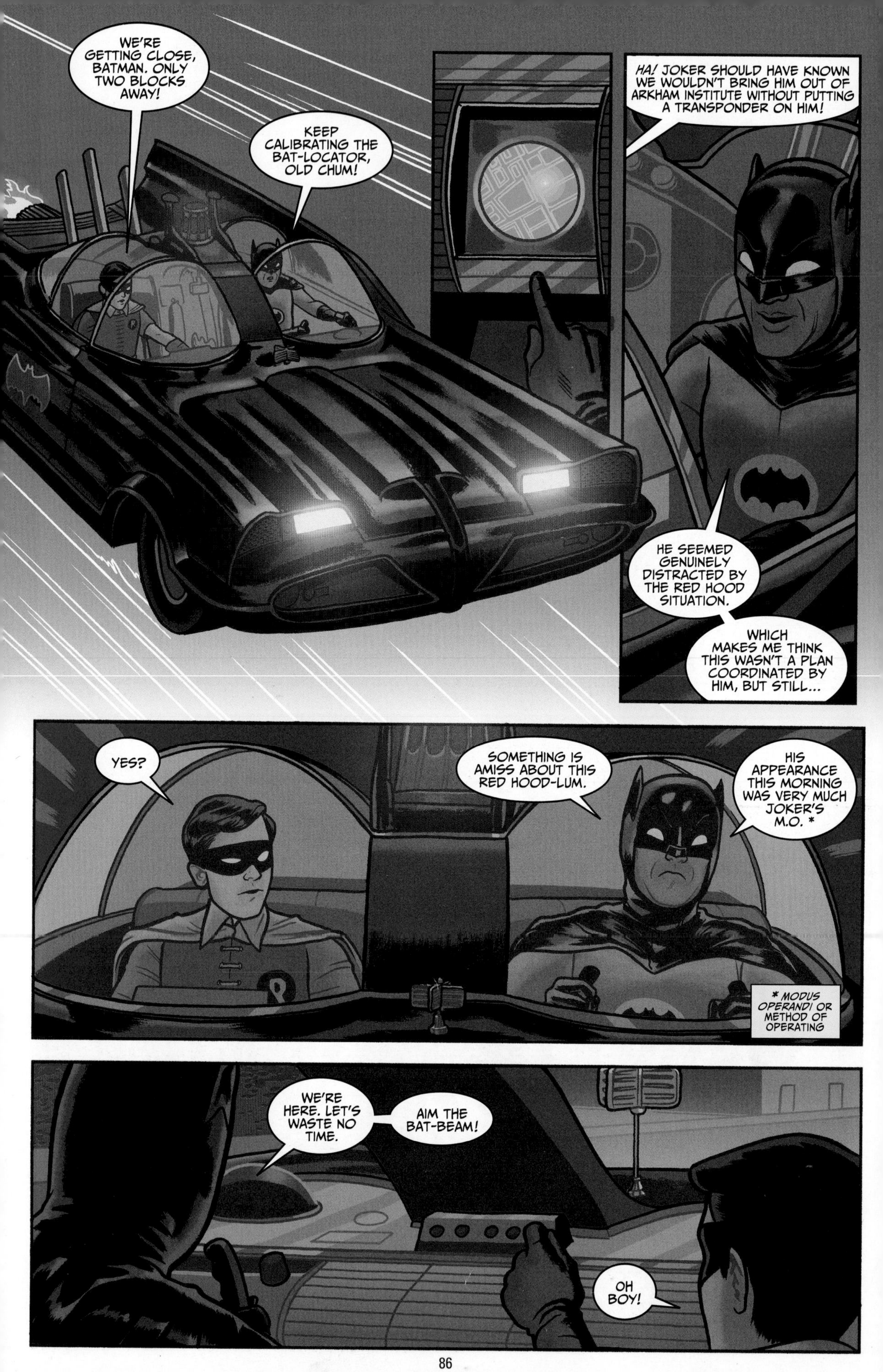
WE'RE GETTING CLOSE, BATMAN. ONLY TWO BLOCKS AWAY!
KEEP CALIBRATING THE BAT-LOCATOR, OLD CHUM!
HA! JOKER SHOULD HAVE KNOWN WE WOULDN'T BRING HIM OUT OF ARKHAM INSTITUTE WITHOUT PUTTING A TRANSPONDER ON HIM!
HE SEEMED GENUINELY DISTRACTED BY THE RED HOOD SITUATION.
WHICH MAKES ME THINK THIS WASN'T A PLAN COORDINATED BY HIM, BUT STILL...
YES?
SOMETHING IS AMISS ABOUT THIS RED HOOD-LUM.
HIS APPEARANCE THIS MORNING WAS VERY MUCH JOKER'S M.O. *
* MODUS OPERANDI OR METHOD OF OPERATING
WE'RE HERE. LET'S WASTE NO TIME.
AIM THE BAT-BEAM!
OH BOY!

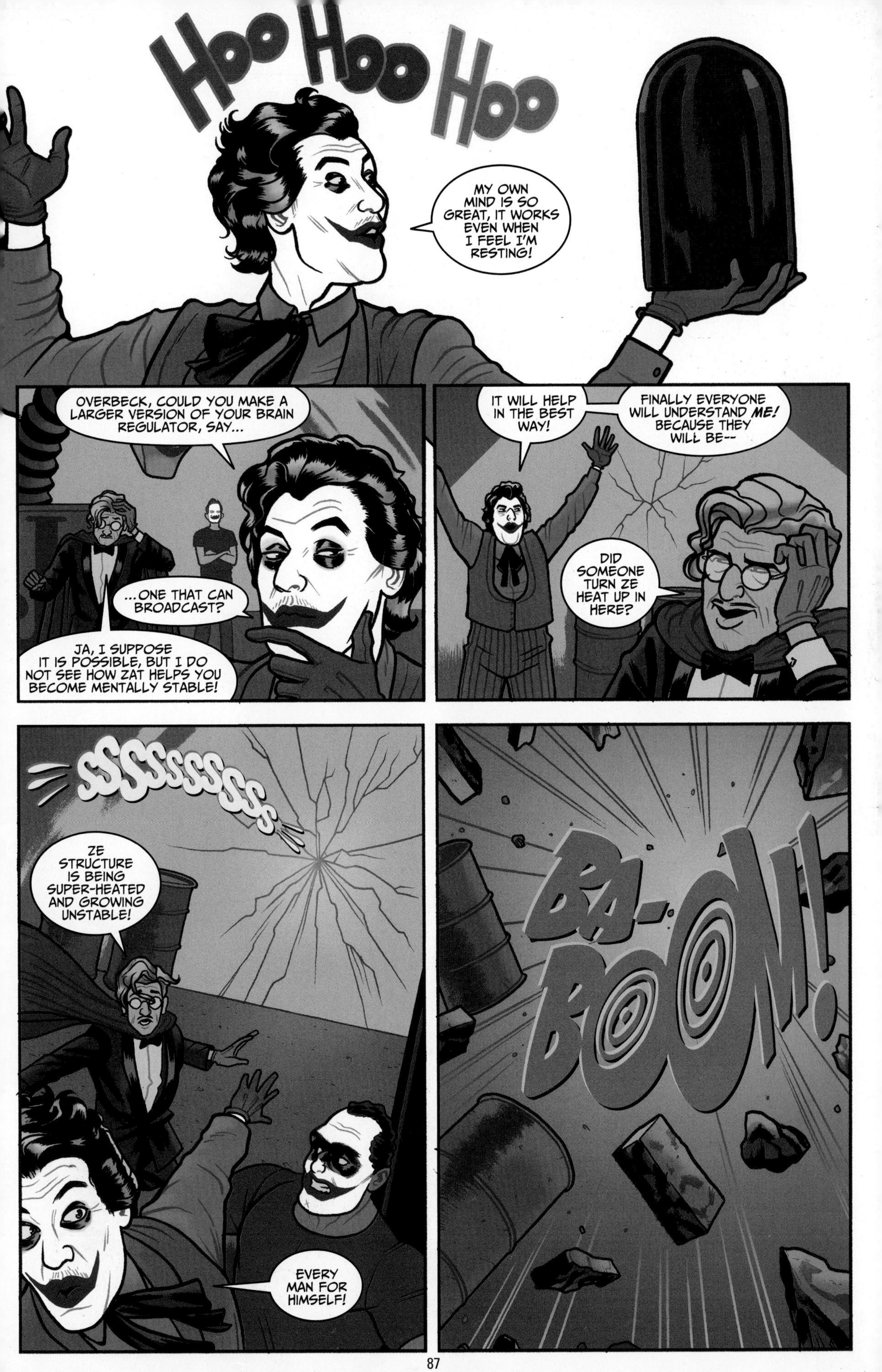
HOO HOO HOO
MY OWN MIND IS SO GREAT, IT WORKS EVEN WHEN I FEEL I'M RESTING!
OVERBECK, COULD YOU MAKE A LARGER VERSION OF YOUR BRAIN REGULATOR, SAY...
...ONE THAT CAN BROADCAST?
JA, I SUPPOSE IT IS POSSIBLE, BUT I DO NOT SEE HOW ZAT HELPS YOU BECOME MENTALLY STABLE!
IT WILL HELP IN THE BEST WAY!
FINALLY EVERYONE WILL UNDERSTAND *ME!* BECAUSE THEY WILL BE--
DID SOMEONE TURN ZE HEAT UP IN HERE?
SSSSSSSSSSS
ZE STRUCTURE IS BEING SUPER-HEATED AND GROWING UNSTABLE!
EVERY MAN FOR HIMSELF!
BA-BOOM!

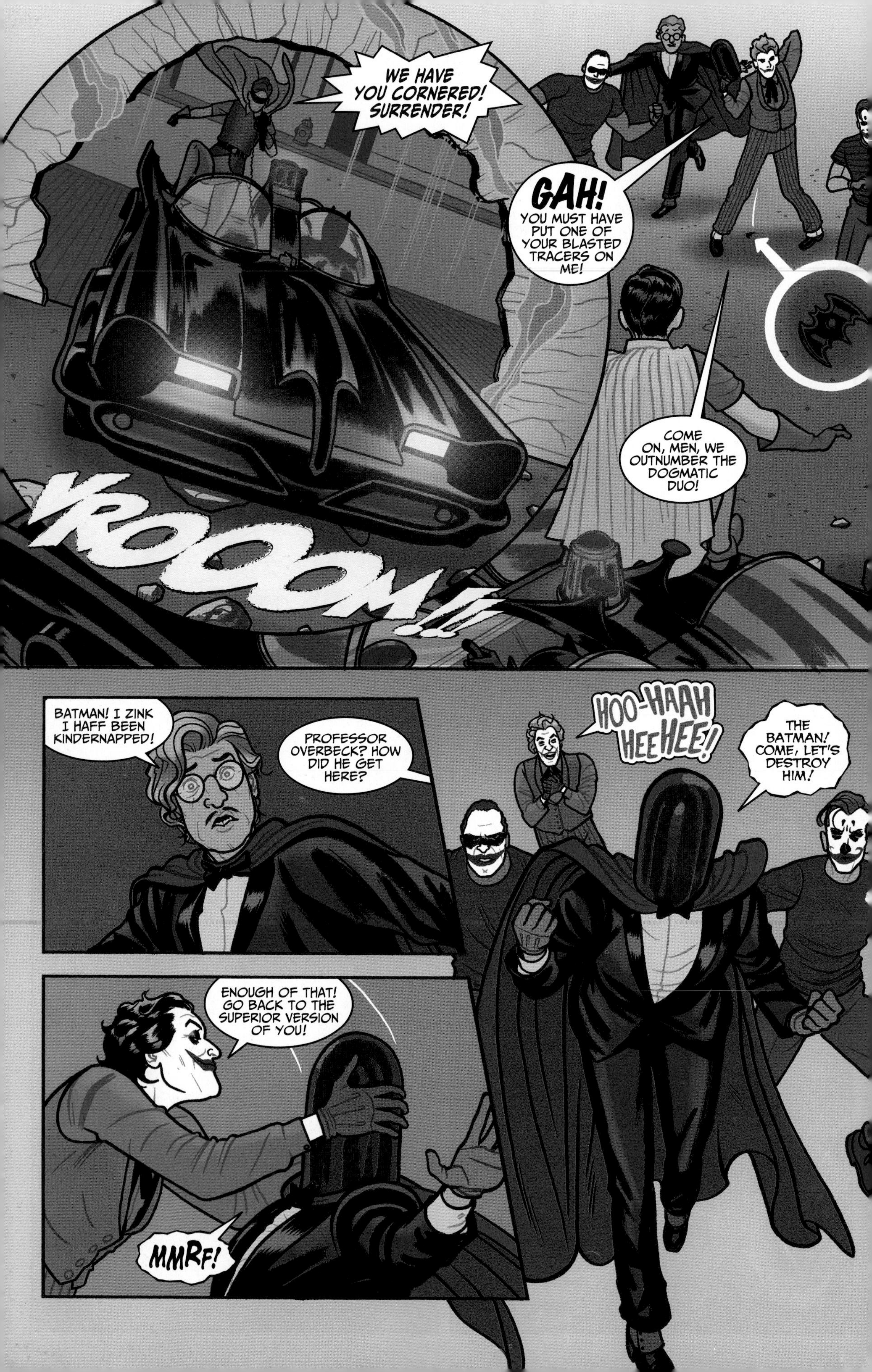
WE HAVE YOU CORNERED! SURRENDER!
GAH! YOU MUST HAVE PUT ONE OF YOUR BLASTED TRACERS ON ME!
COME ON, MEN, WE OUTNUMBER THE DOGMATIC DUO!
VROOOM!!!
BATMAN! I ZINK I HAFF BEEN KINDERNAPPED!
PROFESSOR OVERBECK? HOW DID HE GET HERE?
HOO-HAAH HEEHEE!
THE BATMAN! COME, LET'S DESTROY HIM!
ENOUGH OF THAT! GO BACK TO THE SUPERIOR VERSION OF YOU!
MMRF!

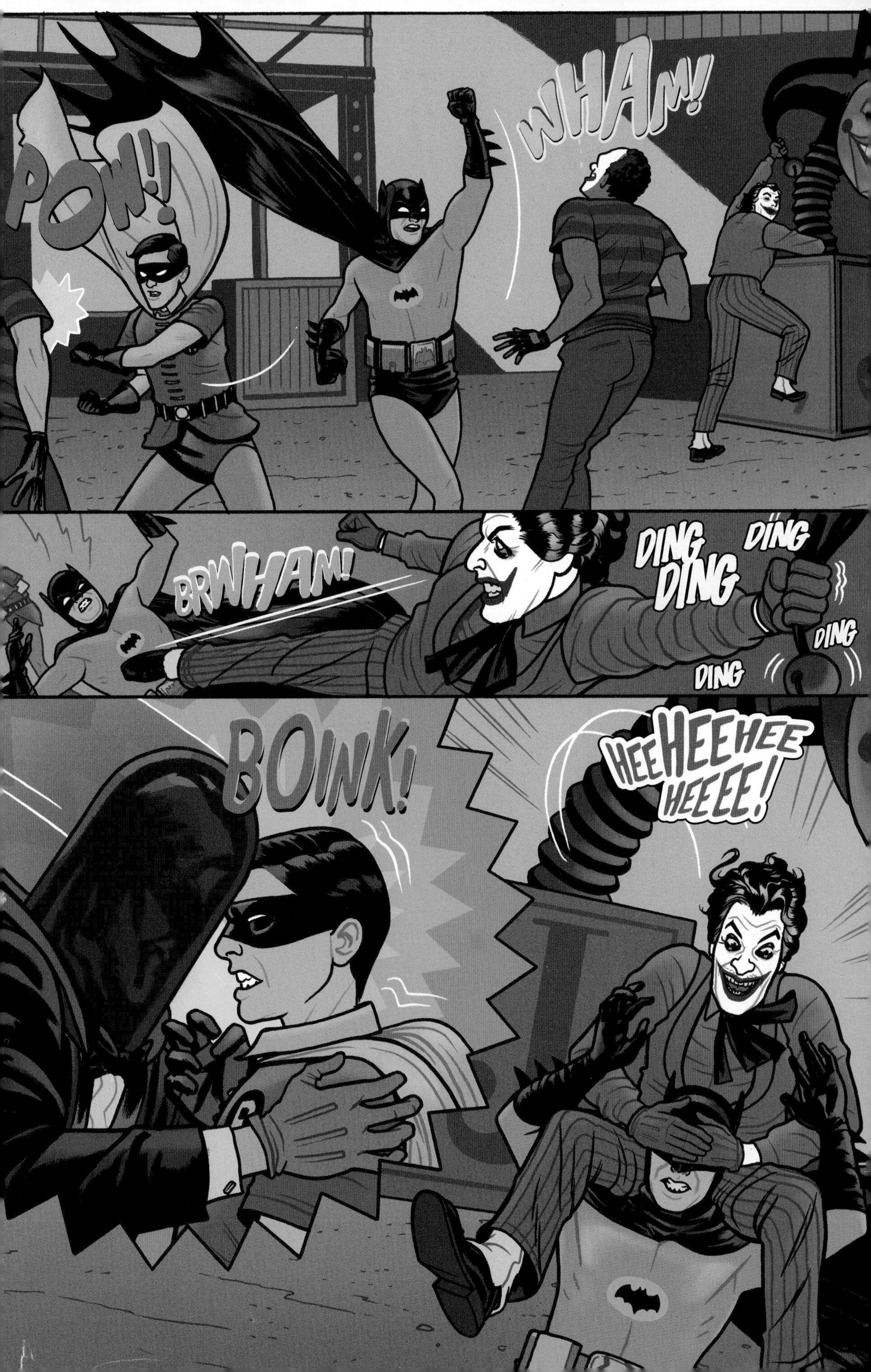
POW!!
WHAM!
BRWHAM!
DING DING
DING
DING
DING
BOINK!
HEEHEEHEE HEEEE!

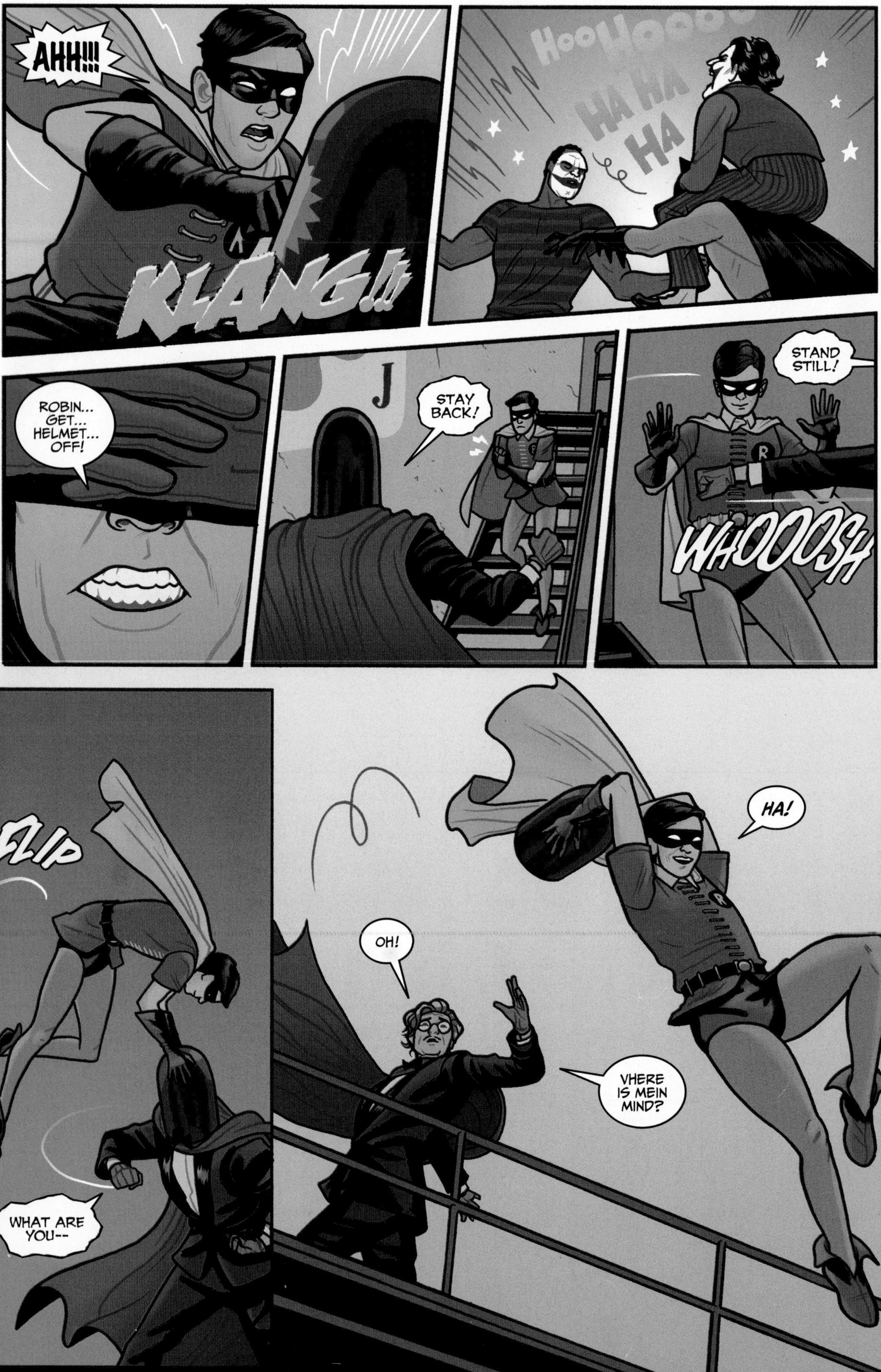
AHH!!!
KLANG!!!
HooHoooo
HA HA
HA
ROBIN... GET... HELMET... OFF!
J
STAY BACK!
STAND STILL!
WHOOOSH
FLIP
WHAT ARE YOU--
OH!
HA!
VHERE IS MEIN MIND?

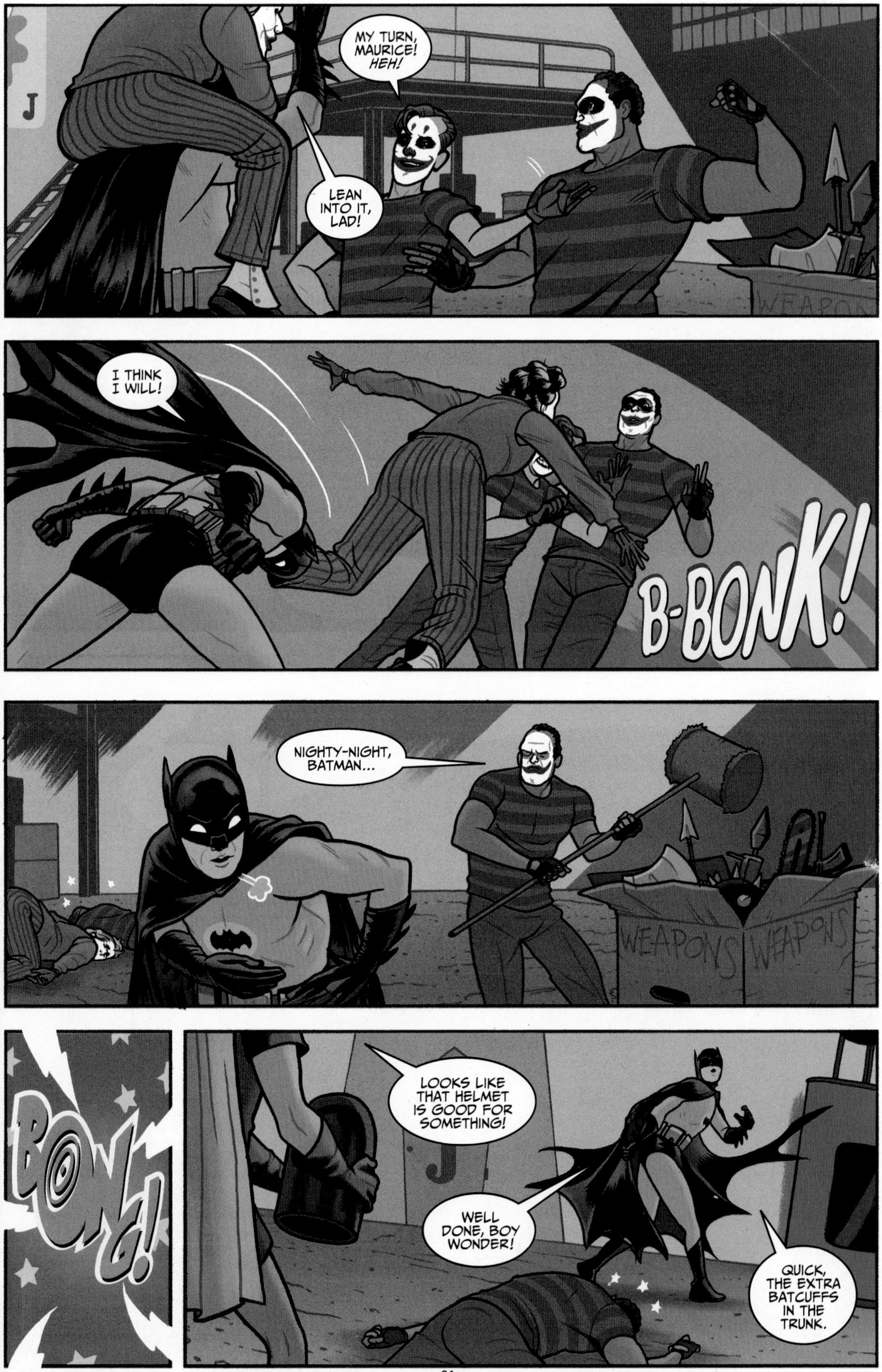
MY TURN, MAURICE! HEH!
LEAN INTO IT, LAD!
I THINK I WILL!
B-BONK!
NIGHTY-NIGHT, BATMAN...
WEAPONS
WEAPONS
BONG!
LOOKS LIKE THAT HELMET IS GOOD FOR SOMETHING!
WELL DONE, BOY WONDER!
QUICK, THE EXTRA BATCUFFS IN THE TRUNK.

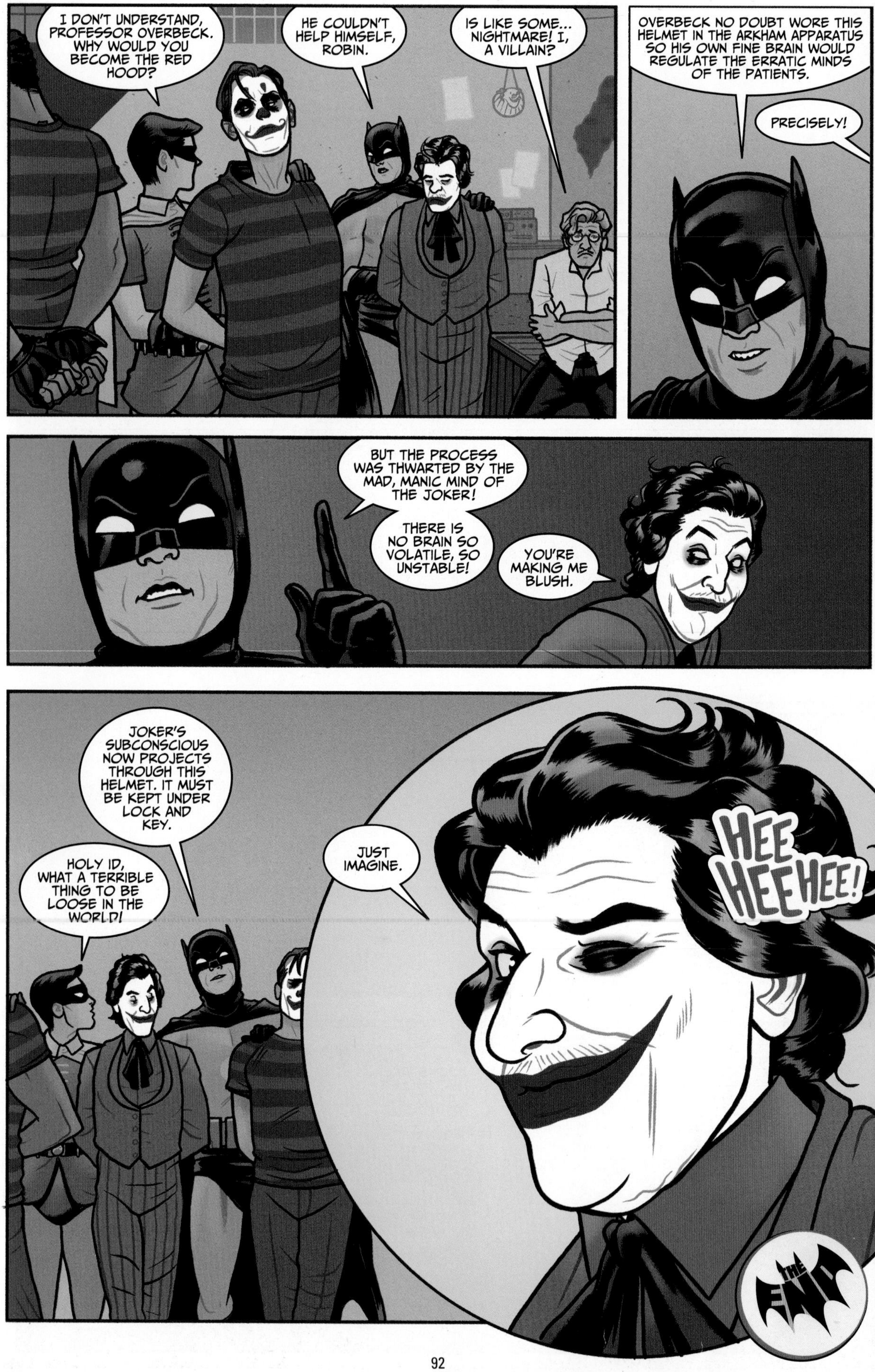
I DON'T UNDERSTAND, PROFESSOR OVERBECK. WHY WOULD YOU BECOME THE RED HOOD?
HE COULDN'T HELP HIMSELF, ROBIN.
IS LIKE SOME... NIGHTMARE! I, A VILLAIN?
OVERBECK NO DOUBT WORE THIS HELMET IN THE ARKHAM APPARATUS SO HIS OWN FINE BRAIN WOULD REGULATE THE ERRATIC MINDS OF THE PATIENTS.
PRECISELY!
BUT THE PROCESS WAS THWARTED BY THE MAD, MANIC MIND OF THE JOKER!
THERE IS NO BRAIN SO VOLATILE, SO UNSTABLE!
YOU'RE MAKING ME BLUSH.
JOKER'S SUBCONSCIOUS NOW PROJECTS THROUGH THIS HELMET. IT MUST BE KEPT UNDER LOCK AND KEY.
HOLY ID, WHAT A TERRIBLE THING TO BE LOOSE IN THE WORLD!
JUST IMAGINE.
HEE HEEHEE!
THE END

THE EGG. A SYMBOL OF LIFE.

ALL OF EGGSISTENCE. IT REPRESENTS POTENTIAL.

A PERFECT PACKET OF INFORMATION THAT LOOKS LIKE ANY OTHER AT THIS STAGE.

LIKE ALL ANIMALS, WE WAIT IN AN EGG UNTIL SPURRED TO DEVELOP INTO SOMETHING MORE.

MOST WILL GROW TO FILL IN THE CRACKS OF SOCIETY, NEVER DISTINGUISHING THEMSELVES.

THEY MIGHT AS WELL REMAIN IN THEIR NASCENT FORM AND STACKED IN A CARTON WITH OTHER UNNOTABLES.

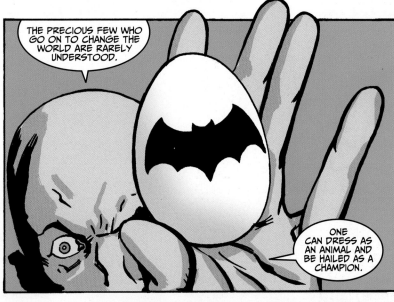

THE PRECIOUS FEW WHO GO ON TO CHANGE THE WORLD ARE RARELY UNDERSTOOD.

ONE CAN DRESS AS AN ANIMAL AND BE HAILED AS A CHAMPION.

WHILE THE TRULY GREAT ARE LABELED...

...EGGCENTRIC.

SKRLCH!

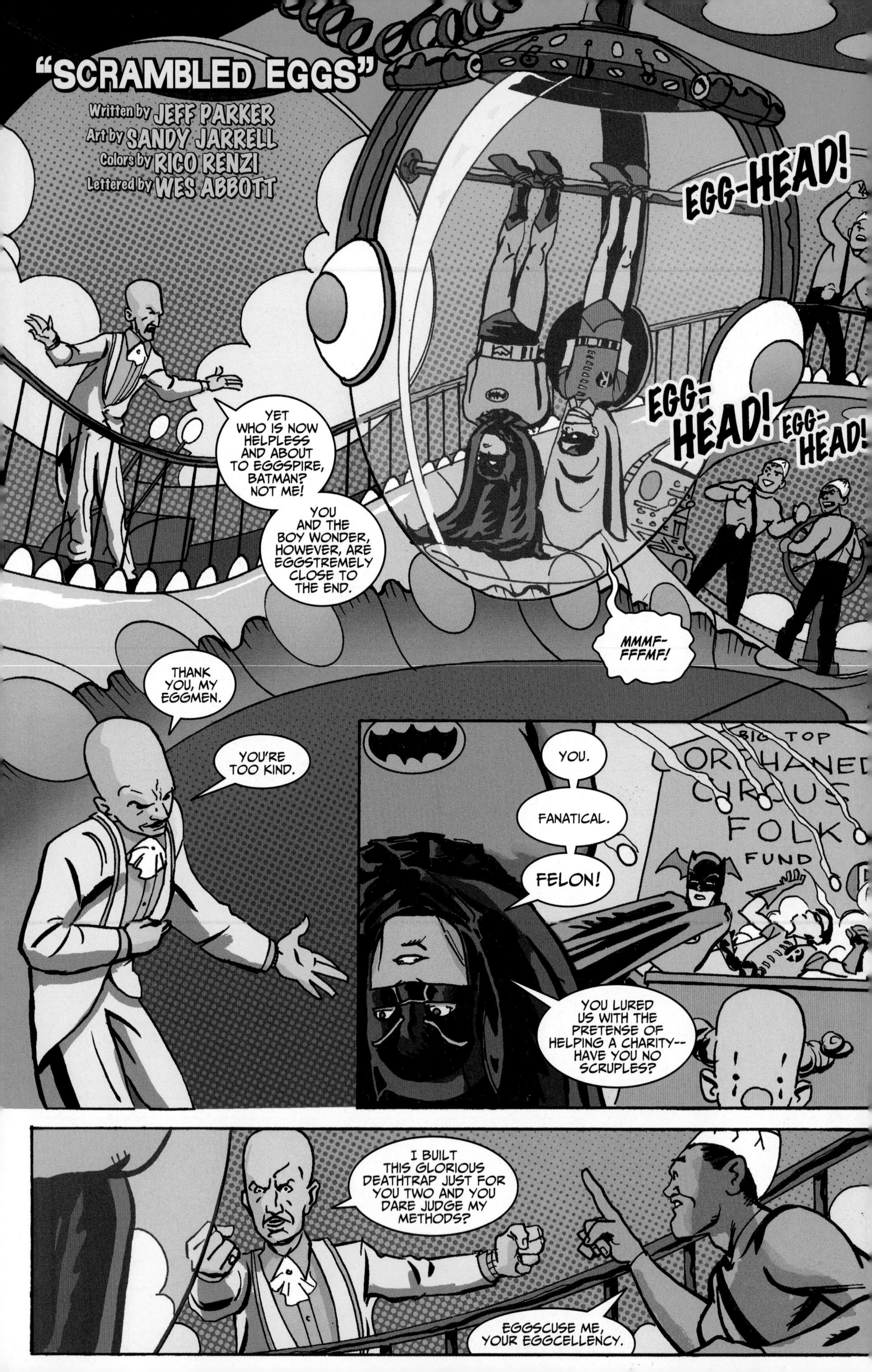
"SCRAMBLED EGGS"
Written by JEFF PARKER
Art by SANDY JARRELL
Colors by RICO RENZI
Lettered by WES ABBOTT
EGG-HEAD!
YET WHO IS NOW HELPLESS AND ABOUT TO EGGSPIRE, BATMAN? NOT ME!
YOU AND THE BOY WONDER, HOWEVER, ARE EGGSTREMELY CLOSE TO THE END.
EGG-HEAD!
EGG-HEAD!
MMMF-FFFMF!
THANK YOU, MY EGGMEN.
YOU'RE TOO KIND.
YOU.
FANATICAL.
FELON!
BIG TOP
FOLK
FUND
YOU LURED US WITH THE PRETENSE OF HELPING A CHARITY-- HAVE YOU NO SCRUPLES?
I BUILT THIS GLORIOUS DEATHTRAP JUST FOR YOU TWO AND YOU DARE JUDGE MY METHODS?
EGGSCUSE ME, YOUR EGGCELLENCY.

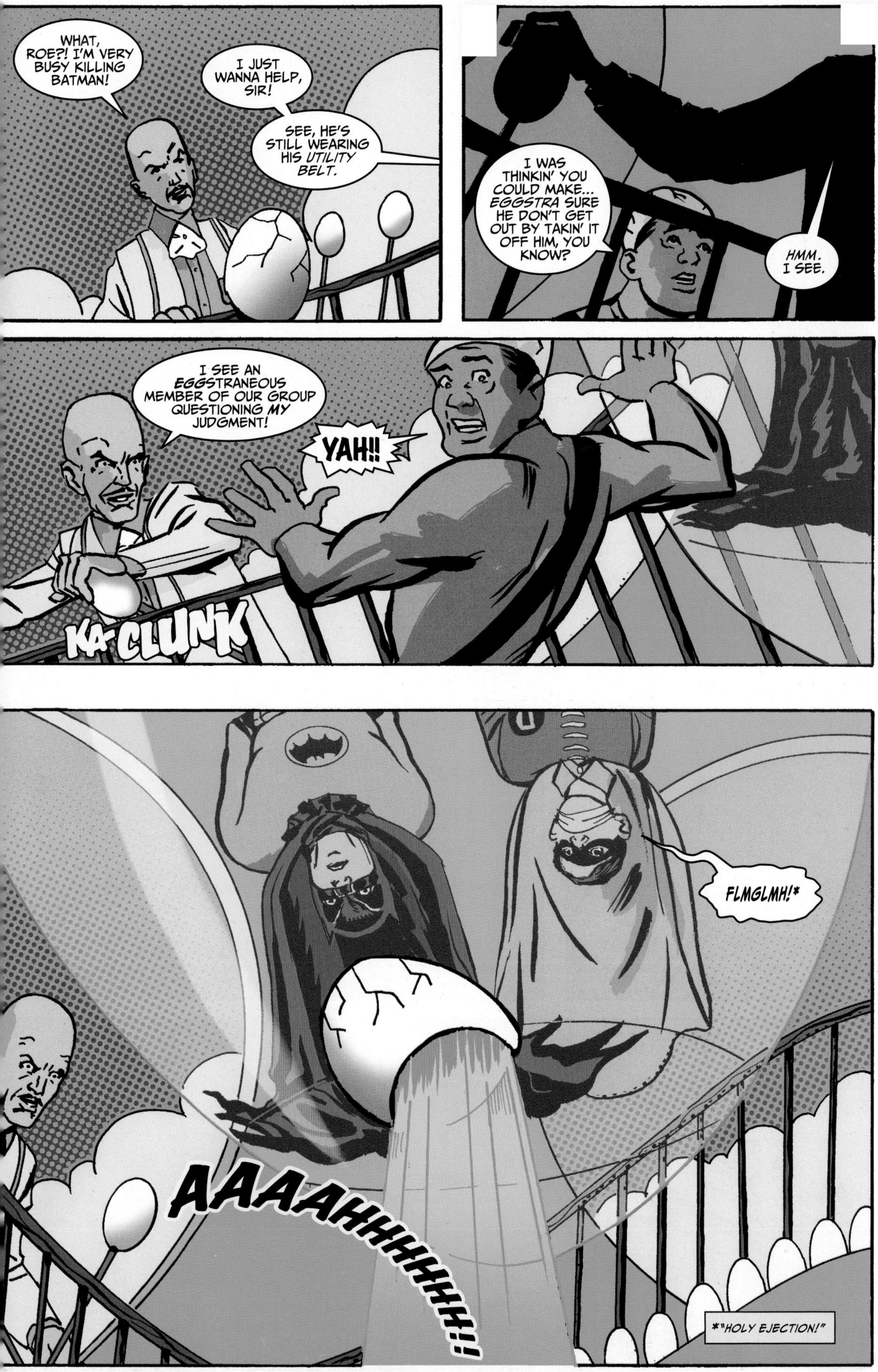
WHAT, ROE?! I'M VERY BUSY KILLING BATMAN!
I JUST WANNA HELP, SIR!
SEE, HE'S STILL WEARING HIS *UTILITY BELT.*
I WAS THINKIN' YOU COULD MAKE... *EGGSTRA* SURE HE DON'T GET OUT BY TAKIN' IT OFF HIM, YOU KNOW?
*HMM.* I SEE.
I SEE AN *EGG*STRANEOUS MEMBER OF OUR GROUP QUESTIONING *MY* JUDGMENT!
YAH!!
KA-CLUNK
FLMGLMH!*
AAAAAHHHHHHH!!
*"HOLY EJECTION!"

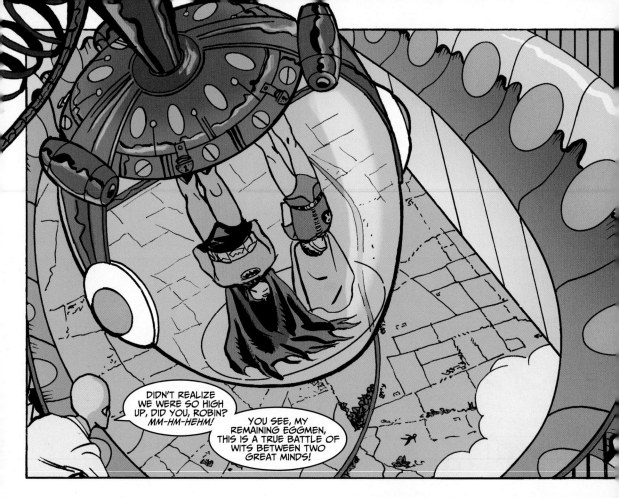

DIDN'T REALIZE WE WERE SO HIGH UP, DID YOU, ROBIN? MM-HM-HEHM!

YOU SEE, MY REMAINING EGGMEN, THIS IS A TRUE BATTLE OF WITS BETWEEN TWO GREAT MINDS!

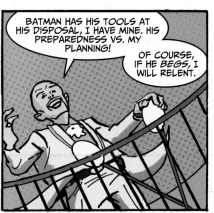

BATMAN HAS HIS TOOLS AT HIS DISPOSAL, I HAVE MINE. HIS PREPAREDNESS VS. MY PLANNING!

OF COURSE, IF HE BEGS, I WILL RELENT.

I WILL... NEVER...

...ASK MERCY...

...OF EVILDOERS.

THEN ENJOY YOUR NEW STATE OF BEING...

KLUNK

...SCRAMBLED!

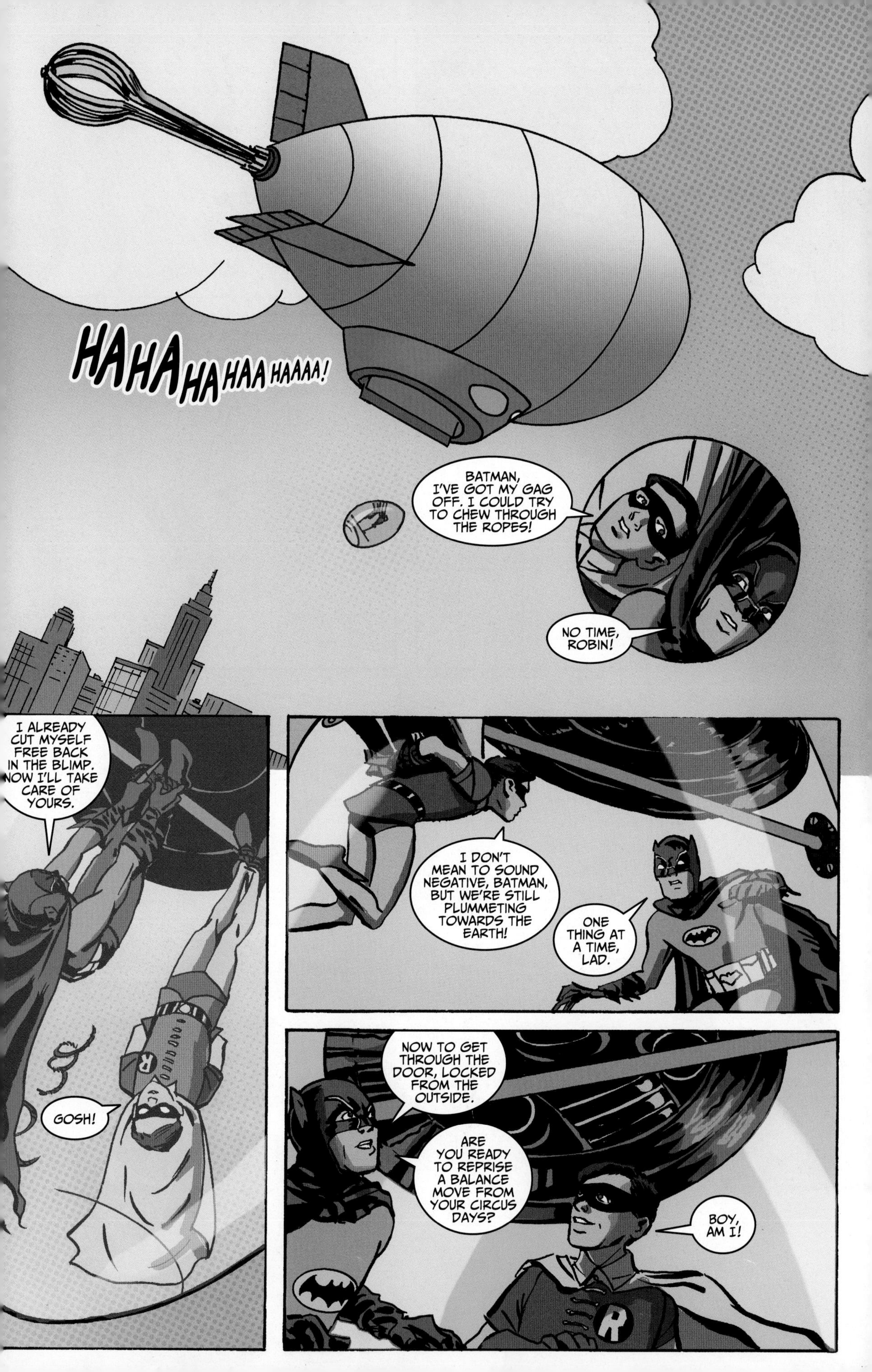
HAHAHAHAAHAAAA!
BATMAN, I'VE GOT MY GAG OFF. I COULD TRY TO CHEW THROUGH THE ROPES!
NO TIME, ROBIN!
I ALREADY CUT MYSELF FREE BACK IN THE BLIMP. NOW I'LL TAKE CARE OF YOURS.
GOSH!
I DON'T MEAN TO SOUND NEGATIVE, BATMAN, BUT WE'RE STILL PLUMMETING TOWARDS THE EARTH!
ONE THING AT A TIME, LAD.
NOW TO GET THROUGH THE DOOR, LOCKED FROM THE OUTSIDE.
ARE YOU READY TO REPRISE A BALANCE MOVE FROM YOUR CIRCUS DAYS?
BOY, AM I!

NO TIME FOR MULTIPLE ATTEMPTS. YOU NEED TO KICK IT OFF ON THE FIRST TRY!

I CAN DO IT! ONE...

...TWO...

...THREE!

WHOOOM!!

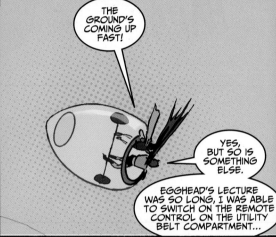

THE GROUND'S COMING UP FAST!

YES, BUT SO IS SOMETHING ELSE.

EGGHEAD'S LECTURE WAS SO LONG, I WAS ABLE TO SWITCH ON THE REMOTE CONTROL ON THE UTILITY BELT COMPARTMENT...

WUBWUBWUBWUB

...TO SUMMON THE **BATCOPTER!**

I SEE IT HEADING FROM THE NORTH. NOW TO START CONTROLLING IT DIRECTLY.

READY YOUR BATARANG, ROBIN.

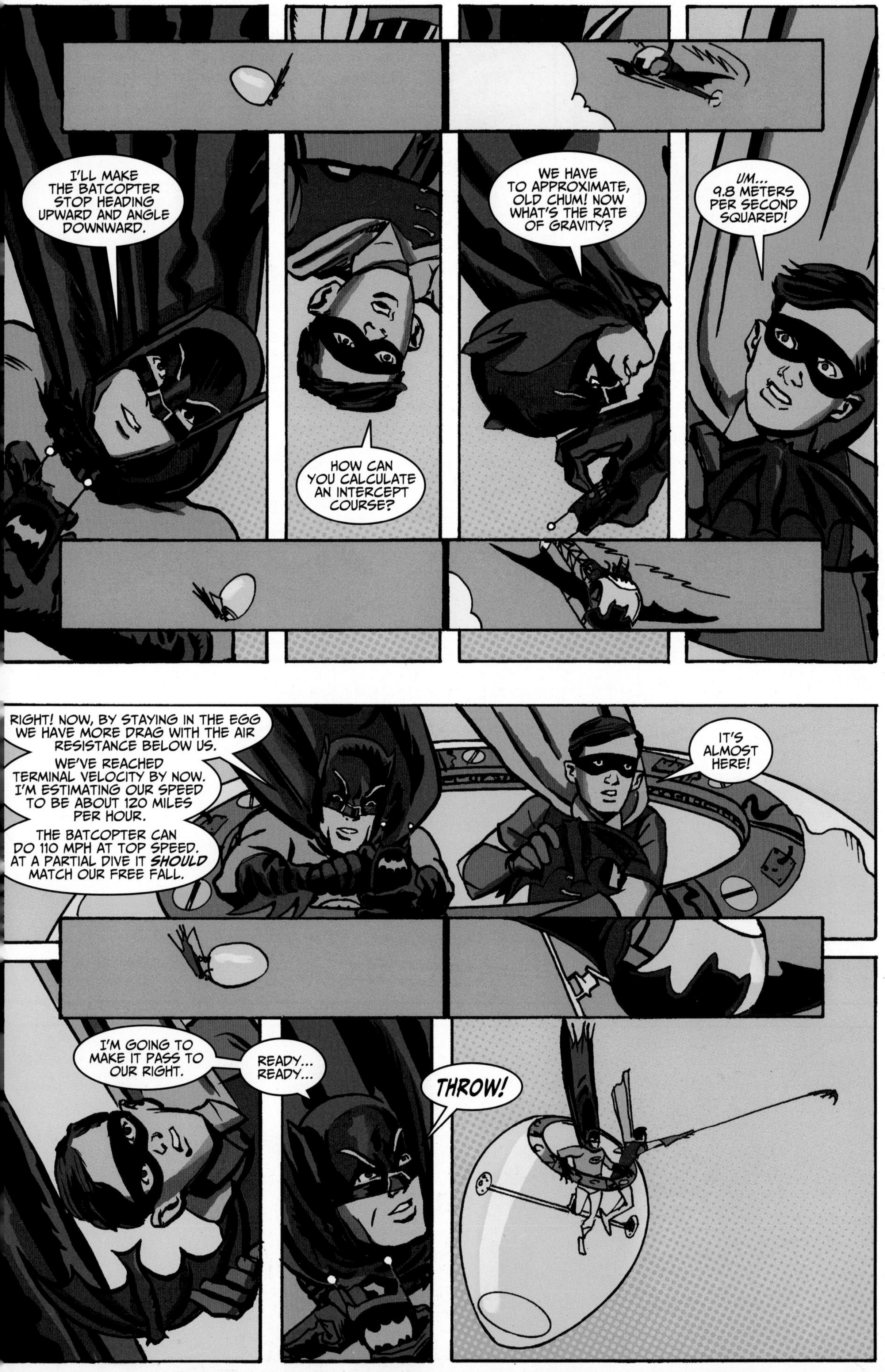
I'LL MAKE THE BATCOPTER STOP HEADING UPWARD AND ANGLE DOWNWARD.
HOW CAN YOU CALCULATE AN INTERCEPT COURSE?
WE HAVE TO APPROXIMATE, OLD CHUM! NOW WHAT'S THE RATE OF GRAVITY?
UM... 9.8 METERS PER SECOND SQUARED!
RIGHT! NOW, BY STAYING IN THE EGG WE HAVE MORE DRAG WITH THE AIR RESISTANCE BELOW US.
WE'VE REACHED TERMINAL VELOCITY BY NOW. I'M ESTIMATING OUR SPEED TO BE ABOUT 120 MILES PER HOUR.
THE BATCOPTER CAN DO 110 MPH AT TOP SPEED. AT A PARTIAL DIVE IT *SHOULD* MATCH OUR FREE FALL.
IT'S ALMOST HERE!
I'M GOING TO MAKE IT PASS TO OUR RIGHT.
READY... READY...
THROW!

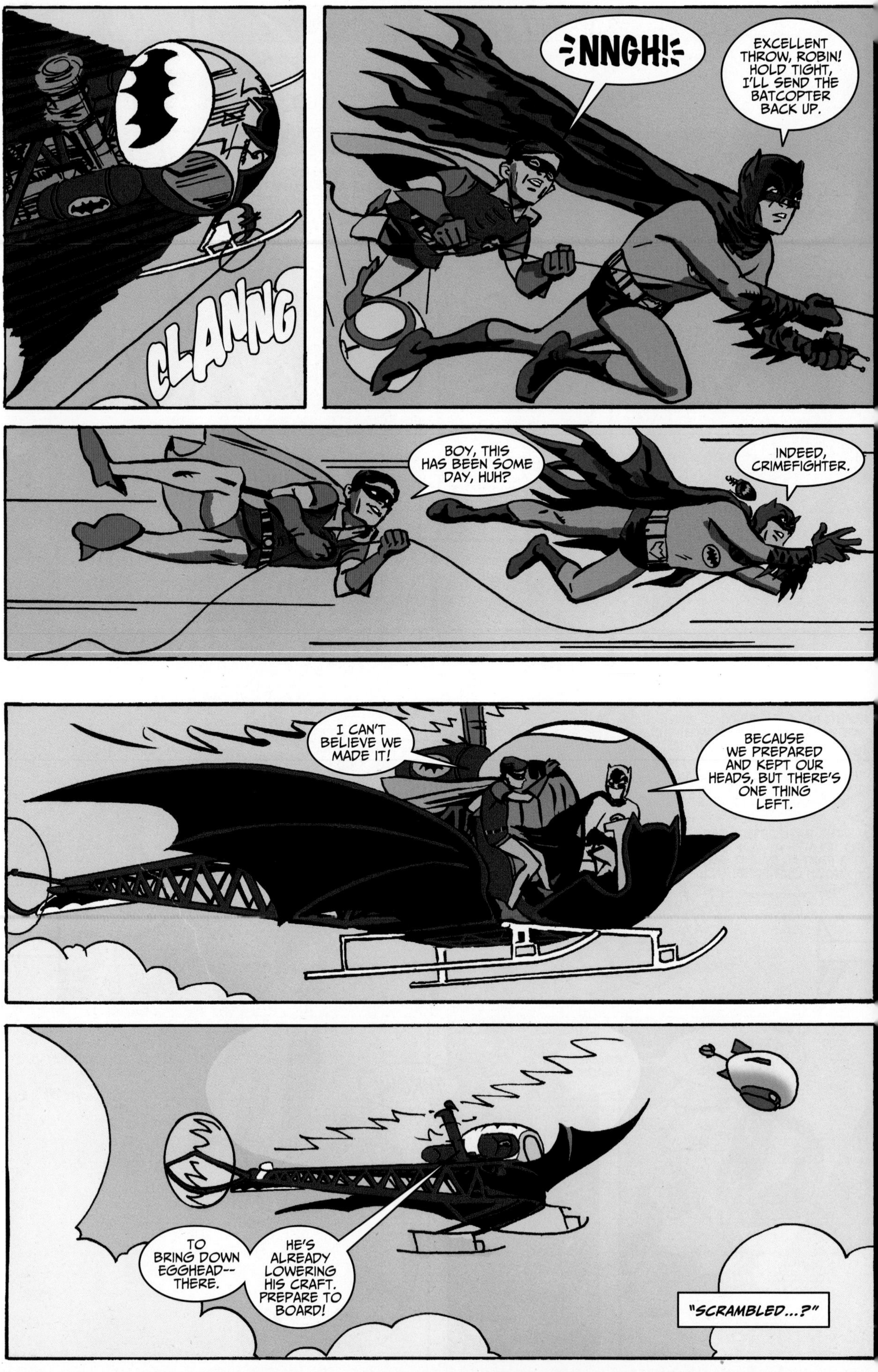
CLANNG
NNGH!
EXCELLENT THROW, ROBIN! HOLD TIGHT, I'LL SEND THE BATCOPTER BACK UP.
BOY, THIS HAS BEEN SOME DAY, HUH?
INDEED, CRIMEFIGHTER.
I CAN'T BELIEVE WE MADE IT!
BECAUSE WE PREPARED AND KEPT OUR HEADS, BUT THERE'S ONE THING LEFT.
TO BRING DOWN EGGHEAD--THERE.
HE'S ALREADY LOWERING HIS CRAFT. PREPARE TO BOARD!
"SCRAMBLED...?"

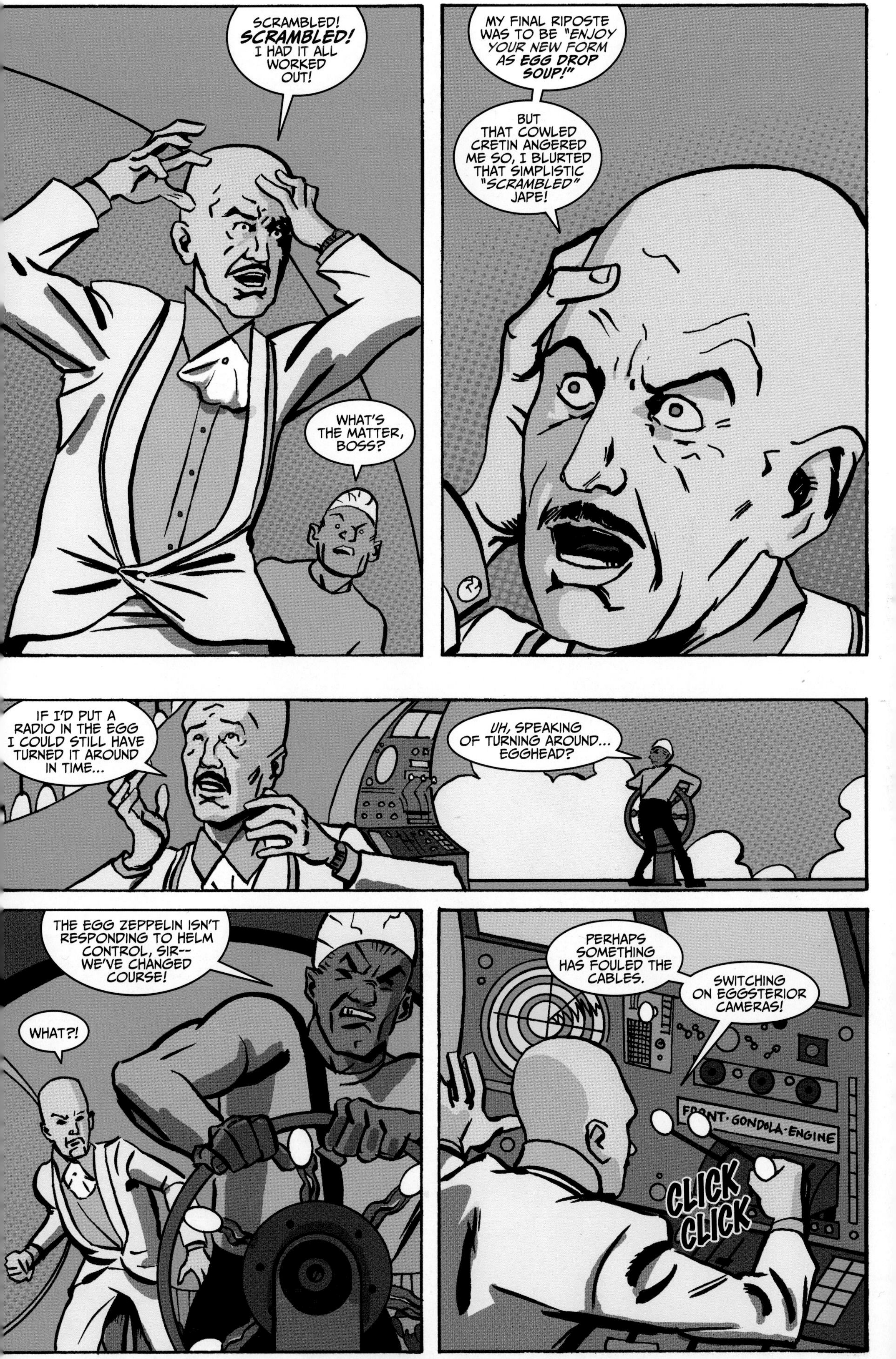
SCRAMBLED! SCRAMBLED! I HAD IT ALL WORKED OUT!
WHAT'S THE MATTER, BOSS?
MY FINAL RIPOSTE WAS TO BE "ENJOY YOUR NEW FORM AS EGG DROP SOUP!"
BUT THAT COWLED CRETIN ANGERED ME SO, I BLURTED THAT SIMPLISTIC "SCRAMBLED" JAPE!
IF I'D PUT A RADIO IN THE EGG I COULD STILL HAVE TURNED IT AROUND IN TIME...
UH, SPEAKING OF TURNING AROUND... EGGHEAD?
THE EGG ZEPPELIN ISN'T RESPONDING TO HELM CONTROL, SIR-- WE'VE CHANGED COURSE!
WHAT?!
PERHAPS SOMETHING HAS FOULED THE CABLES.
SWITCHING ON EGGSTERIOR CAMERAS!
FRONT · GONDOLA · ENGINE
CLICK
CLICK

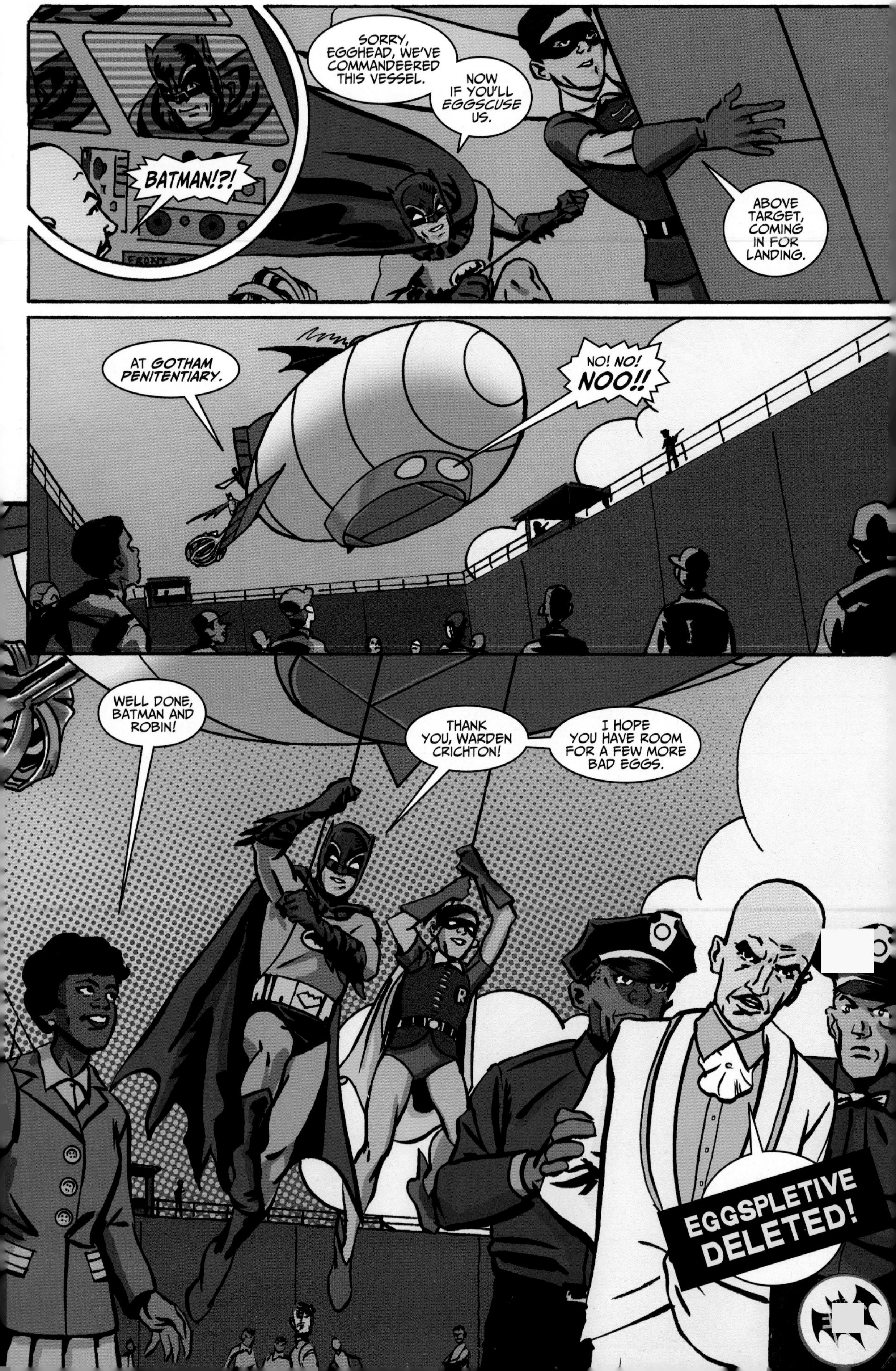
SORRY, EGGHEAD, WE'VE COMMANDEERED THIS VESSEL.
NOW IF YOU'LL EGGSCUSE US.
BATMAN!?!
ABOVE TARGET, COMING IN FOR LANDING.
AT GOTHAM PENITENTIARY.
NO! NO! NOO!!
WELL DONE, BATMAN AND ROBIN!
THANK YOU, WARDEN CRICHTON!
I HOPE YOU HAVE ROOM FOR A FEW MORE BAD EGGS.
EGGSPLETIVE DELETED!

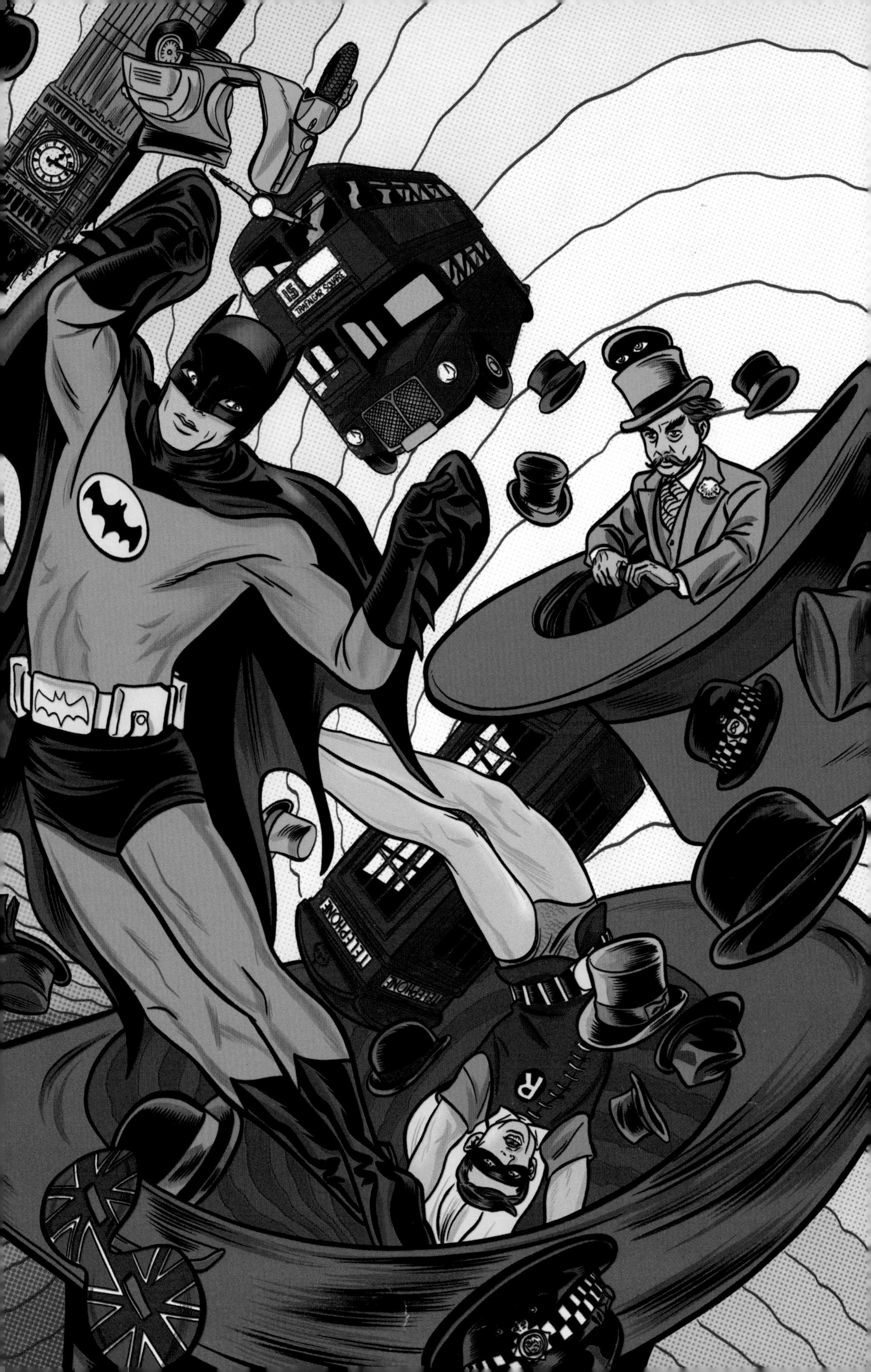
15
TRAFALGAR SQUARE
TELEPHONE

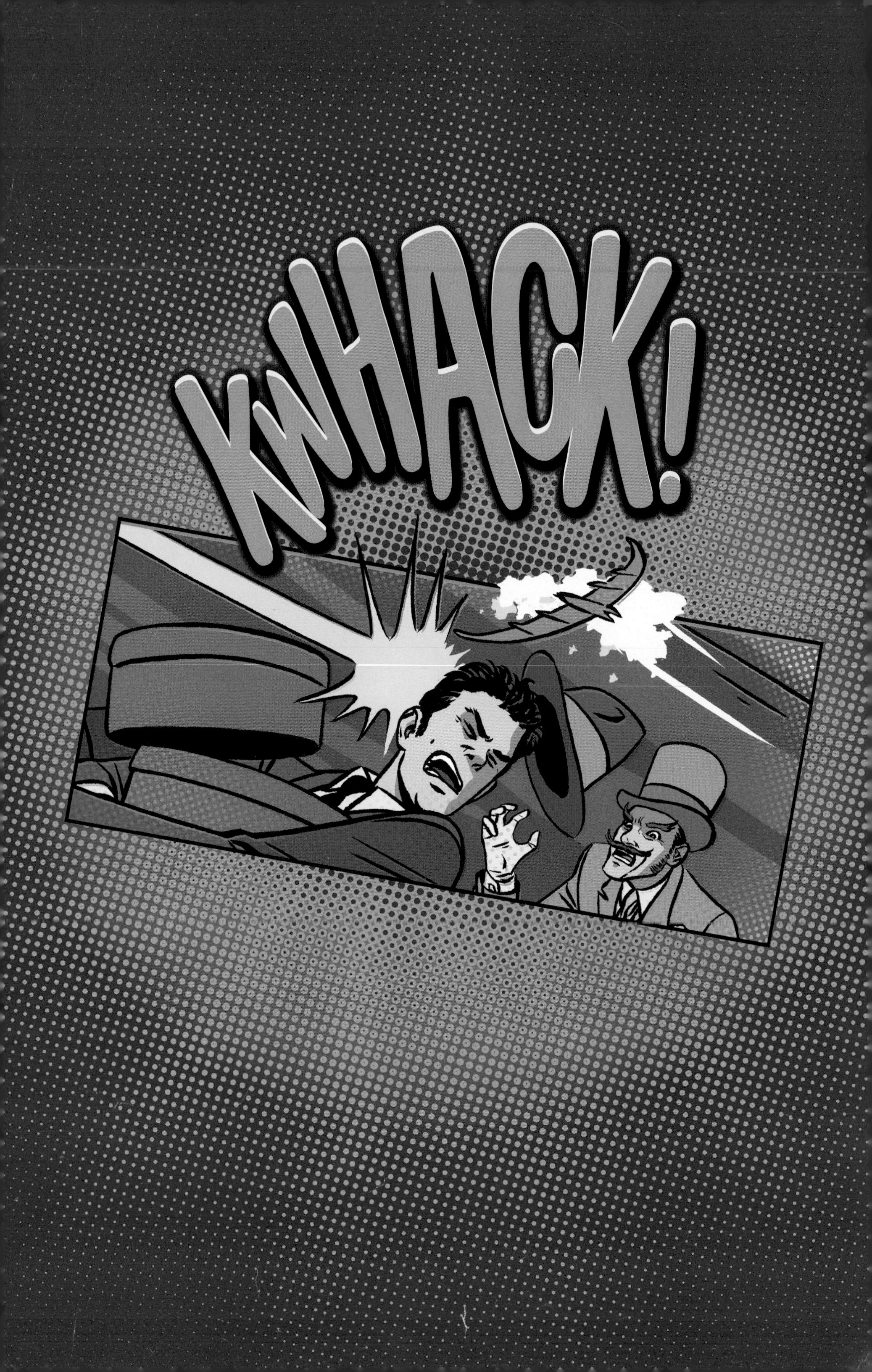
KWHACK!

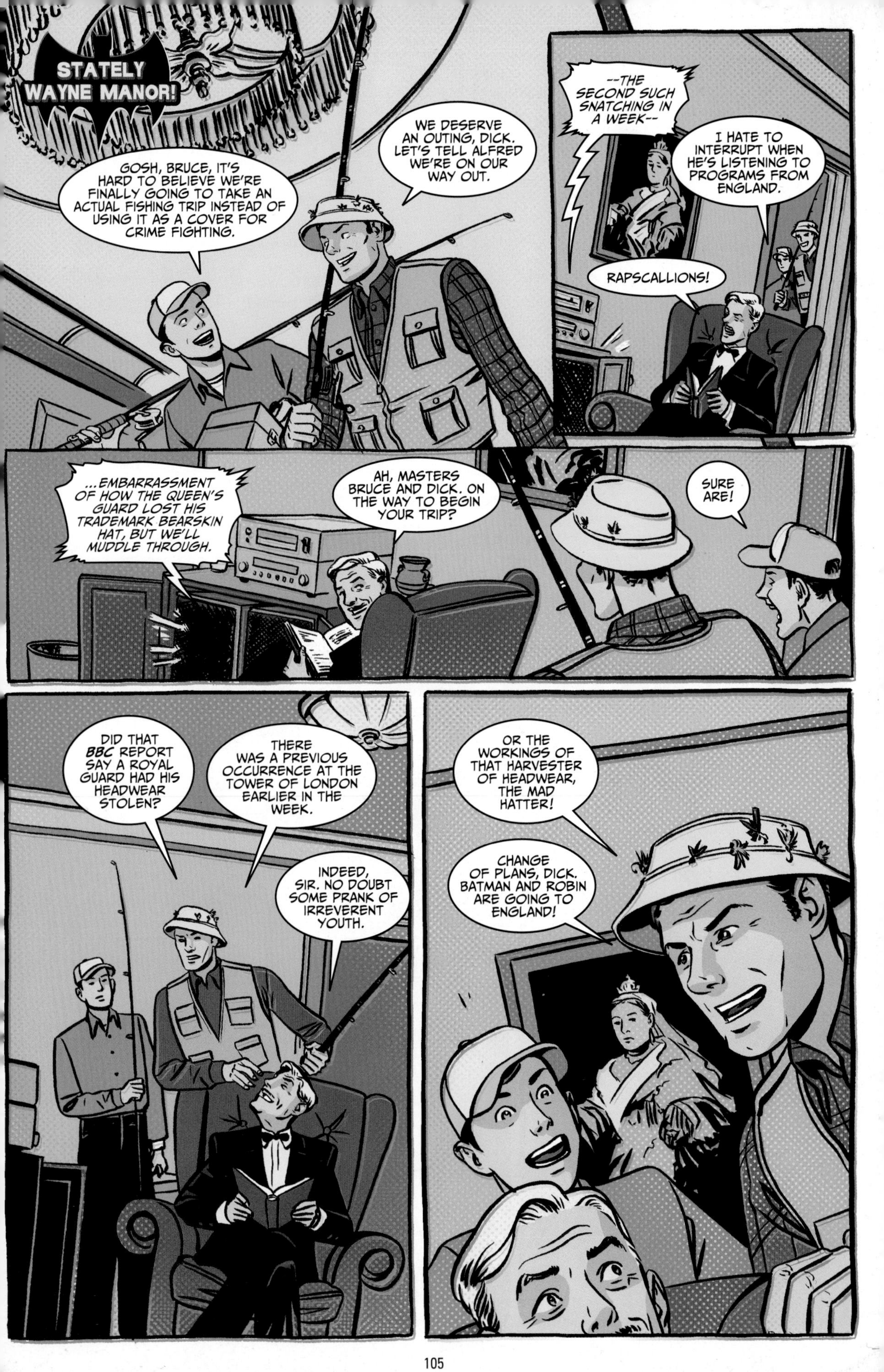
STATELY WAYNE MANOR!
GOSH, BRUCE, IT'S HARD TO BELIEVE WE'RE FINALLY GOING TO TAKE AN ACTUAL FISHING TRIP INSTEAD OF USING IT AS A COVER FOR CRIME FIGHTING.
WE DESERVE AN OUTING, DICK. LET'S TELL ALFRED WE'RE ON OUR WAY OUT.
--THE SECOND SUCH SNATCHING IN A WEEK--
I HATE TO INTERRUPT WHEN HE'S LISTENING TO PROGRAMS FROM ENGLAND.
RAPSCALLIONS!
...EMBARRASSMENT OF HOW THE QUEEN'S GUARD LOST HIS TRADEMARK BEARSKIN HAT, BUT WE'LL MUDDLE THROUGH.
AH, MASTERS BRUCE AND DICK. ON THE WAY TO BEGIN YOUR TRIP?
SURE ARE!
DID THAT BBC REPORT SAY A ROYAL GUARD HAD HIS HEADWEAR STOLEN?
THERE WAS A PREVIOUS OCCURRENCE AT THE TOWER OF LONDON EARLIER IN THE WEEK.
INDEED, SIR. NO DOUBT SOME PRANK OF IRREVERENT YOUTH.
OR THE WORKINGS OF THAT HARVESTER OF HEADWEAR, THE MAD HATTER!
CHANGE OF PLANS, DICK. BATMAN AND ROBIN ARE GOING TO ENGLAND!

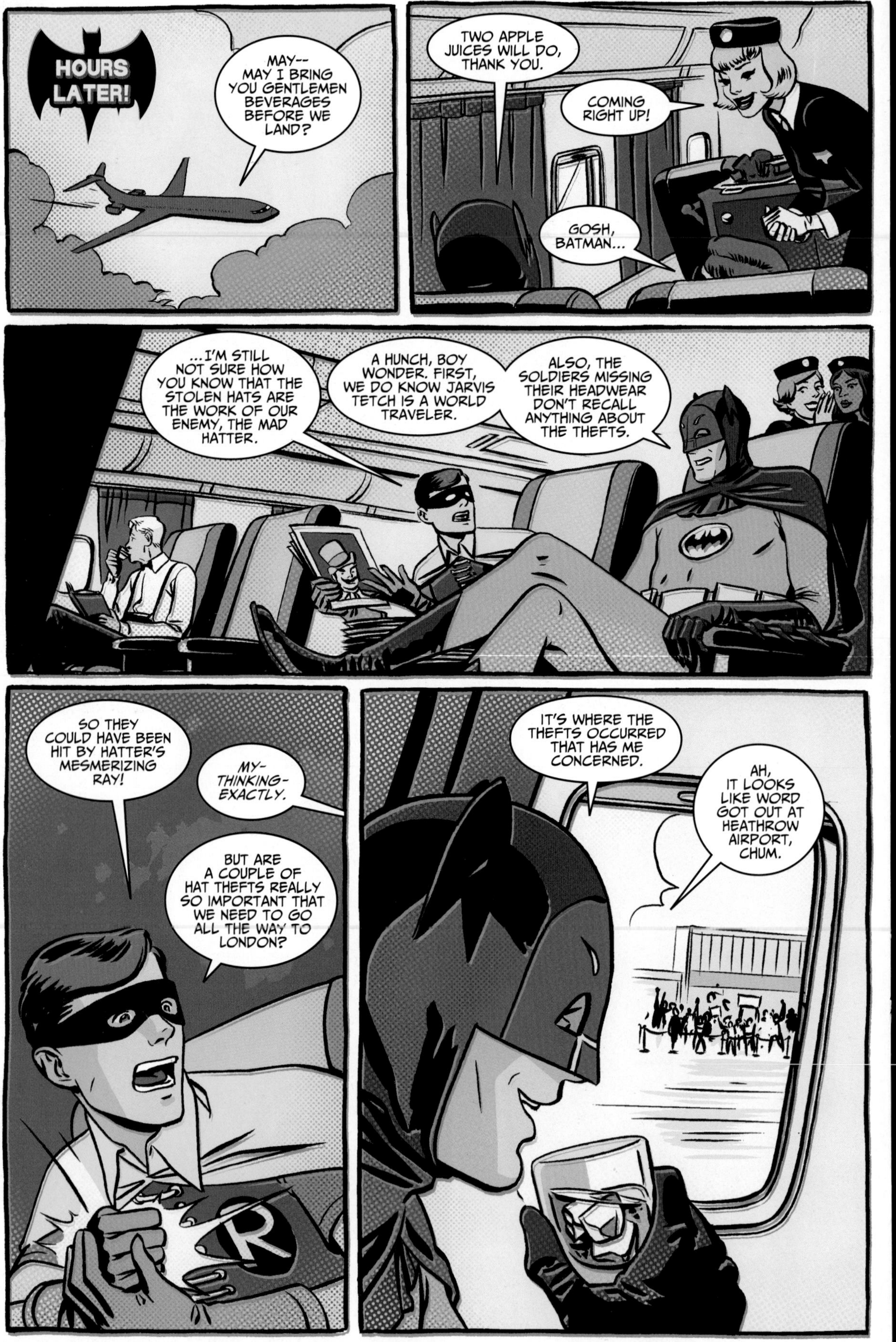
HOURS LATER!
MAY-- MAY I BRING YOU GENTLEMEN BEVERAGES BEFORE WE LAND?
TWO APPLE JUICES WILL DO, THANK YOU.
COMING RIGHT UP!
GOSH, BATMAN...
...I'M STILL NOT SURE HOW YOU KNOW THAT THE STOLEN HATS ARE THE WORK OF OUR ENEMY, THE MAD HATTER.
A HUNCH, BOY WONDER. FIRST, WE DO KNOW JARVIS TETCH IS A WORLD TRAVELER.
ALSO, THE SOLDIERS MISSING THEIR HEADWEAR DON'T RECALL ANYTHING ABOUT THE THEFTS.
SO THEY COULD HAVE BEEN HIT BY HATTER'S MESMERIZING RAY!
MY- THINKING- EXACTLY.
BUT ARE A COUPLE OF HAT THEFTS REALLY SO IMPORTANT THAT WE NEED TO GO ALL THE WAY TO LONDON?
IT'S WHERE THE THEFTS OCCURRED THAT HAS ME CONCERNED.
AH, IT LOOKS LIKE WORD GOT OUT AT HEATHROW AIRPORT, CHUM.

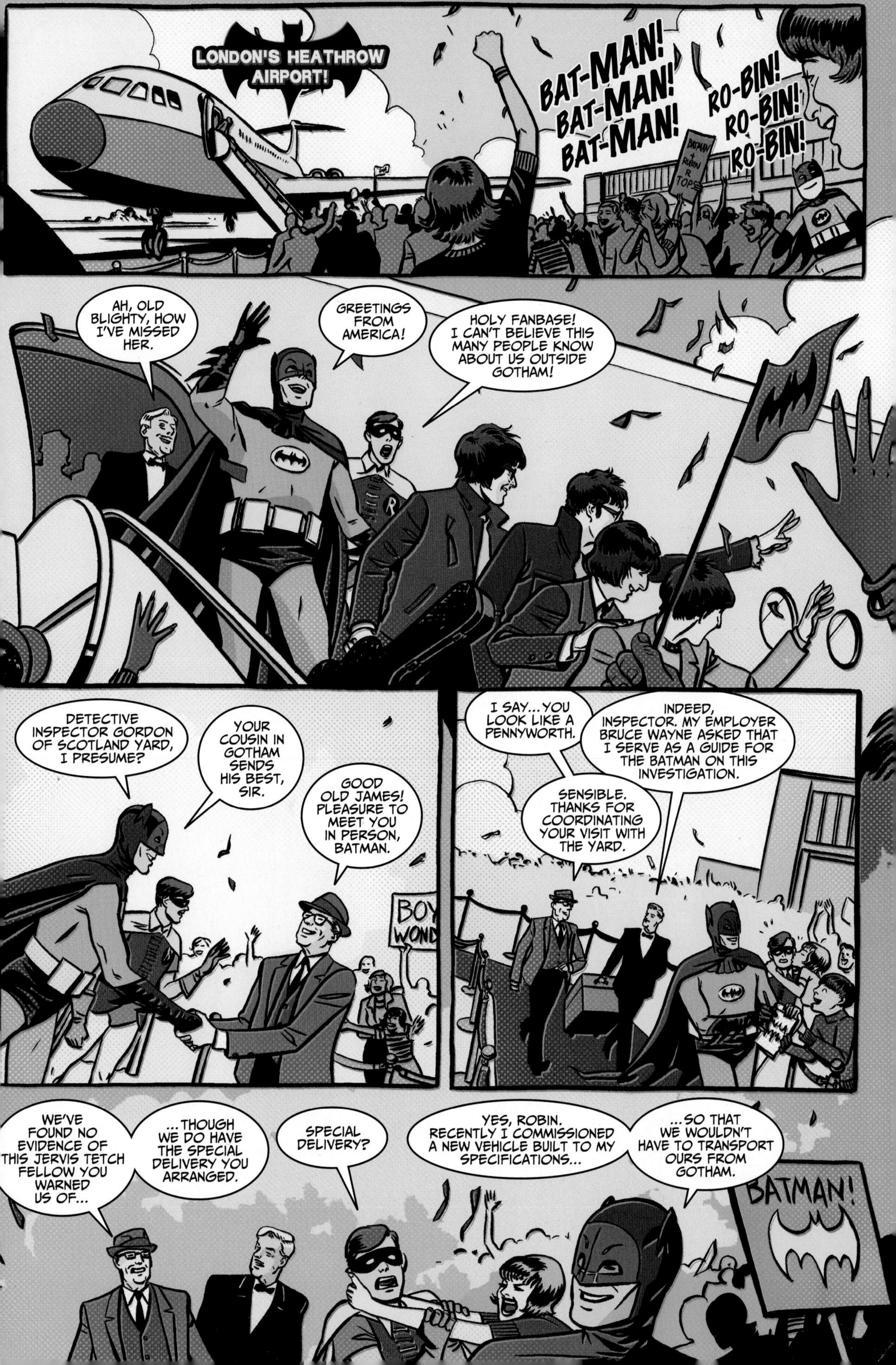
LONDON'S HEATHROW AIRPORT!
BAT-MAN! BAT-MAN! BAT-MAN!
RO-BIN! RO-BIN! RO-BIN!
AH, OLD BLIGHTY, HOW I'VE MISSED HER.
GREETINGS FROM AMERICA!
HOLY FANBASE! I CAN'T BELIEVE THIS MANY PEOPLE KNOW ABOUT US OUTSIDE GOTHAM!
DETECTIVE INSPECTOR GORDON OF SCOTLAND YARD, I PRESUME?
YOUR COUSIN IN GOTHAM SENDS HIS BEST, SIR.
GOOD OLD JAMES! PLEASURE TO MEET YOU IN PERSON, BATMAN.
I SAY...YOU LOOK LIKE A PENNYWORTH.
INDEED, INSPECTOR. MY EMPLOYER BRUCE WAYNE ASKED THAT I SERVE AS A GUIDE FOR THE BATMAN ON THIS INVESTIGATION.
SENSIBLE. THANKS FOR COORDINATING YOUR VISIT WITH THE YARD.
WE'VE FOUND NO EVIDENCE OF THIS JERVIS TETCH FELLOW YOU WARNED US OF...
...THOUGH WE DO HAVE THE SPECIAL DELIVERY YOU ARRANGED.
SPECIAL DELIVERY?
YES, ROBIN. RECENTLY I COMMISSIONED A NEW VEHICLE BUILT TO MY SPECIFICATIONS...
...SO THAT WE WOULDN'T HAVE TO TRANSPORT OURS FROM GOTHAM.
BATMAN!

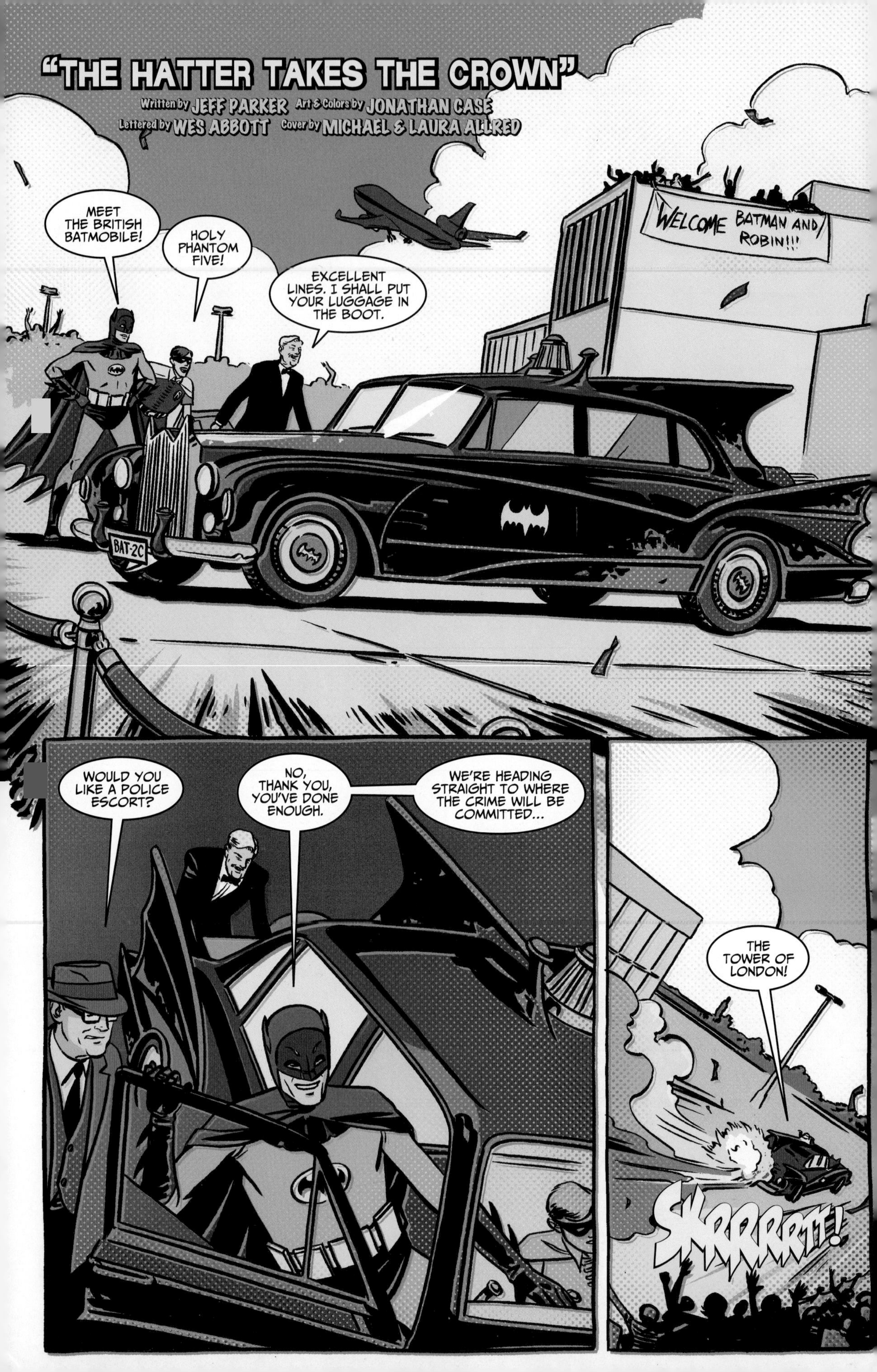
"THE HATTER TAKES THE CROWN"
Written by JEFF PARKER Art & Colors by JONATHAN CASE
Lettered by WES ABBOTT Cover by MICHAEL & LAURA ALLRED
WELCOME BATMAN AND ROBIN!!!
MEET THE BRITISH BATMOBILE!
HOLY PHANTOM FIVE!
EXCELLENT LINES. I SHALL PUT YOUR LUGGAGE IN THE BOOT.
BAT-2C
WOULD YOU LIKE A POLICE ESCORT?
NO, THANK YOU, YOU'VE DONE ENOUGH.
WE'RE HEADING STRAIGHT TO WHERE THE CRIME WILL BE COMMITTED...
THE TOWER OF LONDON!
SKRRRRTT!

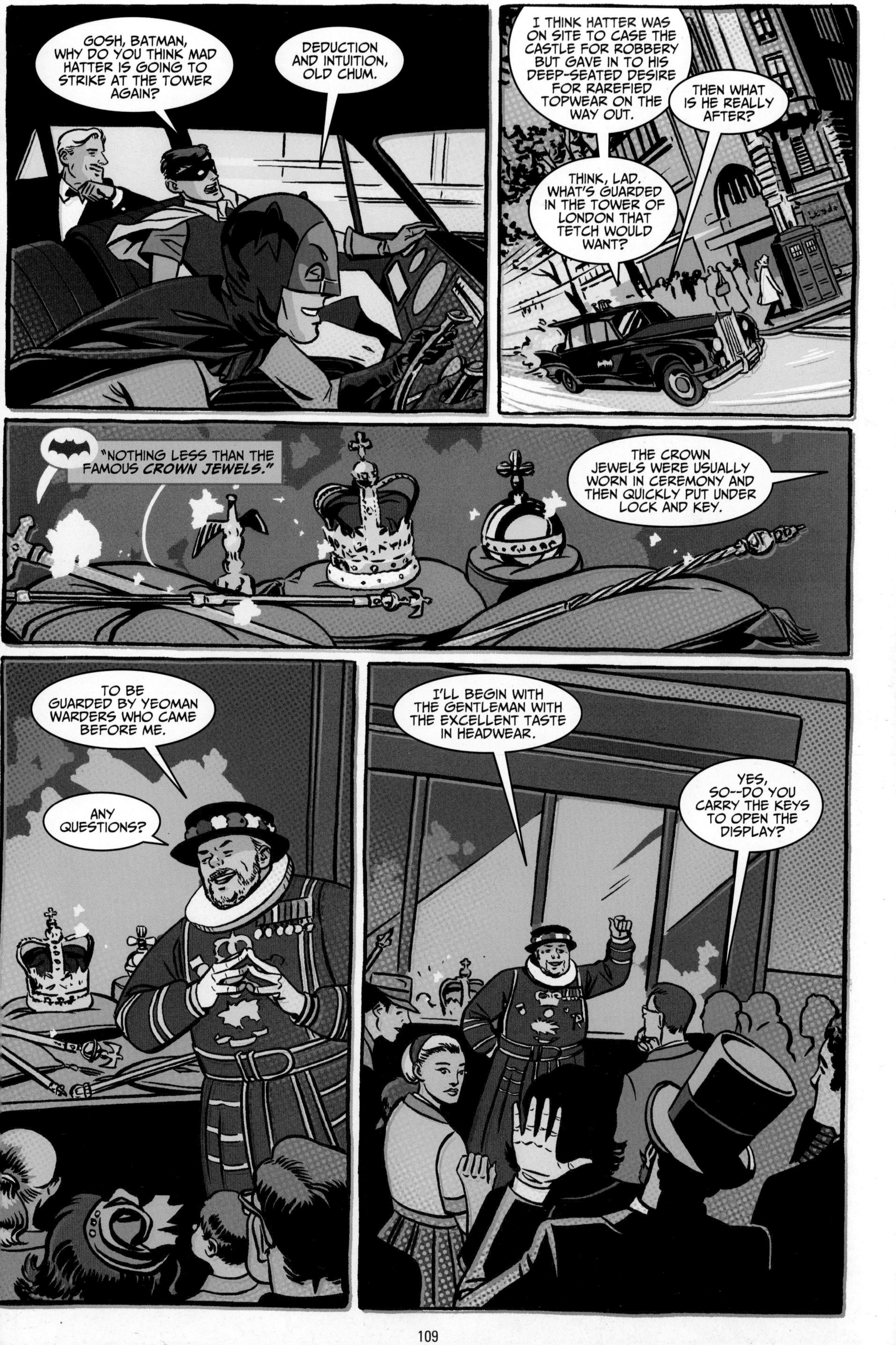
GOSH, BATMAN, WHY DO YOU THINK MAD HATTER IS GOING TO STRIKE AT THE TOWER AGAIN?
DEDUCTION AND INTUITION, OLD CHUM.
I THINK HATTER WAS ON SITE TO CASE THE CASTLE FOR ROBBERY BUT GAVE IN TO HIS DEEP-SEATED DESIRE FOR RAREFIED TOPWEAR ON THE WAY OUT.
THEN WHAT IS HE REALLY AFTER?
THINK, LAD. WHAT'S GUARDED IN THE TOWER OF LONDON THAT TETCH WOULD WANT?
"NOTHING LESS THAN THE FAMOUS CROWN JEWELS."
THE CROWN JEWELS WERE USUALLY WORN IN CEREMONY AND THEN QUICKLY PUT UNDER LOCK AND KEY.
TO BE GUARDED BY YEOMAN WARDERS WHO CAME BEFORE ME.
ANY QUESTIONS?
I'LL BEGIN WITH THE GENTLEMAN WITH THE EXCELLENT TASTE IN HEADWEAR.
YES, SO--DO YOU CARRY THE KEYS TO OPEN THE DISPLAY?

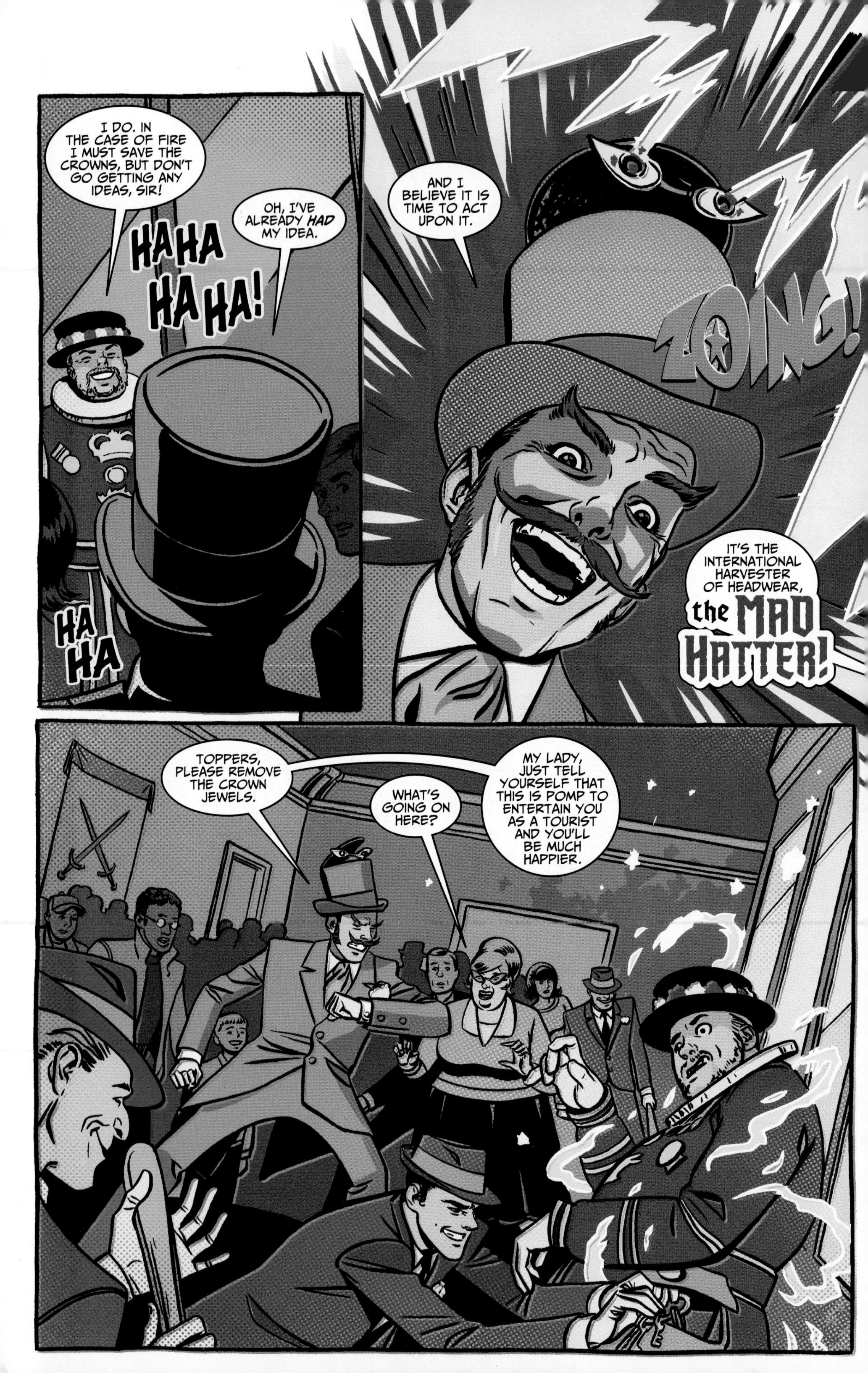
I DO. IN THE CASE OF FIRE I MUST SAVE THE CROWNS, BUT DON'T GO GETTING ANY IDEAS, SIR!
OH, I'VE ALREADY *HAD* MY IDEA.
HAHA HAHA!
HA HA
AND I BELIEVE IT IS TIME TO ACT UPON IT.
ZOING!!
IT'S THE INTERNATIONAL HARVESTER OF HEADWEAR,
the MAD HATTER!
TOPPERS, PLEASE REMOVE THE CROWN JEWELS.
WHAT'S GOING ON HERE?
MY LADY, JUST TELL YOURSELF THAT THIS IS POMP TO ENTERTAIN YOU AS A TOURIST AND YOU'LL BE MUCH HAPPIER.

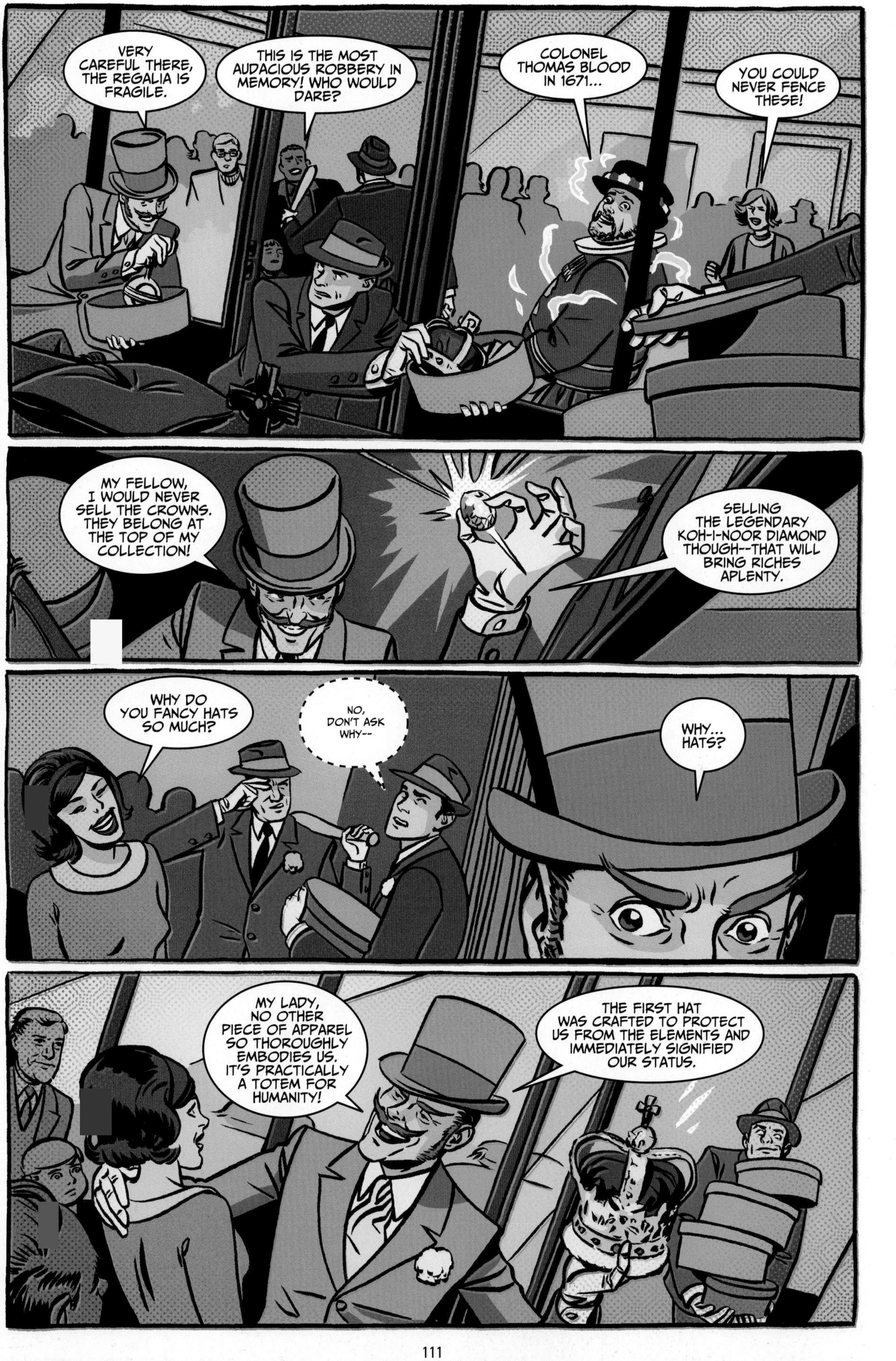
VERY CAREFUL THERE, THE REGALIA IS FRAGILE.
THIS IS THE MOST AUDACIOUS ROBBERY IN MEMORY! WHO WOULD DARE?
COLONEL THOMAS BLOOD IN 1671...
YOU COULD NEVER FENCE THESE!
MY FELLOW, I WOULD NEVER SELL THE CROWNS. THEY BELONG AT THE TOP OF MY COLLECTION!
SELLING THE LEGENDARY KOH-I-NOOR DIAMOND THOUGH--THAT WILL BRING RICHES APLENTY.
WHY DO YOU FANCY HATS SO MUCH?
NO, DON'T ASK WHY--
WHY... HATS?
MY LADY, NO OTHER PIECE OF APPAREL SO THOROUGHLY EMBODIES US. IT'S PRACTICALLY A TOTEM FOR HUMANITY!
THE FIRST HAT WAS CRAFTED TO PROTECT US FROM THE ELEMENTS AND IMMEDIATELY SIGNIFIED OUR STATUS.

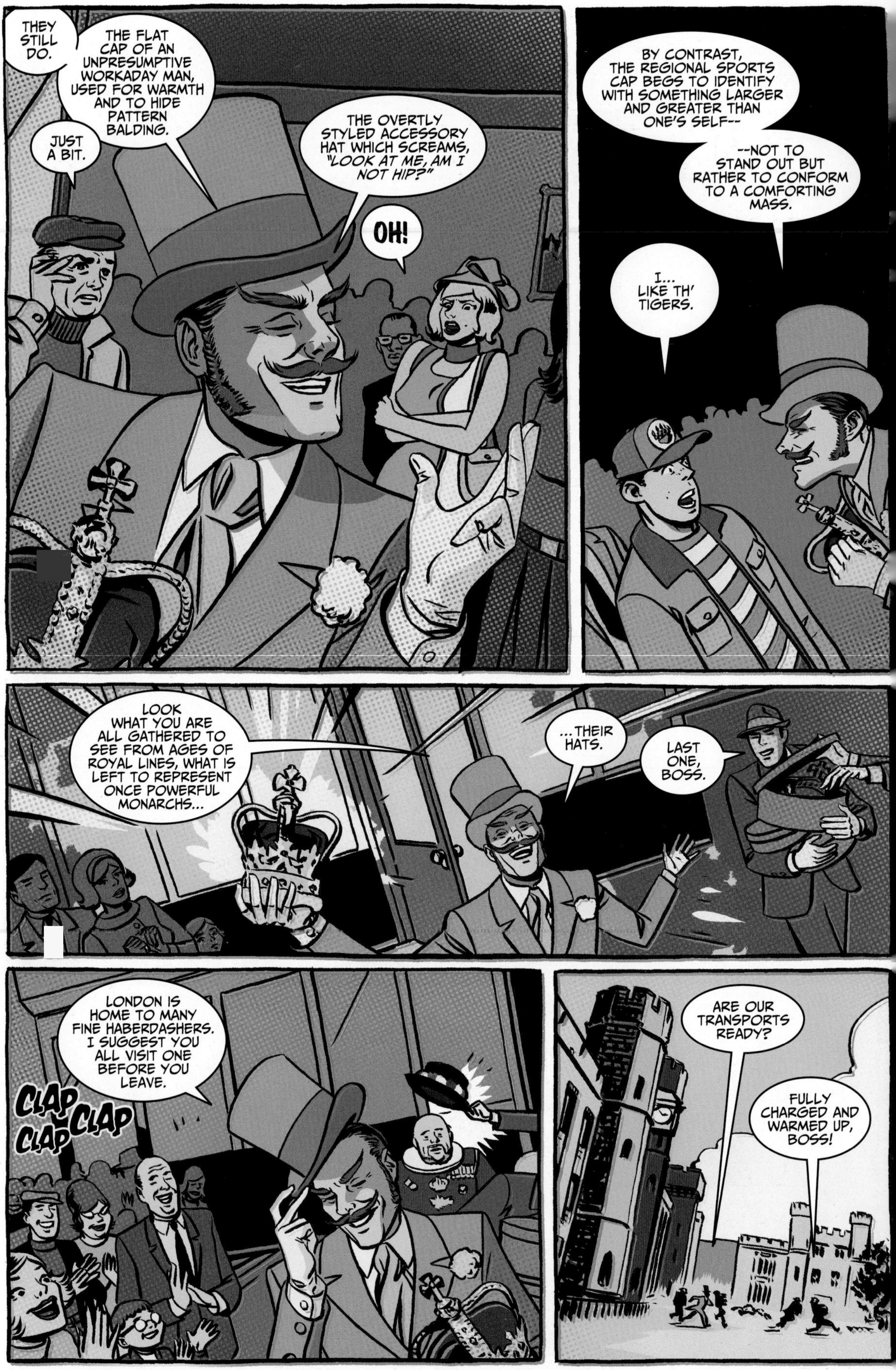
THEY STILL DO.
THE FLAT CAP OF AN UNPRESUMPTIVE WORKADAY MAN, USED FOR WARMTH AND TO HIDE PATTERN BALDING.
JUST A BIT.
THE OVERTLY STYLED ACCESSORY HAT WHICH SCREAMS, "LOOK AT ME, AM I NOT HIP?"
OH!
BY CONTRAST, THE REGIONAL SPORTS CAP BEGS TO IDENTIFY WITH SOMETHING LARGER AND GREATER THAN ONE'S SELF--
--NOT TO STAND OUT BUT RATHER TO CONFORM TO A COMFORTING MASS.
I... LIKE TH' TIGERS.
LOOK WHAT YOU ARE ALL GATHERED TO SEE FROM AGES OF ROYAL LINES, WHAT IS LEFT TO REPRESENT ONCE POWERFUL MONARCHS...
...THEIR HATS.
LAST ONE, BOSS.
LONDON IS HOME TO MANY FINE HABERDASHERS. I SUGGEST YOU ALL VISIT ONE BEFORE YOU LEAVE.
CLAP CLAP CLAP
ARE OUR TRANSPORTS READY?
FULLY CHARGED AND WARMED UP, BOSS!

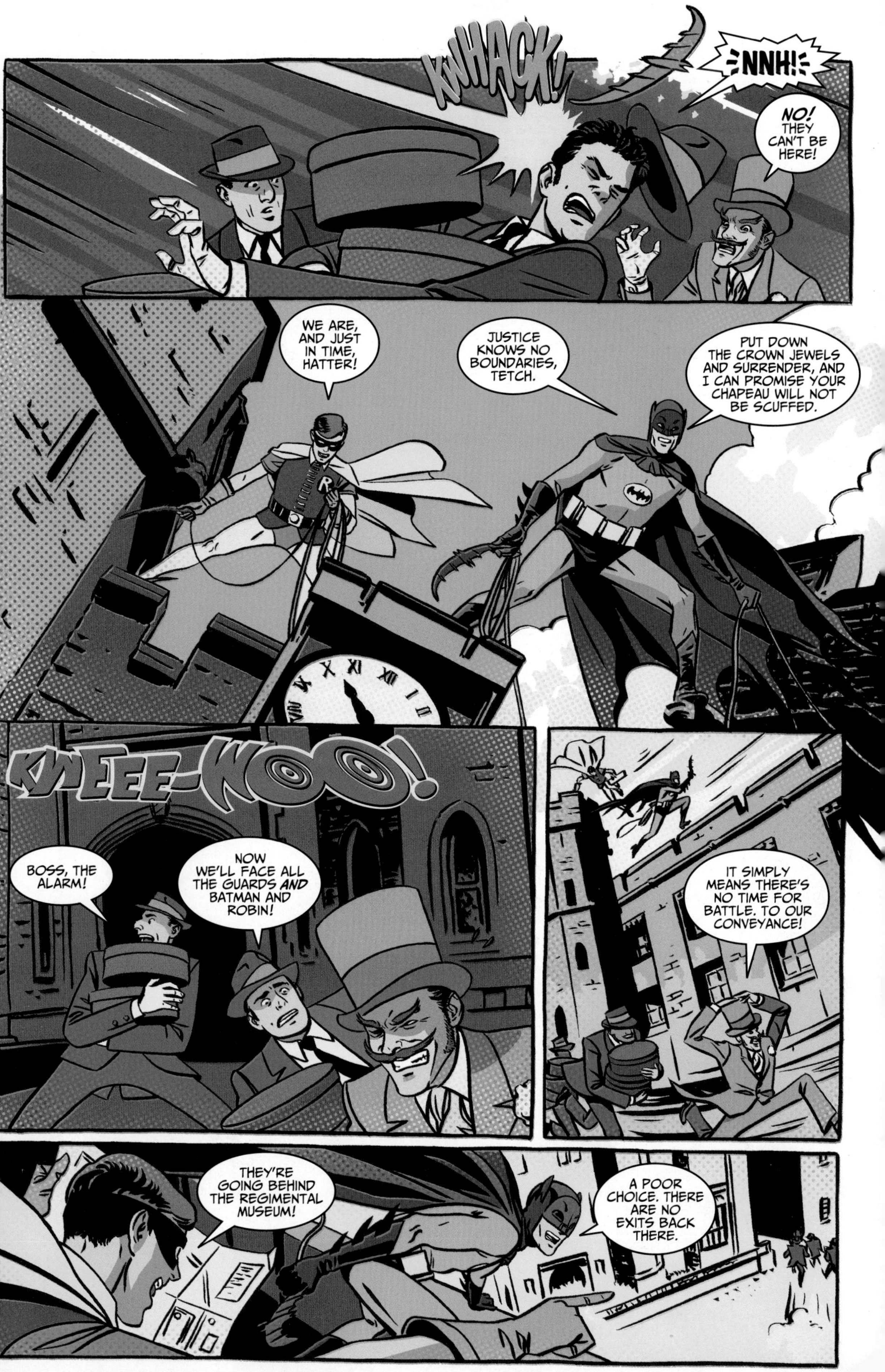
KWHACK!
NNH!
NO! THEY CAN'T BE HERE!
WE ARE, AND JUST IN TIME, HATTER!
JUSTICE KNOWS NO BOUNDARIES, TETCH.
PUT DOWN THE CROWN JEWELS AND SURRENDER, AND I CAN PROMISE YOUR CHAPEAU WILL NOT BE SCUFFED.
KWEEE-WOO!
BOSS, THE ALARM!
NOW WE'LL FACE ALL THE GUARDS AND BATMAN AND ROBIN!
IT SIMPLY MEANS THERE'S NO TIME FOR BATTLE. TO OUR CONVEYANCE!
THEY'RE GOING BEHIND THE REGIMENTAL MUSEUM!
A POOR CHOICE. THERE ARE NO EXITS BACK THERE.

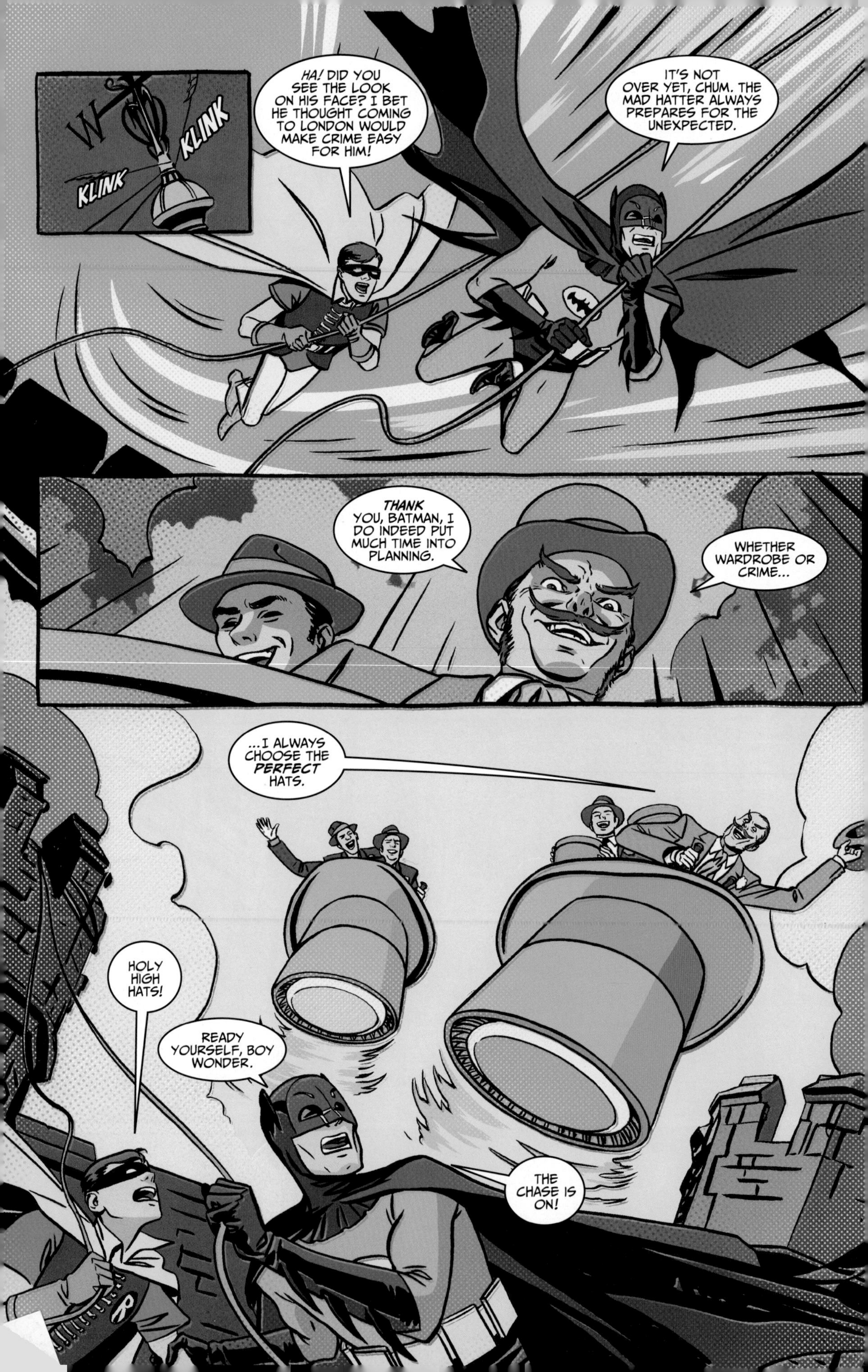
KLINK
KLINK
HA! DID YOU SEE THE LOOK ON HIS FACE? I BET HE THOUGHT COMING TO LONDON WOULD MAKE CRIME EASY FOR HIM!
IT'S NOT OVER YET, CHUM. THE MAD HATTER ALWAYS PREPARES FOR THE UNEXPECTED.
THANK YOU, BATMAN, I DO INDEED PUT MUCH TIME INTO PLANNING.
WHETHER WARDROBE OR CRIME...
...I ALWAYS CHOOSE THE PERFECT HATS.
HOLY HIGH HATS!
READY YOURSELF, BOY WONDER.
THE CHASE IS ON!

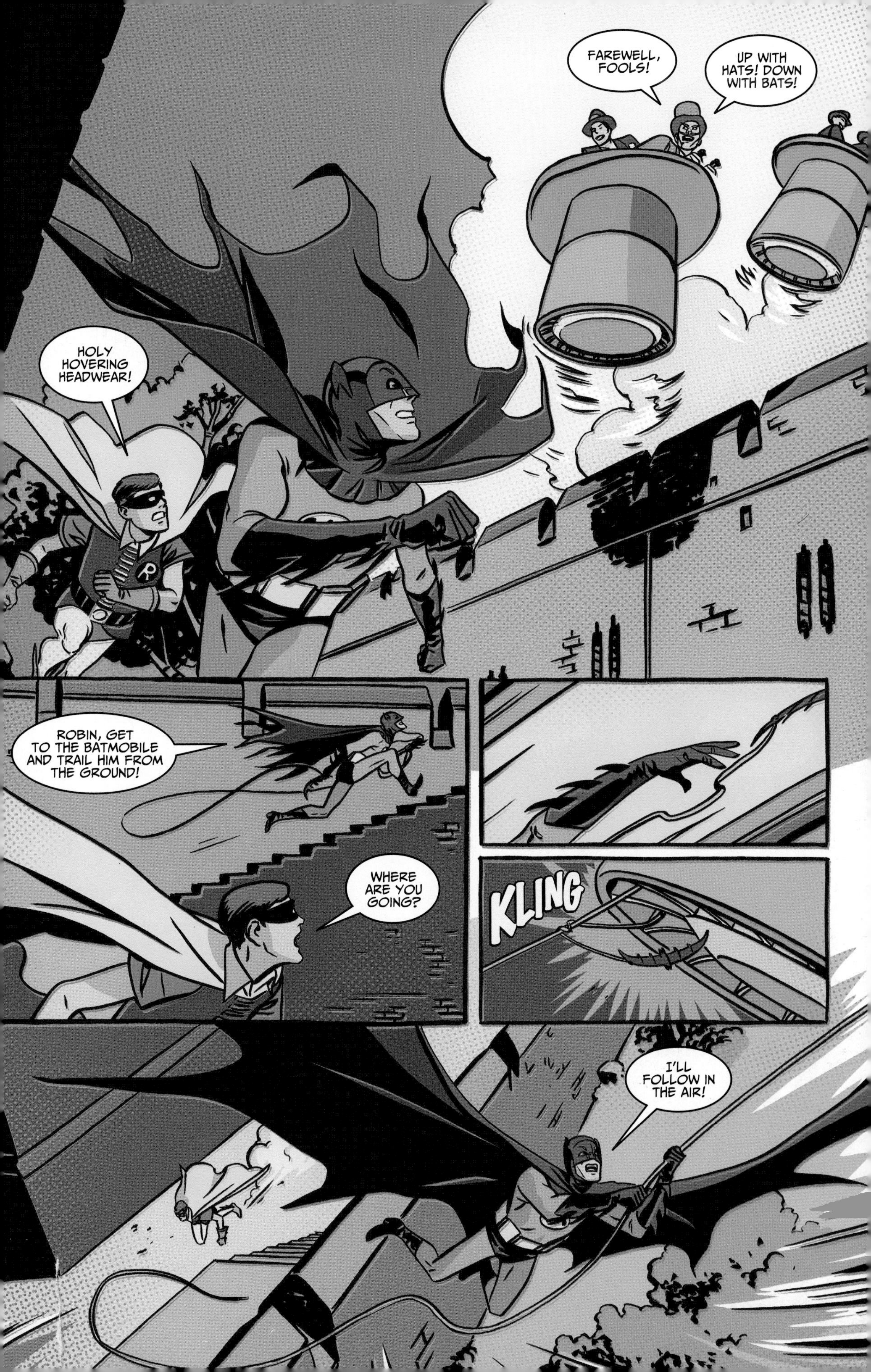
FAREWELL, FOOLS!
UP WITH HATS! DOWN WITH BATS!
HOLY HOVERING HEADWEAR!
ROBIN, GET TO THE BATMOBILE AND TRAIL HIM FROM THE GROUND!
WHERE ARE YOU GOING?
KLING
I'LL FOLLOW IN THE AIR!

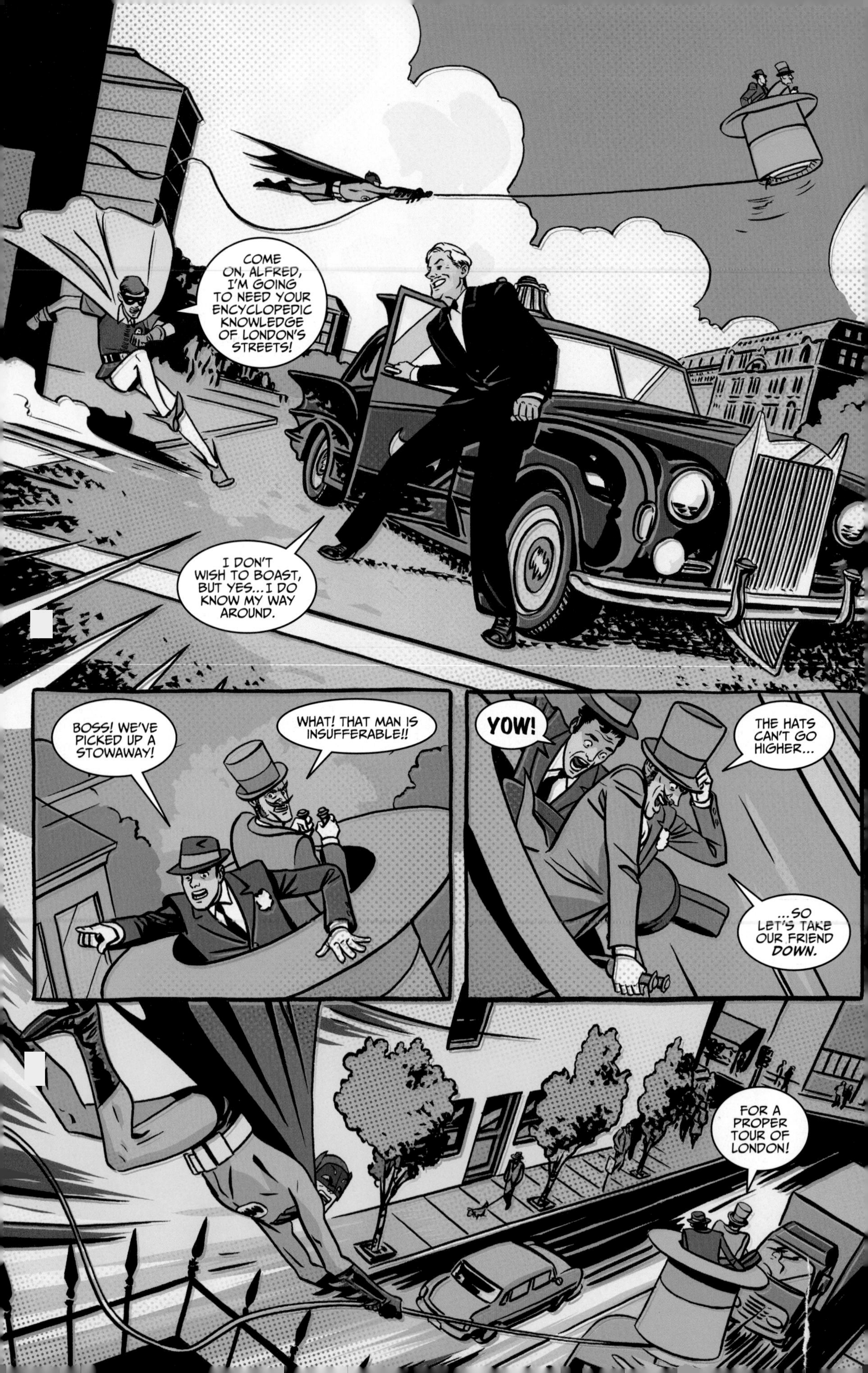
COME ON, ALFRED, I'M GOING TO NEED YOUR ENCYCLOPEDIC KNOWLEDGE OF LONDON'S STREETS!
I DON'T WISH TO BOAST, BUT YES...I DO KNOW MY WAY AROUND.
BOSS! WE'VE PICKED UP A STOWAWAY!
WHAT! THAT MAN IS INSUFFERABLE!!
YOW!
THE HATS CAN'T GO HIGHER...
...SO LET'S TAKE OUR FRIEND DOWN.
FOR A PROPER TOUR OF LONDON!

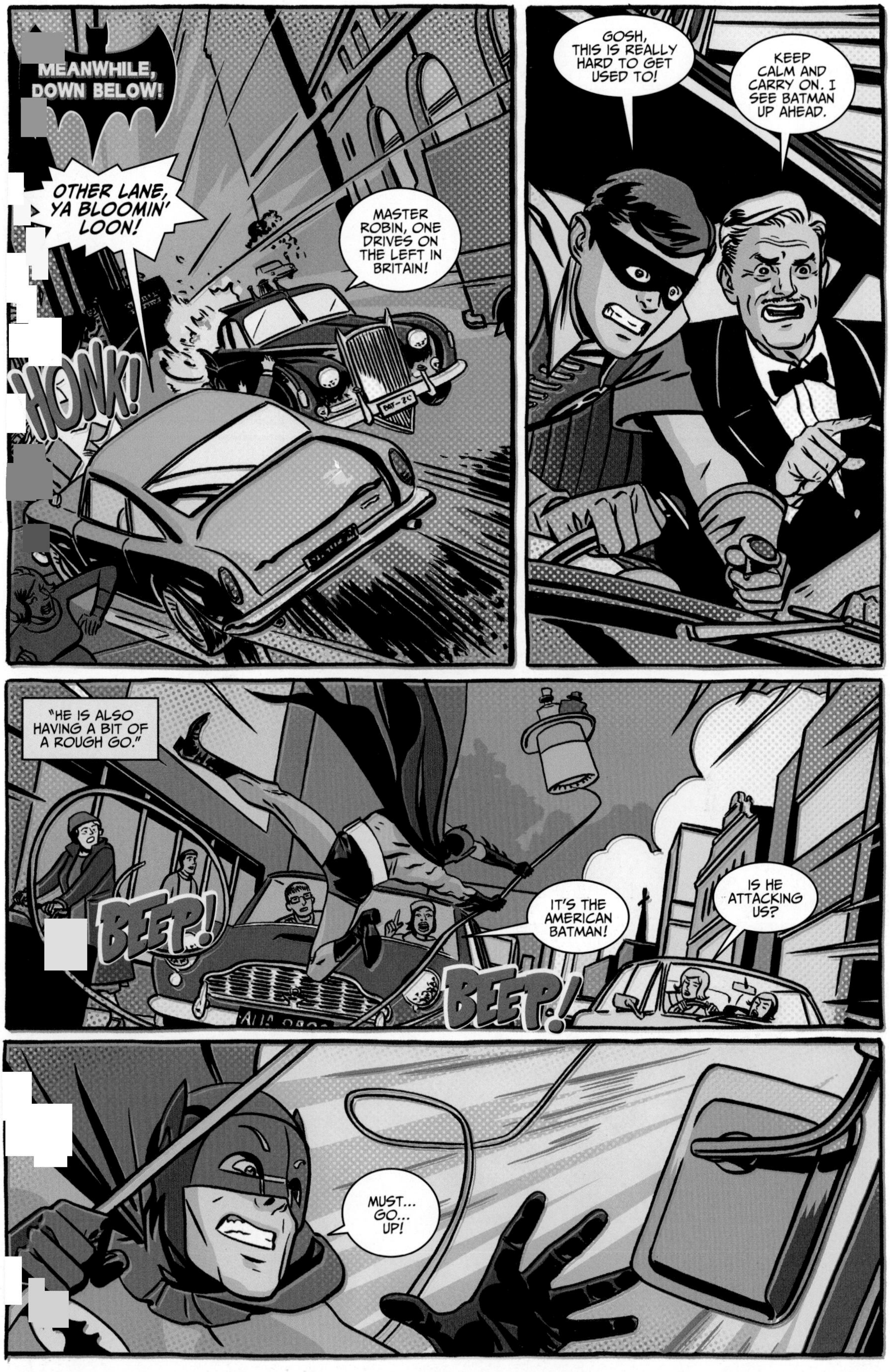
MEANWHILE, DOWN BELOW!
OTHER LANE, YA BLOOMIN' LOON!
MASTER ROBIN, ONE DRIVES ON THE LEFT IN BRITAIN!
HONK!
GOSH, THIS IS REALLY HARD TO GET USED TO!
KEEP CALM AND CARRY ON. I SEE BATMAN UP AHEAD.
"HE IS ALSO HAVING A BIT OF A ROUGH GO."
BEEP!
IT'S THE AMERICAN BATMAN!
IS HE ATTACKING US?
BEEP!
MUST... GO... UP!

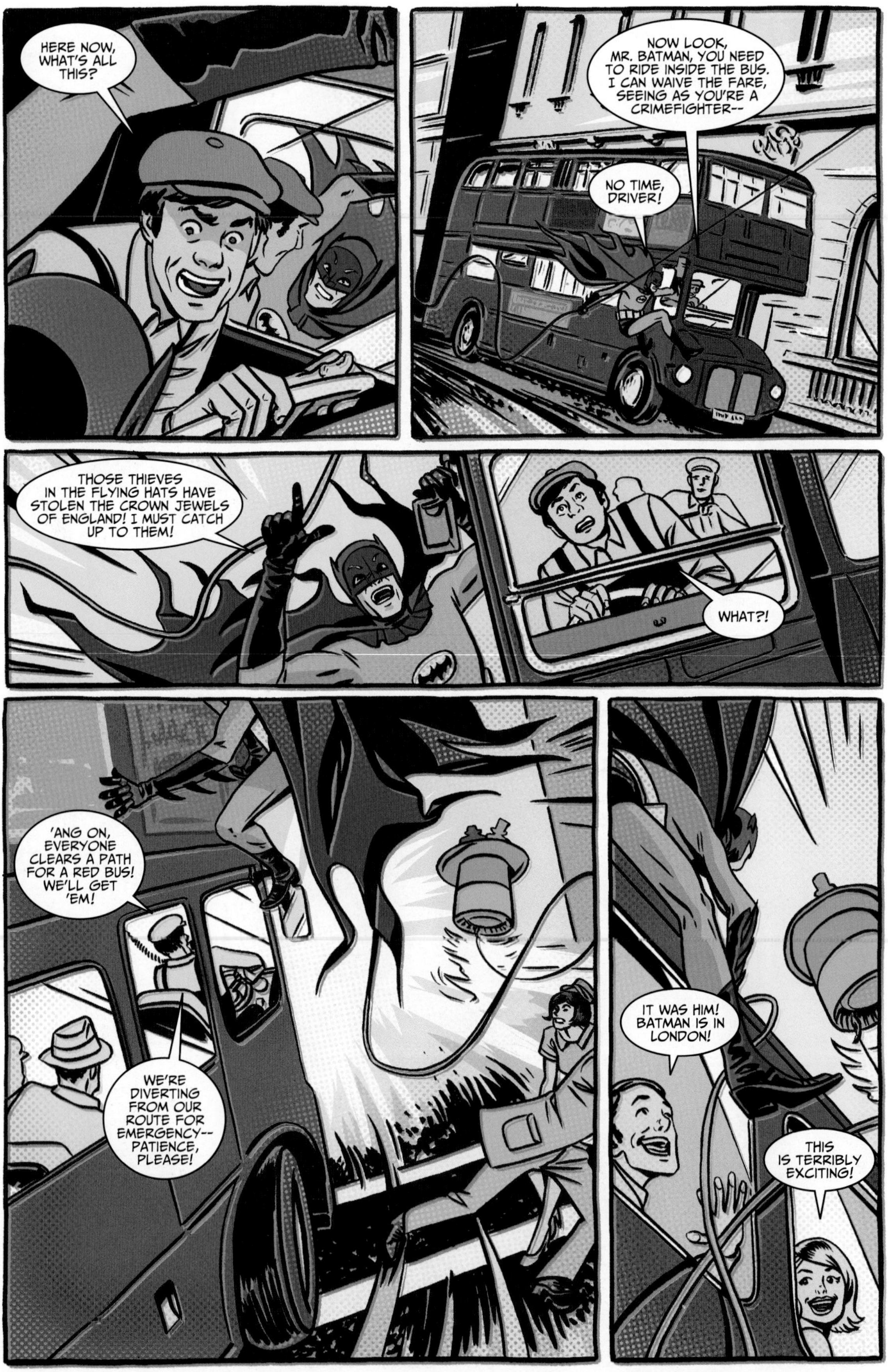
HERE NOW, WHAT'S ALL THIS?
NOW LOOK, MR. BATMAN, YOU NEED TO RIDE INSIDE THE BUS. I CAN WAIVE THE FARE, SEEING AS YOU'RE A CRIMEFIGHTER--
NO TIME, DRIVER!
THOSE THIEVES IN THE FLYING HATS HAVE STOLEN THE CROWN JEWELS OF ENGLAND! I MUST CATCH UP TO THEM!
WHAT?!
'ANG ON, EVERYONE CLEARS A PATH FOR A RED BUS! WE'LL GET 'EM!
WE'RE DIVERTING FROM OUR ROUTE FOR EMERGENCY-- PATIENCE, PLEASE!
IT WAS HIM! BATMAN IS IN LONDON!
THIS IS TERRIBLY EXCITING!

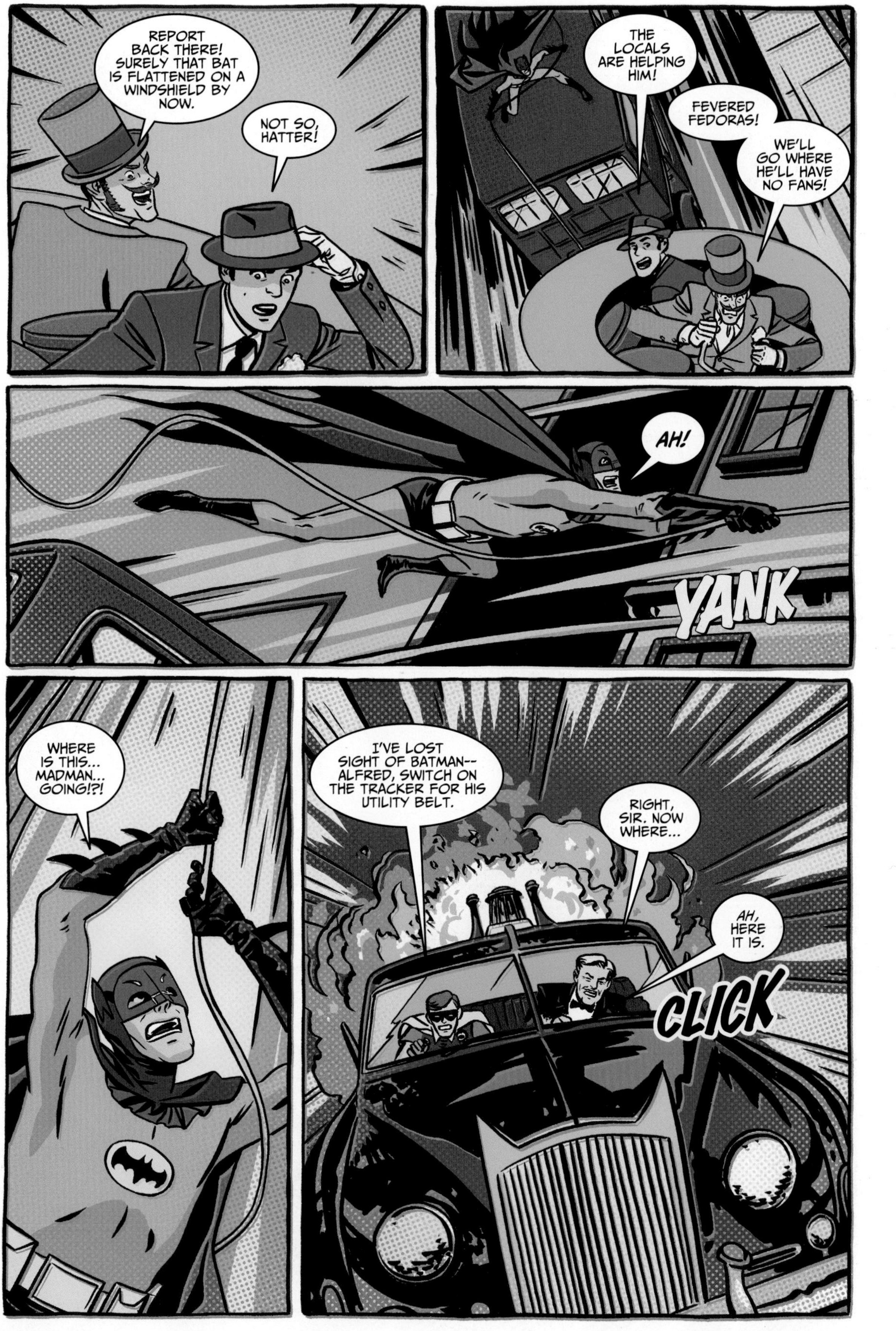
REPORT BACK THERE! SURELY THAT BAT IS FLATTENED ON A WINDSHIELD BY NOW.
NOT SO, HATTER!
THE LOCALS ARE HELPING HIM!
FEVERED FEDORAS!
WE'LL GO WHERE HE'LL HAVE NO FANS!
AH!
YANK
WHERE IS THIS... MADMAN... GOING!?!
I'VE LOST SIGHT OF BATMAN-- ALFRED, SWITCH ON THE TRACKER FOR HIS UTILITY BELT.
RIGHT, SIR. NOW WHERE...
AH, HERE IT IS.
CLICK

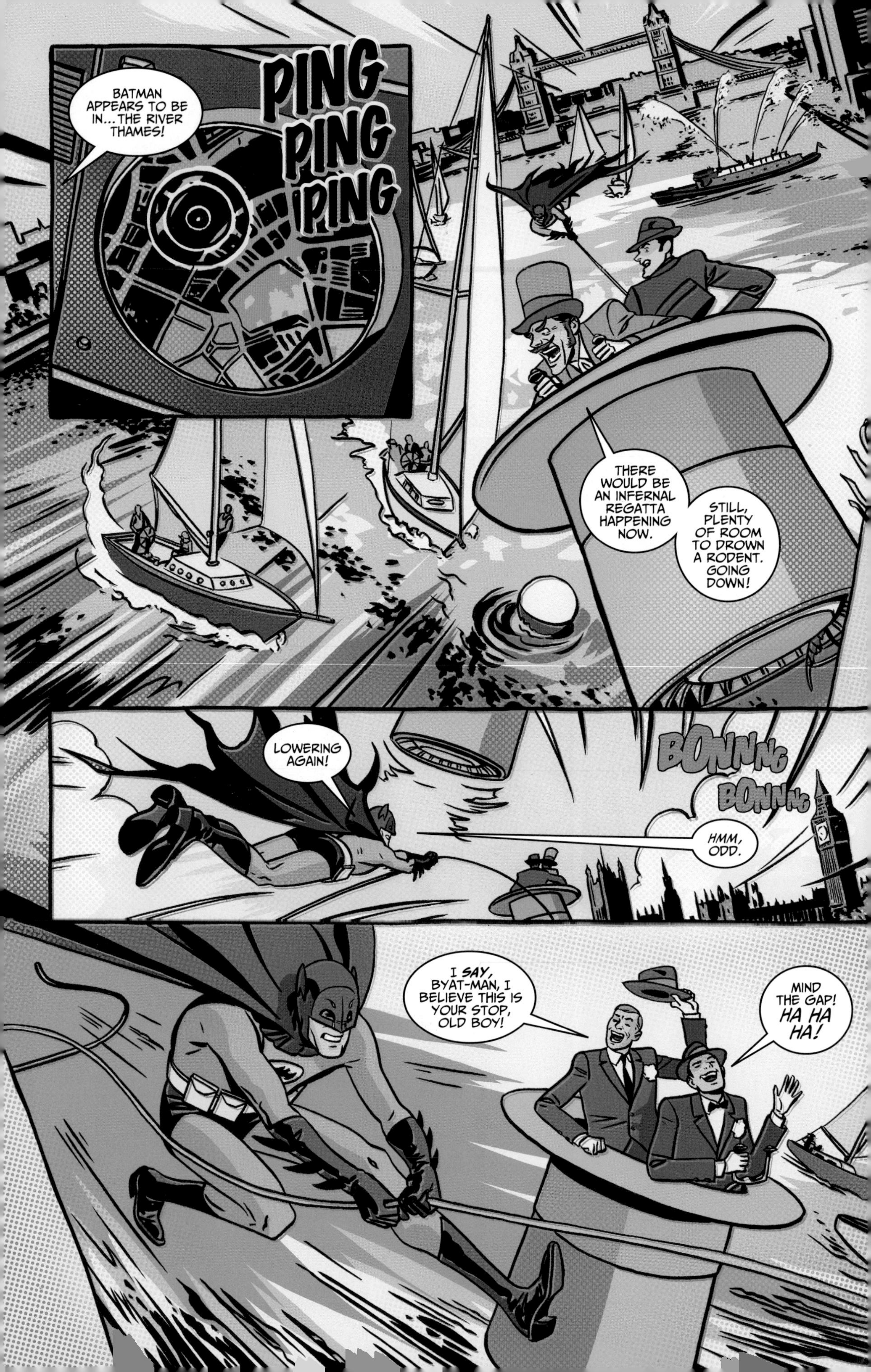
BATMAN APPEARS TO BE IN... THE RIVER THAMES!
PING PING PING
THERE WOULD BE AN INFERNAL REGATTA HAPPENING NOW.
STILL, PLENTY OF ROOM TO DROWN A RODENT. GOING DOWN!
LOWERING AGAIN!
BONNNG
BONNNG
HMM, ODD.
I SAY, BYAT-MAN, I BELIEVE THIS IS YOUR STOP, OLD BOY!
MIND THE GAP! HA HA HA!

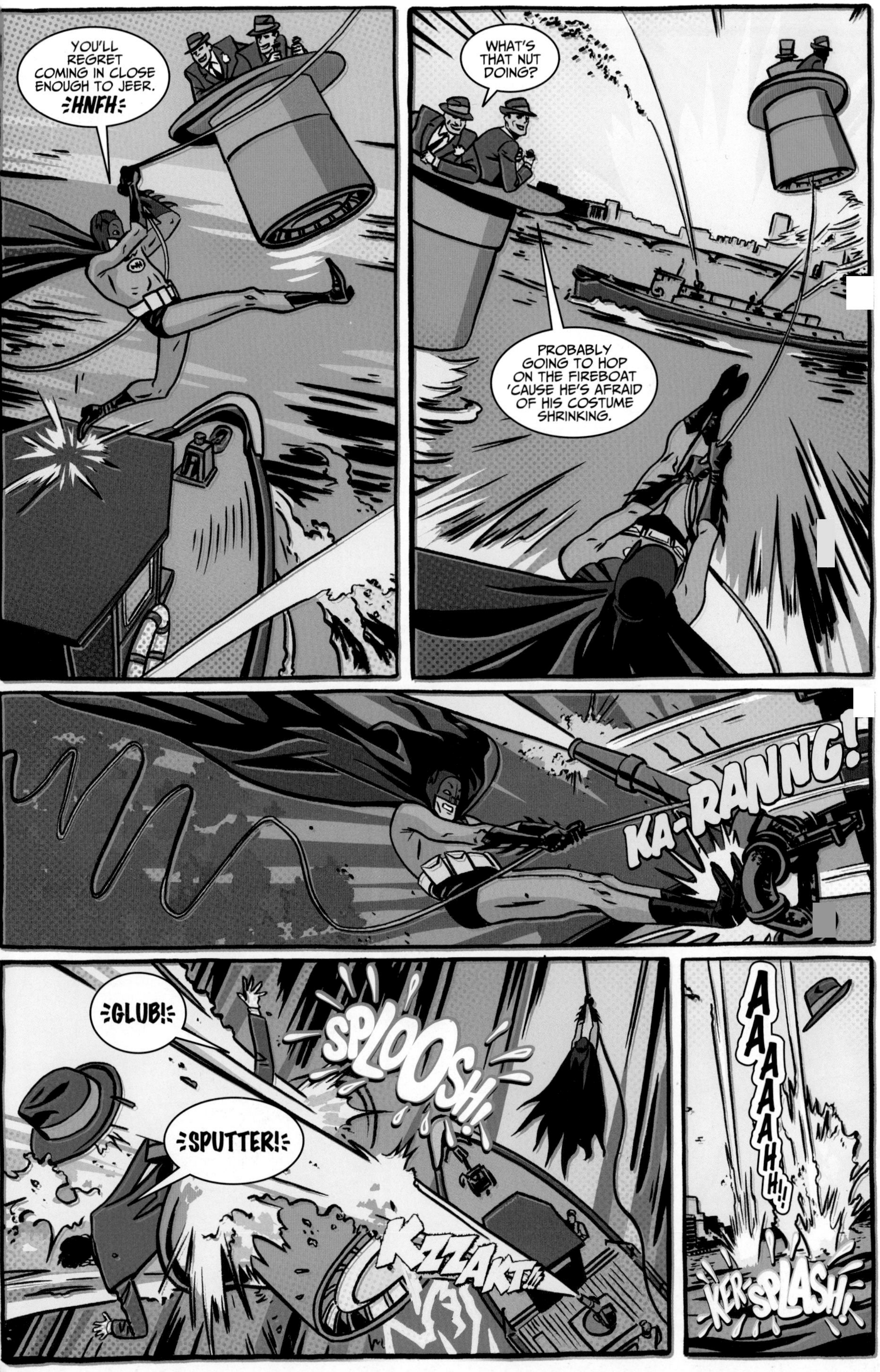
YOU'LL REGRET COMING IN CLOSE ENOUGH TO JEER.
HNFH
WHAT'S THAT NUT DOING?
PROBABLY GOING TO HOP ON THE FIREBOAT 'CAUSE HE'S AFRAID OF HIS COSTUME SHRINKING.
KA-RANNG!
GLUB!
SPLOOSH!
SPUTTER!
KZZZAKT!!
AAAAAAHH!!
KER-SPLASH!

BATMAN, COME IN! CAN YOU HEAR ME?

LOUD AND CLEAR, BOY WONDER!

WE HAVE YOU ON THE BAT-TRACKER HEADING TOWARDS THE WESTMINSTER BRIDGE. ALFRED AND I ARE TURNING ON TO IT NOW.

GOOD WORK, LAD!

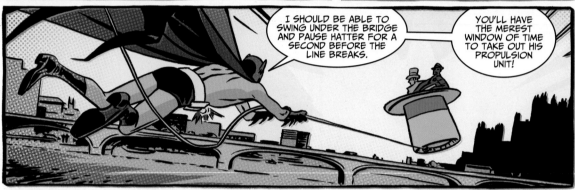

I SHOULD BE ABLE TO SWING UNDER THE BRIDGE AND PAUSE HATTER FOR A SECOND BEFORE THE LINE BREAKS.

YOU'LL HAVE THE MEREST WINDOW OF TIME TO TAKE OUT HIS PROPULSION UNIT!

OKAY, BATMAN, I'M READY.

AND ROBIN...

...HATTER'S CRAFT *MUST* COME DOWN ON THE BRIDGE.

IF HE GOES DOWN IN THE RIVER, THE CROWN JEWELS COULD BE LOST FOREVER.

ULP!

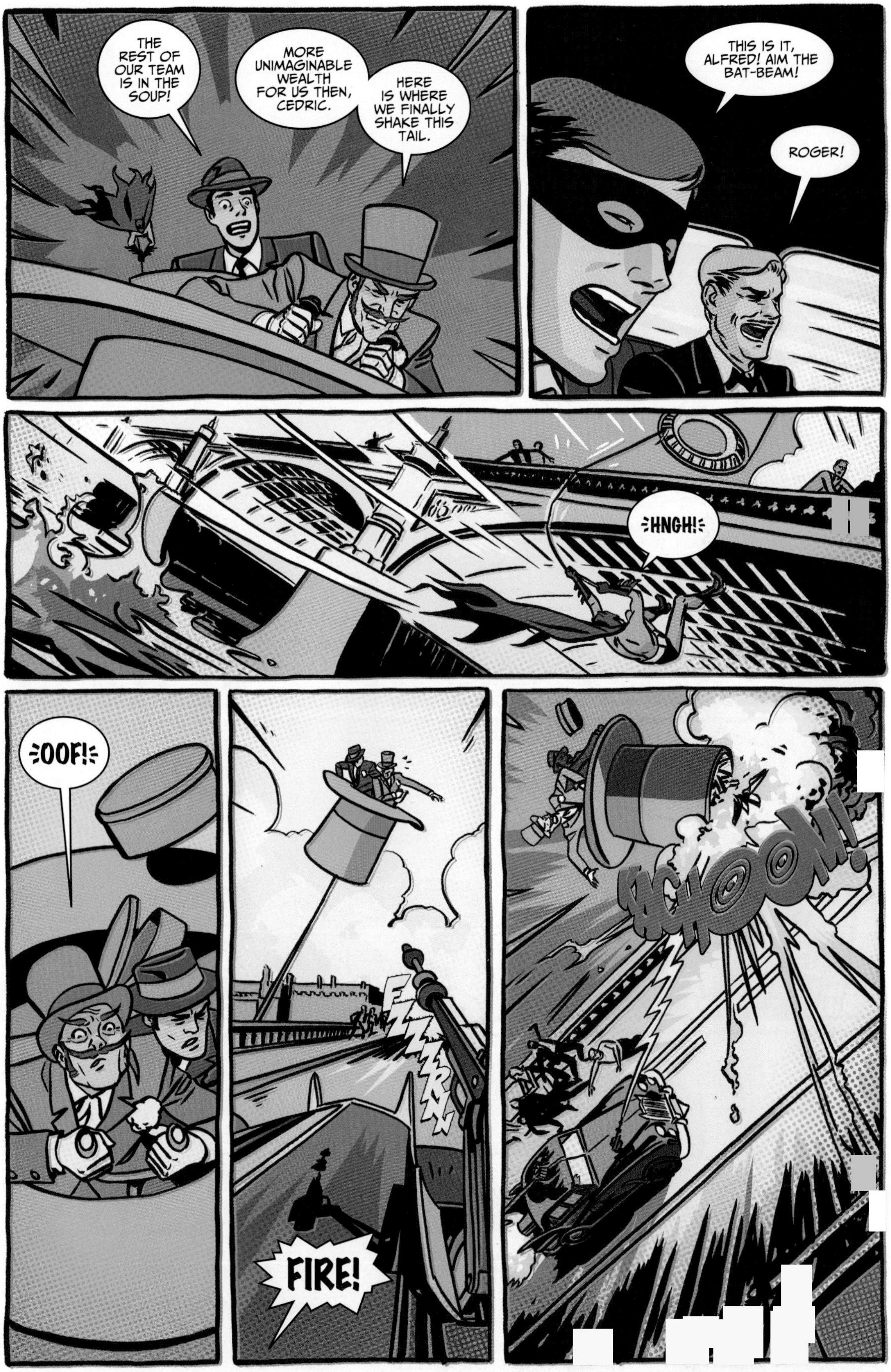
THE REST OF OUR TEAM IS IN THE SOUP!
MORE UNIMAGINABLE WEALTH FOR US THEN, CEDRIC.
HERE IS WHERE WE FINALLY SHAKE THIS TAIL.
THIS IS IT, ALFRED! AIM THE BAT-BEAM!
ROGER!
HNGH!
OOF!
FIRE!

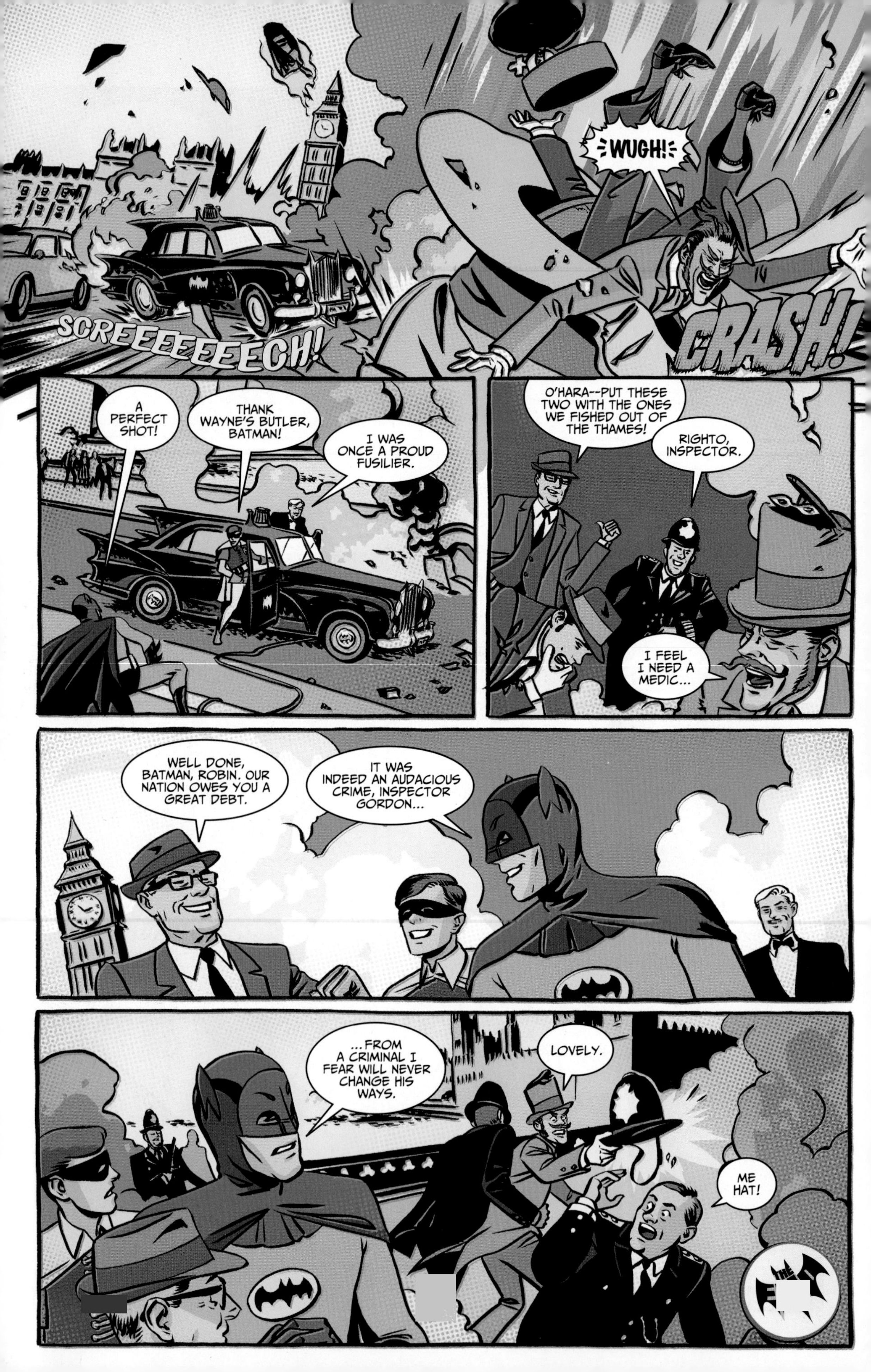
WUGH!
SCREEEEEEEECH!
CRASH!
A PERFECT SHOT!
THANK WAYNE'S BUTLER, BATMAN!
I WAS ONCE A PROUD FUSILIER.
O'HARA--PUT THESE TWO WITH THE ONES WE FISHED OUT OF THE THAMES!
RIGHTO, INSPECTOR.
I FEEL I NEED A MEDIC...
WELL DONE, BATMAN, ROBIN. OUR NATION OWES YOU A GREAT DEBT.
IT WAS INDEED AN AUDACIOUS CRIME, INSPECTOR GORDON...
...FROM A CRIMINAL I FEAR WILL NEVER CHANGE HIS WAYS.
LOVELY.
ME HAT!

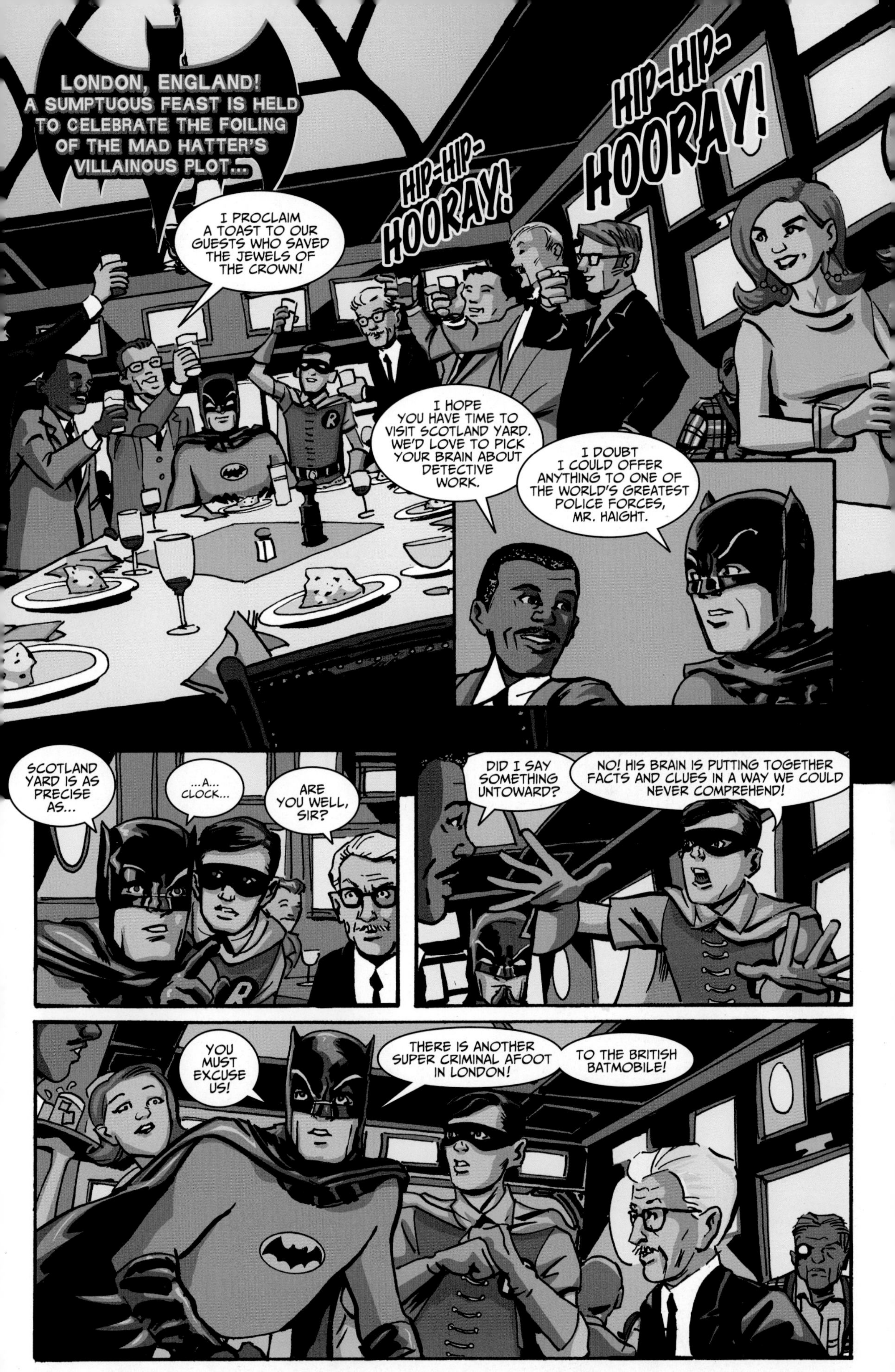
LONDON, ENGLAND! A SUMPTUOUS FEAST IS HELD TO CELEBRATE THE FOILING OF THE MAD HATTER'S VILLAINOUS PLOT...
I PROCLAIM A TOAST TO OUR GUESTS WHO SAVED THE JEWELS OF THE CROWN!
HIP-HIP-HOORAY!
HIP-HIP-HOORAY!
I HOPE YOU HAVE TIME TO VISIT SCOTLAND YARD. WE'D LOVE TO PICK YOUR BRAIN ABOUT DETECTIVE WORK.
I DOUBT I COULD OFFER ANYTHING TO ONE OF THE WORLD'S GREATEST POLICE FORCES, MR. HAIGHT.
SCOTLAND YARD IS AS PRECISE AS...
...A... CLOCK...
ARE YOU WELL, SIR?
DID I SAY SOMETHING UNTOWARD?
NO! HIS BRAIN IS PUTTING TOGETHER FACTS AND CLUES IN A WAY WE COULD NEVER COMPREHEND!
YOU MUST EXCUSE US!
THERE IS ANOTHER SUPER CRIMINAL AFOOT IN LONDON!
TO THE BRITISH BATMOBILE!

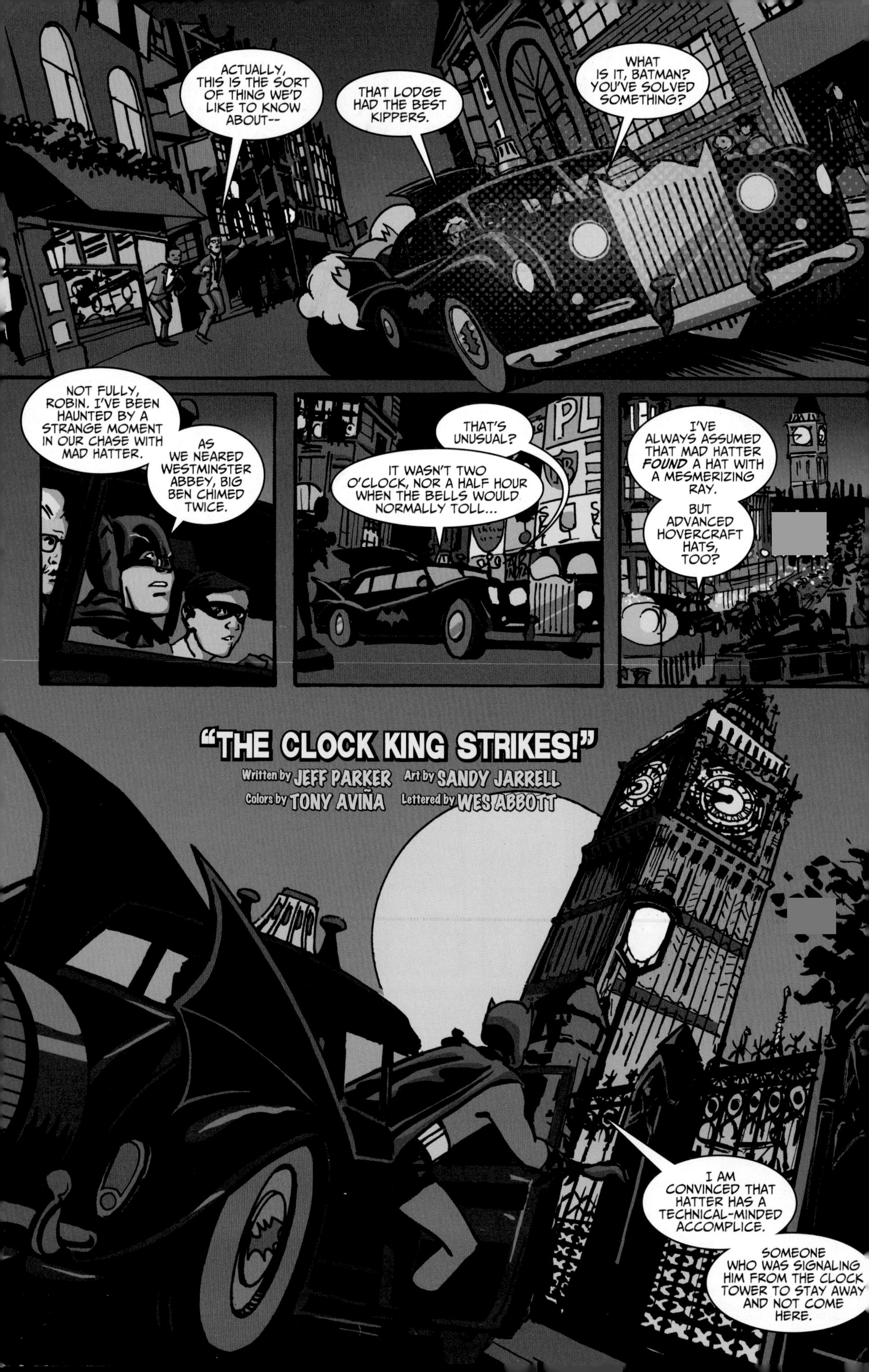
ACTUALLY, THIS IS THE SORT OF THING WE'D LIKE TO KNOW ABOUT--
THAT LODGE HAD THE BEST KIPPERS.
WHAT IS IT, BATMAN? YOU'VE SOLVED SOMETHING?
NOT FULLY, ROBIN. I'VE BEEN HAUNTED BY A STRANGE MOMENT IN OUR CHASE WITH MAD HATTER.
AS WE NEARED WESTMINSTER ABBEY, BIG BEN CHIMED TWICE.
THAT'S UNUSUAL?
IT WASN'T TWO O'CLOCK, NOR A HALF HOUR WHEN THE BELLS WOULD NORMALLY TOLL...
I'VE ALWAYS ASSUMED THAT MAD HATTER *FOUND* A HAT WITH A MESMERIZING RAY.
BUT ADVANCED HOVERCRAFT HATS, TOO?
"THE CLOCK KING STRIKES!"
Written by JEFF PARKER Art by SANDY JARRELL
Colors by TONY AVIÑA Lettered by WES ABBOTT
I AM CONVINCED THAT HATTER HAS A TECHNICAL-MINDED ACCOMPLICE.
SOMEONE WHO WAS SIGNALING HIM FROM THE CLOCK TOWER TO STAY AWAY AND NOT COME HERE.

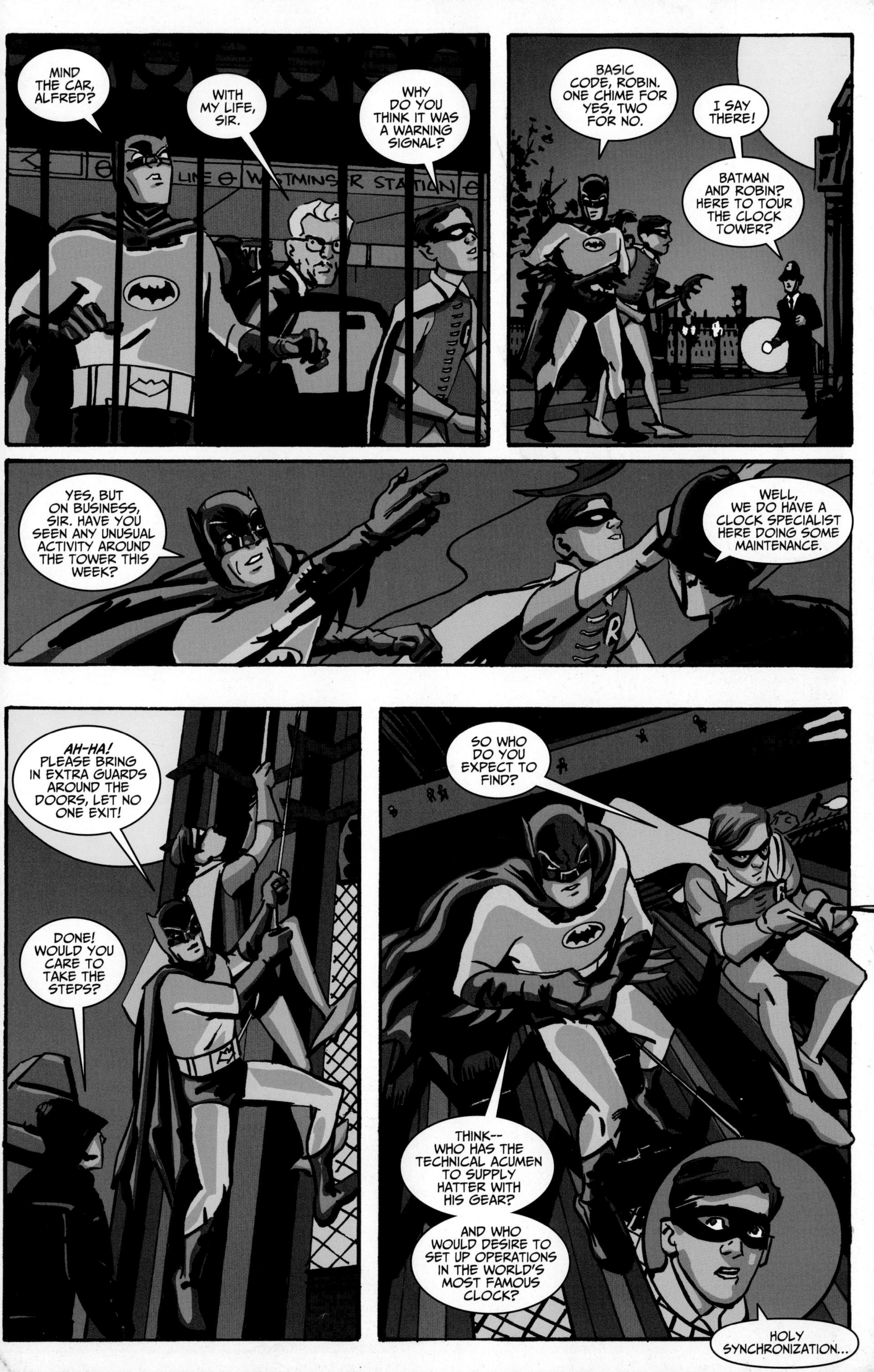
MIND THE CAR, ALFRED?
WITH MY LIFE, SIR.
WHY DO YOU THINK IT WAS A WARNING SIGNAL?
WESTMINSTER STATION
BASIC CODE, ROBIN. ONE CHIME FOR YES, TWO FOR NO.
I SAY THERE!
BATMAN AND ROBIN? HERE TO TOUR THE CLOCK TOWER?
YES, BUT ON BUSINESS, SIR. HAVE YOU SEEN ANY UNUSUAL ACTIVITY AROUND THE TOWER THIS WEEK?
WELL, WE DO HAVE A CLOCK SPECIALIST HERE DOING SOME MAINTENANCE.
AH-HA! PLEASE BRING IN EXTRA GUARDS AROUND THE DOORS, LET NO ONE EXIT!
DONE! WOULD YOU CARE TO TAKE THE STEPS?
SO WHO DO YOU EXPECT TO FIND?
THINK-- WHO HAS THE TECHNICAL ACUMEN TO SUPPLY HATTER WITH HIS GEAR?
AND WHO WOULD DESIRE TO SET UP OPERATIONS IN THE WORLD'S MOST FAMOUS CLOCK?
HOLY SYNCHRONIZATION...

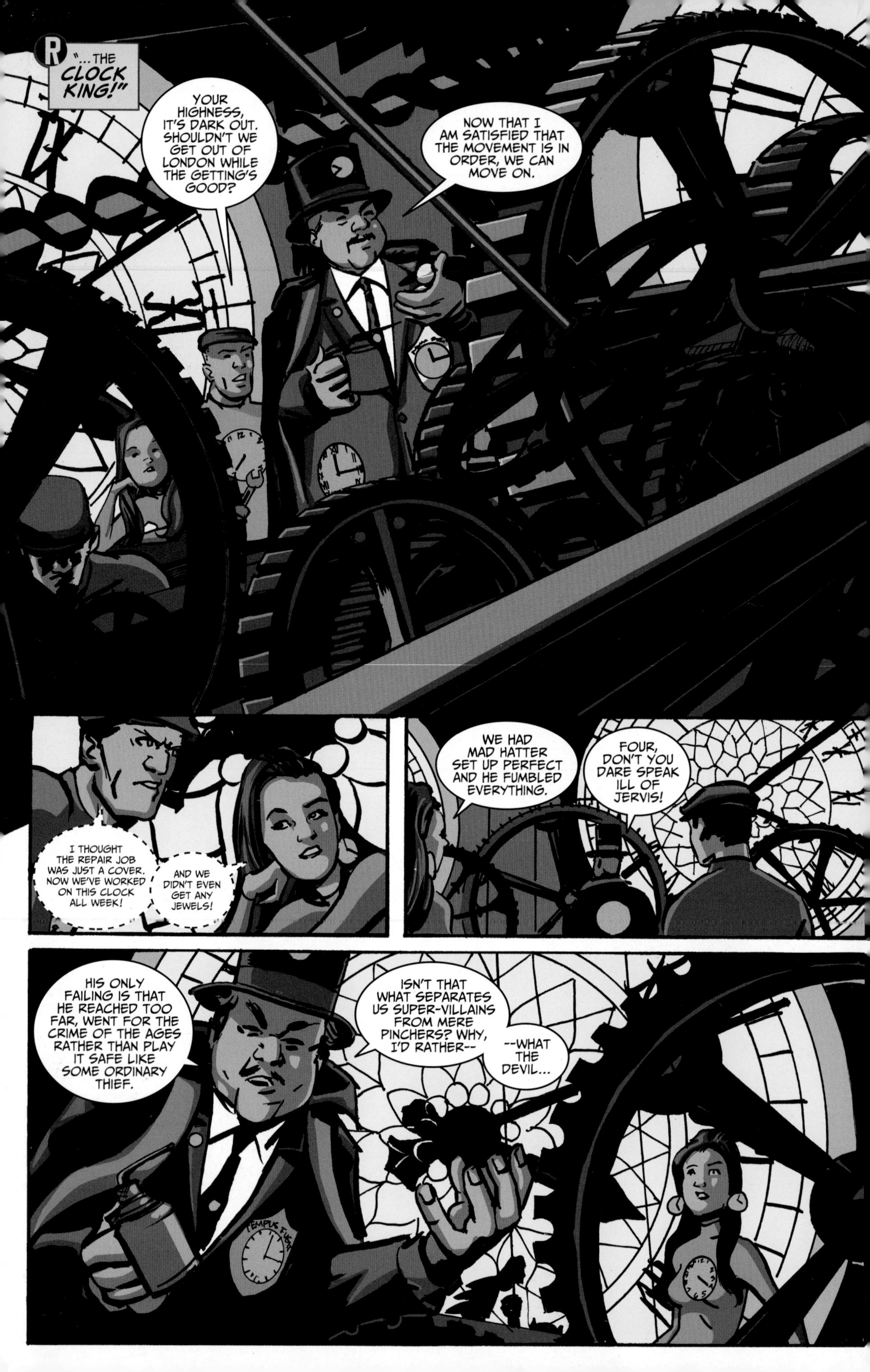

"...THE CLOCK KING!"
YOUR HIGHNESS, IT'S DARK OUT. SHOULDN'T WE GET OUT OF LONDON WHILE THE GETTING'S GOOD?
NOW THAT I AM SATISFIED THAT THE MOVEMENT IS IN ORDER, WE CAN MOVE ON.
I THOUGHT THE REPAIR JOB WAS JUST A COVER. NOW WE'VE WORKED ON THIS CLOCK ALL WEEK!
AND WE DIDN'T EVEN GET ANY JEWELS!
WE HAD MAD HATTER SET UP PERFECT AND HE FUMBLED EVERYTHING.
FOUR, DON'T YOU DARE SPEAK ILL OF JERVIS!
HIS ONLY FAILING IS THAT HE REACHED TOO FAR, WENT FOR THE CRIME OF THE AGES RATHER THAN PLAY IT SAFE LIKE SOME ORDINARY THIEF.
ISN'T THAT WHAT SEPARATES US SUPER-VILLAINS FROM MERE PINCHERS? WHY, I'D RATHER--
--WHAT THE DEVIL...

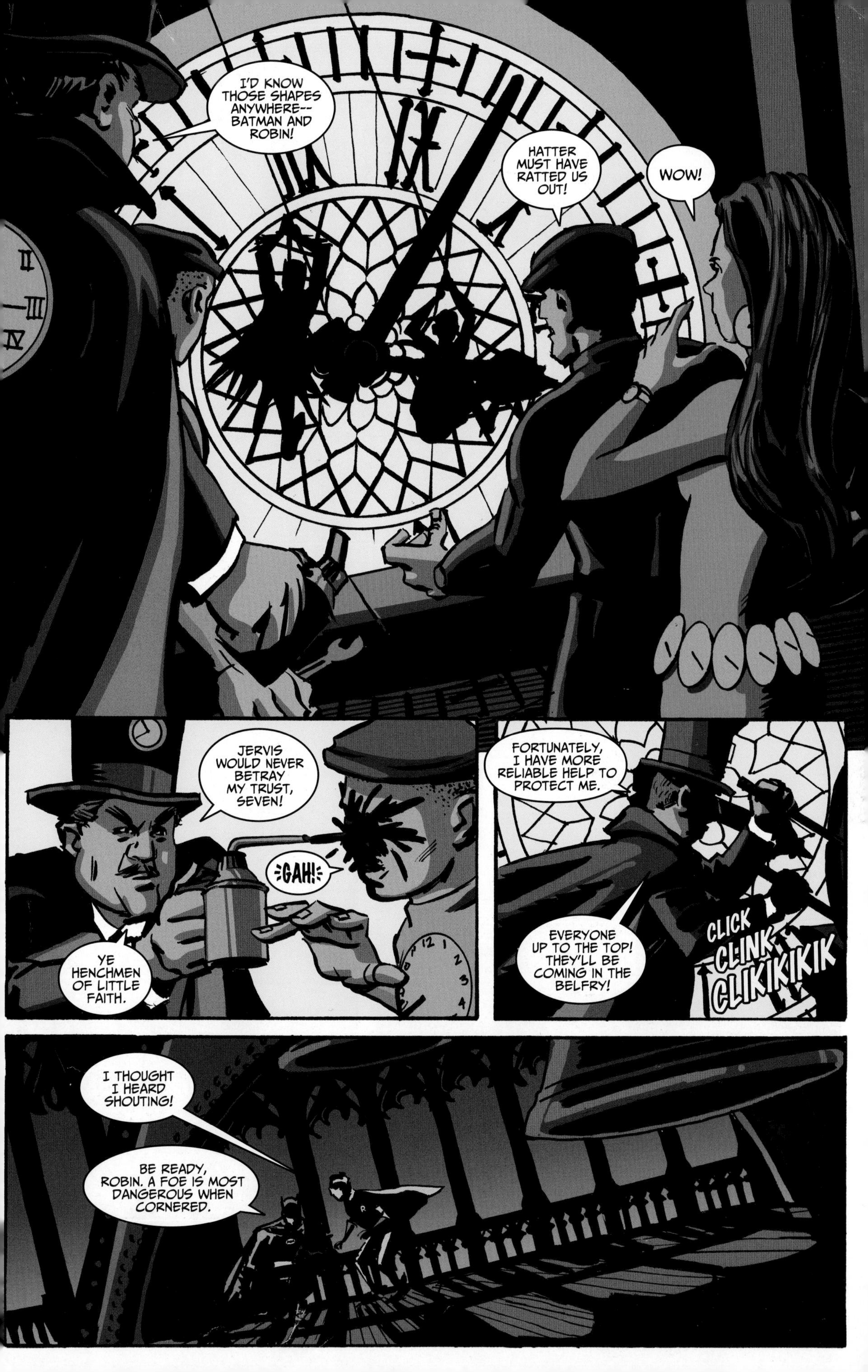
I'D KNOW THOSE SHAPES ANYWHERE-- BATMAN AND ROBIN!
HATTER MUST HAVE RATTED US OUT!
WOW!
JERVIS WOULD NEVER BETRAY MY TRUST, SEVEN!
GAH!
YE HENCHMEN OF LITTLE FAITH.
FORTUNATELY, I HAVE MORE RELIABLE HELP TO PROTECT ME.
EVERYONE UP TO THE TOP! THEY'LL BE COMING IN THE BELFRY!
CLICK
CL-INK
CLIKIKIKIK
I THOUGHT I HEARD SHOUTING!
BE READY, ROBIN. A FOE IS MOST DANGEROUS WHEN CORNERED.

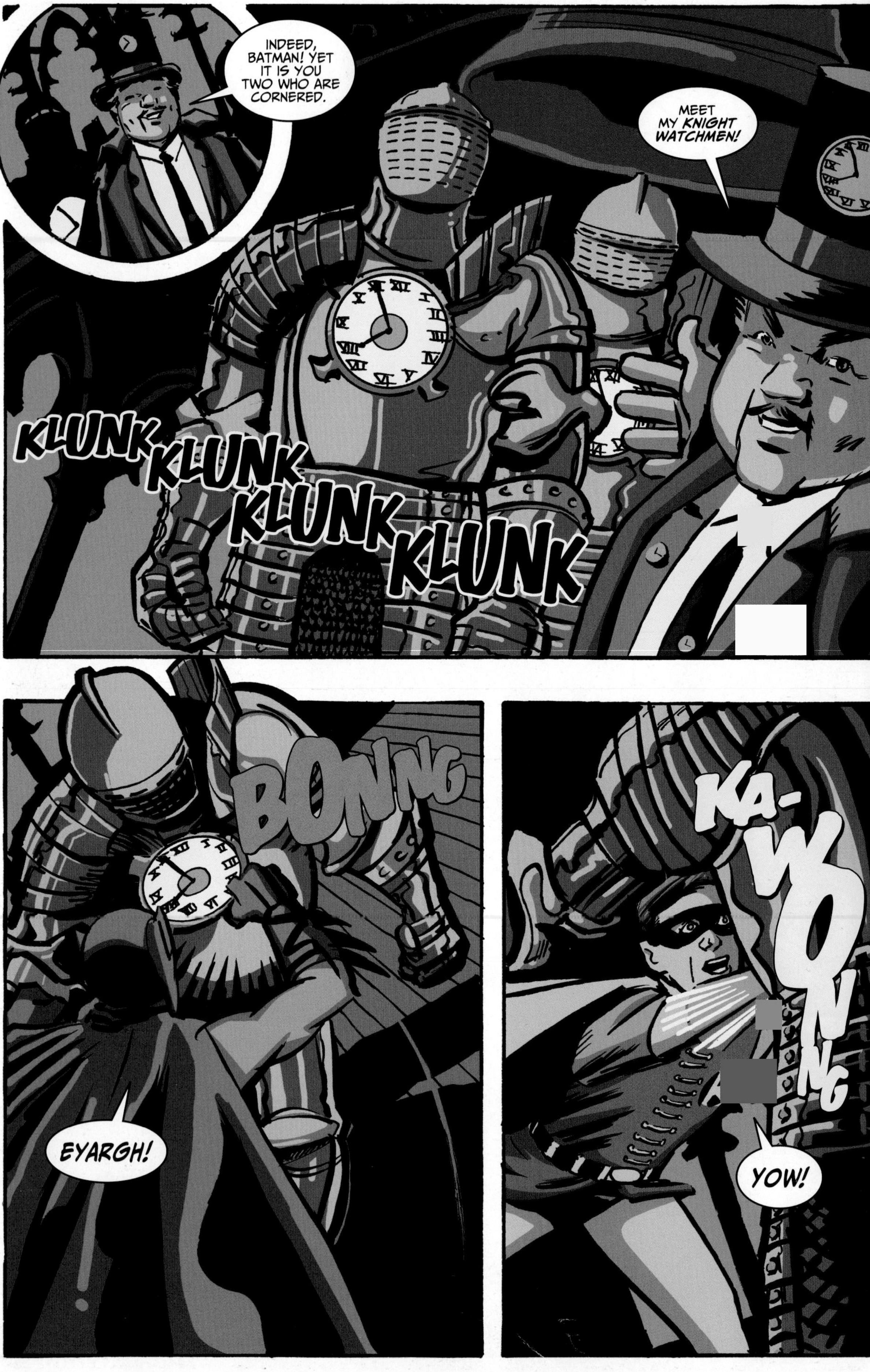
INDEED, BATMAN! YET IT IS YOU TWO WHO ARE CORNERED.
MEET MY KNIGHT WATCHMEN!
KLUNK KLUNK KLUNK KLUNK
BONNG
EYARGH!
KA-WONNG
YOW!

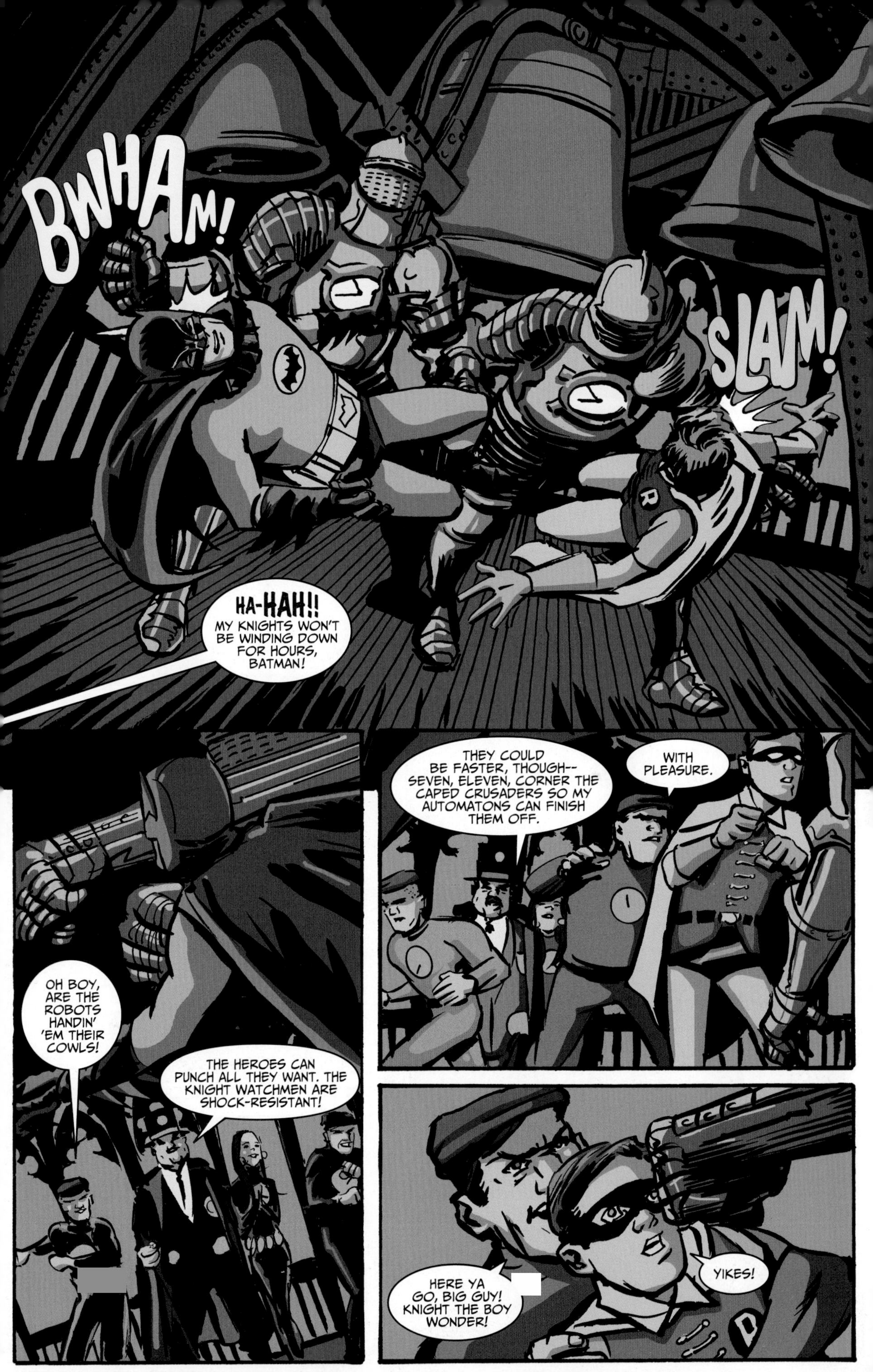
BWHAM!
SLAM!
HA-HAH!! MY KNIGHTS WON'T BE WINDING DOWN FOR HOURS, BATMAN!
OH BOY, ARE THE ROBOTS HANDIN' 'EM THEIR COWLS!
THE HEROES CAN PUNCH ALL THEY WANT. THE KNIGHT WATCHMEN ARE SHOCK-RESISTANT!
THEY COULD BE FASTER, THOUGH-- SEVEN, ELEVEN, CORNER THE CAPED CRUSADERS SO MY AUTOMATONS CAN FINISH THEM OFF.
WITH PLEASURE.
HERE YA GO, BIG GUY! KNIGHT THE BOY WONDER!
YIKES!

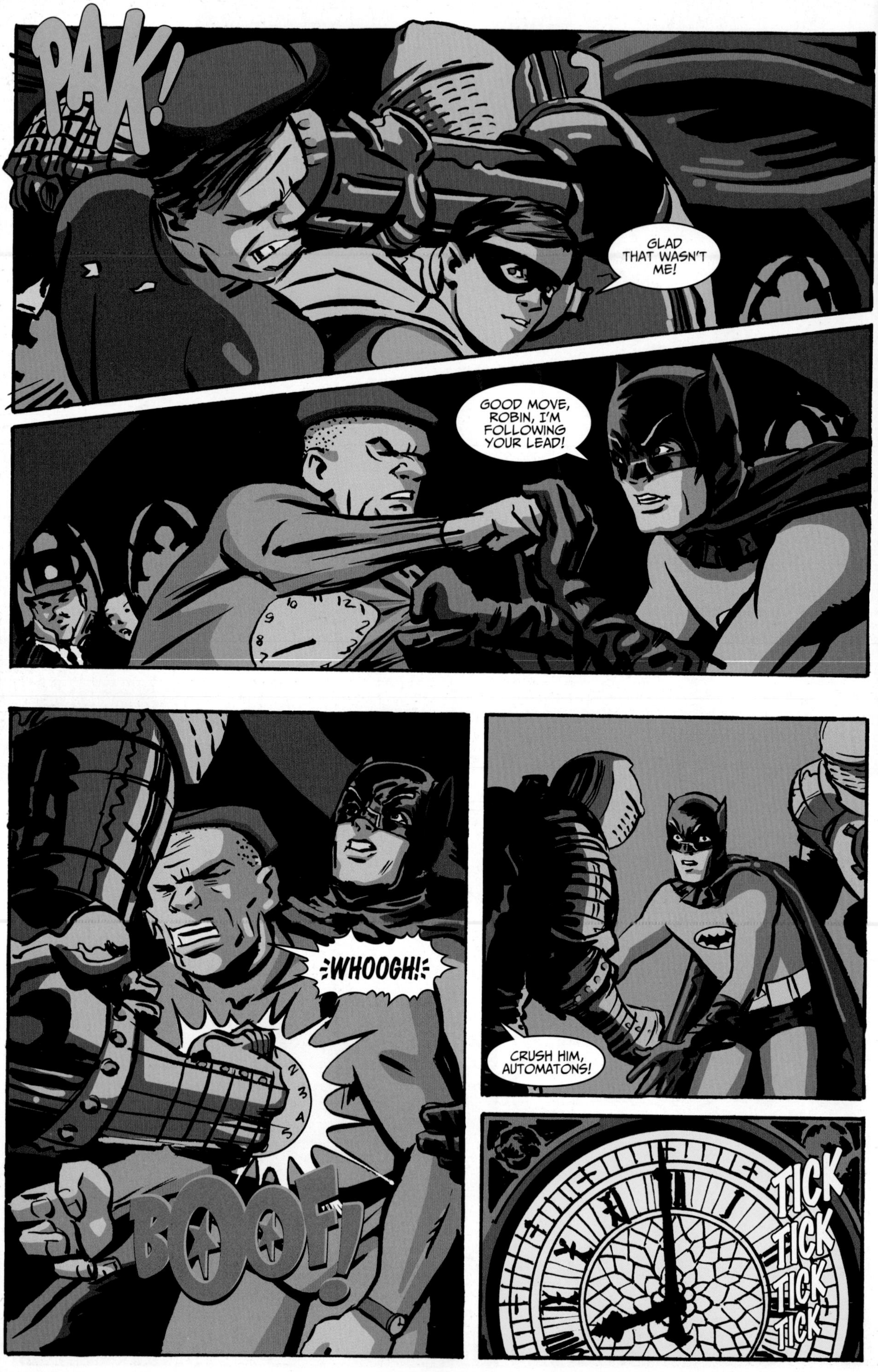
PAK!
GLAD THAT WASN'T ME!
GOOD MOVE, ROBIN, I'M FOLLOWING YOUR LEAD!
WHOOGH!
BOOF!
CRUSH HIM, AUTOMATONS!
TICK
TICK
TICK
TICK

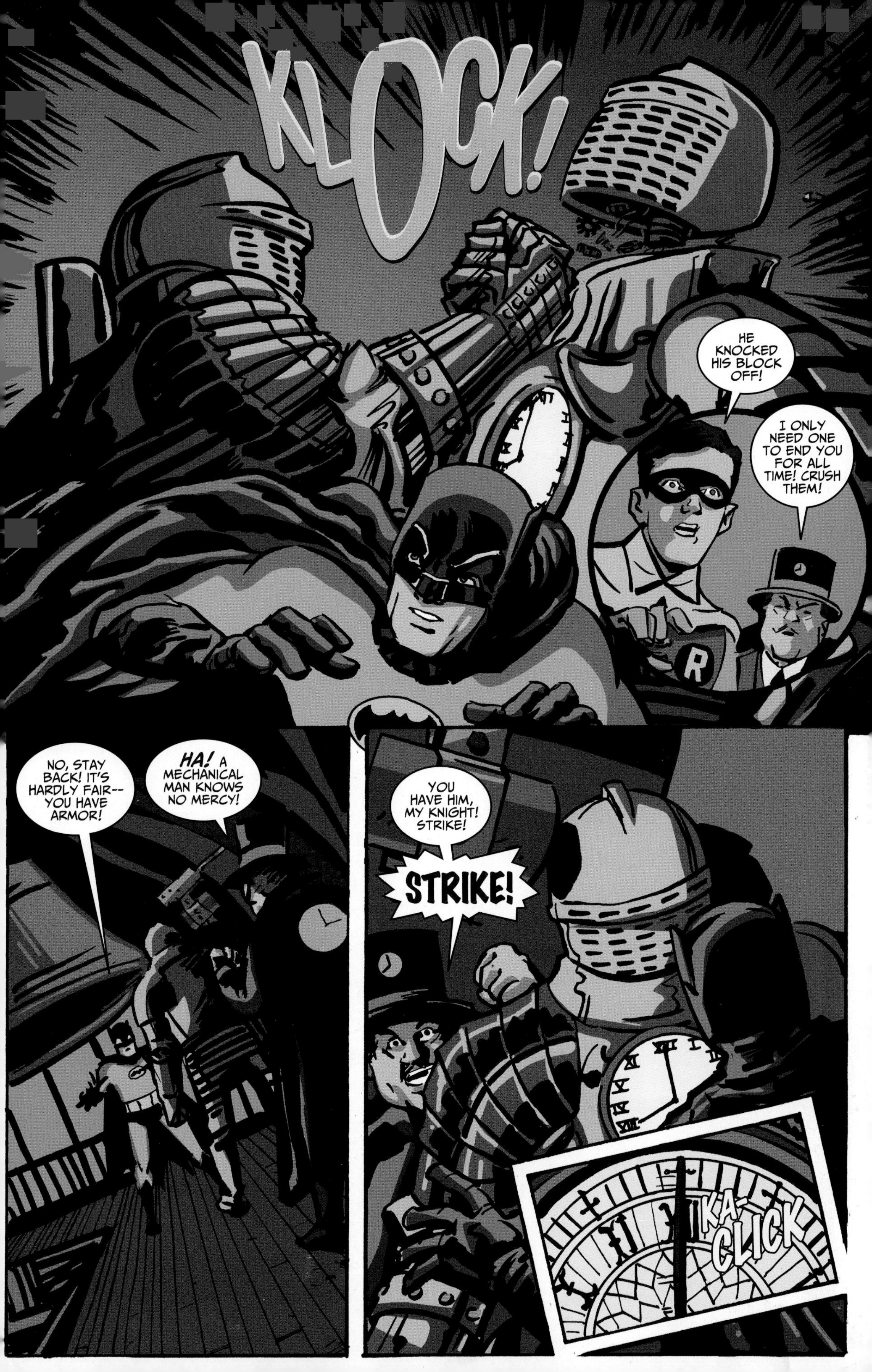
KLOCK!
HE KNOCKED HIS BLOCK OFF!
I ONLY NEED ONE TO END YOU FOR ALL TIME! CRUSH THEM!
NO, STAY BACK! IT'S HARDLY FAIR-- YOU HAVE ARMOR!
HA! A MECHANICAL MAN KNOWS NO MERCY!
YOU HAVE HIM, MY KNIGHT! STRIKE!
STRIKE!
KA-CLICK

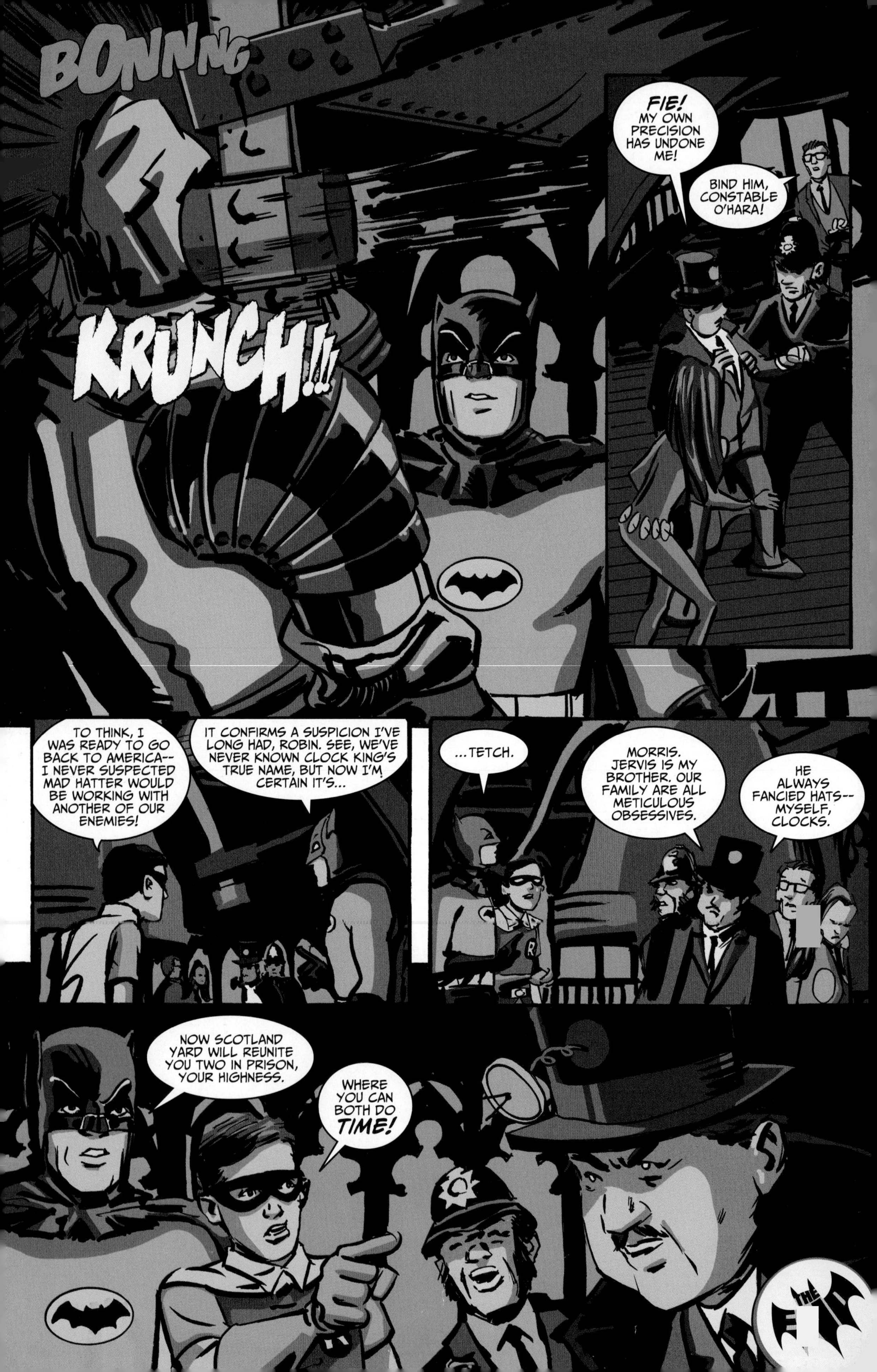
BONNNG
KRUNCH!!!
FIE! MY OWN PRECISION HAS UNDONE ME!
BIND HIM, CONSTABLE O'HARA!
TO THINK, I WAS READY TO GO BACK TO AMERICA-- I NEVER SUSPECTED MAD HATTER WOULD BE WORKING WITH ANOTHER OF OUR ENEMIES!
IT CONFIRMS A SUSPICION I'VE LONG HAD, ROBIN. SEE, WE'VE NEVER KNOWN CLOCK KING'S TRUE NAME, BUT NOW I'M CERTAIN IT'S...
...TETCH.
MORRIS. JERVIS IS MY BROTHER. OUR FAMILY ARE ALL METICULOUS OBSESSIVES.
HE ALWAYS FANCIED HATS-- MYSELF, CLOCKS.
NOW SCOTLAND YARD WILL REUNITE YOU TWO IN PRISON, YOUR HIGHNESS.
WHERE YOU CAN BOTH DO TIME!
THE END

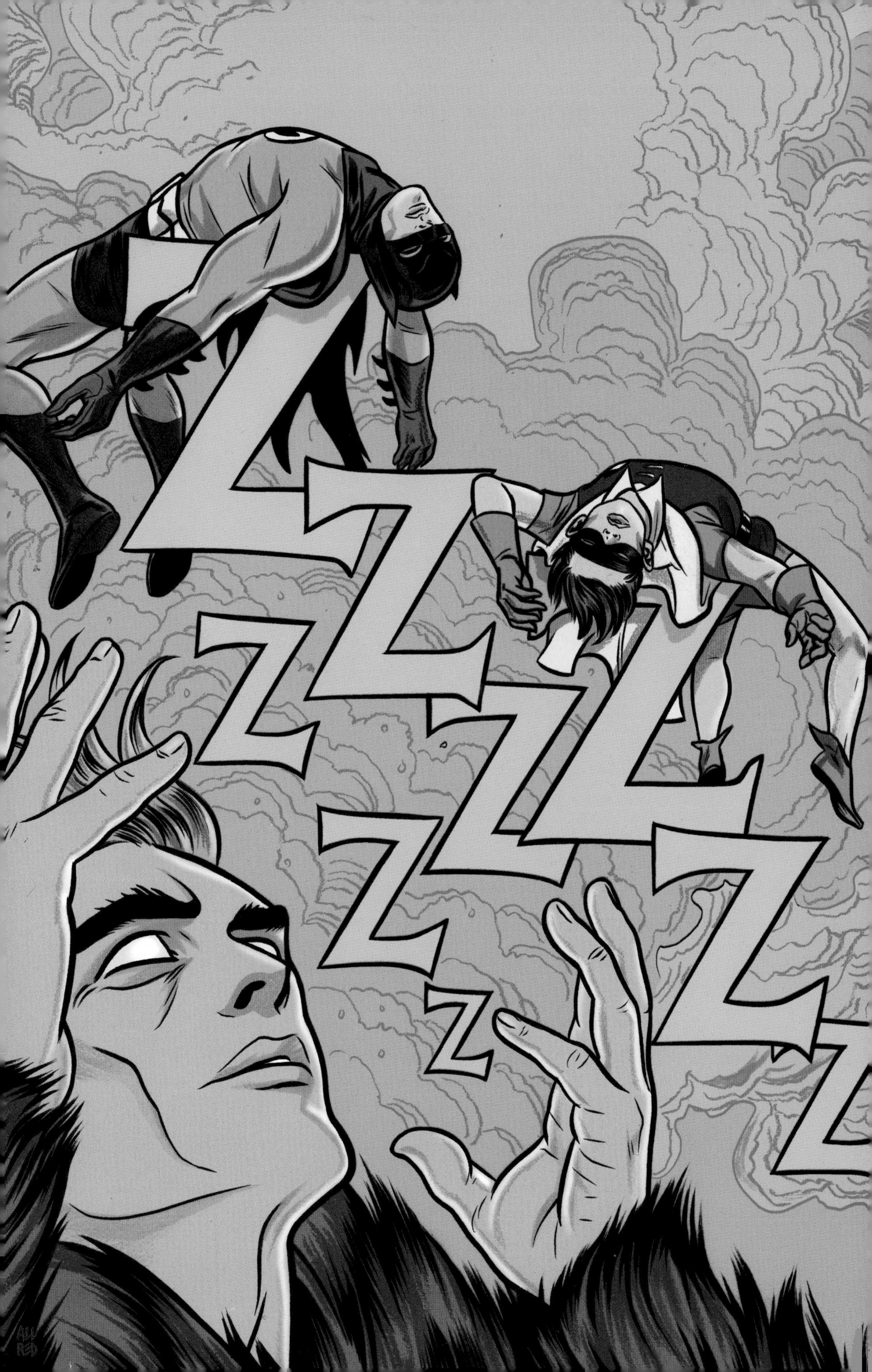
ZZZZZZZZZ

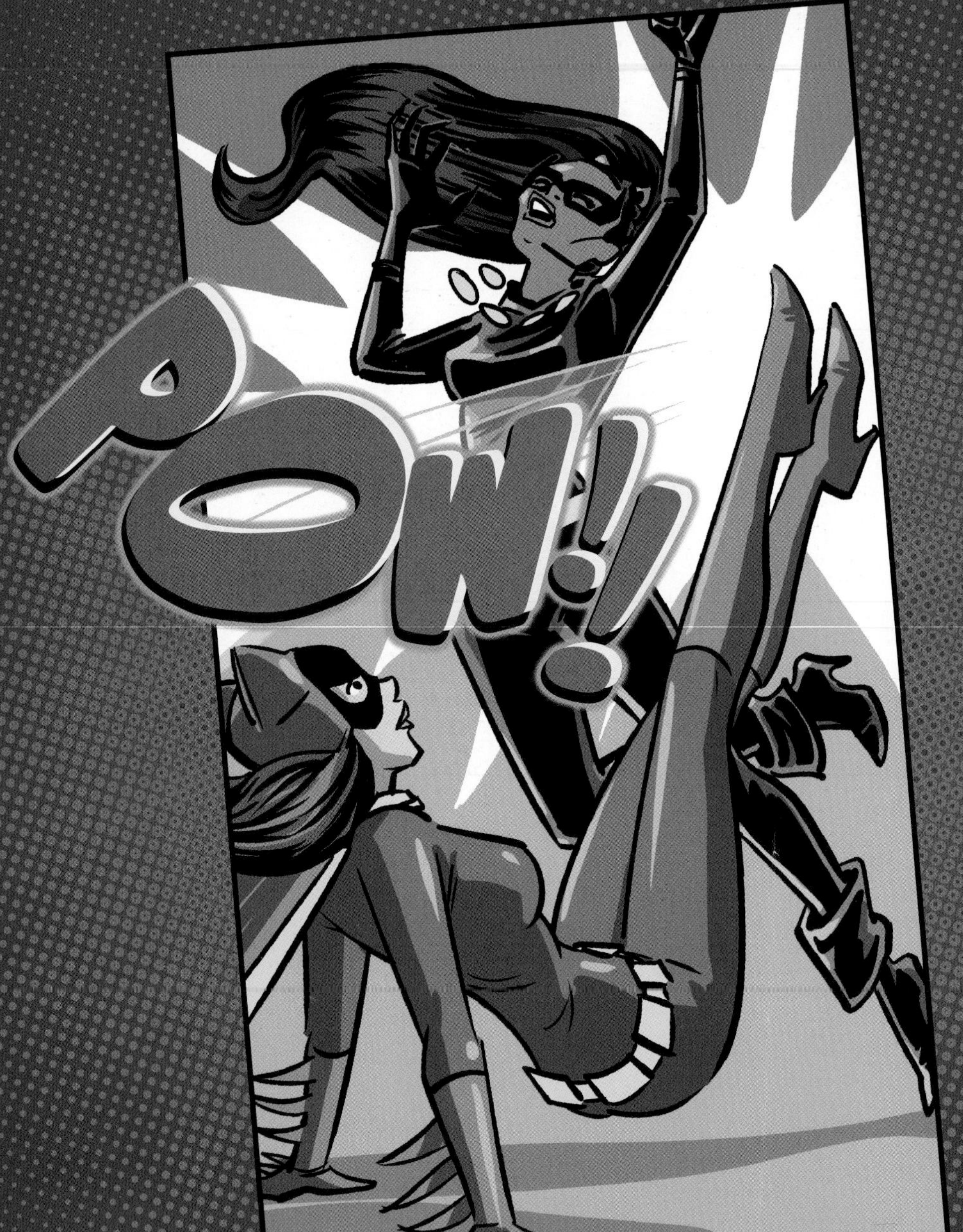
POW!!

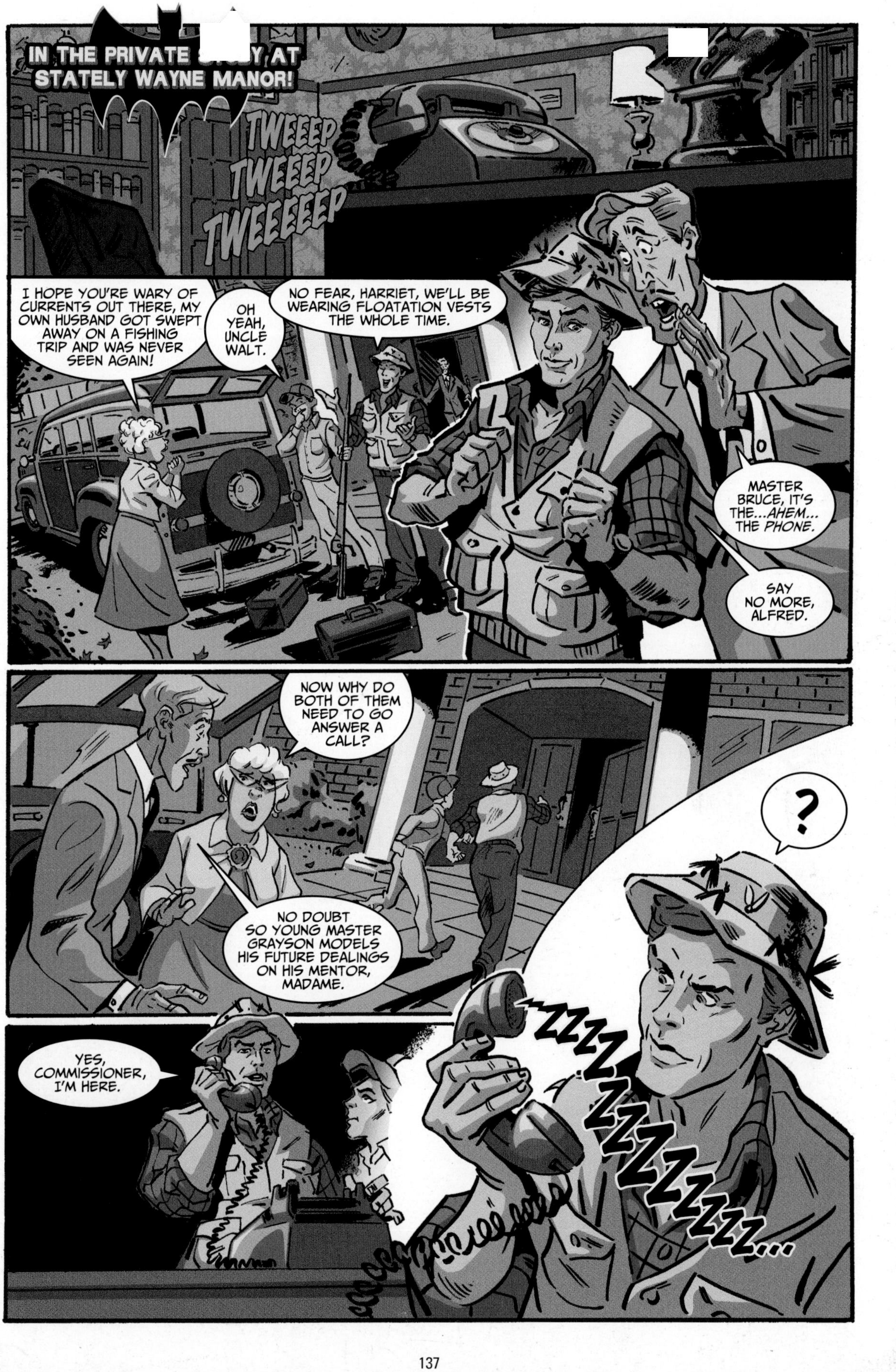
IN THE PRIVATE AT STATELY WAYNE MANOR!
TWEEEP
TWEEEP
TWEEEEEP
I HOPE YOU'RE WARY OF CURRENTS OUT THERE, MY OWN HUSBAND GOT SWEPT AWAY ON A FISHING TRIP AND WAS NEVER SEEN AGAIN!
OH YEAH, UNCLE WALT.
NO FEAR, HARRIET, WE'LL BE WEARING FLOATATION VESTS THE WHOLE TIME.
MASTER BRUCE, IT'S THE...*AHEM*... THE *PHONE*.
SAY NO MORE, ALFRED.
NOW WHY DO BOTH OF THEM NEED TO GO ANSWER A CALL?
NO DOUBT SO YOUNG MASTER GRAYSON MODELS HIS FUTURE DEALINGS ON HIS MENTOR, MADAME.
?
YES, COMMISSIONER, I'M HERE.
ZZZZZZZZZZZZZ...

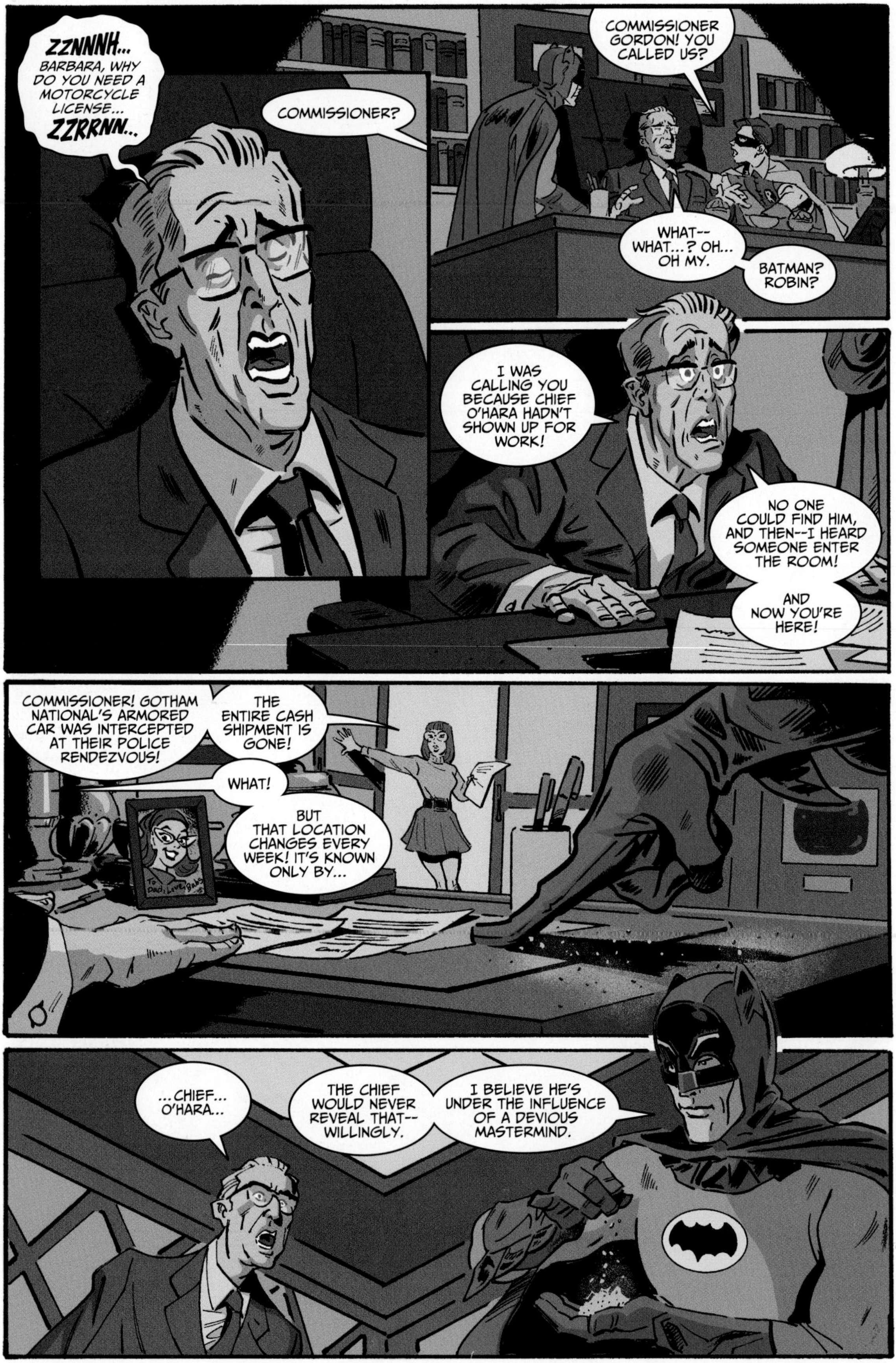
ZZNNNH... BARBARA, WHY DO YOU NEED A MOTORCYCLE LICENSE... ZZRRNN...
COMMISSIONER?
COMMISSIONER GORDON! YOU CALLED US?
WHAT-- WHAT...? OH... OH MY.
BATMAN? ROBIN?
I WAS CALLING YOU BECAUSE CHIEF O'HARA HADN'T SHOWN UP FOR WORK!
NO ONE COULD FIND HIM, AND THEN--I HEARD SOMEONE ENTER THE ROOM!
AND NOW YOU'RE HERE!
COMMISSIONER! GOTHAM NATIONAL'S ARMORED CAR WAS INTERCEPTED AT THEIR POLICE RENDEZVOUS!
THE ENTIRE CASH SHIPMENT IS GONE!
WHAT!
BUT THAT LOCATION CHANGES EVERY WEEK! IT'S KNOWN ONLY BY...
...CHIEF... O'HARA...
THE CHIEF WOULD NEVER REVEAL THAT--WILLINGLY.
I BELIEVE HE'S UNDER THE INFLUENCE OF A DEVIOUS MASTERMIND.

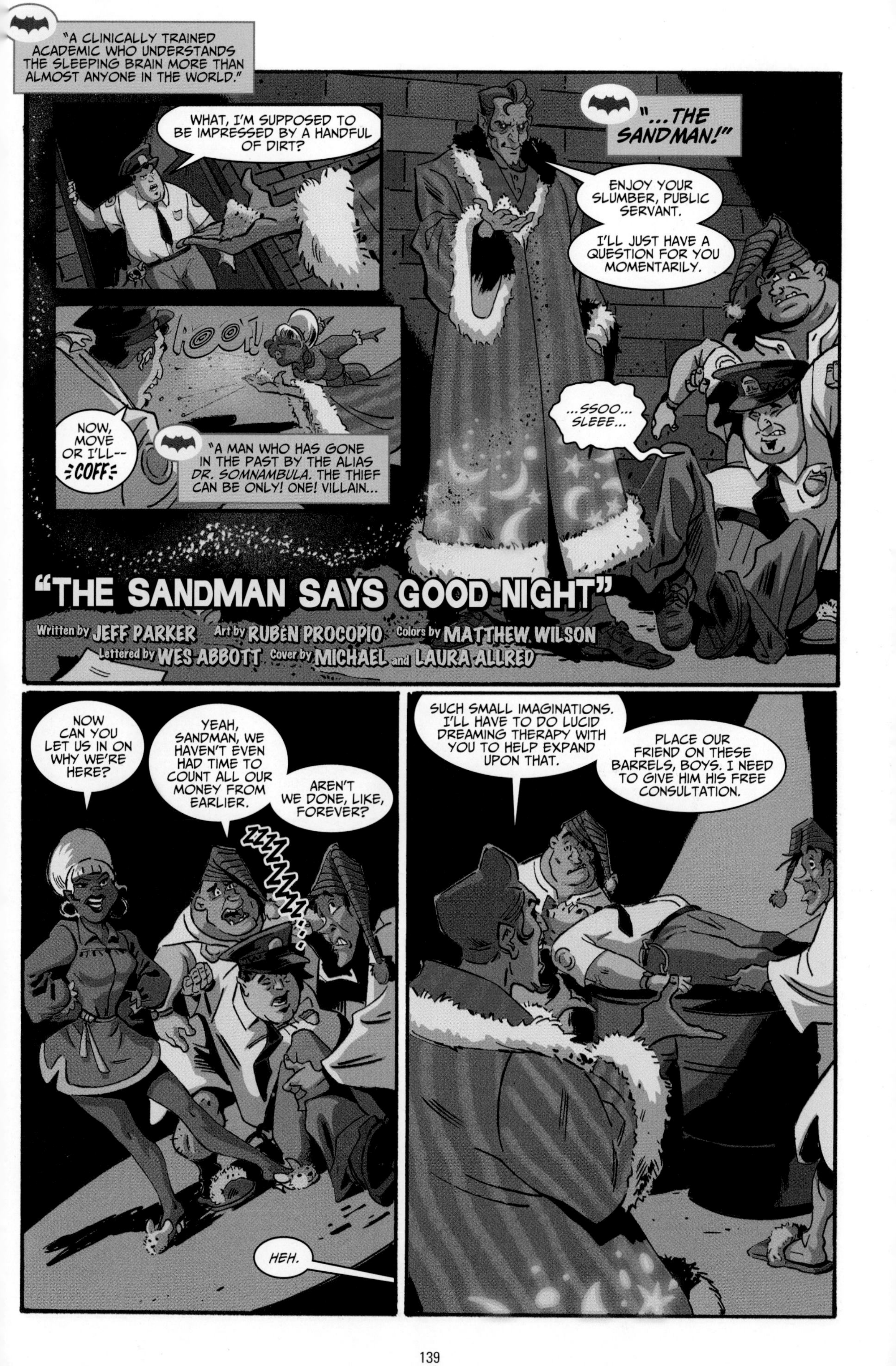
"A CLINICALLY TRAINED ACADEMIC WHO UNDERSTANDS THE SLEEPING BRAIN MORE THAN ALMOST ANYONE IN THE WORLD."
WHAT, I'M SUPPOSED TO BE IMPRESSED BY A HANDFUL OF DIRT?
POOF!
NOW, MOVE OR I'LL--
COFF
"A MAN WHO HAS GONE IN THE PAST BY THE ALIAS DR. SOMNAMBULA. THE THIEF CAN BE ONLY! ONE! VILLAIN...
"...THE SANDMAN!"
ENJOY YOUR SLUMBER, PUBLIC SERVANT.
I'LL JUST HAVE A QUESTION FOR YOU MOMENTARILY.
...SSOO... SLEEE...
"THE SANDMAN SAYS GOOD NIGHT"
Written by JEFF PARKER Art by RUBÉN PROCOPIO Colors by MATTHEW WILSON
Lettered by WES ABBOTT Cover by MICHAEL and LAURA ALLRED
NOW CAN YOU LET US IN ON WHY WE'RE HERE?
YEAH, SANDMAN, WE HAVEN'T EVEN HAD TIME TO COUNT ALL OUR MONEY FROM EARLIER.
AREN'T WE DONE, LIKE, FOREVER?
ZZZZZZ
HEH.
SUCH SMALL IMAGINATIONS. I'LL HAVE TO DO LUCID DREAMING THERAPY WITH YOU TO HELP EXPAND UPON THAT.
PLACE OUR FRIEND ON THESE BARRELS, BOYS. I NEED TO GIVE HIM HIS FREE CONSULTATION.

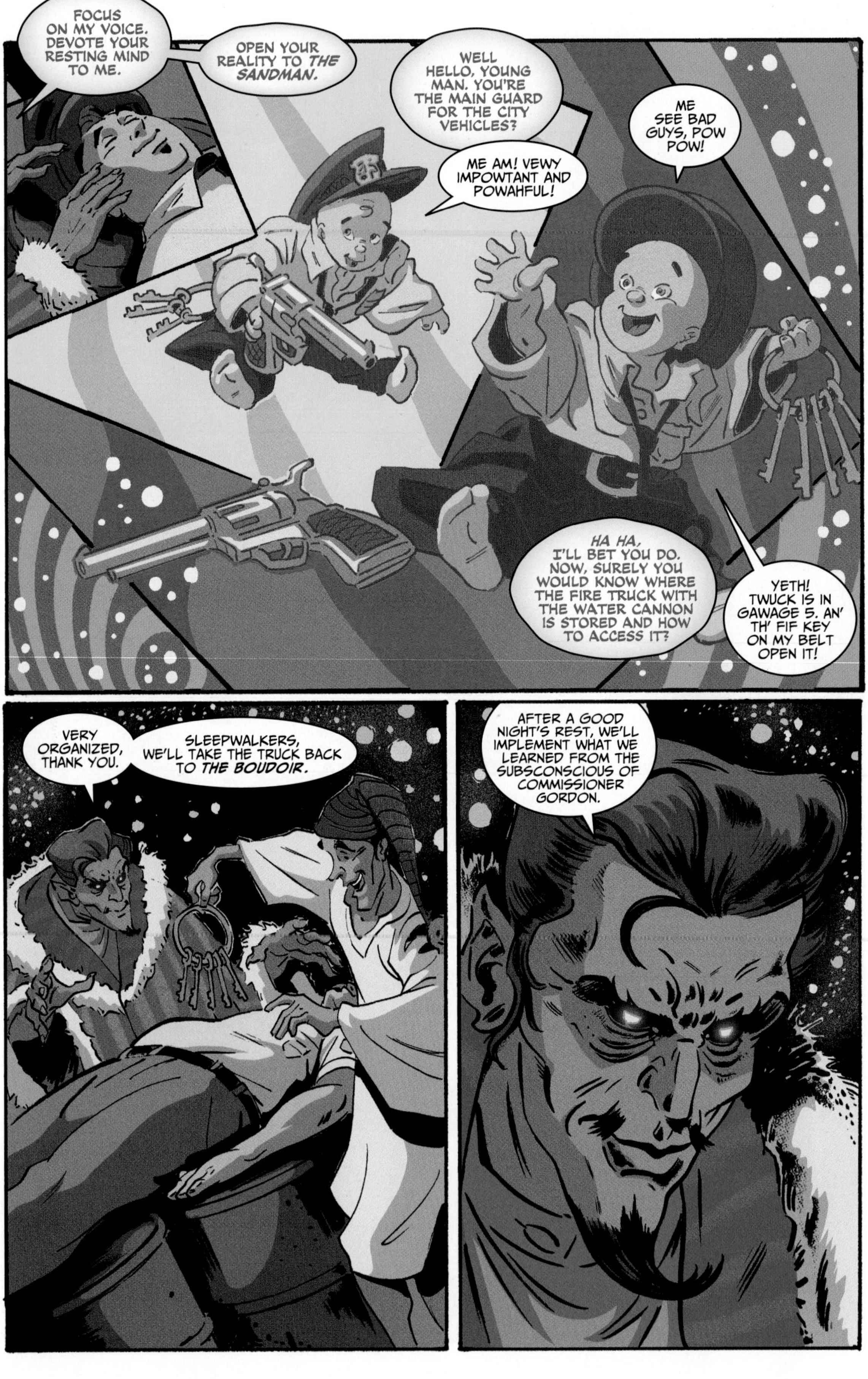
FOCUS ON MY VOICE. DEVOTE YOUR RESTING MIND TO ME.
OPEN YOUR REALITY TO *THE SANDMAN.*
WELL HELLO, YOUNG MAN. YOU'RE THE MAIN GUARD FOR THE CITY VEHICLES?
ME AM! VEWY IMPOWTANT AND POWAHFUL!
ME SEE BAD GUYS, POW POW!
*HA HA,* I'LL BET YOU DO. NOW, SURELY YOU WOULD KNOW WHERE THE FIRE TRUCK WITH THE WATER CANNON IS STORED AND HOW TO ACCESS IT?
YETH! TWUCK IS IN GAWAGE 5. AN' TH' FIF KEY ON MY BELT OPEN IT!
VERY ORGANIZED, THANK YOU.
SLEEPWALKERS, WE'LL TAKE THE TRUCK BACK TO *THE BOUDOIR.*
AFTER A GOOD NIGHT'S REST, WE'LL IMPLEMENT WHAT WE LEARNED FROM THE SUBSCONSCIOUS OF COMMISSIONER GORDON.

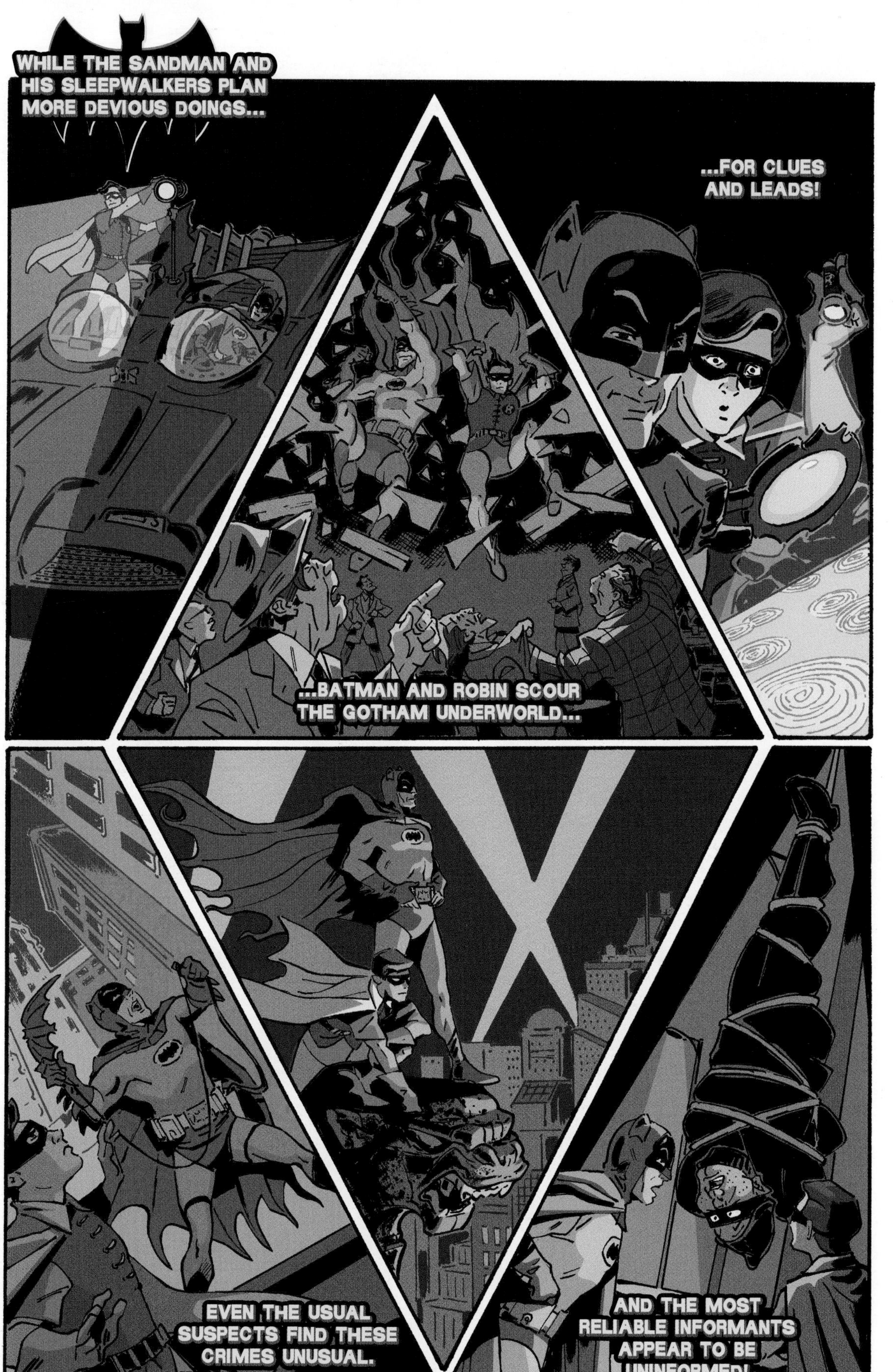
WHILE THE SANDMAN AND HIS SLEEPWALKERS PLAN MORE DEVIOUS DOINGS...
...BATMAN AND ROBIN SCOUR THE GOTHAM UNDERWORLD...
...FOR CLUES AND LEADS!
EVEN THE USUAL SUSPECTS FIND THESE CRIMES UNUSUAL.
AND THE MOST RELIABLE INFORMANTS APPEAR TO BE UNINFORMED!

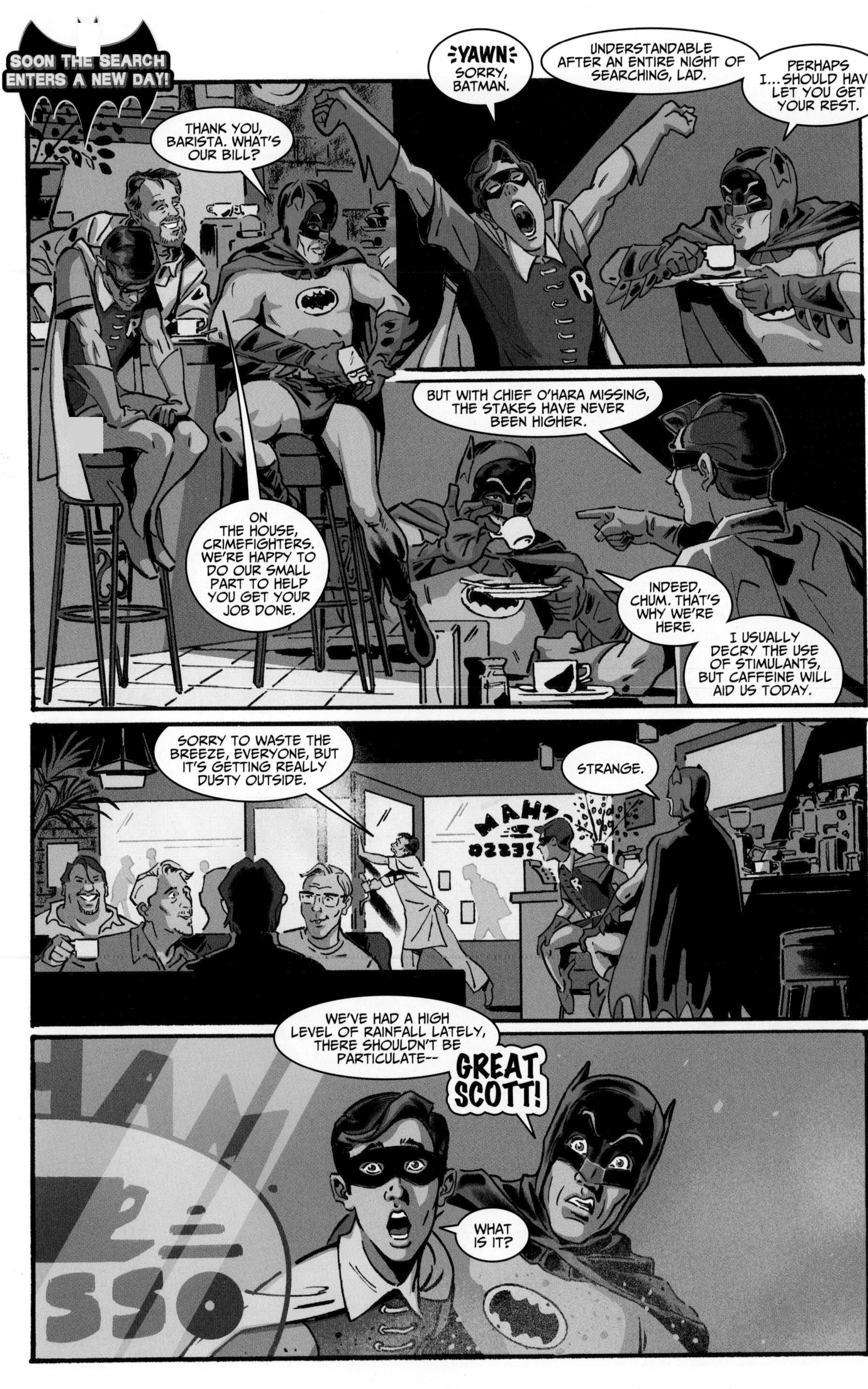
SOON THE SEARCH ENTERS A NEW DAY!
THANK YOU, BARISTA. WHAT'S OUR BILL?
YAWN SORRY, BATMAN.
UNDERSTANDABLE AFTER AN ENTIRE NIGHT OF SEARCHING, LAD.
PERHAPS I...SHOULD HAVE LET YOU GET YOUR REST.
ON THE HOUSE, CRIMEFIGHTERS. WE'RE HAPPY TO DO OUR SMALL PART TO HELP YOU GET YOUR JOB DONE.
BUT WITH CHIEF O'HARA MISSING, THE STAKES HAVE NEVER BEEN HIGHER.
INDEED, CHUM. THAT'S WHY WE'RE HERE.
I USUALLY DECRY THE USE OF STIMULANTS, BUT CAFFEINE WILL AID US TODAY.
SORRY TO WASTE THE BREEZE, EVERYONE, BUT IT'S GETTING REALLY DUSTY OUTSIDE.
STRANGE.
WE'VE HAD A HIGH LEVEL OF RAINFALL LATELY, THERE SHOULDN'T BE PARTICULATE--
GREAT SCOTT!
WHAT IS IT?

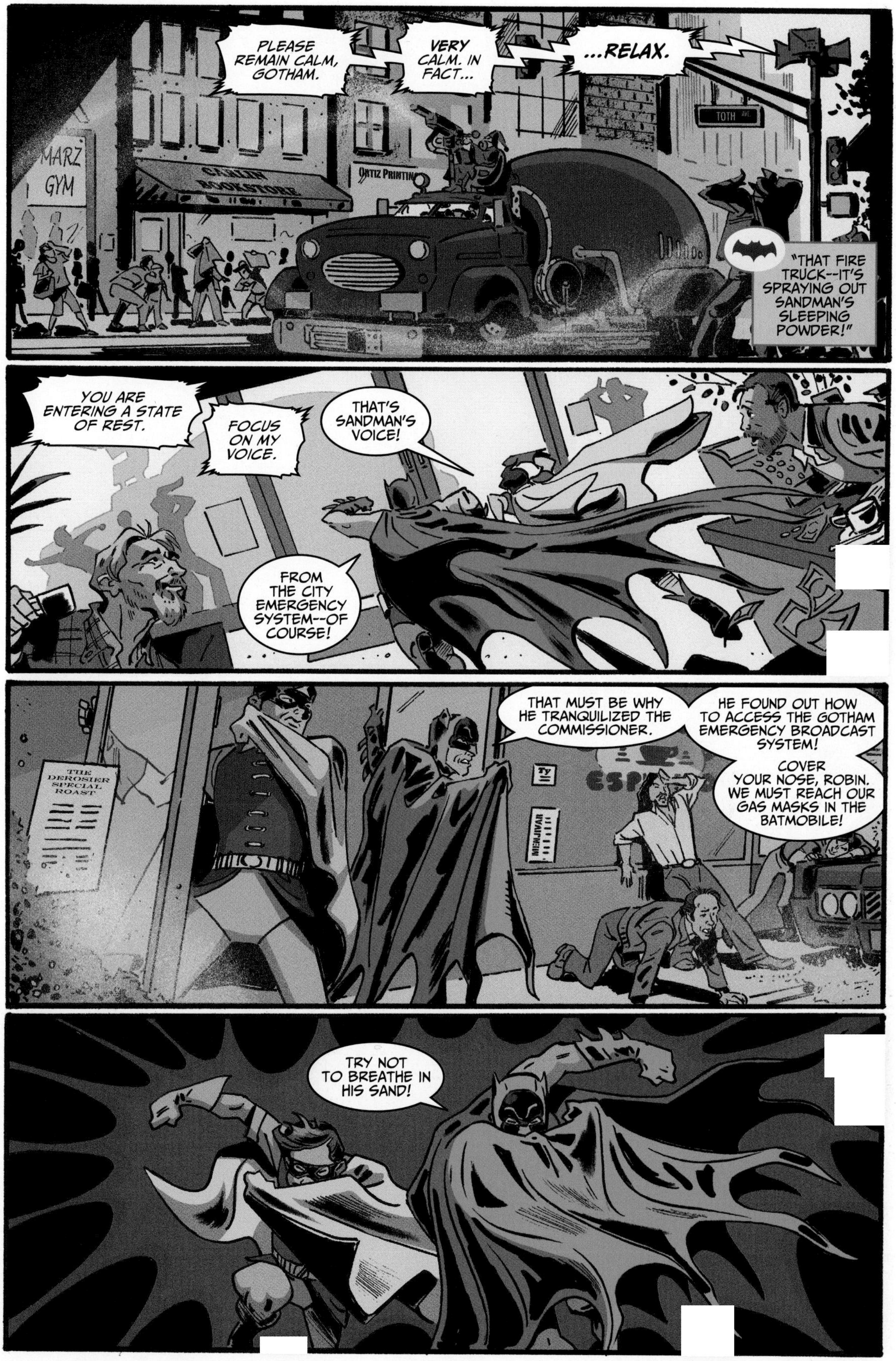
PLEASE REMAIN CALM, GOTHAM.
VERY CALM. IN FACT...
...RELAX.
MARZ GYM
ORTIZ PRINTIN
TOTH AVE
"THAT FIRE TRUCK--IT'S SPRAYING OUT SANDMAN'S SLEEPING POWDER!"
YOU ARE ENTERING A STATE OF REST.
FOCUS ON MY VOICE.
THAT'S SANDMAN'S VOICE!
FROM THE CITY EMERGENCY SYSTEM--OF COURSE!
THE DEROSIER SPECIAL ROAST
THAT MUST BE WHY HE TRANQUILIZED THE COMMISSIONER.
HE FOUND OUT HOW TO ACCESS THE GOTHAM EMERGENCY BROADCAST SYSTEM!
COVER YOUR NOSE, ROBIN. WE MUST REACH OUR GAS MASKS IN THE BATMOBILE!
TRY NOT TO BREATHE IN HIS SAND!

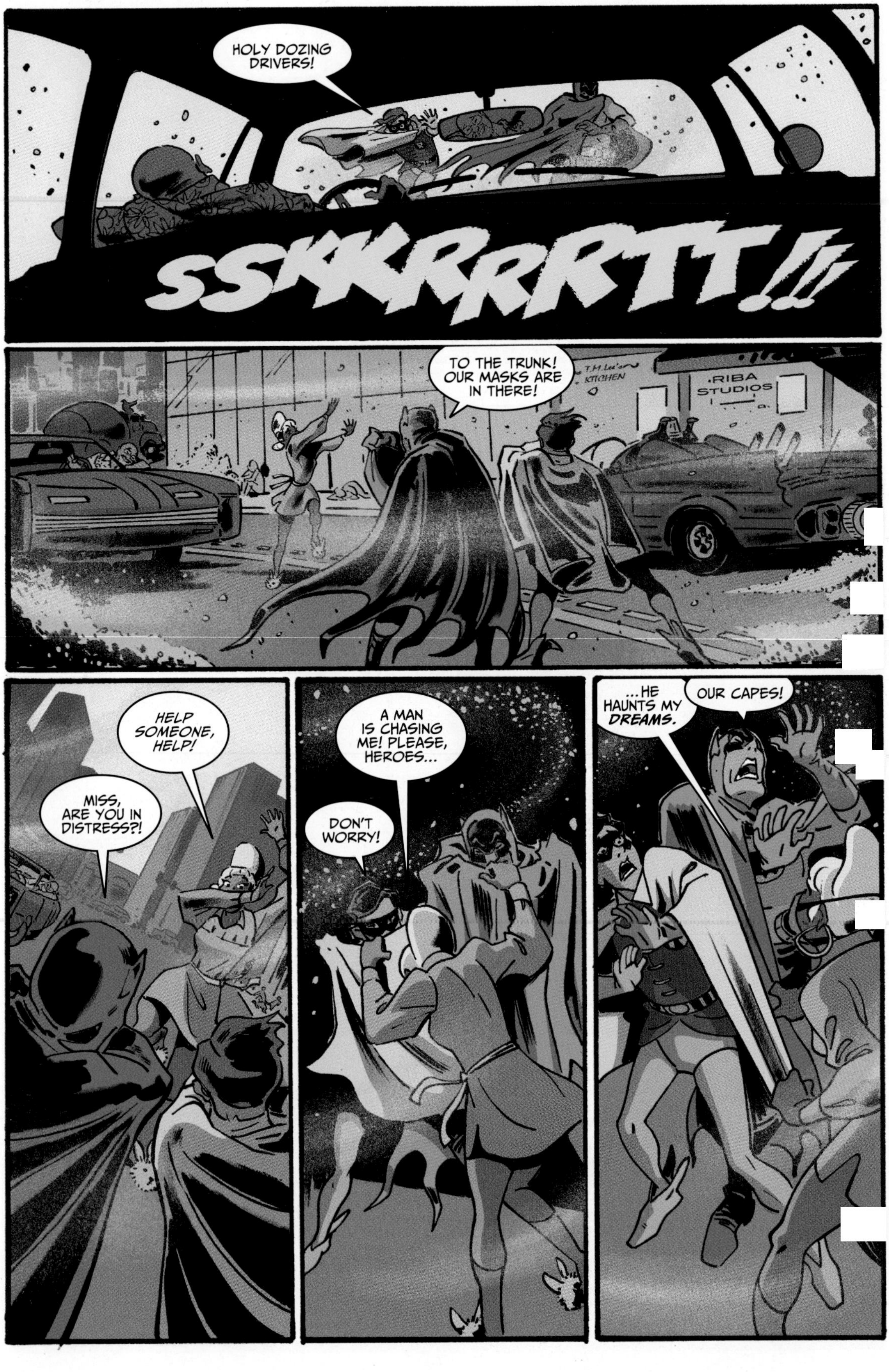
HOLY DOZING DRIVERS!
SSKKRRRTT!!!
TO THE TRUNK! OUR MASKS ARE IN THERE!
T.M. Lee's KITCHEN
RIBA STUDIOS
HELP SOMEONE, HELP!
MISS, ARE YOU IN DISTRESS?!
A MAN IS CHASING ME! PLEASE, HEROES...
DON'T WORRY!
...HE HAUNTS MY DREAMS.
OUR CAPES!

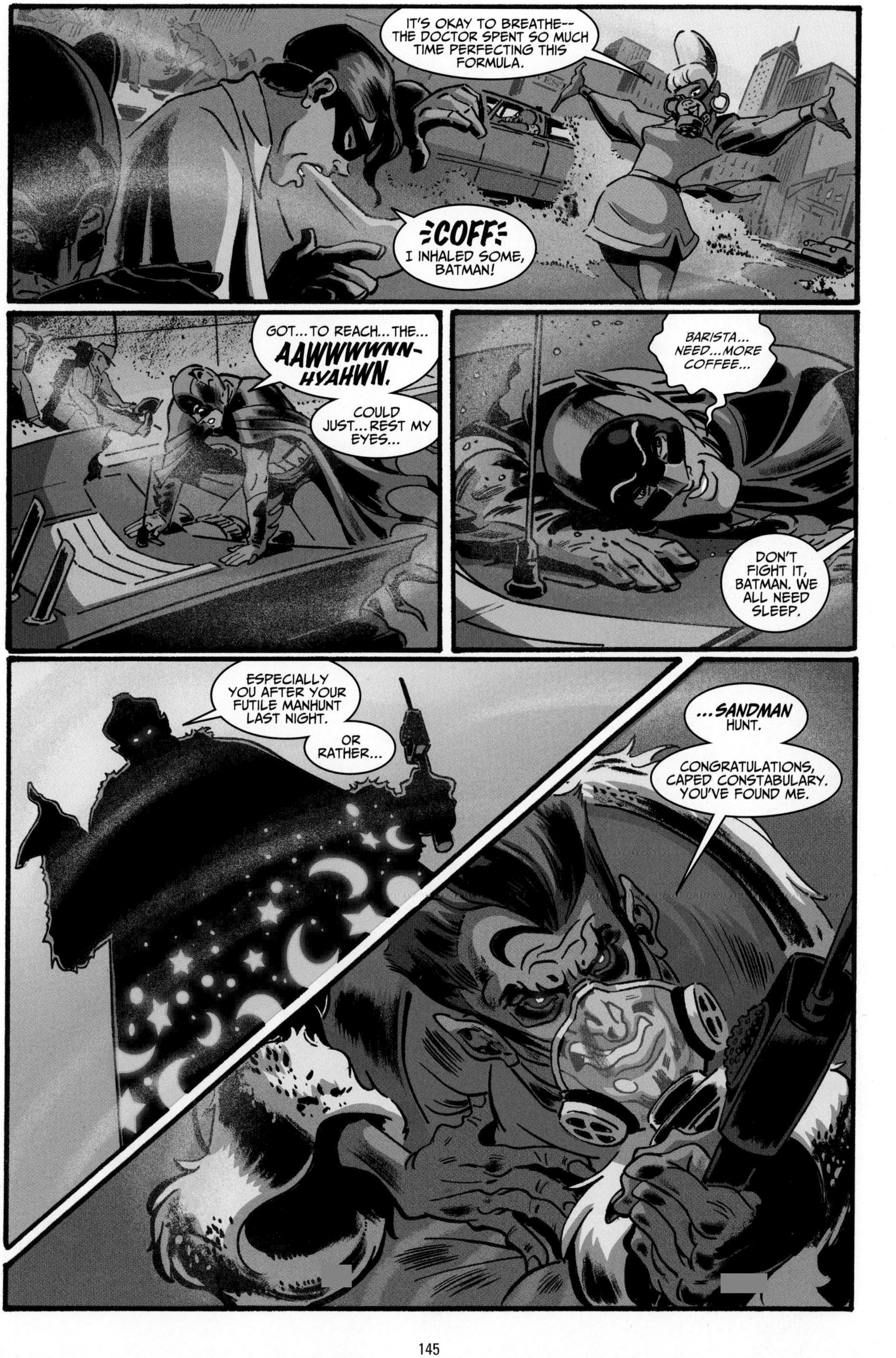
IT'S OKAY TO BREATHE-- THE DOCTOR SPENT SO MUCH TIME PERFECTING THIS FORMULA.
COFF I INHALED SOME, BATMAN!
GOT...TO REACH...THE... AAWWWWNN-HYAHWN.
COULD JUST...REST MY EYES...
BARISTA... NEED...MORE COFFEE...
DON'T FIGHT IT, BATMAN. WE ALL NEED SLEEP.
ESPECIALLY YOU AFTER YOUR FUTILE MANHUNT LAST NIGHT.
OR RATHER...
...SANDMAN HUNT.
CONGRATULATIONS, CAPED CONSTABULARY. YOU'VE FOUND ME.

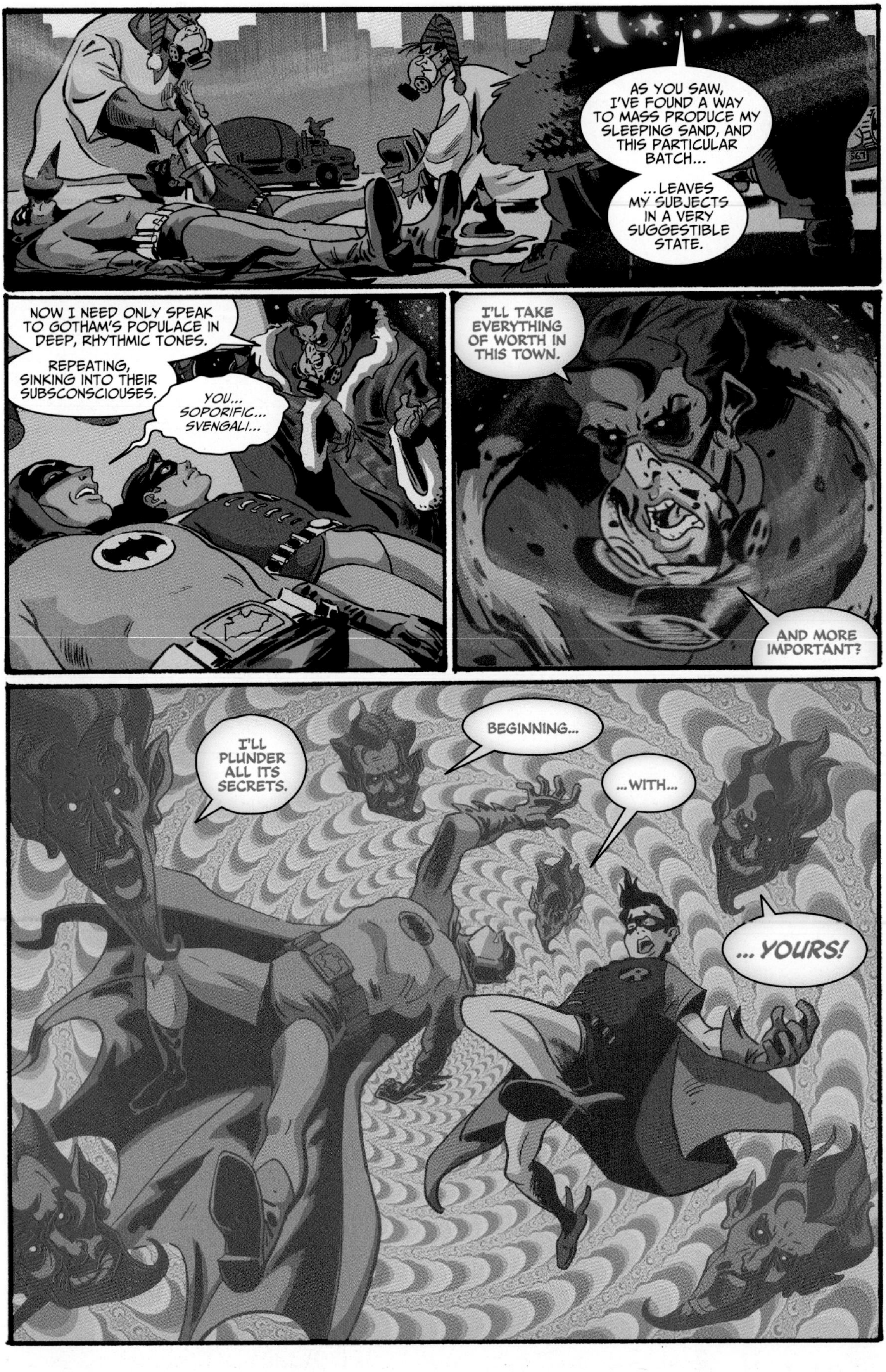
AS YOU SAW, I'VE FOUND A WAY TO MASS PRODUCE MY SLEEPING SAND, AND THIS PARTICULAR BATCH...
...LEAVES MY SUBJECTS IN A VERY SUGGESTIBLE STATE.
NOW I NEED ONLY SPEAK TO GOTHAM'S POPULACE IN DEEP, RHYTHMIC TONES.
REPEATING, SINKING INTO THEIR SUBSCONSCIOUSES.
YOU... SOPORIFIC... SVENGALI...
I'LL TAKE EVERYTHING OF WORTH IN THIS TOWN.
AND MORE IMPORTANT?
I'LL PLUNDER ALL ITS SECRETS.
BEGINNING...
...WITH...
...YOURS!

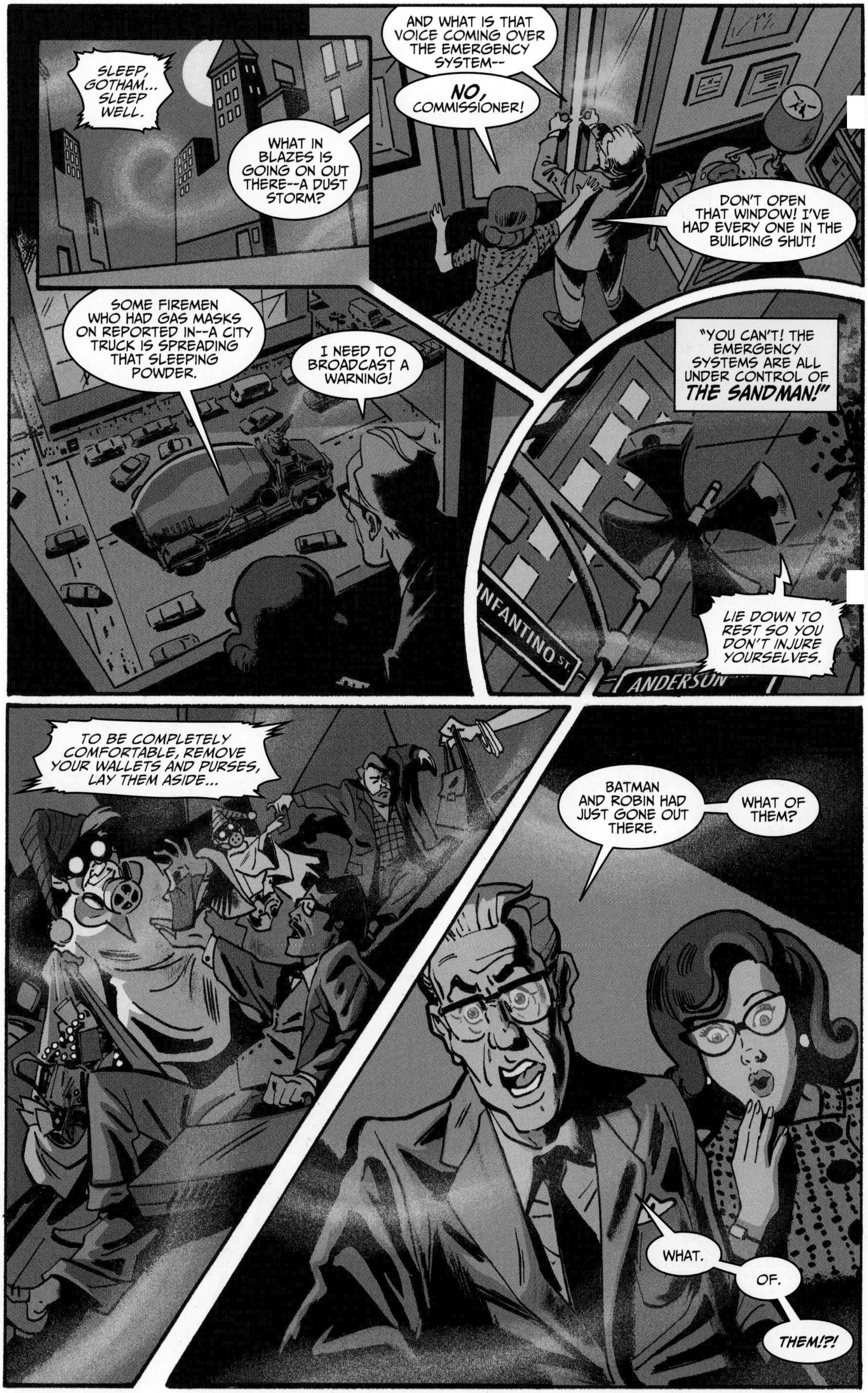
SLEEP, GOTHAM... SLEEP WELL.
WHAT IN BLAZES IS GOING ON OUT THERE--A DUST STORM?
AND WHAT IS THAT VOICE COMING OVER THE EMERGENCY SYSTEM--
NO, COMMISSIONER!
DON'T OPEN THAT WINDOW! I'VE HAD EVERY ONE IN THE BUILDING SHUT!
SOME FIREMEN WHO HAD GAS MASKS ON REPORTED IN--A CITY TRUCK IS SPREADING THAT SLEEPING POWDER.
I NEED TO BROADCAST A WARNING!
"YOU CAN'T! THE EMERGENCY SYSTEMS ARE ALL UNDER CONTROL OF THE SANDMAN!"
INFANTINO ST.
ANDERSON
LIE DOWN TO REST SO YOU DON'T INJURE YOURSELVES.
TO BE COMPLETELY COMFORTABLE, REMOVE YOUR WALLETS AND PURSES, LAY THEM ASIDE...
BATMAN AND ROBIN HAD JUST GONE OUT THERE.
WHAT OF THEM?
WHAT.
OF.
THEM!?!

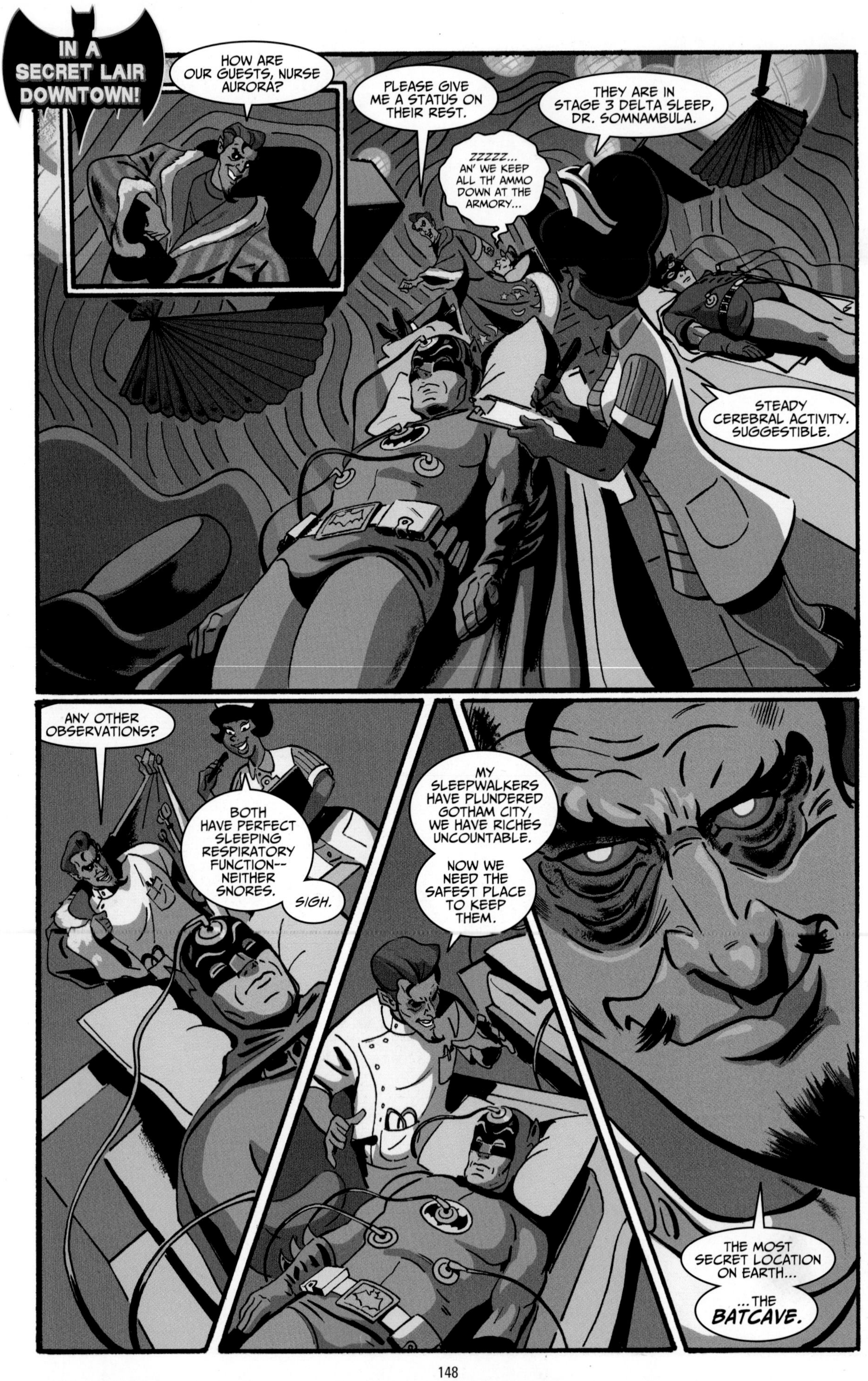
IN A SECRET LAIR DOWNTOWN!
HOW ARE OUR GUESTS, NURSE AURORA?
PLEASE GIVE ME A STATUS ON THEIR REST.
ZZZZZ... AN' WE KEEP ALL TH' AMMO DOWN AT THE ARMORY...
THEY ARE IN STAGE 3 DELTA SLEEP, DR. SOMNAMBULA.
STEADY CEREBRAL ACTIVITY. SUGGESTIBLE.
ANY OTHER OBSERVATIONS?
BOTH HAVE PERFECT SLEEPING RESPIRATORY FUNCTION-- NEITHER SNORES.
SIGH.
MY SLEEPWALKERS HAVE PLUNDERED GOTHAM CITY, WE HAVE RICHES UNCOUNTABLE.
NOW WE NEED THE SAFEST PLACE TO KEEP THEM.
THE MOST SECRET LOCATION ON EARTH...
...THE BATCAVE.

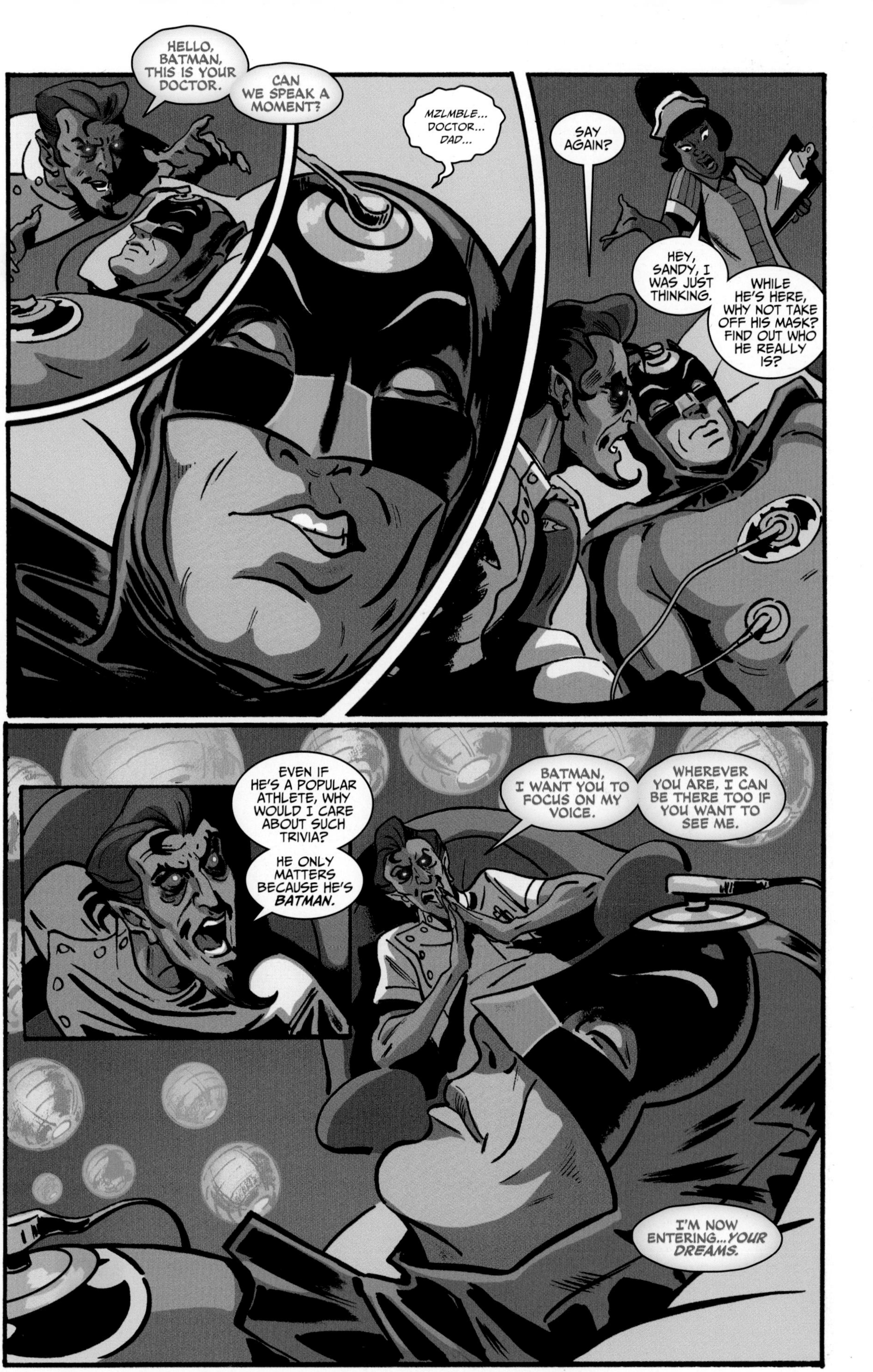
HELLO, BATMAN, THIS IS YOUR DOCTOR.
CAN WE SPEAK A MOMENT?
MZLMBLE... DOCTOR... DAD...
SAY AGAIN?
HEY, SANDY, I WAS JUST THINKING.
WHILE HE'S HERE, WHY NOT TAKE OFF HIS MASK? FIND OUT WHO HE REALLY IS?
EVEN IF HE'S A POPULAR ATHLETE, WHY WOULD I CARE ABOUT SUCH TRIVIA?
HE ONLY MATTERS BECAUSE HE'S *BATMAN.*
BATMAN, I WANT YOU TO FOCUS ON MY VOICE.
WHEREVER YOU ARE, I CAN BE THERE TOO IF YOU WANT TO SEE ME.
I'M NOW ENTERING... *YOUR DREAMS.*

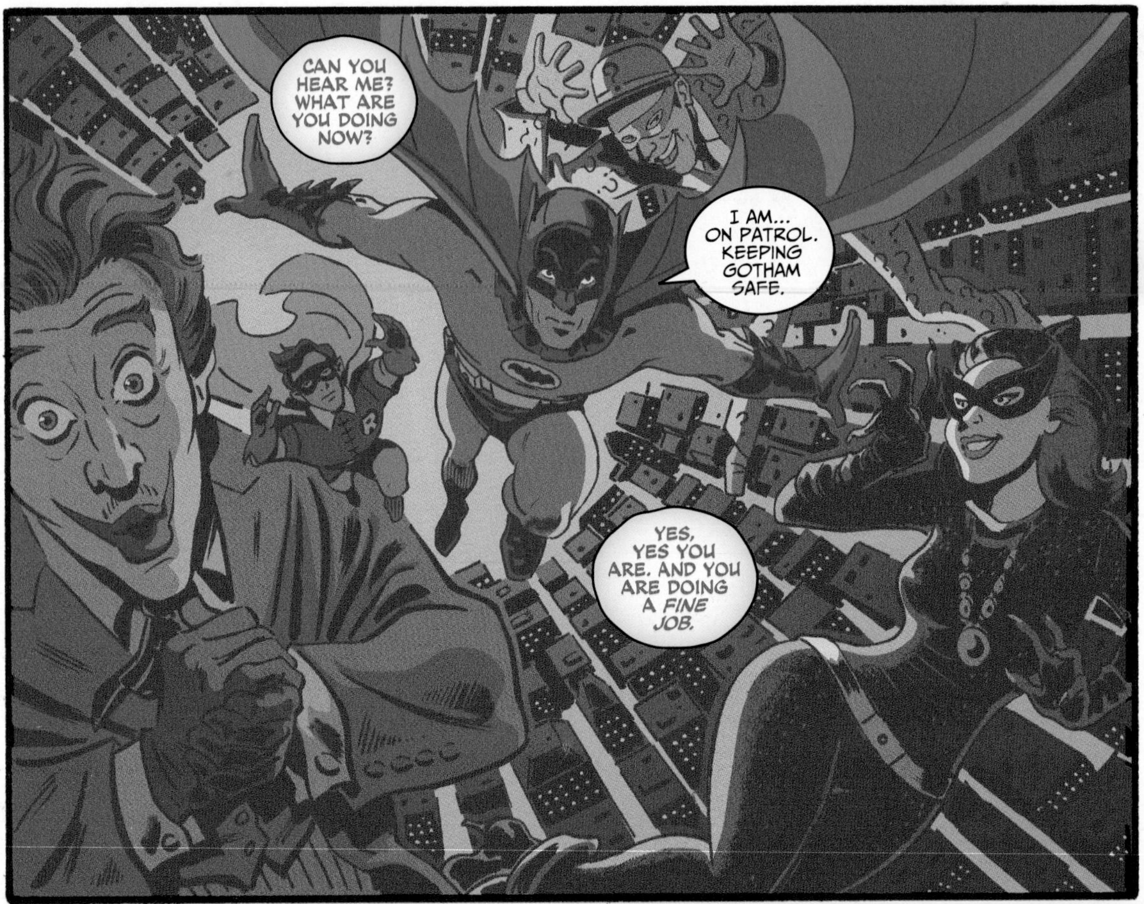
CAN YOU HEAR ME? WHAT ARE YOU DOING NOW?
I AM... ON PATROL. KEEPING GOTHAM SAFE.
YES, YES YOU ARE. AND YOU ARE DOING A *FINE* JOB.

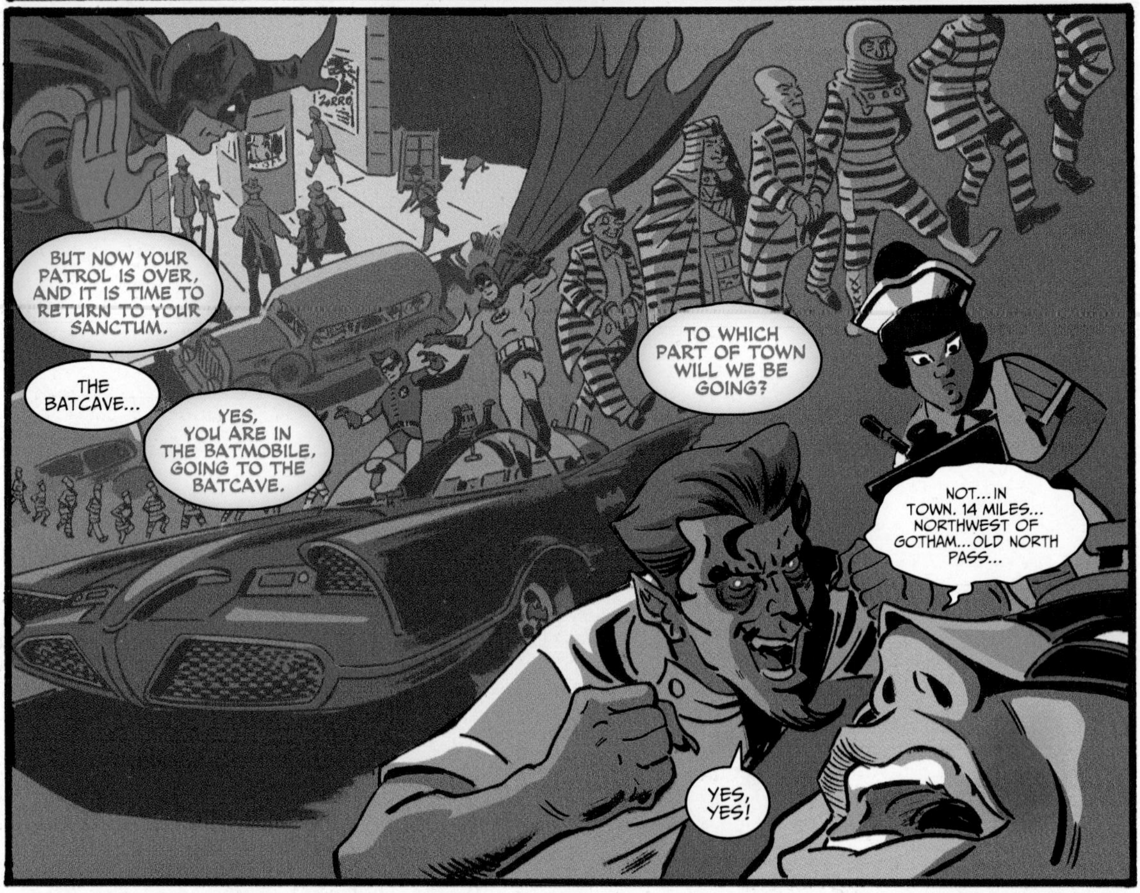
BUT NOW YOUR PATROL IS OVER, AND IT IS TIME TO RETURN TO YOUR SANCTUM.
THE BATCAVE...
YES, YOU ARE IN THE BATMOBILE, GOING TO THE BATCAVE.
TO WHICH PART OF TOWN WILL WE BE GOING?
NOT...IN TOWN. 14 MILES... NORTHWEST OF GOTHAM...OLD NORTH PASS...
YES, YES!

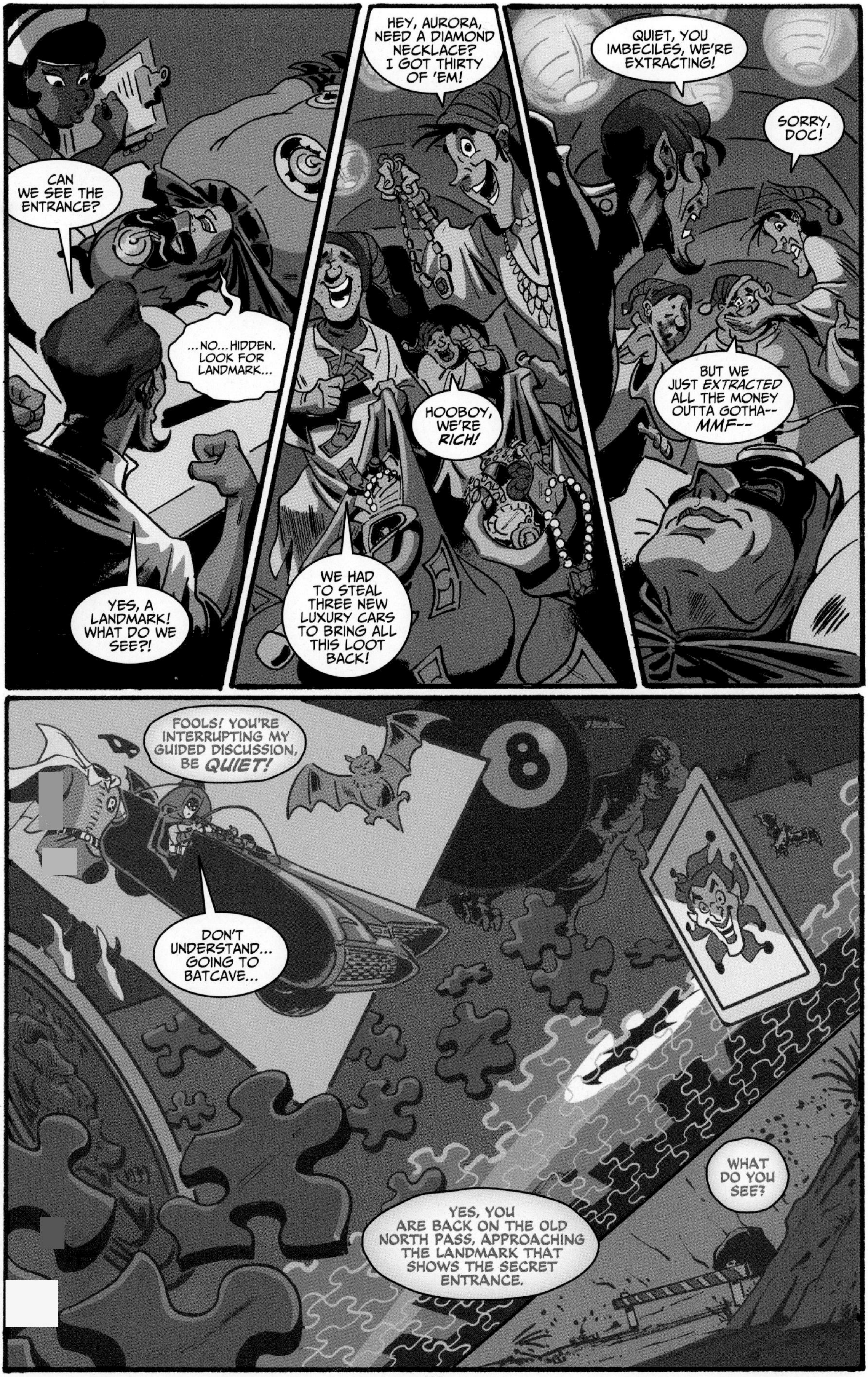
CAN WE SEE THE ENTRANCE?
...NO...HIDDEN. LOOK FOR LANDMARK...
YES, A LANDMARK! WHAT DO WE SEE?!
HEY, AURORA, NEED A DIAMOND NECKLACE? I GOT THIRTY OF 'EM!
HOOBOY, WE'RE RICH!
WE HAD TO STEAL THREE NEW LUXURY CARS TO BRING ALL THIS LOOT BACK!
QUIET, YOU IMBECILES, WE'RE EXTRACTING!
SORRY, DOC!
BUT WE JUST EXTRACTED ALL THE MONEY OUTTA GOTHA-- MMF--
FOOLS! YOU'RE INTERRUPTING MY GUIDED DISCUSSION, BE QUIET!
DON'T UNDERSTAND... GOING TO BATCAVE...
WHAT DO YOU SEE?
YES, YOU ARE BACK ON THE OLD NORTH PASS, APPROACHING THE LANDMARK THAT SHOWS THE SECRET ENTRANCE.

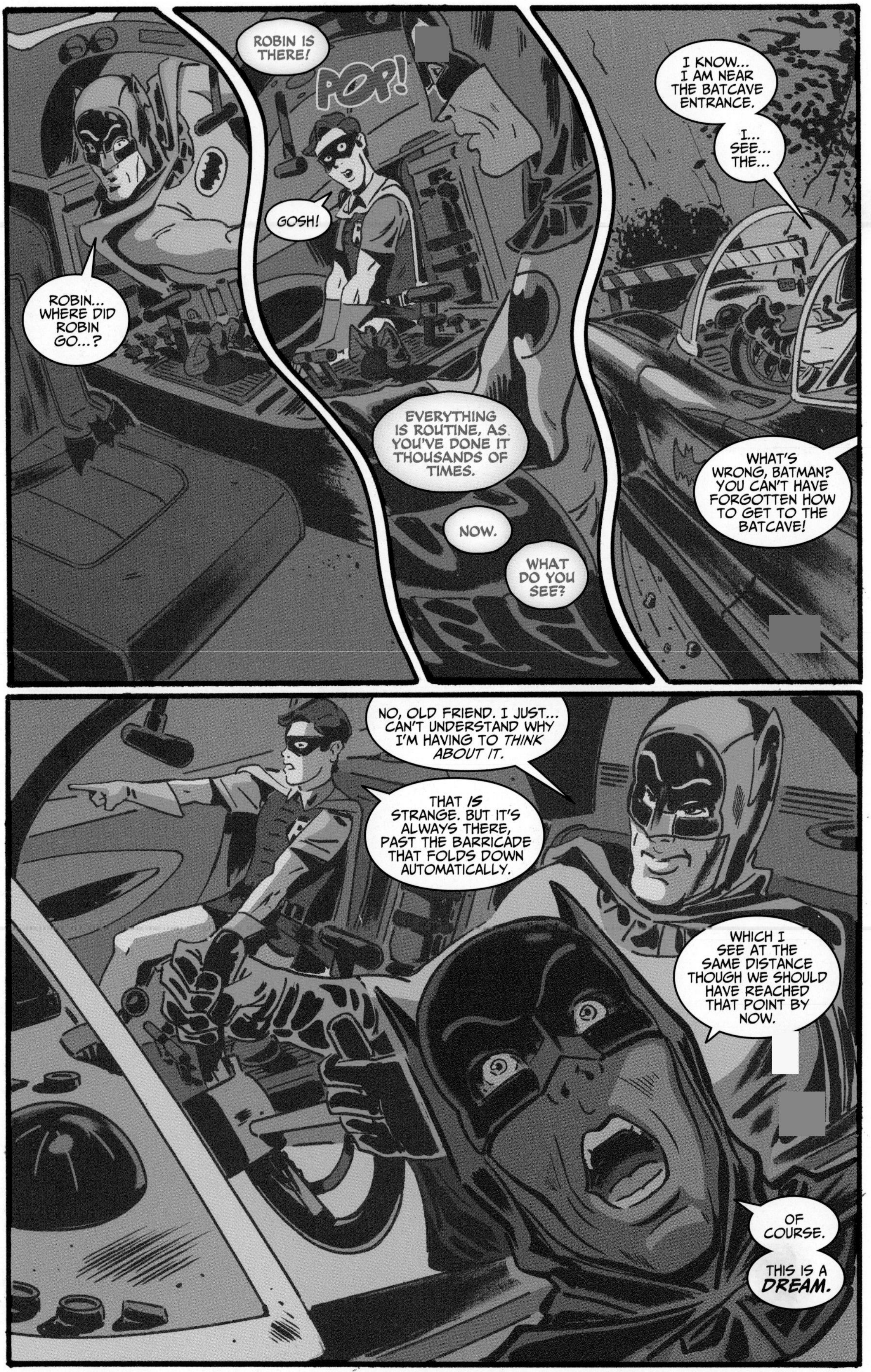
ROBIN... WHERE DID ROBIN GO...?
ROBIN IS THERE!
POP!
GOSH!
EVERYTHING IS ROUTINE, AS YOU'VE DONE IT THOUSANDS OF TIMES.
NOW.
WHAT DO YOU SEE?
I KNOW... I AM NEAR THE BATCAVE ENTRANCE.
I... SEE... THE...
WHAT'S WRONG, BATMAN? YOU CAN'T HAVE FORGOTTEN HOW TO GET TO THE BATCAVE!
NO, OLD FRIEND. I JUST... CAN'T UNDERSTAND WHY I'M HAVING TO *THINK ABOUT IT.*
THAT *IS* STRANGE. BUT IT'S ALWAYS THERE, PAST THE BARRICADE THAT FOLDS DOWN AUTOMATICALLY.
WHICH I SEE AT THE SAME DISTANCE THOUGH WE SHOULD HAVE REACHED THAT POINT BY NOW.
OF COURSE.
THIS IS A **DREAM.**

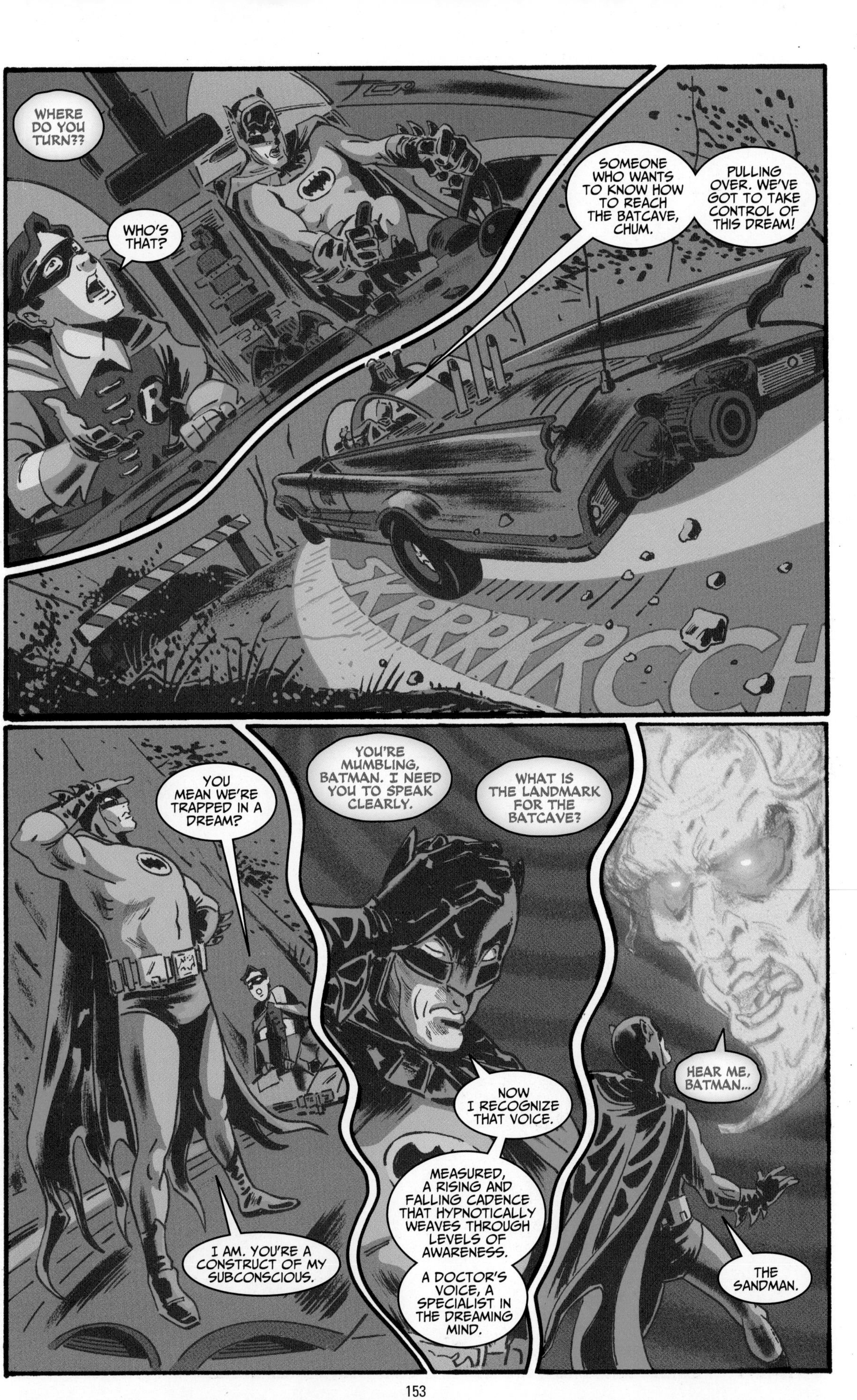
WHERE DO YOU TURN??
WHO'S THAT?
SOMEONE WHO WANTS TO KNOW HOW TO REACH THE BATCAVE, CHUM.
PULLING OVER. WE'VE GOT TO TAKE CONTROL OF THIS DREAM!
SKRRRKRCCH
YOU MEAN WE'RE TRAPPED IN A DREAM?
I AM. YOU'RE A CONSTRUCT OF MY SUBCONSCIOUS.
YOU'RE MUMBLING, BATMAN. I NEED YOU TO SPEAK CLEARLY.
WHAT IS THE LANDMARK FOR THE BATCAVE?
NOW I RECOGNIZE THAT VOICE.
MEASURED, A RISING AND FALLING CADENCE THAT HYPNOTICALLY WEAVES THROUGH LEVELS OF AWARENESS.
A DOCTOR'S VOICE, A SPECIALIST IN THE DREAMING MIND.
HEAR ME, BATMAN...
THE SANDMAN.

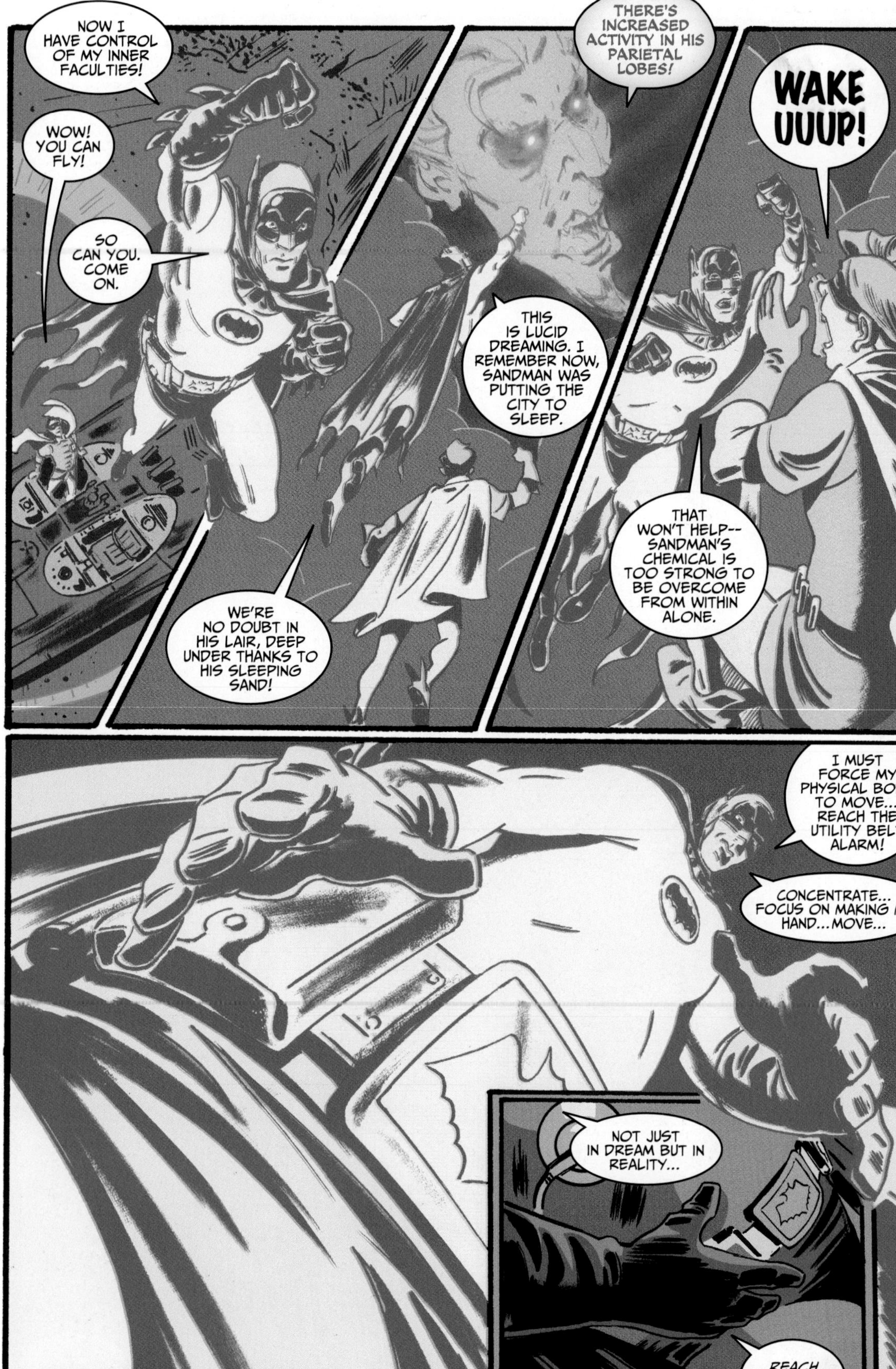
NOW I HAVE CONTROL OF MY INNER FACULTIES!
WOW! YOU CAN FLY!
SO CAN YOU. COME ON.
THERE'S INCREASED ACTIVITY IN HIS PARIETAL LOBES!
THIS IS LUCID DREAMING. I REMEMBER NOW, SANDMAN WAS PUTTING THE CITY TO SLEEP.
WE'RE NO DOUBT IN HIS LAIR, DEEP UNDER THANKS TO HIS SLEEPING SAND!
WAKE UUUP!
THAT WON'T HELP-- SANDMAN'S CHEMICAL IS TOO STRONG TO BE OVERCOME FROM WITHIN ALONE.
I MUST FORCE MY PHYSICAL BODY TO MOVE... REACH THE UTILITY BELT ALARM!
CONCENTRATE... FOCUS ON MAKING MY HAND...MOVE...
NOT JUST IN DREAM BUT IN REALITY...
...REACH... THE... BELT...!

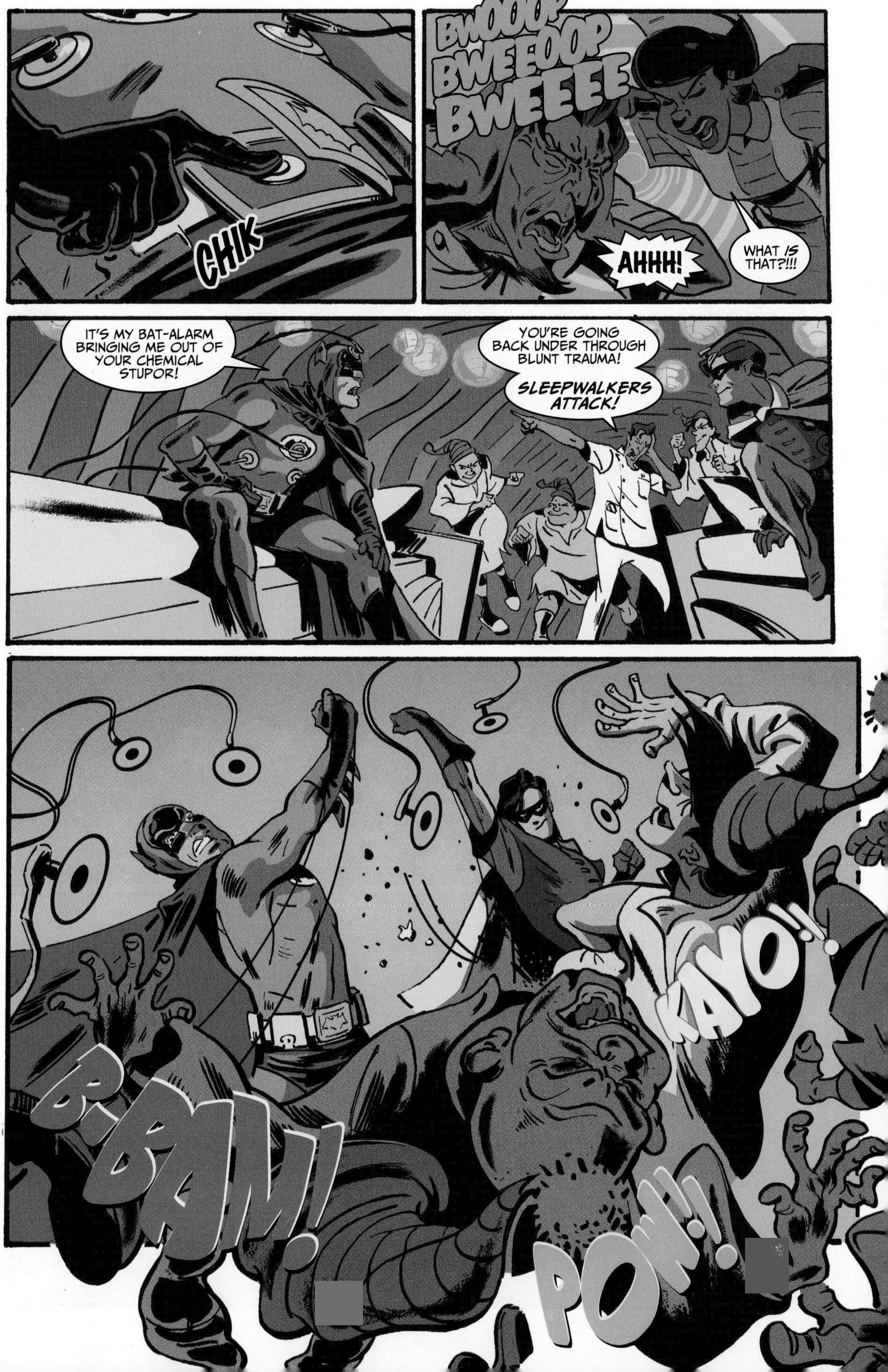
CHIK
BWOOOP BWEEOOP BWEEEE
AHHH!
WHAT IS THAT?!!!
IT'S MY BAT-ALARM BRINGING ME OUT OF YOUR CHEMICAL STUPOR!
YOU'RE GOING BACK UNDER THROUGH BLUNT TRAUMA!
SLEEPWALKERS ATTACK!
KAYO!!!
B-BAM!
POW!!!

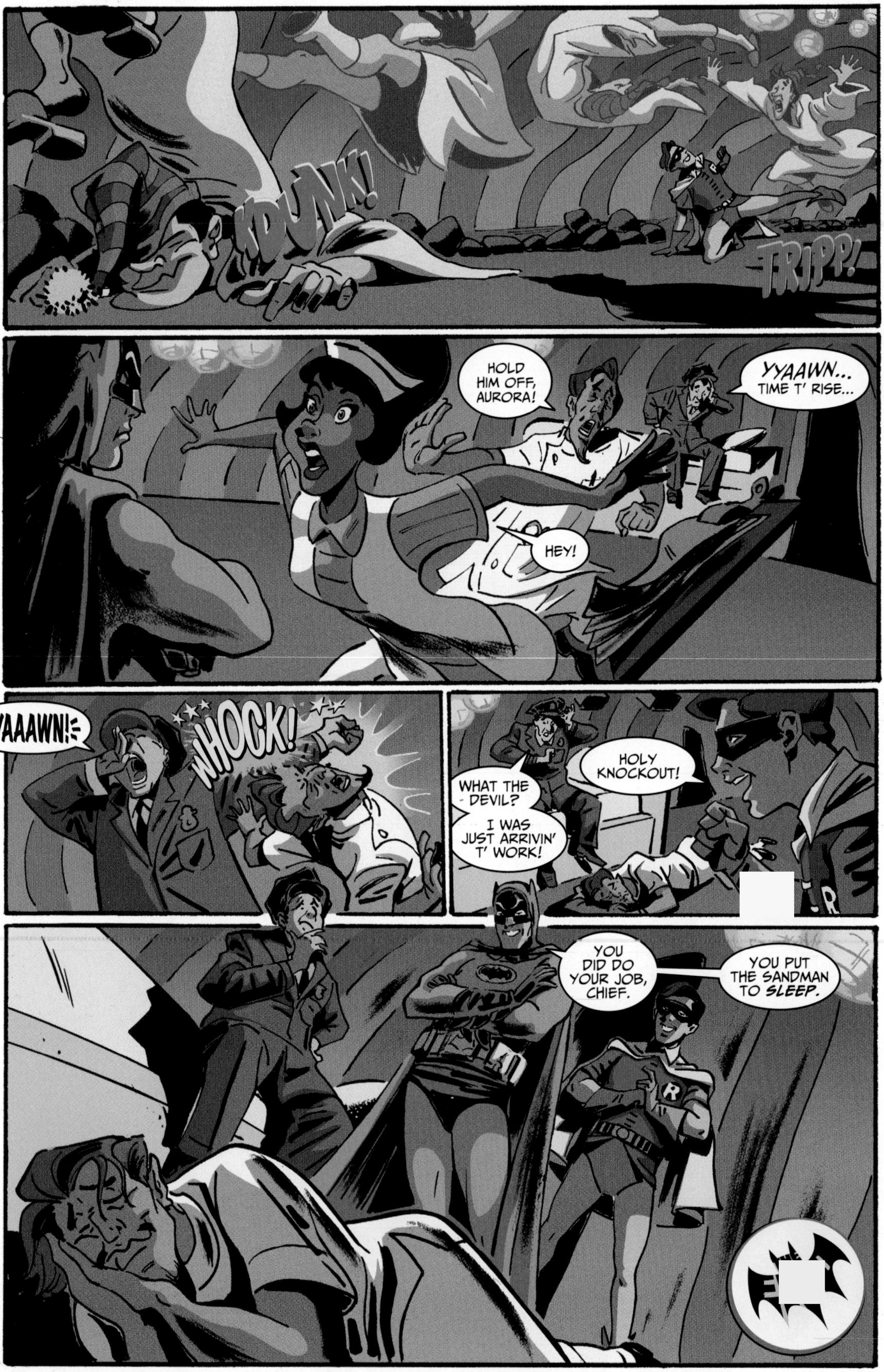
KDUNK!
TRIPP!
HOLD HIM OFF, AURORA!
YYAAWN... TIME T' RISE...
HEY!
YAAAWN!
WHOCK!
WHAT THE DEVIL?
I WAS JUST ARRIVIN' T' WORK!
HOLY KNOCKOUT!
YOU DID DO YOUR JOB, CHIEF.
YOU PUT THE SANDMAN TO SLEEP.

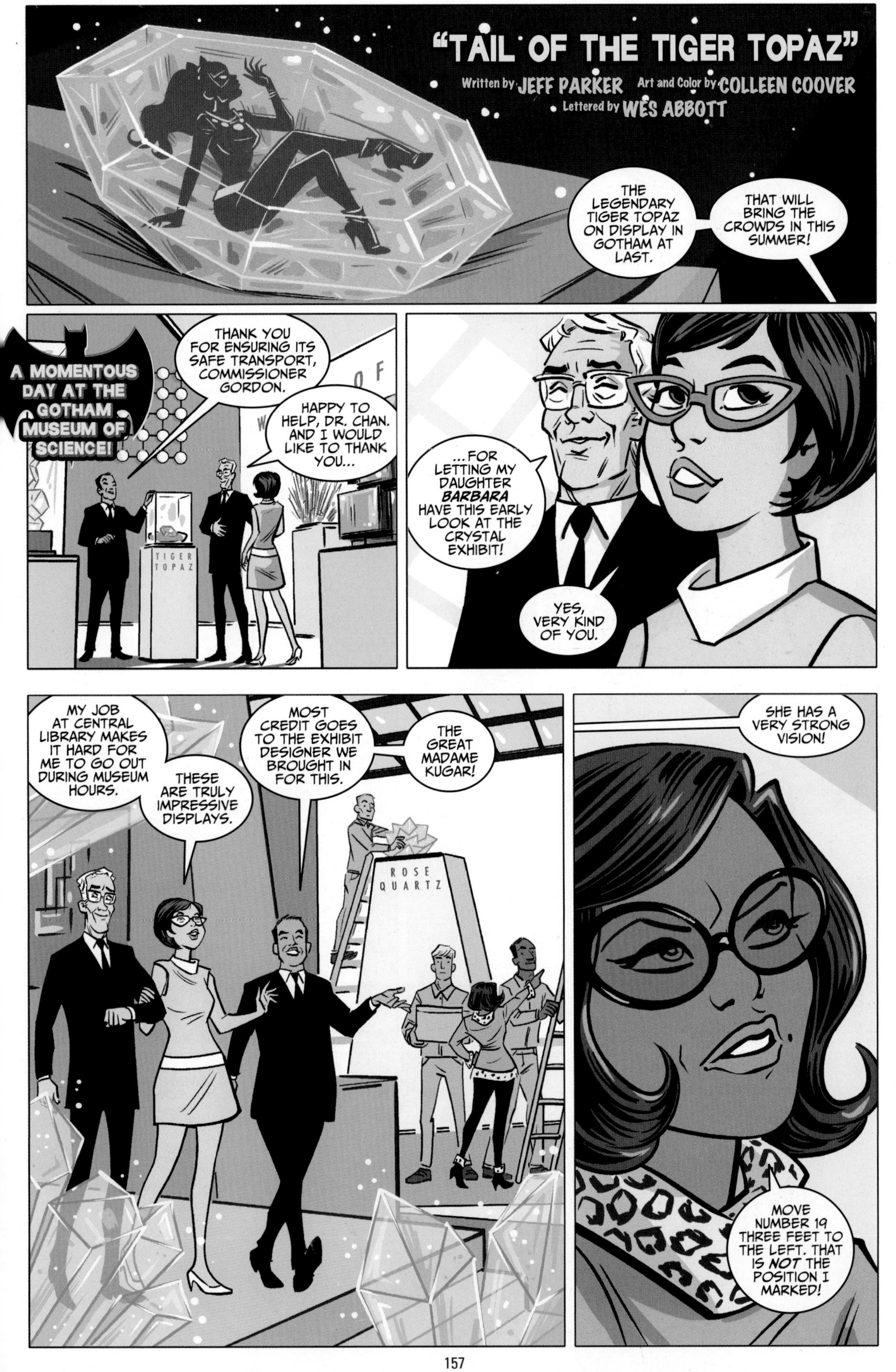

"TAIL OF THE TIGER TOPAZ"
Written by JEFF PARKER Art and Color by COLLEEN COOVER
Lettered by WES ABBOTT
THE LEGENDARY TIGER TOPAZ ON DISPLAY IN GOTHAM AT LAST.
THAT WILL BRING THE CROWDS IN THIS SUMMER!
A MOMENTOUS DAY AT THE GOTHAM MUSEUM OF SCIENCE!
THANK YOU FOR ENSURING ITS SAFE TRANSPORT, COMMISSIONER GORDON.
HAPPY TO HELP, DR. CHAN. AND I WOULD LIKE TO THANK YOU...
TIGER TOPAZ
...FOR LETTING MY DAUGHTER BARBARA HAVE THIS EARLY LOOK AT THE CRYSTAL EXHIBIT!
YES, VERY KIND OF YOU.
MY JOB AT CENTRAL LIBRARY MAKES IT HARD FOR ME TO GO OUT DURING MUSEUM HOURS.
THESE ARE TRULY IMPRESSIVE DISPLAYS.
MOST CREDIT GOES TO THE EXHIBIT DESIGNER WE BROUGHT IN FOR THIS.
THE GREAT MADAME KUGAR!
ROSE QUARTZ
SHE HAS A VERY STRONG VISION!
MOVE NUMBER 19 THREE FEET TO THE LEFT. THAT IS NOT THE POSITION I MARKED!

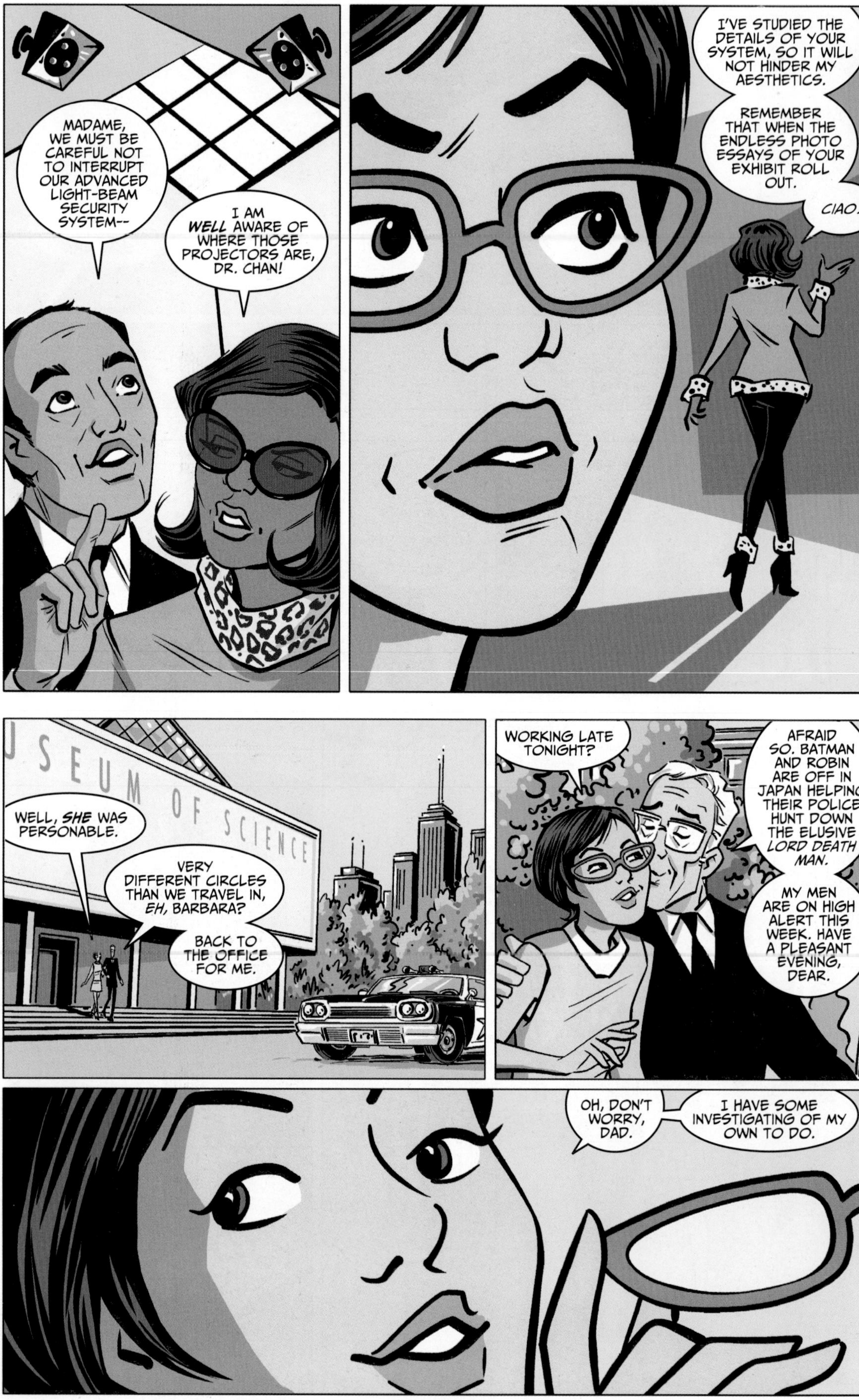
MADAME, WE MUST BE CAREFUL NOT TO INTERRUPT OUR ADVANCED LIGHT-BEAM SECURITY SYSTEM--
I AM WELL AWARE OF WHERE THOSE PROJECTORS ARE, DR. CHAN!
I'VE STUDIED THE DETAILS OF YOUR SYSTEM, SO IT WILL NOT HINDER MY AESTHETICS.
REMEMBER THAT WHEN THE ENDLESS PHOTO ESSAYS OF YOUR EXHIBIT ROLL OUT.
CIAO.
USEUM OF SCIENCE
WELL, SHE WAS PERSONABLE.
VERY DIFFERENT CIRCLES THAN WE TRAVEL IN, EH, BARBARA?
BACK TO THE OFFICE FOR ME.
WORKING LATE TONIGHT?
AFRAID SO. BATMAN AND ROBIN ARE OFF IN JAPAN HELPING THEIR POLICE HUNT DOWN THE ELUSIVE LORD DEATH MAN.
MY MEN ARE ON HIGH ALERT THIS WEEK. HAVE A PLEASANT EVENING, DEAR.
OH, DON'T WORRY, DAD.
I HAVE SOME INVESTIGATING OF MY OWN TO DO.

LATER THAT NIGHT!

SHLLUP

SHIK

SHIKT

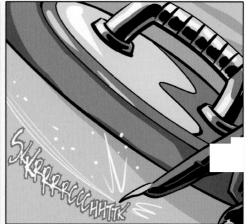

SHKRRAAACCCHHHTTK

POMPH

CRRREEEAAK

TIGER TOPAZ

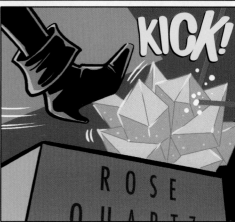

KICK!

ROSE QUARTZ

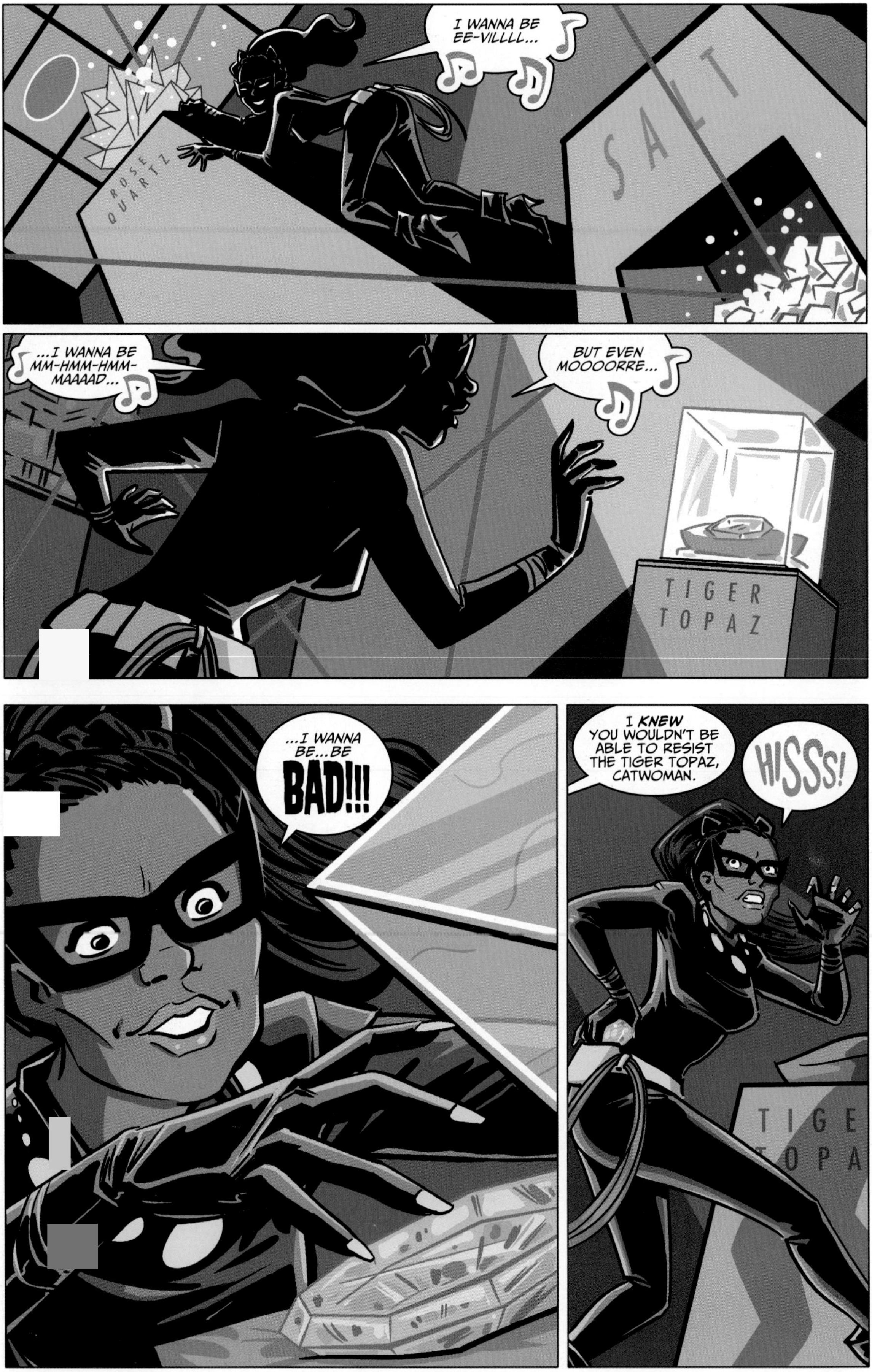

I WANNA BE EE-VILLLL...
ROSE QUARTZ
SALT
...I WANNA BE MM-HMM-HMM-MAAAAD...
BUT EVEN MOOOORRE...
TIGER TOPAZ
...I WANNA BE...BE BAD!!!
I KNEW YOU WOULDN'T BE ABLE TO RESIST THE TIGER TOPAZ, CATWOMAN.
HISSS!

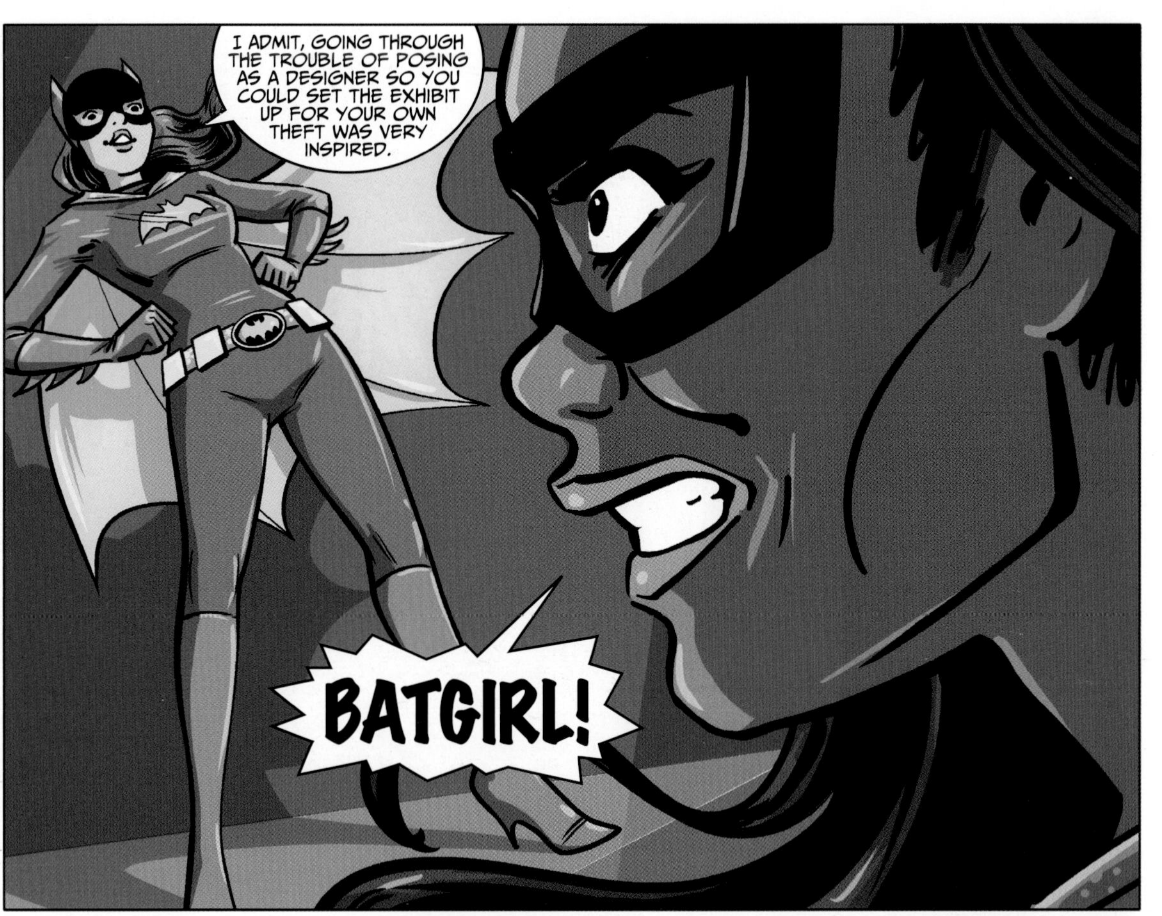
I ADMIT, GOING THROUGH THE TROUBLE OF POSING AS A DESIGNER SO YOU COULD SET THE EXHIBIT UP FOR YOUR OWN THEFT WAS VERY INSPIRED.
BATGIRL!

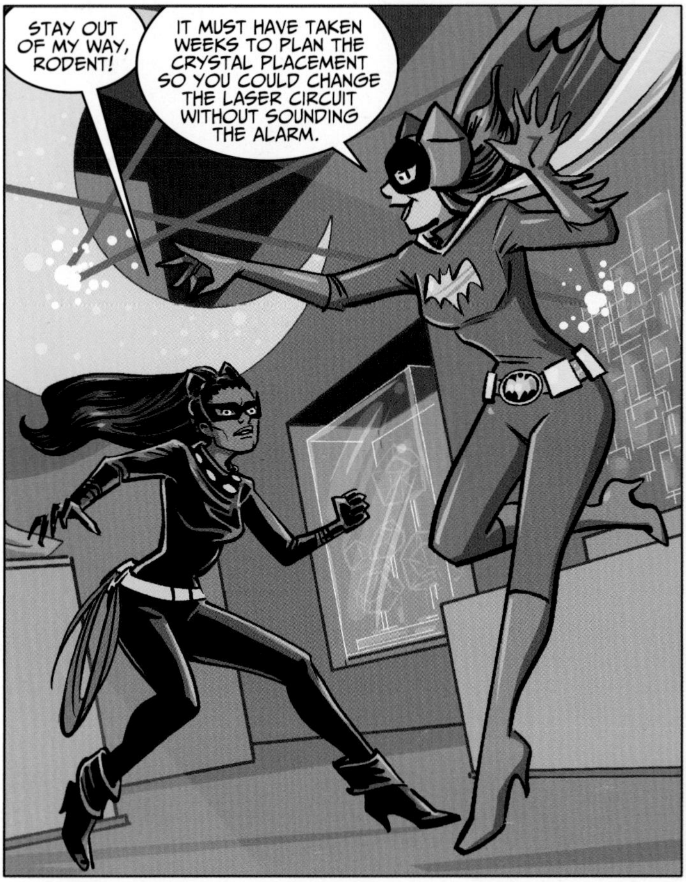
STAY OUT OF MY WAY, RODENT!
IT MUST HAVE TAKEN WEEKS TO PLAN THE CRYSTAL PLACEMENT SO YOU COULD CHANGE THE LASER CIRCUIT WITHOUT SOUNDING THE ALARM.

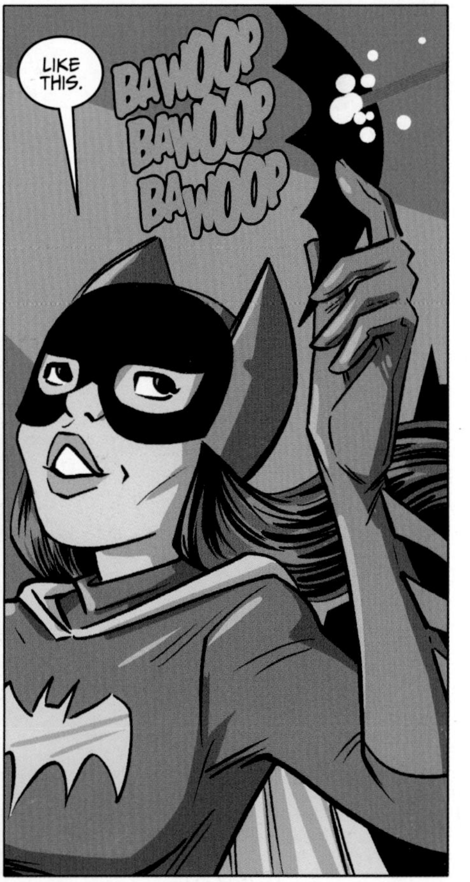
LIKE THIS.
BAWOOP
BAWOOP
BAWOOP

BAH! IT WILL TAKE MORE MINUTES FOR THE POLICE TO ARRIVE THAN I NEED!

I HAVE TIME ENOUGH TO DISCIPLINE A BAT!

WHP-

CRSSH!

WOW!

A-HA!

GOT YOU NOW!

HAHAHAHAHAAA!

KEE-RASSH!

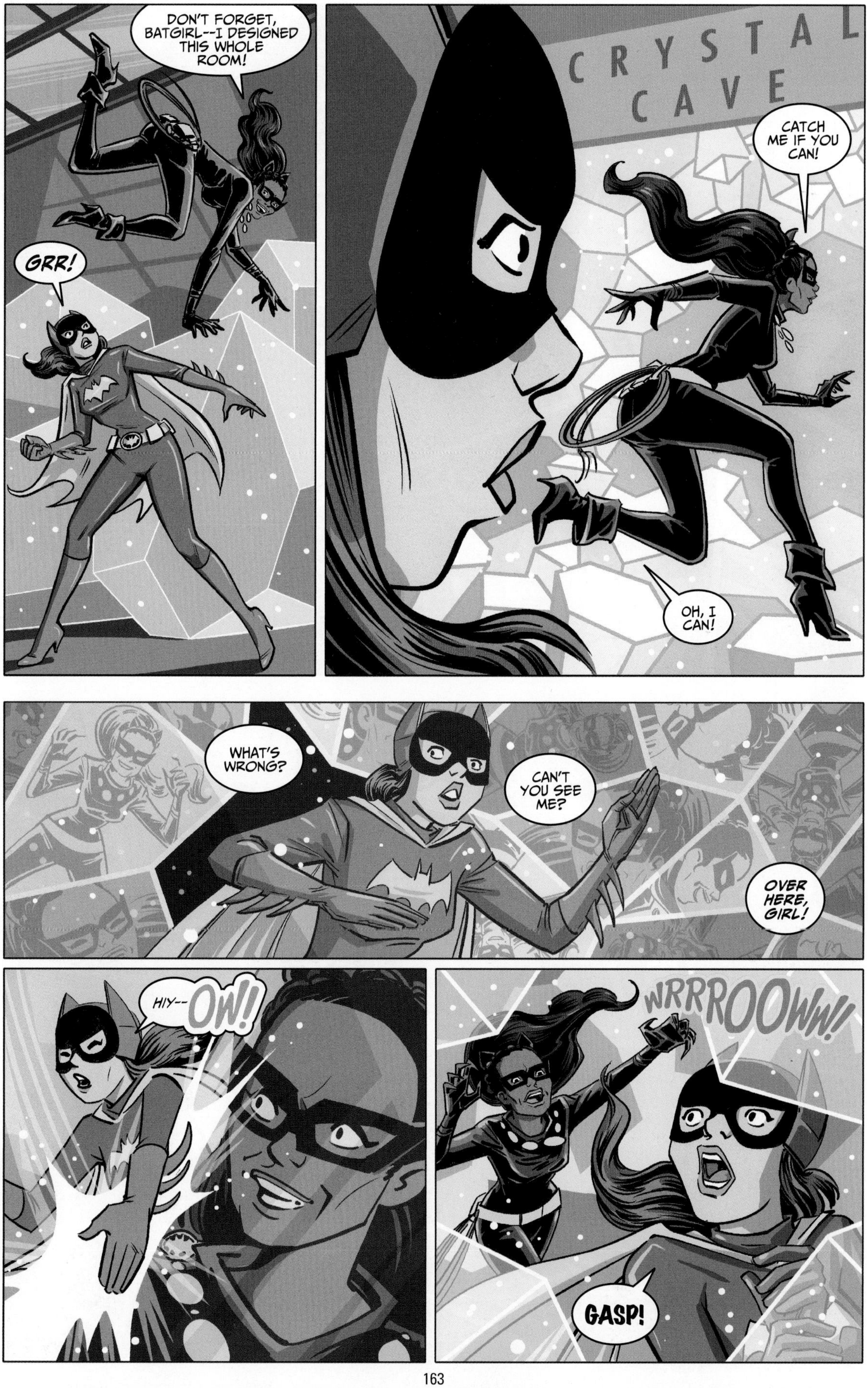
DON'T FORGET, BATGIRL--I DESIGNED THIS WHOLE ROOM!
GRR!
CRYSTAL CAVE
CATCH ME IF YOU CAN!
OH, I CAN!
WHAT'S WRONG?
CAN'T YOU SEE ME?
OVER HERE, GIRL!
HIY--OW!
WRRROOWW!
GASP!

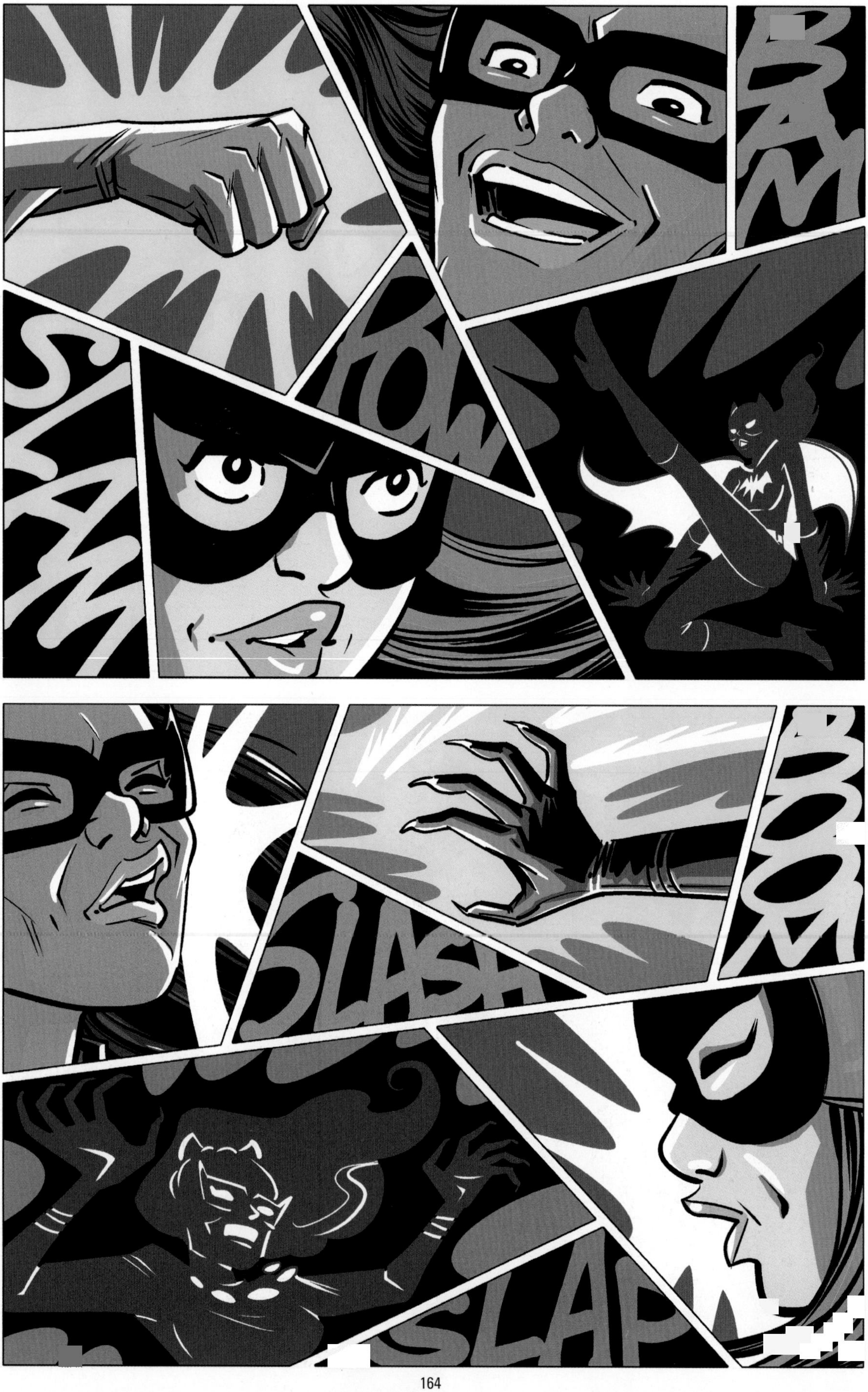
BAM
POW
SLAM
SLASH
BOOM
SLAP

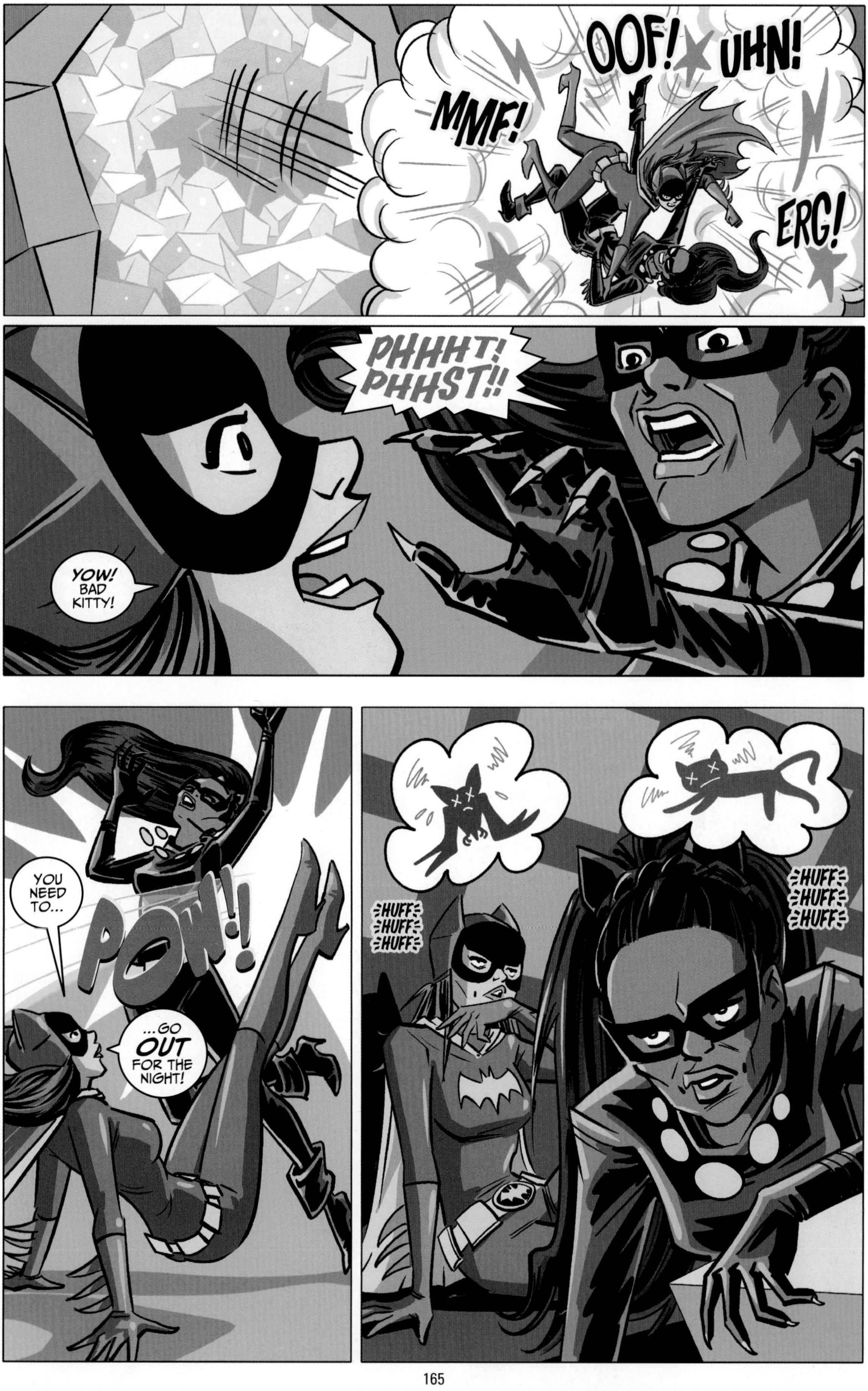
MMF!
OOF!
UHN!
ERG!
PHHHT! PHHST!!
YOW! BAD KITTY!
YOU NEED TO...
POW!!
...GO OUT FOR THE NIGHT!
HUFF HUFF HUFF
HUFF HUFF HUFF

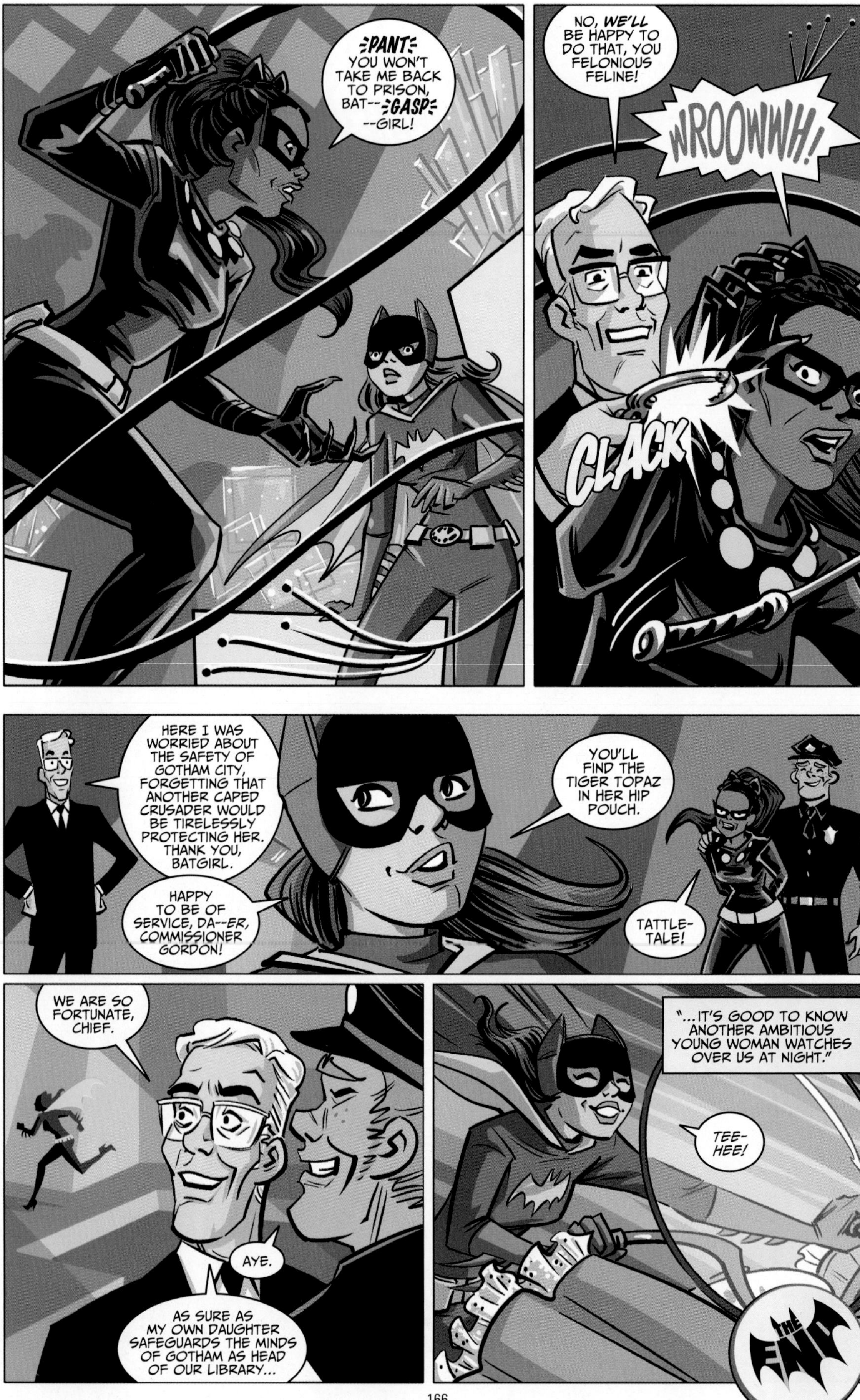
PANT
YOU WON'T TAKE ME BACK TO PRISON, BAT-- GASP --GIRL!
NO, WE'LL BE HAPPY TO DO THAT, YOU FELONIOUS FELINE!
WROOWWH!
CLACK
HERE I WAS WORRIED ABOUT THE SAFETY OF GOTHAM CITY, FORGETTING THAT ANOTHER CAPED CRUSADER WOULD BE TIRELESSLY PROTECTING HER. THANK YOU, BATGIRL.
HAPPY TO BE OF SERVICE, DA--ER, COMMISSIONER GORDON!
YOU'LL FIND THE TIGER TOPAZ IN HER HIP POUCH.
TATTLE-TALE!
WE ARE SO FORTUNATE, CHIEF.
AYE.
AS SURE AS MY OWN DAUGHTER SAFEGUARDS THE MINDS OF GOTHAM AS HEAD OF OUR LIBRARY...
"...IT'S GOOD TO KNOW ANOTHER AMBITIOUS YOUNG WOMAN WATCHES OVER US AT NIGHT."
TEE-HEE!
THE END

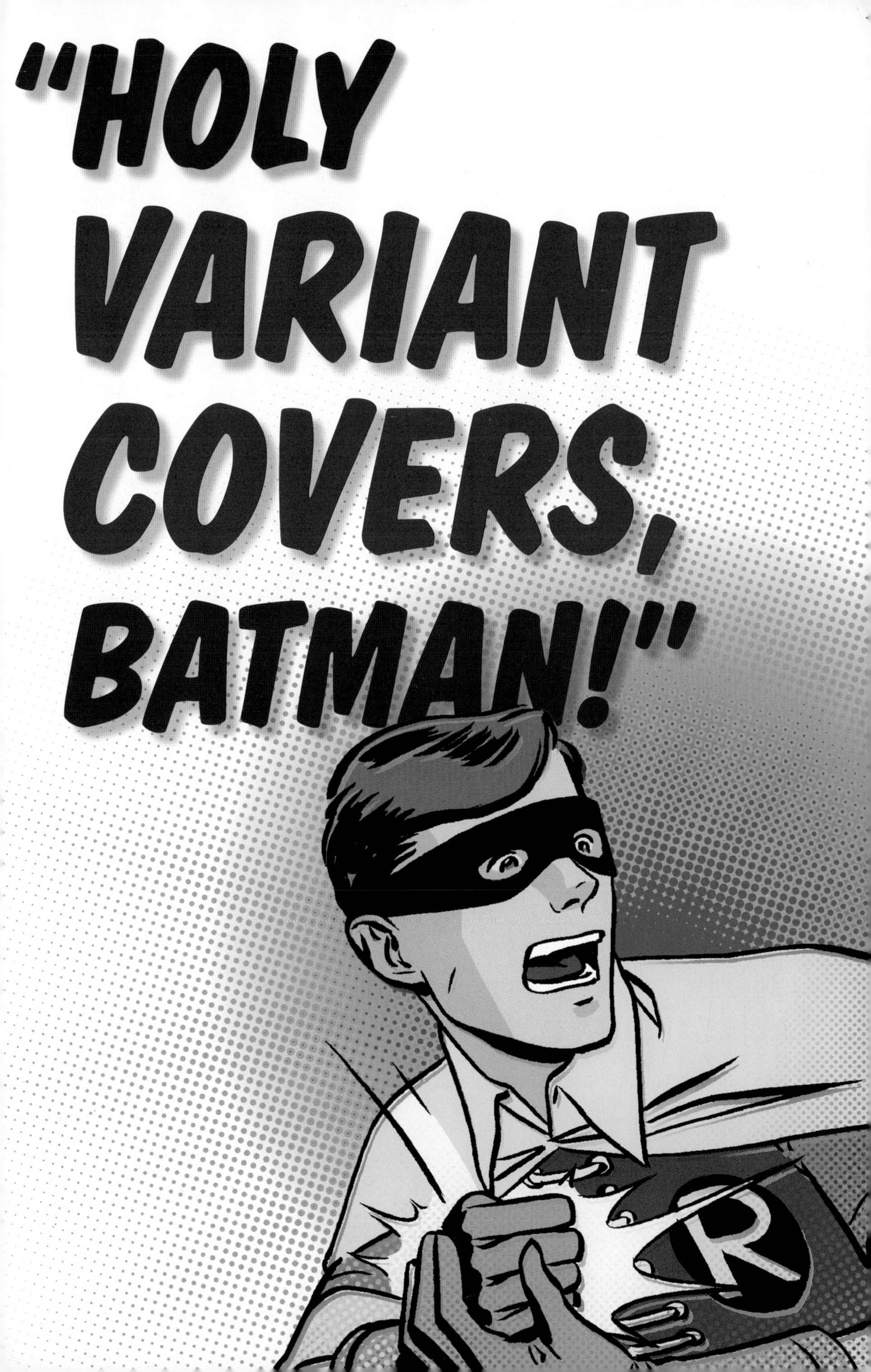
"HOLY VARIANT COVERS, BATMAN!"
R

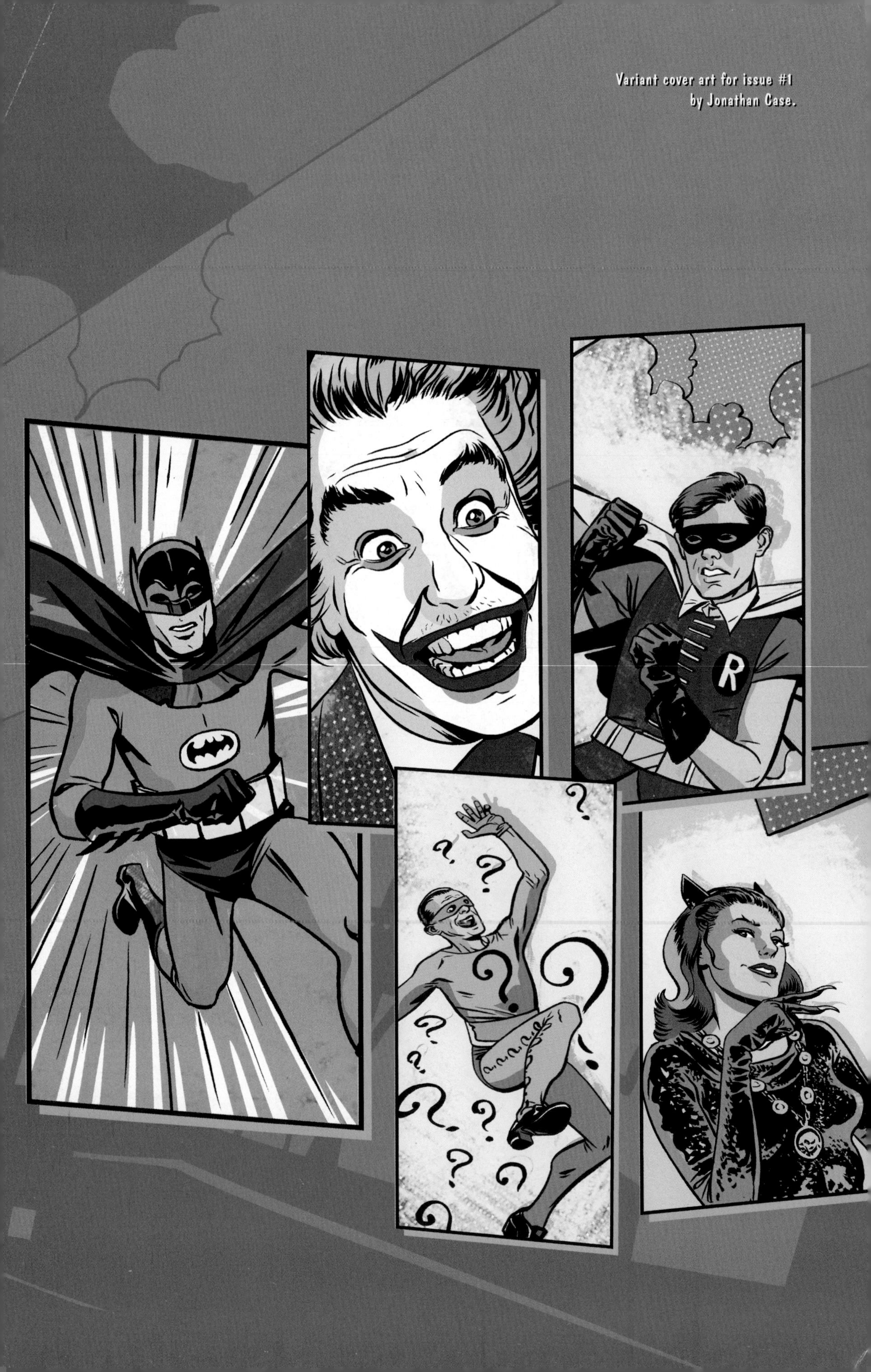
R

Variant cover art for issue #1
by Jonathan Case.

Action figure variant cover for issue #1
created for Comic-Con International in San Diego.

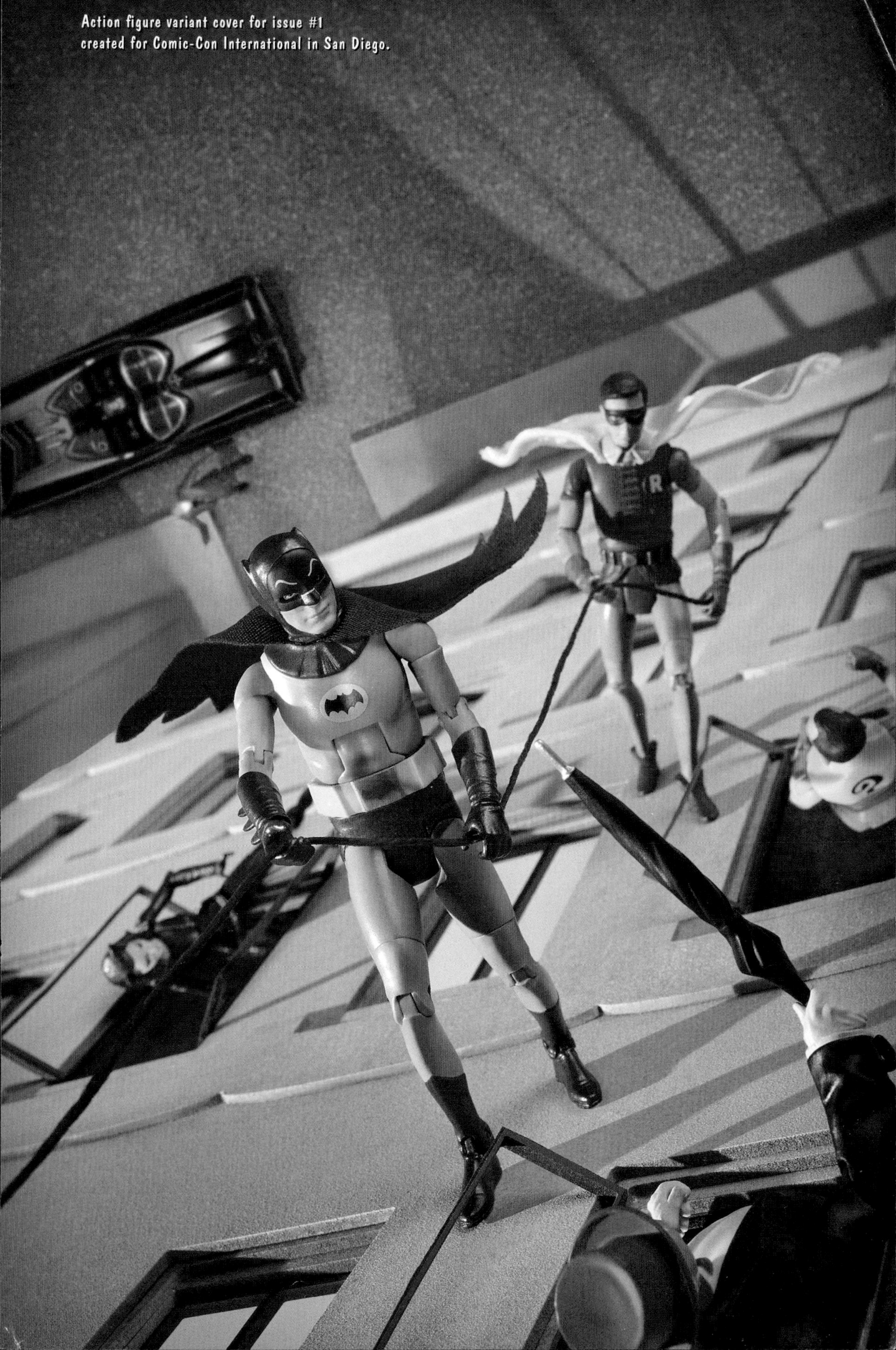

Variant cover art for issue #2 by Kevin Maguire
(color by Rosemary Cheetham).

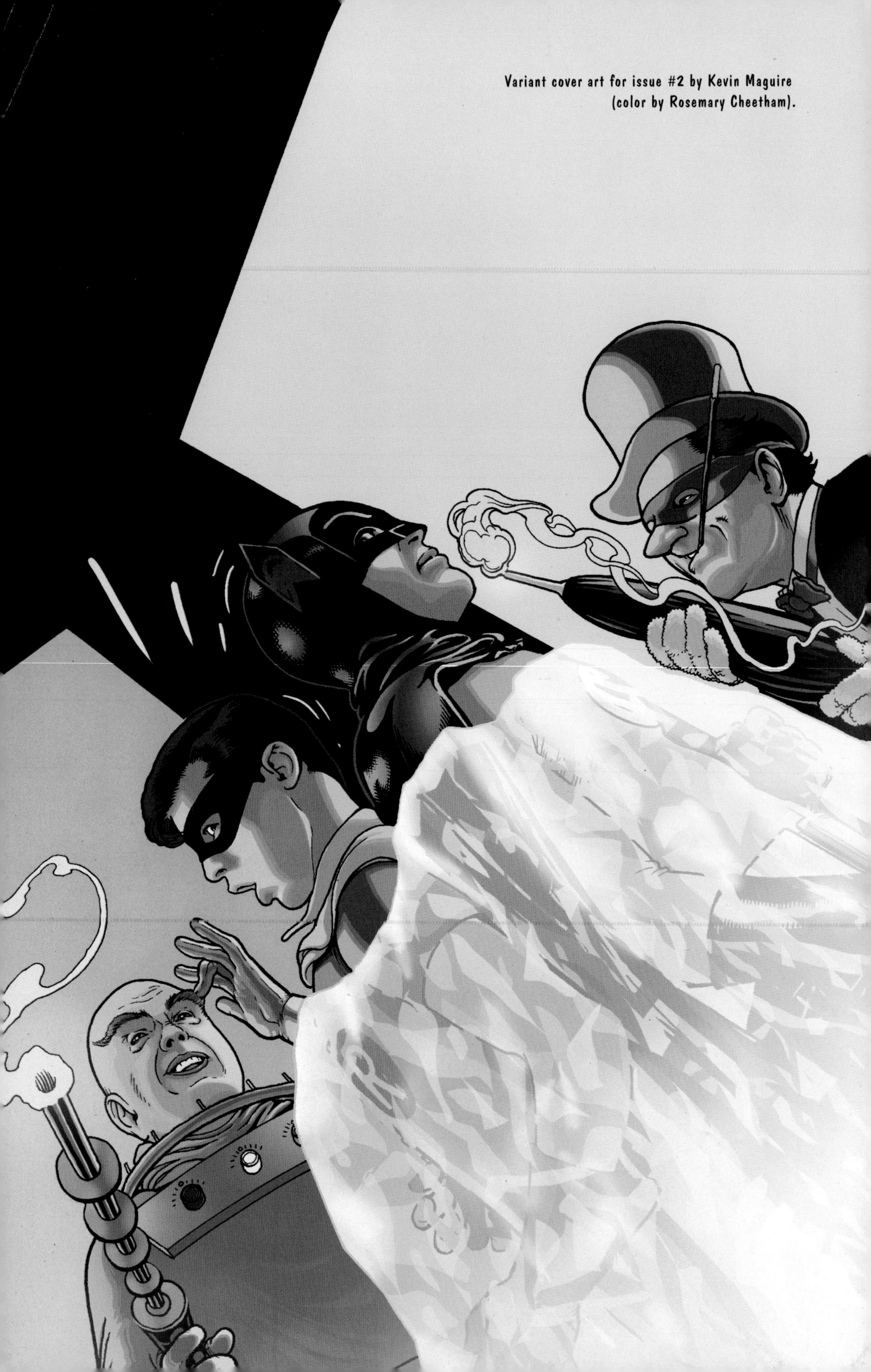

Variant cover art
for issue #3
by Cully Hamner.

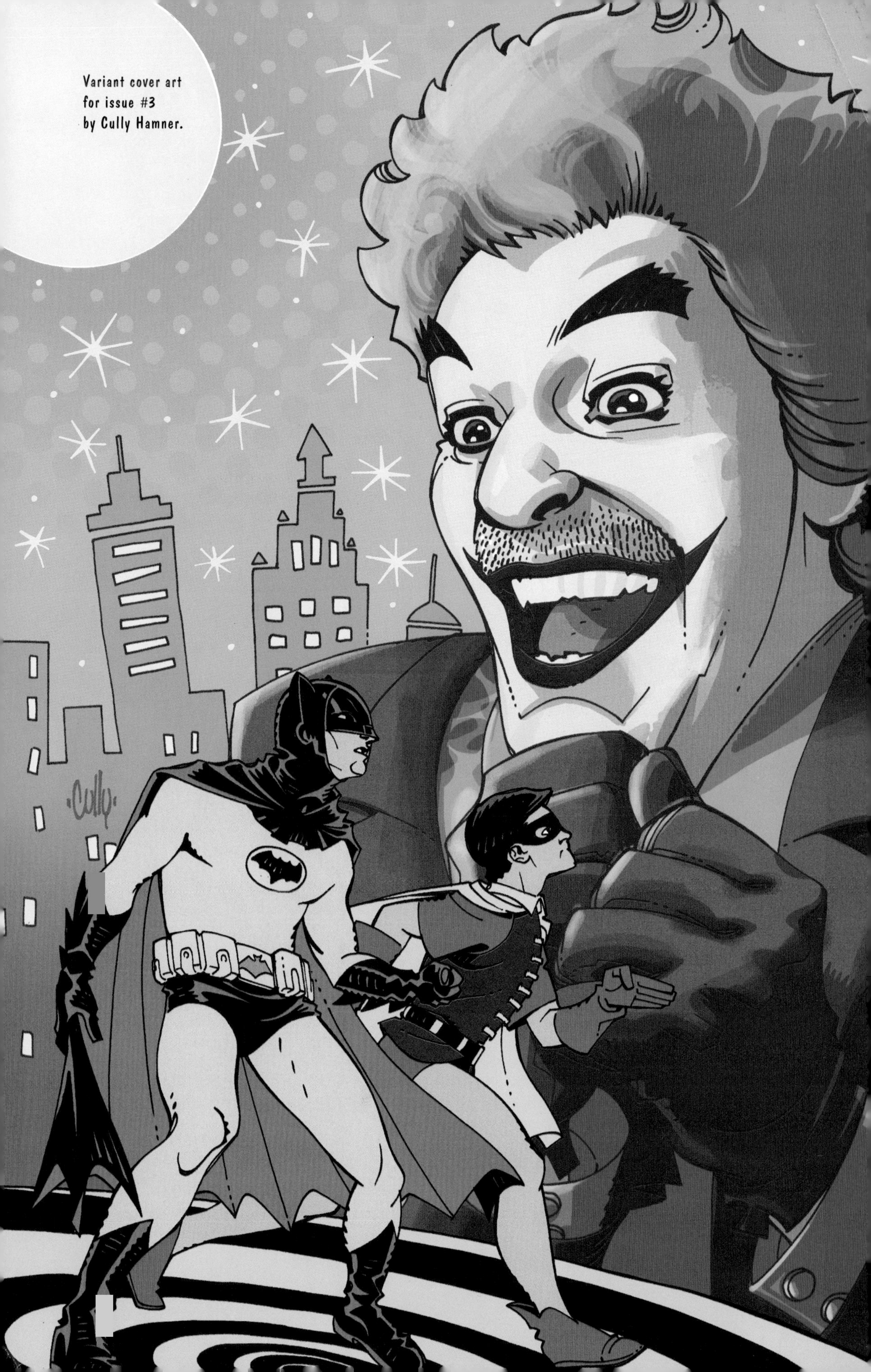
Cully

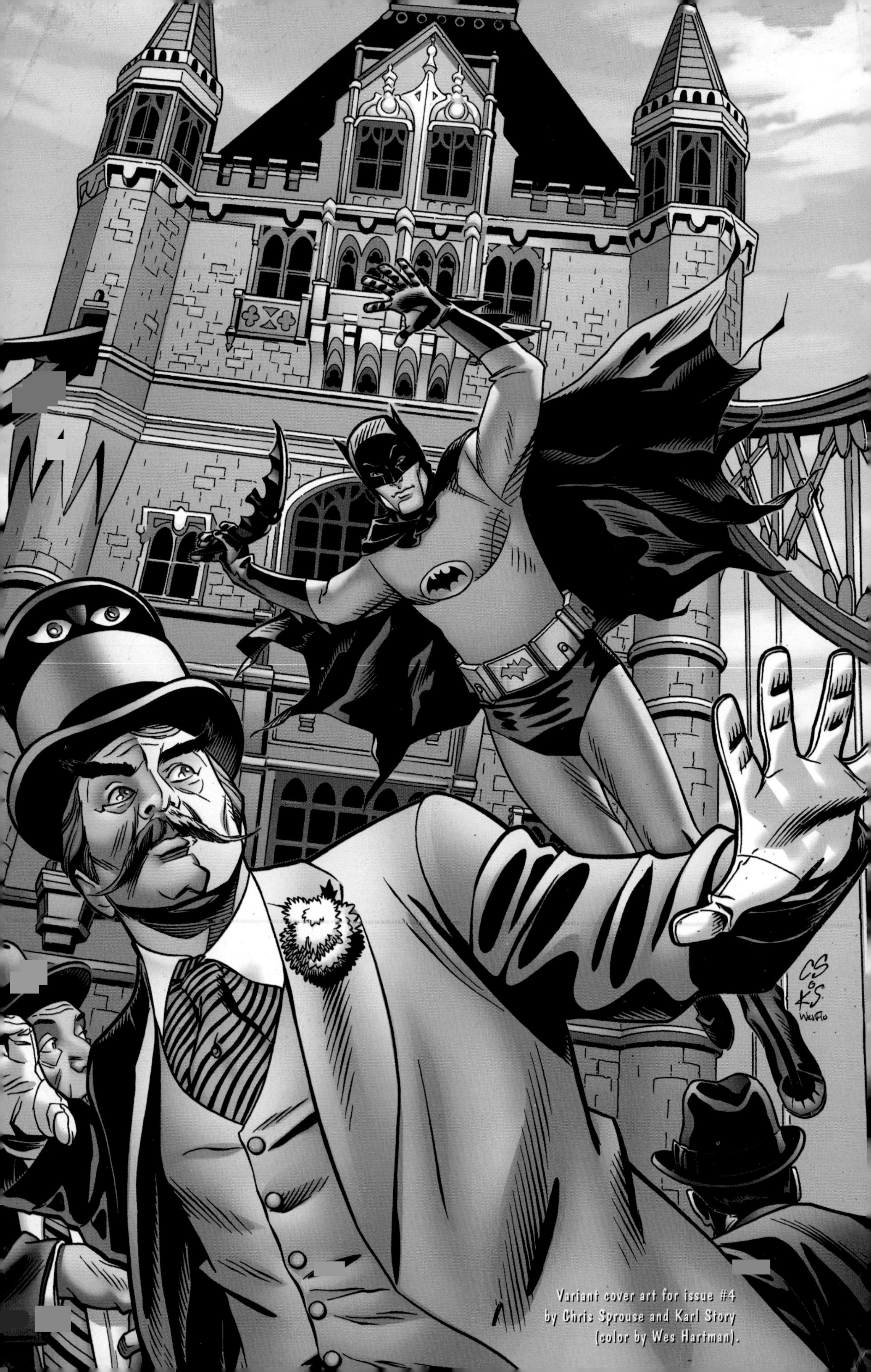

Variant cover art for issue #4
by Chris Sprouse and Karl Story
(color by Wes Hartman).

Variant cover art for issue #5
by Dave Johnson.

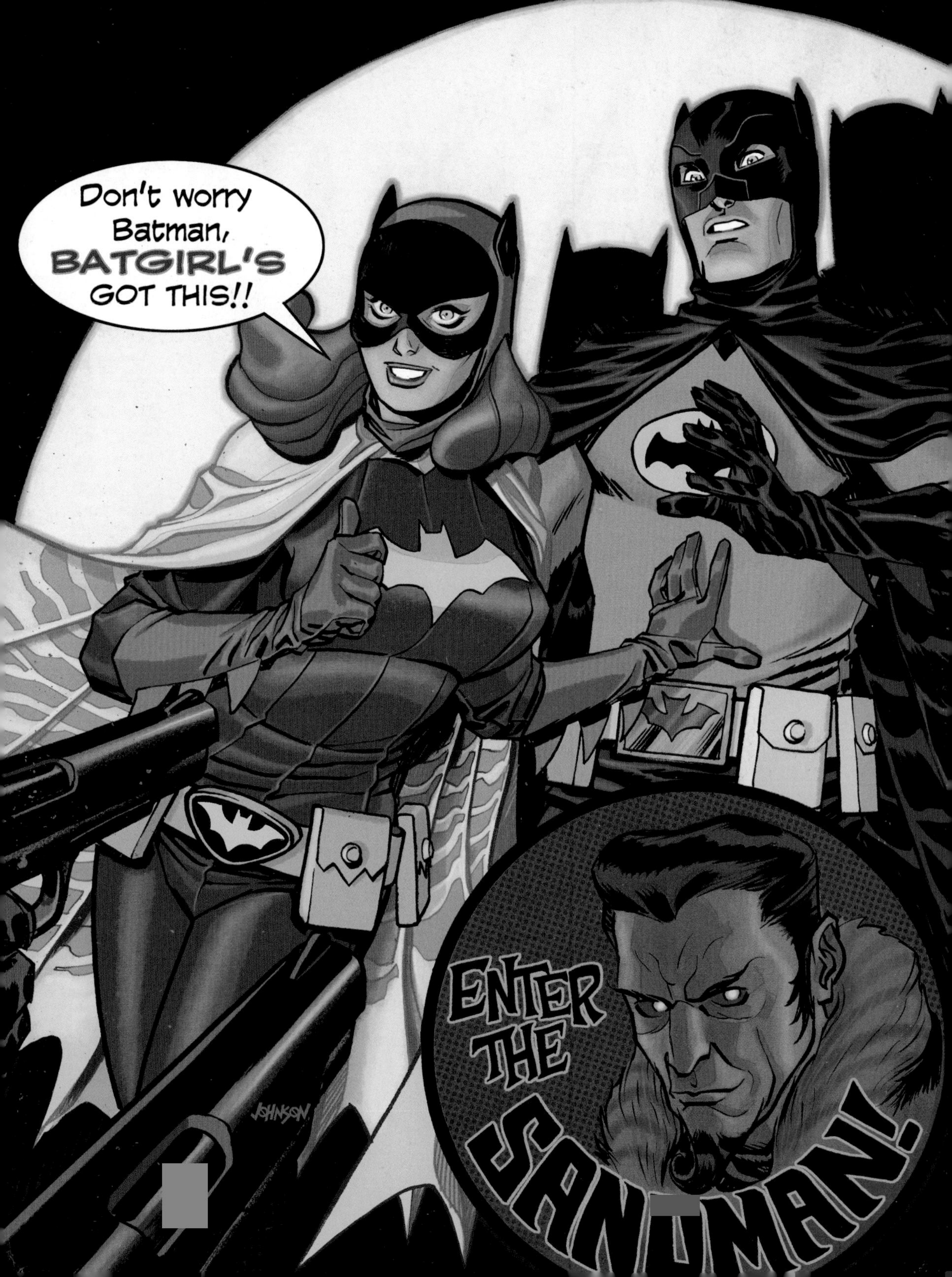

Don't worry Batman, BATGIRL'S GOT THIS!!
ENTER THE SANDMAN!
JOHNSON

"THE LONG HALLOWEEN is more than a comic book. It's an epic tragedy."

—Christopher Nolan (director of Batman Begins, The Dark Knight and The Dark Knight Rises)

"THE LONG HALLOWEEN is the preeminent influence on both movies [Batman Begins and The Dark Knight]."

—David Goyer (screenwriter of The Dark Knight Rises)

# JEPH LOEB & TIM SALE
## BATMAN: THE LONG HALLOWEEN

**BATMAN: DARK VICTORY**

**BATMAN: HAUNTED KNIGHT**

**CATWOMAN: WHEN IN ROME**

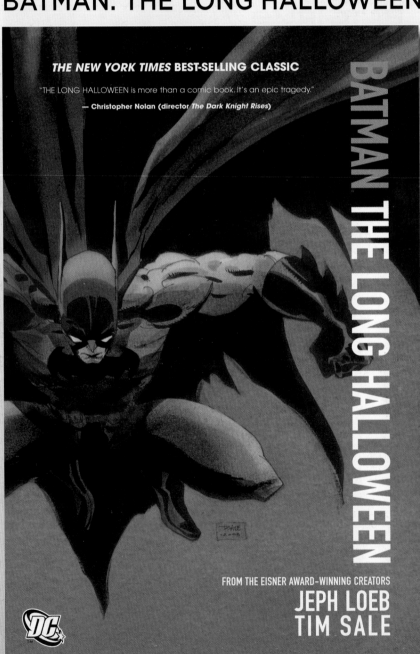

THE NEW YORK TIMES BEST-SELLING CLASSIC

"THE LONG HALLOWEEN is more than a comic book. It's an epic tragedy."
— Christopher Nolan (director The Dark Knight Rises)

BATMAN THE LONG HALLOWEEN

FROM THE EISNER AWARD–WINNING CREATORS
JEPH LOEB
TIM SALE

THE DARK KNIGHT. THE MAN OF STEEL. TOGETHER.

# SUPERMAN/BATMAN: PUBLIC ENEMIES

## JEPH LOEB & ED McGUINNESS

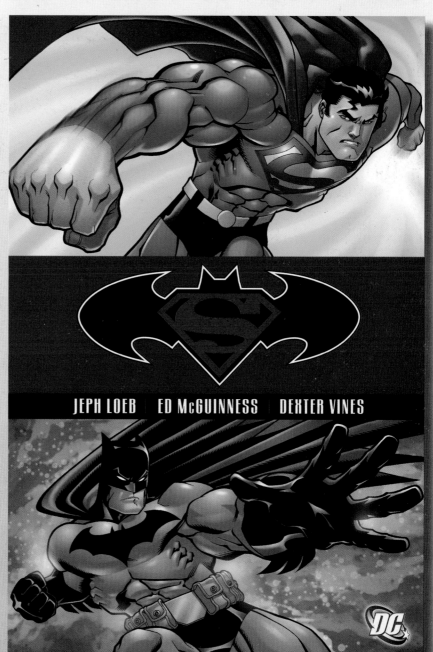

JEPH LOEB | ED McGUINNESS | DEXTER VINES

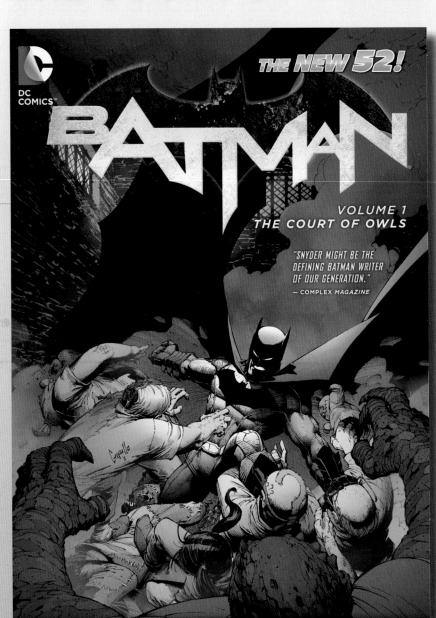